VEIL OF PATRIOTISM

ROMAN BELL

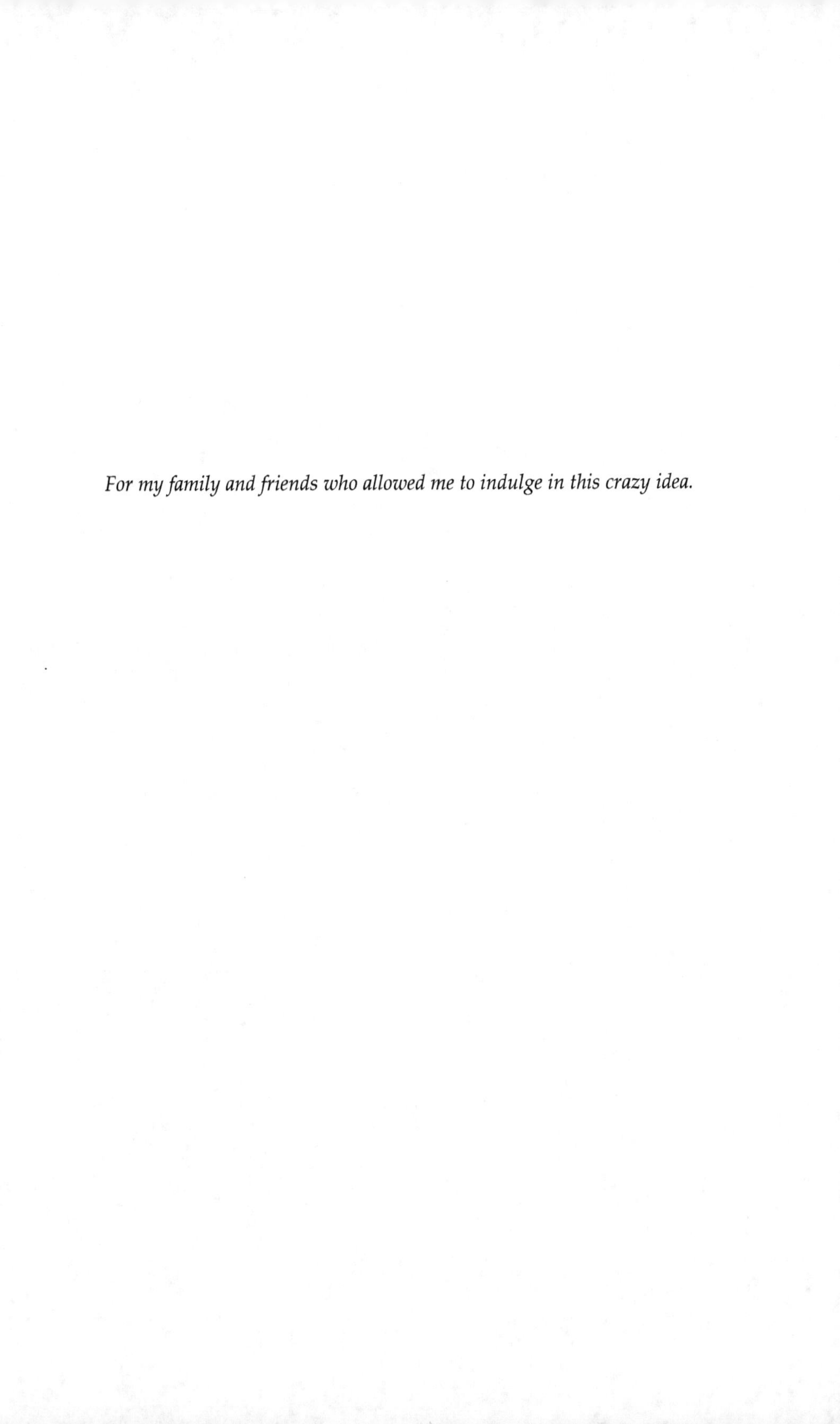

For my family and friends who allowed me to indulge in this crazy idea.

PROLOGUE

AMBITIOUS UNITED STATES Senator Andrew Hayes was being dragged to his death. Of that, he was sure. Just moments ago, the tall, broad-shouldered man had separated him from the group by pushing him out a door and onto the ground outside. When Hayes didn't get up, his assailant grabbed him under both arms and pulled him to another building. Alone with him now, Hayes knew there would be no witnesses.

And worse, the Senator thought, *this man would once more get away with murder.*

The struggle against his assailant's grip was useless. Even if he could break free, Hayes was in no shape to fight back. After four days of sadistic torture, the young Senator's left foot was mutilated, both hands had been drilled through, and his body was covered in expertly placed minor cuts designed for maximum pain while ensuring he didn't bleed out.

Taking a deep breath of the still late-night air, he slowly released the final bit of resistance, along with the air filling his lungs. It was futile and would only prolong an already expired life. The realization that he would soon be dead, free of pain, blanketed him with a peaceful warmth.

His body had suffered enough for three lifetimes and couldn't bear another day. His mind was far worse than his bruised, broken, and mangled body.

His captures were possibly the worst men who had ever walked the earth. Their delight in causing agony to their captives was evident with each moment that they savored, inflicting horrendous pain on the five of them. During one of the few quiet moments, a fellow Senator and captive remarked that the men holding them hostage had been *'sent by the Devil himself because no rational human being could take such pleasure in the pain they caused others.'*

Earlier in the day, their captors would break from what had become their routine. Instead of choosing two of the hostages to string up by ropes dangling from the roof and beating them mercilessly, they pulled only one out of the windowless room that had been their prison cell.

Several moments would pass before Hayes and the other three captives left in the room would hear her blood-screeching screams. The loudest abruptly cut off mid-cry.

The Senator from West Virginia didn't return. All they brought back was her head.

That was the moment when hope left his failing spirit. Hayes' mind fractured into pieces as he looked into his mentor's lifeless eyes, staring back up at him just as the wedge of light shining in from the door slid out of the room.

When the door opened next, the man Hayes feared most in the world stepped in.

This doesn't make sense, Hayes thought as he struggled to understand what was happening. Had he organized all this? Was he pulling the strings and giving the orders to brutally torment the five of them?

In Hayes' fragile state of mind, there was only one possible reason why, out of all the people in the world, this man was here— he was behind it all.

The irony of the situation wasn't lost on the junior Senator from Iowa. Hayes had spent the last year investigating the tall, rugged man standing above him holding a gun for alleged war crimes. The accusations of ruthlessly murdering innocent women and children were severe enough that they caught the attention of the free world's press. For Hayes, it had become a personal mission to ensure justice was served for those who had died at this man's hands.

The far-reaching probe launched by the Senator had included scores of witness interviews, months of evidence collection, and one very public, very contentious Foreign Relations Committee hearing just two weeks ago. During this, Hayes and his fellow party members blatantly accused the man of murder and vowed to see him behind bars, if not executed, for his crimes. A personal mission turned into an obsession.

Now, in a physically and mentally broken state, Hayes was sure he would be his next victim.

Reaching the opposite side of the dirt road, the man lifted Hayes off the ground and seated him against a wall.

For the first time since being taken hostage, Hayes was outside. Forcing his tired, bruised eyes open, all he saw was the tall man's back as he looked at the door they had exited. The nighttime air was chilly, even for early summer.

"It would be a lot easier if you made an effort to move instead of me having to drag you," the man said after a moment.

"I don't have it in me."

He bent down to take a knee beside the Senator, placing his gun on the ground next to Hayes' left leg. He put both hands on his face and tilted his head to one side and the other. Seeming satisfied with whatever he was looking at, he used his gloved hands to lift each of Hayes' eyelids roughly. The hurried action scraped the Senator's right eye, but he didn't protest or cry out in pain. That time had passed, and he would not give the man the satisfaction.

Once he had finished, he turned away from Hayes' face to focus on his foot, lifting it off the ground and moving it at the ankle before placing it back in the dirt.

"Your foot is in bad shape; I'll have to carry you."

Mustering his most resilient facial expression, Hayes replied, "No!"

In the dim light of a nearby street lamp, Hayes took notice of the smirk on the man's face as he turned back toward him.

This was the first time tonight that Hayes saw his assailant's eyes. A tremor of fear ran through his body as he noticed how different they looked tonight.

The two men had previously met on several occasions. They had shaken hands, had meetings, and even shared a coffee not too long ago. So, it wasn't the first time they had ever made eye contact or shared a gaze. Yet, looking up at him now, Hayes was mystified by what he saw.

These were not the eyes of a raged killer teetering on the edge of insanity. Nor were they the eyes of a man finding pleasure in the work as his captures had while they smashed his foot with a sledgehammer or drilled through his hands using an electric drill.

No, these eyes staring back at him had an unmistakable purpose.

There's no talking my way out of this.

He might have been able to reason with a crazed man on the brink of doing something stupid. Hell, maybe even find a way to bargain for his life if the tall man enjoyed inflicting the unspeakable misery the other captors had. Perhaps he could have lived if he had seen either scenario in the eyes looking back at him.

But the cold, calculated eyes of a man on a mission weren't usually found in those of someone susceptible to being talked down or reasoned with.

The Senator knew this.

He was a talented politician who had risen to national stardom quickly because of how well he could read and manipulate others.

Breaking the stare, Hayes glanced down at the gun at his side and then back up.

Taking notice. "Are you thinking about grabbing my rifle to shoot me?" The man asked.

"Why did it have to be you?"

"It was always going to be me, Senator. Our fates have been tied together."

Hayes looked back at the gun on the ground beside him once more. He was no longer considering if he should try to grab it. Instead, he was mesmerized that the bullet that would end his life was already in the chamber, ready to be fired.

Taking in a deep breath and slowly exhaling. "Are you going to kill me now?"

CHAPTER
ONE

SOME DAYS LINGER IN TIME.

Whether a world-altering event that rewrites history or an ominous personal ordeal, certain days stay suspended in the conscious and unconscious mind no matter how many weeks or years may pass. Time, the great equalizer, has not worn these harrowing memories down the same way it erodes our favorites. This was such a day.

The rain had not let up for hours. It wasn't the drizzle of an afternoon shower that accomplished little more than getting the ground wet enough to track dirt into the house on your boots. Nor was it the torrential downpour we needed in Southern California to help lower the ever-increasing risk of brush fires. No, these heavy drops of water were the worst kind of rain. It moved in from the West with a prophetic feeling and seemed to have decided that this house was the best place to take up residence. Thus contributing to the somber mood that was always part of leaving for a deployment.

Ty and Beth had been sitting on the twin wooden rocking chairs that were usually nothing more than decorations for the wrap-around front porch of their home for more than an hour. Or what he felt was an eternity.

"What happens from here?" Beth asked calmly, not to wake their beloved boxer, Murphy, sleeping at their feet.

Mustering just enough courage to look at her, Ty replied, "I'm not sure, but it doesn't change the fact that I have to leave."

"I know."

They both stood up to realize how numb their butts had become from sitting so long in the rocking chairs. Each stretched while Beth rubbed her backside for a moment before they stepped towards one another to enjoy one last embrace before Ty walked down the four porch steps into the rain.

As they kissed goodbye, she pulled back just a little to look into his eyes in the porch light. Smiling slightly, Beth said, "You're a pain in my ass, and this is always so hard because I am addicted to you."

This playful gesture was a sign that while she was still distraught at Ty leaving her and the kids again, she understood he had to. It was his job. His duty as a Marine.

"Trust me. I know that I'm a pain in the ass. I get reminded almost weekly," he chuckled in response before turning more serious, "Just know that it's yours and the kids' love that brings me home."

"Be safe, and message me as soon as you can. I love you with all my heart, Ty." This was Beth's way of releasing him.

"I love you, too. Please tell the kids -,"

Interrupting her husband, "They know how much you love them and that you'll be home as soon as you can."

"I'll call you soon."

Ty kissed her once more before turning to go down the porch steps.

The last person he needed to say goodbye to was blocking his path. Ty kneeled and used both hands to rub Murphy behind the ears. "You're in charge while I am gone. I expect you to take care of Mommy, Audrey, and Jake until I return."

Murphy didn't offer a response. He just leaned into Ty's hand a so that he would give that ear a little more attention.

Ty rose and, with a fleeting look, stepped out into the rain.

The drive to the base was only fifteen minutes, but tonight, it was filled with years of reminiscing.

The usual sorrow for Ty leaving for deployment was overshadowed by the recognition that this last embrace between him and his bride felt like it was their last. Worse, it wasn't the fear of dying in combat that made him feel like it was the last time he would feel her close to him and be able to inhale her scent. No, it was the debilitating anxiety that she wouldn't be waiting for him when he returned.

They had met before Ty became a United States Marine. For Beth, this meant she was his priority because she was part of his life first.

· · ·

As per his norm in college, Ty was running late to class. "Who the hell signs up for a 9 a.m. financial markets class over the summer?" Quipped his roommate as he left their two-room apartment to head to campus for his first class.

"The dumb ass who needs it to graduate on time," Ty replied as he headed out the door.

In the early 2000s, the University of Central Florida was a big school that was trying to be bigger than it was by competing with colleges like the University of Florida and Florida State to attract both athletes and students.

It had done a decent job.

The student population had exceeded thirty thousand, and it was joining the Mid-American Conference in sports. While exciting, it also had some downsides. Students were little more than a number attending classes, with many being over two hundred. This meant that occasionally, you would be forced to take an early morning class due to the lack of available courses. Which was never anyone's favorite.

When Ty registered for two summer classes, he was frustrated that his required financial markets class was only available at 9 a.m. To make matters worse, since it was a condensed summer semester, he would have to attend Monday through Thursday. While he was a finance major, studying how the global economy and financial markets interacted wasn't a topic he wanted to start his day with. Running to campus, Ty thought, *There's not enough coffee in my apartment to do this four days a week for the next six weeks.*

But, his mood towards having an early class changed as soon as he walked in.

Room 107 was a small lecture hall with four rows of tables and chairs arranged in the traditional "U" shape, with a large projector screen and a teacher's desk at its focal point. This shape allowed the sixty-plus students to feel like active participants and easily hear the instructor. While it was Ty's first class in this particular room, he had been in several of the carbon copies that made up the business college's two buildings.

This also meant that he knew that the room had two separate doors, and based on the current rush of students into class, he went to the door that would give him the best chance to grab a seat in the back.

His favorite seats were always in the rear of the classroom. He wasn't a bad student or troublemaker. Ty was a decent honors student who preferred the back row so he could people-watch.

Some students took detailed lecture notes while others doodled in their notebooks or chatted with their neighbors. His vice while listening to a lecture was to watch what fellow bored students were doing to pass the time.

Luckily, his plan worked flawlessly.

Ty chose the right door, walked in, and quickly reached the top rear row to find the perfect spot, about 4 to 5 seats from the edge. Dropping his backpack to sit down, he took his first look over the room.

There she was, sitting in the front row opposite his side.

She was beautiful. Short, shoulder-length blonde hair, a great smile that she was sharing with the girl sitting to her left, and the skirt she was wearing was chosen that morning by design to show off her legs while she sat like a good student in the first row.

Holy shit! Was the only thing he could think. Yet, based on the looks he got from a couple of the students around him, the words might have slipped out of his mouth. Ignoring the looks, Ty grabbed his backpack to rush back to the door.

With it on his shoulder, he quickly exited through the door he had just entered with a new plan. Darting toward the second classroom door, Ty was moving swiftly enough so that others took notice, but he didn't care.

He was a man on a mission.

He gave a quick thank you nod to the two guys who stepped out of his way as he made the sharp right back into the room. With two quick steps in, he relocated next to the cute blonde girl. The seat to her right was open, and she was still talking with the girl next to her.

Ty made his approach.

With as much confidence as he could muster. "Hi, is this seat taken?"

She turned to him with a heart-melting smile, "No."

Not saying anything back, Ty took the seat with much less proclamation of ownership than his first seat on the opposite side.

Ty didn't speak again before the class started. After letting him know the seat was open, the girl returned to her friend and continued their conversation until the instructor called the room to order a few minutes later.

It wasn't overly warm in the class, nor was Ty not feeling well, but he felt feverish.

The palms of his hands were sweaty, heart fluttering, and he dared not look towards her. He knew she was there. It was all he could do to pay attention as the instructor brought up a presentation and started his lecture on… well, something Ty doesn't remember.

The class was coming to its natural conclusion when the cute blond turned towards Ty to put her laptop in her backpack.

That's when Ty noticed it.

A small, elegant gold ring nestled at the base of her ring finger on her left hand. No diamond. Just a thin band.

The words out of his mouth were either brilliant or a sign of an utterly desperate guy.

"Are you engaged?"

Beth looked up from her bag. With their faces just a mere foot apart, their eyes locked for a moment before she glanced down at her left hand, clutching her bag as if realizing what he had just asked.

"Ummm, no. It is a promise ring."

"What did you promise?" Was the next stupid thing that came out of his mouth as the classroom emptied around them.

She offered a knowing smile to show him she was catching what he was hopelessly getting at and replied, "I guess nothing." She paused briefly before continuing, "But we've been together for a while, and he gave it to me for my birthday."

There wasn't an opportunity for a response. The cute girl had successfully put everything away and rose out of her seat.

Walking past him toward the door, she said, "Have a good day. Hopefully, I'll see you tomorrow."

As Ty came to a slow stop at a red light just a couple blocks from the base's main gates, he couldn't help but smile at this memory of Beth and his first words. He had walked into that classroom four years ago with the cocky edge one would expect from a frat boy showing up on the first day of a class. But, the guy who rushed into that second door to ask a cute girl if he could sit beside her was different.

CHAPTER
TWO

THE MARINE SENTRY snapped to attention as Ty pulled up and rolled down his window just enough to slip out his identification in the pouring rain. The Department of Defense standard-issue badge was new. The 1-inch by 1-inch picture was only taken a few months ago after Ty's old one got cracked.

The photo was the same as every other Marine's. His dark brown hair was high and tight. Shaved face, pointed, strong chin. The most distinguishable feature was Ty's light blue eyes.

Just below his expressionless face, it read in large, all-caps font.

TYLER C. HUDSON
O-2 First Lieutenant

After reviewing the badge, the sentry handed it back through the cracked window, stepped back to offer a salute, and waved Ty onto Marine Corps Base Camp Pendleton, California.

Situated strategically between San Diego and Los Angeles, Camp Pendleton is a sprawling base and training grounds for the Marine Corps. It is the home garrison for the Corps' largest and most prestigious unit, I Marine Expeditionary Force.

Due to the war on terrorism, the First Marine Expeditionary Force, or I MEF, had swollen in size to sixty-thousand Marines spread across several global bases and combat theaters. Ty had been part of Force

Company, 1st Reconnaissance Battalion, First Marine Division for the last two years.

This morning, he was arriving at 1st Recon's headquarters for a final briefing before the battalion of nearly 450 Marines loaded onto transports to Iraq for the third time since 2001. This particular rotation was unplanned and was the Pentagon's response to an increase in Iraqi insurgency.

Elements of I MEF, including 1st Recon, had just rotated back to Camp Pendleton five months earlier after an intense eleven-month deployment that included both battles for Fallujah in 2004. This rotation home allowed the Marines to see family, rest, relax, and, more importantly, replenish their depleted ranks.

More than half of the Marines in the battalion had been replaced with recruits since their return stateside. These newbies included a new battalion commander, Lieutenant Colonel George Aimes, and Captain Marcus Williams, Ty's new boss. He was much more excited about Williams being in command of Force Company than Aimes.

Aimes had a reputation for being an extremely tough officer. Even by Marine Reconnaissance standards, his approach to training, physical conditioning, and Corps traditions was considered over the top.

Marcus Williams had a completely different reputation than Aimes. He was a Navy legacy, with his grandfather and father serving distinguished careers as enlisted sailors.

Despite a rich family tradition, Marcus paved his own path. He attended the United States Naval Academy at Annapolis and was commissioned as a Second Lieutenant in the Marines after graduating in 2001.

He and Ty met in Spring 2003 when they both attended Basic Recon Course at Camp Pendleton. The nine-week course was the initial qualification required to become a Recon Marine. Both were fresh off their first deployments to Afghanistan.

Their friendship formed quickly because they were from two infantry regiments and were already quite familiar with Camp Pendleton, its training grounds, and, more importantly, its nearby nightlife. This last bit of knowledge made them popular among their classmates.

After completing BRC, Ty was assigned to 1st Recon, whereas Williams went to 3rd Recon and served under Aimes. Both saw action in Iraq during the early months of Operation Iraqi Freedom.

Two years later, they were again heading into a final briefing before returning to war.

The rain had not let up as Ty pulled into the closest parking spot he could find. Despite the rain and just before 4 a.m., the parking lot was almost full as the building was buzzing with activity. Two more sentries were standing guard at the headquarters, or HQ, main doors to check IDs, and several Marines were standing under the building's canopy. Without even being part of the conversation, Ty knew that they were trying to figure out which province the battalion was being deployed to.

It had been nearly a year since Saddam Hussein had been captured while disgracefully hiding in a hole. With his collapse, a severe power vacuum had been created. Tribal warlords and al-Qaeda acted quickly to trap as much territory and critical resources as they could. Regular officer briefings on the war had turned into a whack-a-mole game of which province was this week's hotbed of activity.

Grudgingly stepping out of his truck, Ty rushed into the building.

Just inside the lobby area, Ty noticed Williams and several Marines gathered around a small TV.

"Hudson, settle a disagreement for us," the Captain barked.

Walking up to the group, Ty replied, "Sir?"

Gesturing toward the TV, Williams asked, "Our next president or not?"

Ty looked at the TV to see a news reporter giving an interview. Glancing at the infographic on the screen below, the well-dressed, mid-forty-year-old man read Senator Andrew Hayes of Iowa. He couldn't make out the discussion, nor did he care. "I don't even know who that is."

"You should. He's gaining popularity by bashing the war."

Ty shrugged his shoulders with indifference. Politics wasn't his thing. Sure, he voted, but he preferred to see his enemies. The idiots in Washington were the least of his concerns.

Before Williams could say anything else, the Marines standing in the lobby started to make their way to the briefing room.

Before entering, Ty placed his cell phone in a steel box on a table outside and scanned his badge to open the heavy door. He had done this hundreds of times before, yet it never lost its seriousness.

The room layout was designed so that the four company commanders who made up the battalion's leadership were all situated at the front table, just in front of a large television screen. The following rows of tables were first come, first served for the other officers.

In a break from Marine norms, Colonel Aimes, their battalion commander, emphasized communications and preferred to have both the commissioned and non-commissioned officers present for essential briefings. That way, nothing was missed or misinterpreted when the officers debriefed their sergeants. Because of this, the briefing room was packed.

It wasn't difficult for Ty to locate his platoon sergeant among the more than thirty people inside. The six-foot four-inch broad-shouldered Staff Sergeant Cody Tiller was not hard to spot even when sitting. Noticing Ty walking into the room, Tiller stood to greet him.

Tiller was a big, corn-fed guy from Kansas. While he looked like he might have been able to play linebacker for either the Kansas Jayhawks or their in-state rivals, the Kansas State Wildcats, he was not a fan of what he often called *'lame-ass group sports.'* Instead, he was an individual fitness freak who once told Ty he had joined the Corps for a *'good workout.'*

Besides being in phenomenal shape, he was a good-looking guy with green eyes and dirty blonde hair. There was a way about him that even Beth noticed. Needless to say, Tiller didn't get many invites over to the house for dinner.

Well-respected, Tiller was known to be one of the better operators in the battalion. Ty often remarked that his platoon sergeant was the poster boy of a badass Marine. Having him as his number two made Ty the luckiest platoon commander in 1st Recon.

Extending his hand to shake Ty's, Tiller asked, "How'd Beth take it?"

"It's been a tough morning," he replied, "We never went to sleep and spent the last several hours talking on the porch." To help illustrate the severe nature, Ty gestured quotation marks with his hands as he said 'talking on the porch.'

"Shit. Are you worried?"

Before he could answer, Aimes walked into the room. Tiller and Ty paused their conversation as they were called to attention and then released to take their seats.

As the room came to order, Aimes spoke with a civilian dressed in worn jeans and an untucked polo shirt. While it wasn't uncommon for civilians to be in briefings, seeing one in jeans and an untucked polo wasn't the norm.

Most civilians who attended were private sector informants or contractors with specific knowledge about a region, a weapons system, or a target package. On rare occasions, a member of the Central Intelligence Agency or another clandestine service would be included in a briefing. Given his attire and Aimes speaking with him before addressing the battalion leadership, Ty assumed he was CIA, and he was correct.

"Can we get the lights?" The unkempt man confidently asked, stepping towards the center of the room and away from his conversation with Aimes.

The lights went out as the large TV screen lit up with a map of Iraq. "My name is Newbold, and I'll lead the first part of your briefing this morning."

Holding a cup of coffee in one hand and a remote in the other, the guy looked half asleep. Other than the dark bags below his eyes, nothing much stood out about Newbold. He had an average build, short salt and pepper hair, and spoke with a slight New England accent.

Seated next to Ty, another officer leaned over to whisper something unintelligible. Second Lieutenant Jamie Lauder was part of the battalion's replenishment and tended never to take anything seriously.

Ignoring him, Ty didn't bother to look in his direction. Instead, he shook his head, dismissing his ill-advised choice to whisper during a briefing. This wasn't high school, and in the past, Ty had witnessed Aimes jump a Marine's ass for speaking during a briefing.

Why Lauder decided to do it now was lost on Ty. Aimes took notice at the front of the room and glared at both men.

Ty always felt uneasy around the Colonel and didn't believe the old man liked him. The last thing he wanted was for Lauder to draw unnecessary attention to him.

Unaware, Newbold continued, "1st Recon is being sent to Forward Operating Base Sykes in the Ninewah Province. From here, you'll relieve Task Force 324."

A new slide with a map was brought up on the screen. "Elements of the 82nd Airborne and SEALs have forced insurgents into the mountains in the northeast region. This terrain has changed the mission and requires 1st Recons unique skill sets."

Ty didn't know if it was the excitement of being deployed for the first time or if he had too much coffee, but once more, Lauder leaned towards him to say something.

This wasn't going unnoticed.

"Lauder!" Aimes snapped. "You and Hudson seem to know the mission already, and you can't seem to shut up. Want to fill the rest of us in?"

This was classic Aimes. He had no problem calling an officer out and humiliating them in front of their peers. Lauder was an idiot who deserved this, but Ty was pissed for being caught up in his stupidity by simply sitting next to him.

"Sir, I don't-" Lauder whimpered before getting cut off.

"No, you don't fucking know," Aimes yelled. "How about you, Hudson? Do you know anything?"

Shit! Ty hoped that with Lauder's fumbling response, he would not be called on and escape the situation unharmed. It was wishful thinking.

When Aimes would call a Marine to the carpet in situations like this, others didn't dare look at the person in his crosshairs. In this case, three people were looking at Ty. Aimes and Newbold were at the front of the room with a blank expression, waiting for him to respond. Yet the third person, Captain Williams, had turned in his chair to face his two platoon leaders so he could share a wide-eyed look that screamed, *Are you fucking kidding me?*

Ty had two choices. Retreat like Lauder and look just as stupid, or show that he was paying attention. He chose the second.

"Sir, I suspect the mission is a simple search and destroy in the Zagros Mountains on the border of Turkey and Iran. This is what makes it complicated and requires the 1st Recon's skill set."

The two men at the front of the room shared a quick look. Newbold looked back at Ty, "What else?"

Ty had not expected a follow-up question. *Why did they look at each other, and why did he ask what else I knew?*

Ty had just repeated what Newbold had said and connected it to the map of northern Iraq on the screen. It wasn't difficult to deduce that their particular skill set was long-range reconnaissance and that the insurgents had been pushed into the nearby mountains. Nor was it a giant leap to know that the Turkish and Iranian borders were a complication. U.S. and coalition intelligence had known for years that al-Qaeda had used the border as a safety shield whenever possible. *So, what was Newbold asking, and why was everyone looking at me?*

Confidently, Ty continued, "The 82nd and SEALs aren't equipped to sustain long-range reconnaissance into Iran and order fire missions when targets reenter Iraq, sir."

Newbold stood there expressionless. It was only a few seconds, at most, but it felt much longer with all the eyes in the room still on him. As Ty waited for either him or Aimes to say something, he noticed some of his fellow officers starting to comprehend the weight of his words. Glancing towards Williams, Ty watched as he unconsciously lifted his eyebrows to recognize the *oh-shit* moment everyone in the room was now having.

"You're correct," Newbold said, "Your mission is to infiltrate Iran to provide intel on insurgency movements while calling in fire missions on critical targets as they cross back over."

There was a low murmur in the room. The news of crossing the border into Iran took the spotlight off Ty and Lauder.

The rest of the briefing went uninterrupted as Aimes took over for Newbold with specific operational details he was only equipped to do. Lauder had learned his lesson, and Ty thought he had escaped unharmed.

CHAPTER
THREE

THE COMPLEMENT of Marines emptied into the hallway to grab their phones as they headed out of the HQ to their respective barracks. The battalion had just a couple of hours to prep before they boarded the transport planes shortly after sunrise.

Ty found Williams and Lauder standing further down the hall as he left the room. It was clear they were speaking rather intently. Well, at least Williams was speaking. Ty knew precisely what it was about. After grabbing his phone, he decided to go ahead and take his licks for being a distraction.

Ty walked up just as the ass-chewing concluded. All he heard was Lauder firmly stating, "Understood, sir. It won't happen again."

Williams gave a firm nod and turned to provide Ty with what was sure to be the same ass-chewing.

Much to his surprise, that wasn't what his Captain started with. "That was pretty impressive. How did you jump to the Iran conclusion so fast?"

Ty smiled. "I thought it was pretty obvious, given where we are going and who we're replacing."

"Well, I'm pretty sure you got Aimes' attention."

"Why do you say that, sir?"

"Because here comes the Sergeant Major."

Stepping to them, the battalion Sergeant Major ordered, "Williams, Hudson, you're needed back in the room."

Ty shared a glance of concern with his commander before pivoting to follow the Sergeant Major.

Only Williams and Ty reentered. Still, by the large TV, Colonel Aimes and Newbold were looking at a detailed projection of a topographical map.

In a deep voice, Aimes shouted, "Up here, gentlemen!"

At the front, Ty was greeted. "I'm Morgan Newbold. As I'm sure you've guessed, I'm with the CIA."

Exchanging handshakes, Newbold continued, "You were spot on in your assessment, with one caveat. This is not only a search-and-destroy mission, we have a specific target."

He handed Ty a large photo of a group of men with a blue circle around one of them.

Why am I being handed the photo? Ty thought.

This entire exchange was very odd. It was standard for intel to be passed to the highest-ranking officer first, so when Newbold handed Ty the photo, it caught him by surprise. He was sure Williams was feeling the same way but showed no sign.

Instead, the Captain stood there stoically.

Ty examined the photo for a long minute before looking up, hoping Newbold would continue with additional information. He wasn't to be disappointed.

"That's Shakir Nasser, or who you'll know as Black Jack. He's the Syrian explosives expert responsible for more than sixty deaths and three times that number wounded. It was his IED that claimed the lives of four Army Rangers last week."

Black Jack was well known to any Marine who had spent time in Iraq. After a stint in the Syrian army, he joined al-Queda and spent his time making improvised explosive devices and teaching others his skills. This last part was what made him a top kill or capture priority.

The nickname Black Jack represented his Jack of Clubs position in the fifty-two-card deck given to soldiers at the onset of the war. These playing cards listed Iraq's fifty-two most important targets during the invasion. Saddam Hussein was the Ace of Spades, followed by Ali Hasan, or who we knew as Chemical Ali, as the King of Spades and so forth. After the spades came the club cards. Shakir Nasser was a wanted man with a significant, multi-million dollar bounty on his head.

"Sir, if I might ask," Williams said, looking at Newbold before turning his question to Aimes, "Why was this not included in the briefing?"

"That's a fair question, Captain. Force Company's mission will differ slightly from that of the rest of the battalion. You will be responsible for hunting Black Jack down, no matter which side of the border he's on."

Williams nodded but then looked towards Ty, using his eyes to ask the earlier question about why he was in the room and being handed the photo first.

Newbold must have recognized why Williams was giving Ty a puzzled expression. "Captain, the plan was to fill you in once we landed at Sykes and have you assign the mission. However, given Lieutenant Hudson's astute observation, we recommend his platoon take point. And since you were both still in the hall, there was no reason to wait."

Aimes clarified, "Captain, it's your company, and you can choose a different platoon if you feel-."

"No, sir. Lieutenant Hudson and 1st Platoon are exactly who I would've tasked."

Newbold turned to the table behind him. Opening a black backpack, he pulled out a vanilla folder with *Top Secret* in large, bright red letters on the cover and handed it directly to Ty.

"This will bring you up to speed on the target mission. Review it and have an ops plan ready to review when we land."

"Yes, sir."

Ty and Williams knew that was their cue to leave. The two Marines exited the briefing room for a second time.

Breaking the silence, Williams finally spoke as they left the building. "Is the 1st Platoon up for this?"

"Of course, sir."

But Ty knew that wasn't what was being asked. Williams asked if Ty could prepare an operations plan by the time the battalion landed in Iraq. More importantly, he wanted Ty to ask him for his help. Ty was smart enough to recognize these underlying questions. "Once airborne, sir. I would like your help in developing an ops plan."

With a satisfactory smile, "Perfect, I'll see you at the barracks."

CHAPTER
FOUR

IT'S scary how certain activities can become normalized through repetition.

1st Recon was being deployed for the second time in as many calendar years. Despite the repetition, mobilizing a battalion of nearly 500 Marines, the equipment, and support staff was no easy feat.

As Ty packed his gear in Force Company's barracks, he couldn't help but notice how relaxed the Marines in his platoon were as they chatted easily with one another while preparing for a combat deployment.

This was a good thing, but what does it say that going off to war had become so routine that it required little to no thought to finish preparation?

Without being asked, Tiller said, "Platoon present and accounted for, sir."

"Fantastic, Sergeant. We're on deck at zero-eight hundred for a final check. If the men have families seeing them off, they need to get their goodbyes in as soon as they're packed."

As long as it could happen, most military units deploying to war usually allow family members to see them off. This means a lot of tears, hugs, kisses, and promises of returning. These last few minutes together were tough on everyone. Spouses, girlfriends, partners, and kids would almost all be crying. While most would fight back their tears, it was equally hard for a Marine.

Ty remembered the first time Beth saw him off before his first deployment in 2002. They had been married for about seven months, and she was five months pregnant with Audrey. Standing there in a long embrace, he had no idea if he would see her or meet his daughter.

He recalled how surreal it felt to have so much love for someone and want to spend every moment of your life with them while also feeling the tug of patriotism and duty to country.

It was torture.

Not only for himself but even more so for his pregnant wife.

Ty didn't remember which Marine said it, but he vividly remembers overhearing someone telling another, *'If I can survive that, I can survive anything the Iraqis throw at me.'*

After 1st Platoon had cleared out of their barracks to say their good-byes, Ty got a firm knock on his office door. "Sir, your family is here to see you off," Tiller exclaimed excitedly.

Ty was shocked. He had not expected to see them again after kissing Audrey and Jake goodnight and leaving Beth on the porch when he stepped into the rain a few hours ago.

He gathered his equipment and rushed out the door.

Audrey was two and a half years old, while Jake was seven months. Both were born while Ty was on two separate deployments in Iraq. After graduating from UCF, Beth and Ty married on a Sunday, and the following Thursday, he signed up to join the Marine Corps after a quick honeymoon in St. Augustine.

Audrey wasn't conceived on their honeymoon, but she was before Ty departed for Officer Candidate School. After OCS, it was the First Marine Division and Operation Iraqi Freedom. For Beth, it was starting her career as an elementary school teacher and a challenging pregnancy while her new husband was at war.

A little more than a year later, the young couple said goodbye for Ty's second deployment in 2004, this time with 1st Recon. Beth informed him that she was pregnant again during this send-off.

As Ty cleared the back corner of the Humvee, he could see his wife with the dual stroller. Audrey saw him simultaneously and bounced from her seat to run towards him. Dropping to his knee to scoop her up in a huge hug, Ty carried her back to Beth and Jake.

He dropped to a knee, leaning over to kiss Jake's forehead. "You can't believe how much I needed to see you again."

Ty unclasped the stroller seatbelt to pull Jake into his right arm as he shifted Audrey to his left hip. With both kids in his arms, Ty stood up with tears in his eyes. Beth was also teary-eyed. She leaned into her husband and kids, kissing him on the lips while putting her arms around all three of them in a family hug.

With a sly joking hint, Beth said, "So…"

Ty laughed hard. "Oh, trust me. That has crossed my mind."

He pulled back a little to look at her. She tried to keep a straight face, but it quickly gave into a big smile. "No, love. I don't think we have to worry about that this time."

The next fifteen minutes went by in a flash.

Just moments after that fun exchange, the large group of families around them started to say their final goodbyes. Everyone felt an emotional wave as one after another gave their last hugs and kisses.

Ty kissed Jake, putting him back in the stroller, and whispered, "Daddy loves you so much, and I'll see you very soon."

Audrey was a bit tougher on her daddy. She wasn't letting go. Being two and a half, she didn't fully understand how long he would be gone or why, but she knew he was going. She hung tight to his neck and told him several times not to go.

The tears were falling freely now for both Ty and Beth.

To help him, Beth took Audrey from Ty's arms and held their daughter tight. With her in her mom's arms, Ty gave Audrey a daddy-daughter kiss. A special kiss that only the two of them shared.

With Audrey still reaching and grabbing him, Ty focused on Beth, taking her and their daughter into a loose hug.

"Thank you for this. I needed to see you again."

"I had to see you, too. I couldn't let you deploy with how we left things this morning."

"I love you so much, more than you know," Ty said as they kissed goodbye again.

CHAPTER
FIVE

CAMP PENDLETON, California, to Forward Operating Base Sykes in the Ninewah Province was an eighteen-hour flight on a C-17 Globemaster.

The desolated runway was once an Iraqi military airfield called Tal Afar Airport. However, the word 'airport' was misleading. The single runway was long enough for the C-17s to land and take off. This could only be done because the jets were nowhere near their weight capacity. If they had been carrying M-1 Abrams tanks or other heavy equipment, the runway wouldn't have been long enough to come to a stop safely. Even now, the large engines had to immediately go into reverse to stop once the jet touched down.

Exiting the rear of the jet onto the runway reminded Ty that he was no longer in California. Yes, the sun setting in the western desert was the same one he would see lowering into the Pacific Ocean, but it looked different, and its warmth was stranger.

Instead of a soothing evening retreat into the ocean, this sun made a burning descent into the sand. Even this late in the afternoon, its long rays radiated off the desert to scorch his exposed face. The temperature this time of the year had already started to break ninety degrees, and the late spring days were turning into longer summer ones as the sun hung around.

As the company moved into formation away from the C-17s, Ty looked around the base. The few buildings still standing were severely war-torn, and only a few had lights on inside. To the north end of the airfield was the secure entrance to the living quarters from the runway side. Heavy steel and concrete barricades were arranged in alternating patterns to prevent a direct assault on the gate from a suicide vehicle.

To the east of Sykes was the reason why the 1st Recon was sent here.

The Zagros Mountain range started to take shape a few miles away. Insurgents used this vast mountain range to hide, train, and launch attacks on coalition forces in northern Iraq and then strategically retreat to caves or across the border into Iran.

The Army's 82nd Airborne, supported by SEALs, had pushed most of the fighting deep into the mountains but had become bogged down by the disappearing, reappearing act the enemy had mastered. To make a difficult situation worse, it was well known that Iran, backed by Russia and China, was supplying the insurgents with weapons, aid, and training when they were on that side of the border.

Even before Ty had stored the contents of his pack in the foot locker at the end of his bunk, he was hearing the news that would only speed up their response—and, by proxy, the ops plan that he and Williams had worked on during the flight.

Clearing his throat, Aimes looked at the two Marines standing in the briefing room before beginning, "Gentlemen, approximately seventy-five minutes ago, a Blackhawk came under fire and went down. On board were four SEALs who were en route back here after a 2-week scouting rotation. UAV footage from a few minutes ago shows no survivors."

Neither Ty nor Williams could respond. This unfortunate event took seven lives and the much-needed intelligence the four SEALs would have been sharing upon their return to Sykes. Worse, both knew that the downing of a helicopter meant there would be more insurgents roaming the mountains where they had to transverse.

"Word out of command is this does not change our mission," Aimes said, "So, Lieutenant Hudson, how does this affect your plan?"

"Sir, this certainly complicates things. If I could ask, what's the status of the recovery mission?"

"Two gunships are already overhead to protect the crash site. A search and rescue team will be onsite in forty minutes."

With confidence, Ty replied, "Then this tragedy opens up an opportunity for us to cross the border tonight, sir."

"How so?" Newbold asked.

Ty knew insurgents would not dare approach the crash site with two AH-64 Apaches roaming above with night vision systems and the weaponry to rain down hell. They would be slow to make their way toward the downed helicopter and converge on it late tomorrow afternoon after the bodies of the fallen soldiers had been recovered.

He knew this because of simple human nature. Insurgency leadership couldn't pass up the opportunity to take pictures and videos of themselves next to a fallen symbol of American military power. This show of progress in defeating the United States was one of the ways they kept their followers motivated to remain isolated in caves for months at a time.

This was possible because, during a recovery effort, multiple units converged on the site for hours. No one on the ground would notice a couple more helicopters coming in and out of the area. An insertion closer to the border would eliminate the team from trudging over a mountain range for miles, risking an engagement with no support at any turn. By going now, they could bypass days of intense hiking and lower the risk of their mission.

"When can you and your team be airborne?" Aimes asked after Ty finished outlining his new plan.

Ty suspected Newbold would be included in the team, so looking at the CIA case worker, he stated, "Sir, we can be airborne within the hour."

Newbold took the statement precisely as he intended: a two-part question about whether he was coming with them and whether he could be ready in the next forty-five minutes.

With a sly smirk, Newbold replied, "That works for me."

Hustling out of HQ toward 1st Platoon's barracks allowed Ty and Williams to speak for the first time since landing in Iraq.

"Ty, a lot is being asked of you right now. Are you good?" Williams asked.

Using his first name helped Ty distinguish that Williams was asking as a friend, not as his commanding officer. This had been his way with Ty since they first met at Recon training a couple of years ago.

"Honestly? I am more worried that I've overstepped with you."

Grabbing Ty's right arm, Williams brought their brisk pace to a sudden halt. "Wait, what? Why do you think you overstepped with me?"

"I've never been in a situation where Aimes was asking my opinion and not going to you."

"Shit, Ty. How long have you been worried about this?"

"Since we left the office at Pendleton."

Williams started to shake his head and chuckled as he turned back toward the barracks. "Man, I wish you would have said something on the flight. This is a really good thing for you."

Ty didn't respond at first, but his curiosity gave way. "How is this good?"

"It shows Aimes has trust in you. He did the same thing with me when we were deployed a year ago. This is how he works. He tests his officers and allows them to think and act for themselves. If he had doubts, he would've said something."

Stopping outside the barracks, Ty considered Williams' points.

Sensing his hesitation, Williams said with a much more serious tone, "Ty, we're good. Go in there, select your fire team, and complete this mission."

A quick twenty minutes had passed from the time Aimes approved the operation to when the four Marines and Newbold gathered for a final briefing.

Half paying attention to the Colonel giving the final details, Ty couldn't help but evaluate the team standing before him. These men were being asked to cross into a country that the president had called part of the axis of evil not too long ago. Due to the downing of the Blackhawk just ninety minutes ago, they had zero intelligence on insurgency movements nor their combat strength. This was going to be a very difficult and risky operation. The good news Ty thought as he looked over his Recon Marines was the excellent balance of experience and skills.

Sergeant Jackson Henry was their point man. He was a proud black man with a small stature of five feet eight inches and weighed one hundred seventy pounds. From the coal mining region in eastern Kentucky, Henry was a master outdoorsman. This keen outdoor ability made him perfect for his job. He would be responsible for navigating the team through the mountains filled with insurgents. Ty liked Henry. He was easy-going and liked to have fun.

Darren Knight was the last member of the team. He was the lowest rank as a Corporal and was highly important in a firefight. This was because he carried the team's only belt-fed light machine gun, the M-249. Commonly referred to by its popular acronym, SAW, the Squad Automatic Weapon was ideal for putting down cover fire or assaulting hardened positions by putting a lot of rounds down range very quickly.

But Knight's weapon wasn't the only thing that made him imposing. He was the same height as Ty, six foot one inch, but he had at least thirty pounds of pure muscle on his lieutenant. Knight was a big guy even by Recon standards, making him ideal to wield the SAW in combat.

The team's five members, including Tiller and Newbold, would rely on each other in the coming days and, perhaps, weeks. Once they touched down in the mountains, they were on their own.

If Ty's plan was successful, the only time they would need to fire their weapons would be to eliminate Black Jack. Until then, they were to evade enemy contact at all costs. This was the mission of a Recon Marine.

THE SUN HAD LONG SET, and the crescent moon was still low in the sky. The stars were covered by the same fast-moving clouds the moon played peek-a-boo behind. Even with the temperature starting its usual rapid drop this time of year as the day gave way to the blackness of night, it was ideal conditions for an incursion behind enemy lines. Well, if there had been any lines in this war.

Two helicopters, the Blackhawk that carried the team and the Apache gun-ship as an escort, flew low and fast over the desert below. Ty was certain that in the far distance to the northeast, other aircraft were taking part in the recovery efforts of the seven dead Americans.

The flight was bumpy but luckily short. After seventy-five minutes, the Blackhawk pilot came over the headphones. "Two minutes out."

The helicopter slowed and circled once to come to a hover twenty meters over the ground. An Army crewman dropped a thick, 2-inch rope out of the open door just in front of Ty. Turning to glance again at the four men with him, Ty reached for the rope, taking a firm hold of it.

Knight grabbed Ty's right shoulder and squeezed it hard to give him the all-clear to fast rope to the ground.

It was called fast roping because it was a lightly controlled free fall. Sure, the rope was threaded through his clasped feet and both hands, but Ty's grip on it was to throttle his speed down as he got closer to the ground. All Ty had to do was fall out of a helicopter fifty feet above the ground and use a 2-inch rope as a breaking mechanism before he crashed into the ground below.

As the team had practiced for years, by the time Ty was halfway down the rope, Knight would be on to steady it, and the remaining Marines and Newbold would follow suit until Tiller hit the ground last and the Blackhawk lifted way with the rope still dangling.

All four Marines and Newbold were down in thirty seconds.

As fast as it arrived, their transport was gone. The Apache did two quick sweeps over their heads and then accelerated away to catch up with the Blackhawk.

Ty moved up to Henry, who was on one knee looking at a map under a dull infrared light. "We're twelve klicks away from the border," the Sergeant said in a hushed voice.

Ty never understood why the term *klick* was still used in the modern military to denote distance. He knew the term's history dating back to World War I, but *why not just say kilometer?*

Hiking uphill on a mountain range with a very rough trail surface, with each member carrying rifles and about sixty pounds of gear, would take them at least seven hours to reach the border. Assuming they didn't encounter insurgents, Ty estimated they would reach it just an hour or two before sunrise.

"Set a good pace, Sergeant. I want to cross the border before the sun is up," Ty instructed.

Henry nodded in response and swiftly pushed off the ground to move out.

Romeo Team's first two days hiking into Iran were as expected.

The dense forests of the Zagros Mountains along the border were sparsely populated, and the steep terrain was difficult to traverse. As the team got closer to the valley Black Jack was suspected of being in, they had three unique challenges.

First was the elevation. When the team fast-roped down from the Blackhawk in Iraq, they were at an elevation of fifteen hundred meters. Their first twelve klicks to the border were relatively flat, but once in Iran, that quickly changed.

The path Newbold and Ty had agreed on was intended to reduce the risk of enemy contact. However, it took them directly over a four thousand meter mountain and then back down into the valley on a steady slope to two thousand meters.

The next challenge was the weather. Though it was early summer, the days were warm, and the nights were frigid. The forty-degree temperature swing was the worst part for Ty as his sweat-drenched undershirt caused by the heat of the day chilled him to his bones at night.

Last, several small villages were scattered throughout the area and all of them had to be avoided. Coming into contact with a farmer herding goats, a woman making her way to a nearby creek for water, or a child playing was just as bad as being discovered by a roaming al-Queda patrol. It was game over for the mission, and worst, they would have to hightail it back to the Iraqi border before it became a firefight in Iran.

In the early morning hours of the third day, Romeo Team crossed the peak and started down the eastern slope into the valley.

"Romeo One, this is Three. We've reached rally point alpha," Henry said.

Team member-to-team-member communications were of the utmost importance during any operation. To simplify this and prevent using names on communication channels, team members were assigned a numerical designation according to their order of command on the team. As team commander, Ty was One, and Tiller was Two. Henry and Knight were next, followed by Newbold, a CIA operative, rounding out the team as Five.

"Roger that," Ty replied. "Team set up overwatch and hunker down for the rest of the night."

Ty had established a position as rally point alpha as a fallback spot if things went sideways and the team needed to exit quickly. It would act not only as a rallying point but also as a central base of operations to make radio calls to Aimes and for the team to meet in person whenever needed.

"Heads up, everyone. Insurgents are about to start target practice at the west end of the camp. I say again, combatants are starting target practice," Tiller whispered into the radio just a moment before the crack of several AK-47s broke the morning silence.

Even from his position, three hundred meters higher than where Tiller was, Ty could see the four insurgents firing in the distance.

The bright morning sun illuminated the valley's full layout. A thousand meters below, Ty could see the camp directly in front of his position.

Much further to the south and on the team's right flank was the Iranian village of Galaz. Nestled at the end of the valley, the village had a small river that cut through it, flowed past the training camp, and continued to the north. Galaz was small and home to no more than thirty families, with only one road in and out. Most of its surrounding land was flat and used for farming or raising livestock. Power and telephone lines came from a larger town twenty kilometers to the southeast.

The team had been given several aerial and satellite photos, but a couple of new buildings have been erected since the last flyover. In total, there were seven buildings. The two newer ones lacked the distinctive war-torn damage from bullets and explosions that the other five had from previous decades. One of the two new buildings was two stories and had a balcony that overlooked the creek to the north. This two-story building was residential, but Ty was unsure if it was a single residence for a particular individual or a barracks for the camp.

The second new building was nearly one hundred meters to the southwest of the others. Its rectangle shape looked to be forty meters long and twenty wide with no visible windows and a set of double doors facing their direction. Ty suspected this was their armory and storage building for bombs. While there were plenty of reasons why a long, narrow building would be built a football field away from the others, and many more reasons why it had no windows, he would still put money on this building being highly explosive.

As Ty examined the camp, Newbold radioed, "Romeo One, I am moving to you."

"Copy."

A few minutes later, Newbold joined Ty in the large clump of bushes that had become his nest. While he had no clue what type of plants they were, their thick branches and leaves provided three-hundred-and-sixty-degree coverage while giving him a great view of the camp, the creek, and at least half the village further down the valley.

"What do you make of the two new buildings?" Ty asked.

"The far one looks like weapon storage, and the two-story baffles me. It's a home, but for whom I don't know."

"Black Jack?"

"Possible, but it's not his style. He might stay in it now, but I doubt it was made for him. This begs the question, who was it built for?"

After a few more minutes of discussing possibilities and agreeing that they needed more intelligence, Ty acted, "Romeo Two, come in."

"Two here," Tiller replied.

"We need eyes in the two new buildings. Who lives in the house, and what is being stored in the building to the west? Tonight, I want you and Three to get a peek into the distant building."

"And the house?"

"I have a good path to it. Report in before you move and avoid all contact."

"Copy that, Two out."

The team had been on site for less than twenty-four hours and already needed to move into camp to get a closer look. The movement was risky, but it needed to happen.

When it was time, it took Ty three hours to reach the valley floor. While he could've easily made the descent quicker, stealth, not speed, was the most important factor.

Seeing the camp at level for the first time, Ty paused at the edge of the forest before it opened to a wide area. It was well past midnight. The lights at the camp had gone out hours ago. The three guards who were on patrol had clumped together near the river on the opposite side of the two-story house.

This was both good and bad.

This meant that Ty had a clear path to move to the side of the house. But, he had no idea when one might walk about the corner. Instead, he had to rely on Knight to monitor his movement from further up the mountain.

"One, you're all clear to the house's edge," Knight said.

Ty scanned the area, the house, and surrounding buildings to ensure Knight hadn't missed a roaming guard. After this scan, he moved towards the house in a squatted, fast walk with his silenced M4 pointing in any direction he looked. He covered the forty meters, reaching the house.

The grayish mud brick wall was still warm from the sun's intense rays from hours earlier. Squatting just above him was one of two windows on this side of the house.

These were not windows in the sense that a person living in the States would think. They were square holes in the wall with closed wood shutters. There was no glass, bars, or obstruction other than a center latch that would prevent someone from entering. The other window was for the second story, and the shutters had been closed all day.

Ty stood to look through the cracks to ensure no one was there. Even with night vision goggles on, the room was difficult to see. The shutter's slots were millimeters thin and did not provide enough visibility.

Ty made a daring decision.

He gently pulled his five-inch knife from its holster on his chest and inserted its narrow blade below the latch. With an easy swipe up, the latch lifted out of its locked position before he slowly pushed the shutters open.

The base of the window was at chest height, so with his pistol at the ready position, Ty leaned his head in through the window to see that the room was clear. Then, he hoisted himself upwards with one hand on the ledge and slipped his left leg in.

Straddling the wall, he paused momentarily to listen. Confident that no one was nearby, Ty swung his right leg inside and silently placed both feet on the floor.

CHAPTER
SEVEN

THE ROOM TY had entered was mixed-use. Towards the back was a wood-burning stove, a deep sink, and a closed cupboard along the same wall he entered from. From his line of sight, Ty could not see a table or a refrigerator. To his right was an open sitting area with a small wooden table separating two worn couches facing each other. On the same wall was the front door. Ten feet in front of him was a wall. No pictures, no art, just a plain wall. It was off-center in the room and ended just a few feet short of the couches. By the way the light was coming from around the corner, Ty knew the staircase to the second floor was on the other side.

Moving left from the window, Ty entered the kitchen. Each of his steps against the concrete floor was deliberate. Placing his heel down before rolling onto the ball of his foot to tread lightly.

In the kitchen, he saw that the wall directly in front of the window hid a small square table pushed against it, with three chairs in each of the remaining seating spots. There was a small refrigerator against the wall and, next to it, a wood door. By the direction of the layout, this door faced the creek and the three guards, who he hoped were still clumped along its edge.

He immediately went to a trash basket beside the refrigerator. Looking in it, he didn't find anything. Either no one lived here, or the trash had been removed earlier in the day.

Turning back to the open kitchen area, there were no letters, papers, electronics, or anything from which he could collect intel. The only two areas in the kitchen he hadn't searched were the closed cupboard and the fridge. Since he was standing next to the refrigerator, Ty slowly cracked the door to look inside.

As he gently pulled it open, there it was.

The intel he was looking for was resting dead center on the top shelf next to a small glass container of milk. It told him who lived in this house and why he needed to immediately return to rally point alpha.

This intel was worth breaking radio silence!

As big deals go, this was a big deal.

Perhaps even mission-changing, but that would be a decision for Aimes. Ty needed to break the team's radio silence before their scheduled call and share the new intelligence.

Ty had found modern, Western medicines used to treat HIV in an area of the world where the astronomical prices a person would pay in the States would be multiplied several times over. The person staying in that house was spending thousands of dollars, perhaps even as high as ten thousand a month, to treat the incurable disease. That's not a price an insurgent could pay, but an arms dealer who has made tens of millions of dollars over the last decade could easily afford it and would have the connections to get them supplied wherever he was.

Ty suspected he knew who they belonged to.

Dragomir Babic made a splash in the Yugoslav wars in the 1990s by supplying weapons to all sides. He was a Colonel in the Serbian Army who used connections within Russia to funnel weapons into Croatia in the early part of the decade. Later, offering his services to all sides in the Kosovo and Bosnian wars.

In the years since Babic had continued to supply weapons to anyone with deep pockets and a desire to kill in mass. This included al-Qaeda, the Taliban, and anyone wanting to kill Americans in either Iraq or Afghanistan.

For more than a decade, he had been a priority target for the CIA but had eluded the agency by using his blood-soaked money to line the pockets of corrupt country leaders in exchange for safe harbor. Sometime before September 11th, the CIA learned he had contracted HIV and was using that intel to track him.

But once Osama bin Laden and al-Qaeda killed nearly three thousand Americans, Babic became old news. The agency's resources shifted to the War on Terror, finding bin Laden, and stabilizing Iraq and Afghanistan.

Or, so the recruiting posters said.

. . .

"Verona base come in. Verona come in." Ty said into the radio's handset as Tiller and Newbold looked on.

In saying the words, he couldn't help but smirk at the choice to use the name of the city where Romeo met Juliet as the code name of command.

An unknown voice answered. "Romeo One, we hear you loud and clear. What's your sitrep?"

"Things have changed on the ground and need operational guidance."

Simply saying the phrase *'need operational guidance,'* Ty informed the person he needed to speak directly to Colonel Aimes. They would not waste time asking for a situation report but instead get Aimes on the radio as soon as possible.

"Roger that, stand by."

After a few minutes, Aimes said, "Romeo One, go for Verona Main."

In a calm voice, Ty said, "Verona Main, we've set up overwatch and have had intel on a possible link to Dragomir Babic. No visual confirmation yet on Black Jack or Babic. Need a kill decision if the latter is confirmed."

"Romeo One, go with new intel," Aimes replied in a steady voice.

The Colonel listened as Ty explained what he had seen in the refrigerator and that Tiller had found several one-thousand-pound bombs in the building at the far end of the camp. Bombs that were most likely supplied by Babic.

After being silent for a moment, Aimes ordered, "Black Jack remains the priority, but if you get eyes on both targets, you are green-lighted to engage. I repeat, if both are present, you are cleared to engage."

"Roger that Verona, Romeo One out."

Closing his eyes, Ty pinched the bridge of his nose before speaking to Tiller and Newbold. "If we can get eyes on both, we are green-lighted to engage"

Looking back and forth between the three standing there, Tiller asked, "Ty, you mean engage as in weapons hot?"

Ty nodded in response to Tiller, then asked Newbold, "Does Aimes have that authority?"

Newbold rubbed his chin. "No, but I suspect he'll take the blowback."

Tiller spoke again, "Wait… can we go back to weapons hot inside of Iran?"

"I am shocked, too. But shit, guys, what did we expect?" Ty said. "We gave them intel on Babic and what…You thought they weren't going to give us a kill order?"

Needing a moment to think, Ty returned to the clump of bushes he had been using for cover, took off his pack, and pulled out a half-eaten ration. The developments of the early morning had been all-consuming, and he had yet to eat anything.

While rushing to call in the new intel on a possible connection to Dragomir Babic, none of them had considered the Colonel's reaction. Ty had no idea how to proceed and needed a moment alone.

In the quiet beauty of the mountainside, Ty's thoughts drifted between how to get the job done and what would happen if it went sideways. The scenario where he found himself and his team pulled up painful memories from several months earlier.

Ty and Beth were visiting one of her friends, Maria, when she got the news that her partner was killed in action. A roadside bomb had blasted through the Humvee that Corporal Angie Hernandez was traveling in, and a chaplain and officer from the regiment had come to tell Maria that she was dead.

The two had been together for a few years and planned to marry once Angie returned from deployment. They had always joked that they wouldn't ever get engaged because that was too much of a commitment, and just saying they were dating provided them both with an escape route.

The notification of death experience had been modeled well throughout the years in war movies. A vehicle, usually a military one, pulls up to the house, and a senior officer dressed in their Class A uniform and a member of the faith that the soldier identifies with would step out. If the partner or spouse sees the two exit the vehicle or as soon as they answer the door, it's at that moment that they know their loved one has been killed.

There are no words needed.

There is no reason for the officer to convey the sad news.

No, the reason for the visit is known not only to the family of the fallen but to any neighbors who might have witnessed the two visitors arriving.

While Hollywood gets the notification of death accurately, the movies don't capture what happens in the painful hours that follow. The agony of asking why or how it happened and often not getting an answer is always missed. If there are kids who are in school, then a family friend pulls them out. If they're at home, they must be comforted, too.

Calls must be made to other spouses in the regiment to initiate support for the family.

Within the hour, the home is swarmed with spouses and partners, offering condolences and helping feed, organize, and answer the constant phone calls. In a time of war, it's possible for regimental spouse support teams to have to conduct this routine multiple times a week. All in the shadow of the knowledge that their loved one could be next. And instead of being the supporter, they would be supported.

As an officer's wife, Beth was a support team lead and had been forced into this unwanted role several times. But, with Maria, it hit closer to home. They knew each other from work and had become good friends.

I can't let this happen to Beth.

The thought of not returning to Beth and the kids ignited a fire inside him. This was not an option, nor was letting emotions cloud his judgment. He had to focus on the mission and its new objective.

It's a simple situation. Stop overthinking it, Ty scolded himself. Aimes had given him a kill order on a second high-value target and authorized the team to go weapons hot in Iran if needed. All he needed to do was figure out the team's assault plan for when one or both of the targets arrived.

Looking out from the bushes at the camp, Ty took in the scene down in the valley. It wasn't an ideal spot for a direct assault. The camp's superior numbers and layout gave them an overwhelming advantage. Each of the different scenarios Ty played out in his head risked taking casualties. This was unacceptable.

Shit… All we need is a single tomahawk missile, and this would all be over, Ty mused.

His eyes went wide in realization as the meaning of his words hit him.

Pushing his radio button on his chest, Ty said, "Romeo Two, come back."

The audio cracked as Tiller replied, "Go for Two."

"You and Five come back to point alpha."

Wiping his mouth with the back of his hand after he drank from his canteen, Tiller asked, "Whatcha got going on?"

"How do we get the bombs in that building to go off at a time of our choosing?"

Tiller looked at Ty, then Newbold, and back out toward the building where the bombs were being stored. Ty knew that Tiller was working through the inventory of munitions and equipment the team had on them, trying to solve the same problem he had started working.

"The initial explosion is pretty simple, but the time of our choosing might not be an option."

"We don't have any way of creating a delayed fuse or trigger?" Newbold asked.

"Fuse, no. Someone would still have to be close enough to ignite it, which wouldn't give them enough time to get clear. As for a timed trigger, that might work, but someone still needs to start the time and exfil before it goes off," Tiller explained.

Newbold shook his head. "Wait… Someone would need to place the charge with a timer to explode when, or if, Babic and Black Jack show up in camp, and then… what?"

Smiling, Ty chuckled, "They would need to run like hell up a mountain to clear the massive blast while evading detection."

Tiller didn't add any colorful commentary. He nodded in agreement as the two Marines looked at each other, knowing that this was not only their best option but their only one.

He knew the answer, but Ty asked Tiller, "You've seen the building. Could an outside charge work?"

"No, the walls are too thick for anything we have. The charge would need to be placed inside."

"So this will be easier than we thought," Ty started. "We prep a timed charge, wait for visual confirmation of both targets, or at least Black Jack, someone places the charge inside the building, and run back up the mountain."

"All while being undetected," Newbold added.

Sarcastically, Ty responded, "Oh, yeah! All while being undetected. Thanks for the reminder."

With a confused look, Tiller asked, "Are we really considering this?"

CHAPTER
EIGHT

NEWBOLD LOVED IT.

Tiller had started to think his Lieutenant had lost his mind. "You're kidding, right?"

"Nope, we're getting this done," Ty told them.

He gave the team three more days on-site to get visual confirmation. If they didn't get eyes on, they would retreat to Iraq. If they did get eyes on target, depending on the scenario, they would take one of three courses of action.

If Black Jack arrived alone, Romeo Team would execute the mission as initially planned and exfil undetected.

The second scenario was the plan Aimes had authorized. If they got eyes on both targets and they were going to leave before nightfall, the team would go weapons hot and eliminate both Babic and Black Jack.

The third scenario was if Babic and Black Jack arrived and stayed overnight in the camp. If that happened, then Ty would place a timed charge inside the building under the cover of darkness and eliminate the targets in a massive explosion.

As expected, Tiller objected to this part of the plan. "I should place the charge. I've seen inside the building."

"I understand, but you're the best shot on the team, and I need you to cover my ass. And since I am faster than you, I can make it up the mountain quicker."

This second fact wasn't something that the First Sergeant could argue with. Tiller is an excellent Marine. He is a genuinely daunting man who could outperform Ty across many aspects, except one. His tall stature, long legs, big feet, and wide frame made him slow. Since he would be positioned well above the camp, Tiller would have more time to escape the blast zone. The person placing the charge and initiating the timer would have to transverse more ground very quickly to reach safety. That was Ty.

Tiller was an expert marksman who was needed for sniper cover. Ty also knew Tiller would not reposition with the rest of the team while he placed the charge.

In Ty's mind, this compromise kept him in action while giving the mission the best possible chance of success.

When Ty informed the team, they reacted as expected and found new energy. There were a few general questions about tactics, movements, and call signs. Most came from Henry, who was lobbying to stay in the valley with Tiller and Ty to provide additional cover.

Since Ty would be placing the charges if both Blackjack and Babic showed up, he needed to easily access the storage building. This meant he needed to get closer. As he moved down, the mountain gradually flattened, and he no longer looked over the camp. Instead, Ty could see it through the trees in front of him.

He hadn't been on level ground since the team's first night when he crept into the house and found the drugs that suggested Babic was or had been there.

The feeling of being exposed now that he was just a hundred meters from the building was eerie. At this level, Ty could be seen by a guard as easily as he could see them. Whatever cover he selected had to be good.

This looks promising, he thought as he came across a set of large boulders.

Several were the size of a small car and even more the size of a suitcase. These could conceal him but would only work as suitable cover if he could maintain visibility of the camp. Ty slowly made his way into the crevices between two larger ones. They were leaning on each other, and if he took his pack off, Ty could squeeze between them.

Lightly burying his pack with loose leaves and debris near the opening, Ty slipped his rifle sling from around his shoulder before laying flat on the ground. With his suppressed M4 in his hands, Ty slid between the boulders on his stomach. The area was large enough for him to move back and forth and deep enough to conceal his entire body. But, he would be in a lying position for the duration.

The good news was he had a great line of sight on the camp's storage building. The bad news was that he had no visibility behind him and entirely relied on Henry, positioned further up the mountain, for cover.

And then the sun came up, and morning turned into day.

Damn, Ty… what the hell were you thinking.

He didn't consider that rocks radiated heat. The last few days had become warmer, with the late afternoon temperature peaking in the low eighties. But, squeezed between two boulders that were not under any shade from the surrounding trees and with no breeze to help, Ty was roasting.

He was lying on his stomach, looking through the trees while wiping sweat from his forehead at what seemed like every second. It was strangely exhausting. Ty knew he was starting to dehydrate but was stuck here until nightfall. He couldn't risk moving out from under the boulders during the day.

He would have to become comfortable with slowly being cooked alive.

"Romeo One, how you doing down there? " Henry asked as his voice broke through the silence of the woods in Ty's earpiece.

He wasn't sure if Henry had been able to follow his movements through the night as he roamed looking for suitable cover. But hearing him confirmed that the Sergeant knew where Ty was and knew he would be miserable. But Ty wasn't going to give them the satisfaction.

"All good. It's a cool sixty degrees in here."

Laughing, Henry choked, "Yeah, okay. Keep telling yourself that, and maybe it'll be true."

This was not Ty's best moment but Tiller spoke before he could jab back at Henry, "Three vehicles approaching from the village. ETA less than five mikes."

Using military slang for minutes.

"There's a flurry of activity at the camp, too," Knight added.

In a calm voice, Ty asked, "Any sight of the HVTs?"

"Negative. They're not in the lead truck, and the dust is too thick to see the trailing SUVs. Stand-by."

Two long minutes passed before Tiller said, "Vehicles are approaching the front gate. Romeo Four, you have the best angle."

"Roger Two. The truck has pulled to the side, and SUVs are close to the house." Knight said, "Black Jack. I say again, Black Jack."

Knight had eyes on their primary target, Shakir Nasser. The Syrian bomb maker who had been accountable for the deaths of scores of Americans had finally arrived.

This was as exciting as it was terrifying. Ty had a sudden adrenaline rush, and the heat radiating from the boulders was now a distant thought. Romeo Team had just achieved a critical milestone toward their mission's first objective of getting eyes on Black Jack.

"No one has exited the other SUV. Three men got out of the one carrying Black Jack. Hold one moment. Bingo, Bingo!"

Shit. This just got real. Ty thought as he heard Knight call out the code name for Babic.

"One, this is Four. HVTs are talking outside the home, and everyone is gathering around. Wait, Black Jack is climbing into the back of the truck."

From Ty's position, he could see a straggler jump up from a chair and jog toward the house. If Black Jack were climbing into the back of the truck, he would most likely give a speech or make an announcement.

"Black Jack is talking."

"Romeo Team, if they get back into the vehicles, we go weapons-free on Two's count," Ty ordered.

As per their orders, if both men were to show up and go to leave, they would go weapons hot and eliminate both targets. The signal would be a countdown that Tiller would give before he took the first shot at the target he had the best line of sight to.

The idea was that Tiller could immediately terminate one of the two HVTs from his position before the rest of the team engaged. If they executed the plan well, both men would be eliminated with the first few shots. Then, the team would rotate out of their positions while moving up the mountain, a movement that gave them a tactical advantage by giving them the higher ground as they exited the valley.

After a few minutes of silence, the crackle of AK-47 fire erupted, and the once quiet valley sounded like a war zone.

Afraid that the team had been spotted and was taking fire, Ty barked, "Four-"

"They're firing into the air, not engaging us. Everyone hold," Knight said. "Black Jack is off the truck, and both targets are going into the house. I say again, HVTs are going into the house."

• • •

That afternoon was very active as Knight became the team's play-by-play announcer, providing commentary with any movement. Especially when Babic and Black Jack came out of the house about an hour after entering.

Most of the camp returned to the normal activities the team had witnessed over the last few days: cleaning various items in the creek, doing small group exercises, and sitting around doing nothing. But when the two men came out and began to walk to the storage building at Ty's end of the camp, all the insurgents sprung up from what they had been doing to follow them.

Now, at the end of the camp, Ty could see both targets through the trees as they entered the building and exited it just a few minutes later. Despite the fanfare surrounding them, there was no big speech or acknowledgment of the ten other men following them.

The two were talking, and Babic was waving his hands and pointing at different things around the building. While it didn't look like an argument, Ty sensed that the arms dealer was either unhappy with how the building was being guarded or wanted a small stack of wooden crates along the side moved. Black Jack appeared to listen before the two men returned to the house. Knight informed the team a minute later that they had gone inside.

Dusk was settling in as the afternoon sun moved to create long shadows on the ground before the team had any more excitement.

After hours of no activity, Tiller's voice cracked in Ty's ear. "Everyone on standby. Three men have approached the SUVs and are talking next to them."

This might be it. It was the first time since arriving that anyone had approached the vehicles, a sign that they were getting ready to leave. If the men showed signs of leaving, it was going to be a firefight.

The sweat that had plagued Ty most of the day had made his hands wet to the point that his fingertips were slightly wrinkled. It was as if he had spent an hour in a pool relaxing or, more aptly, had been inside a sauna.

As he had done hundreds of times throughout the day, Ty wiped the sweat from his brow under his helmet with his right hand before drying it on his left sleeve.

Tightening his dried hand tighter around the pistol grip on his rifle, Ty pulled its sights up to his eye while stretching out his trigger finger a few times to wake it up from a long nap. With his thumb, Ty switched his M4 from safety to fire.

Anticipating Tiller's countdown, he aimed at the three guards outside the storage building. Two were sitting. The one standing would be his primary target because he was the only one with a weapon in hand.

From his angle, Ty could easily take out the insurgent standing and another one facing him without having to move his aim very much. It would be a quick burst, and both targets would be down, just in time for him to aim at the third before he got his AK-47 to his shoulder. Once the three guards were down, Ty would need to move from his position between the boulders, grab his pack, and move toward the camp to engage targets of opportunity. He would entirely rely on Tiller and the rest of the team to eliminate Babic and Black Jack.

He just needed the countdown.

CHAPTER
NINE

THE MEN STANDING NEXT to the vehicles chatted for fifteen minutes before they decided to get into each of the two SUVs and the lead truck. This was the sign they had been waiting for.

Even from Ty's position, a hundred meters away, he would swear that he could faintly hear the engines turn over.

There was a certainty that Babic and Black Jack were about to come out of the house when one of the insurgents he was targeting stood up to take a better look at the running vehicles. There were now two targets standing and one sitting. Ty quickly readjusted his target pattern to eliminate the two standing holding their weapons.

His heart was pounding so hard on the rough surface of the boulder below him that he was certain it would put a crack through it. He had been a Marine for several years, and this wasn't his first deployment. But there was something different about this operation and this moment. Maybe it was that they were in Iran or how significant of a mission this had become for the ongoing war on terrorism. If he were honest, the difference was because of how things were left with Beth.

But Ty couldn't think about that.

He focused on his breathing. Slowly taking in deep, sustained breaths and releasing each just as slowly. As soon as he heard Tiller start his countdown, Ty would need to hold his breath for accuracy while putting down the first two targets.

That moment never came.

The three men who got into the vehicles weren't getting ready to leave. They were moving them away from the front of the house.

"Stand down, I say again, Romeo team, stand down," Tiller said. "They're moving the vehicles away from the house. There is no movement from the HVTs."

As nighttime came, the temperature rapidly declined. The sweat that had tortured Ty during the day found new ways to create misery. Instead of dripping into his eyes and all the unspeakable parts of his body, his damp clothes attracted a chill that cut through him as only a wet, brisk cold could.

He would have to make peace with this situation for several hours. Ty would need to block out both the stickiness and the frigid temperature while he waited for the right time to exit his hiding spot and prepare to move to the storage building.

If Ty's plan were successful, the camp would be destroyed in a massive blast that would kill Babic and Black Jack. That, by definition, was a successful mission. His survival would only be a bonus.

The team's movement time was scheduled for zero one hundred hours. At this time, the team and Newbold would start to move back up the mountain to the other side of the peak. Tiller would move to his overlook position. Ty would hold for another thirty minutes before planting the initial charge.

He would deal accordingly with any guards, and once the charge was placed inside, Tiller would move out while Ty ran up the mountain as quickly as possible. With a bit of luck, he would get out of the blast range before the timer hit zero.

After five long hours, at precisely 1 a.m., Tiller ordered, "Romeo team, start your movement."

With the team moving behind him, Ty stayed between the boulders. He could still see one guard sitting, leaning against the building. The man had not moved for the last hour, and Ty suspected he was asleep. Regardless, he had to be dealt with because he was between Ty and the door. The plan was for Tiller to take a silent shot on Ty's mark as he moved out of the woods and into the clearing.

However, the brisk cold Ty had been suffering from was pushed by a steady breeze. A sniper shot in this wind would be too risky. A miss could awaken the guard and lead him to alert the rest of the camp. Ty would need to deal with the lone guard.

If the last five hours had felt slow, these past thirty minutes since Tiller ordered everyone to move out had flown by. Ty had been nervously looking down at his watch every few minutes with heavy anticipation.

It finally read 01:28. That was good enough.

Slowly backing out of the crevice between the two boulders, Ty retrieved his pack before conducting a final check on the charge and timer that Henry had prepped. Pulling out the small demolition charge, he clicked on the timer to ensure it worked as planned but was sure not to initiate the countdown. The dull green light on its face lit up and showed the start time of twenty minutes.

Ty's eyes went wide in realization.

Once he started the count, he had twenty minutes to climb the mountain and out of the blast zone. Tiller, Newbold, and he had agreed on the time, but seeing it in his hands took on a new significance.

"Holy shit! Why did I suggest this?" Ty murmured.

He switched the timer off before placing it back into his pack and pulling out his night vision goggles. Snapping them in place on his helmet, he slung his pack over his shoulders and strapped it around his chest and waist. With his rifle, he turned on his night vision and pulled the goggles over his eyes.

The world went green as he quickly looked around to orientate himself.

He was ready.

"Two, this is One. I'm ready to move."

"Roger. I have you in sight. You're cleared to the edge of the woods. Good luck."

Tiller's comment didn't warrant a response. This wasn't a sad goodbye, nor a moment that needed to be made into something bigger. All Ty was doing was taking a stroll through the woods at night.

Using the thick trunks of the trees at the mountain's base to his advantage, Ty moved from one to another. Keeping his rifle ready and his eyes down range as he slowly moved to the edge of the clearing.

The trek from the boulders to the edge of the woods took less than ten minutes. As he approached the opening, Ty kneeled behind a tree. The insurgent was still leaning back against the building and had not moved. Now, at the clearing, Ty could see the entire side of the camp and even the house that Babic and Black Jack were in.

And as if on cue, Tiller said, "All clear, one target at the front of the building. You're good to make your move."

Not wasting a moment, Ty pushed off the ground and moved into the opening. Staying in a deep crouched position, looking down the scope of his rifle with his right eye and keeping his left open to see the peripheral. He advanced toward the side of the building at an angle that would put him coming up to it just to the right corner of where the insurgent was leaning. The dot in his rifle's sight was honed in on the side of his head. Ty was ready to pull the trigger and drop him if he made even the slightest movement.

Ty decided on a different tactic as he got closer to him.

Gently dropping his rifle to hang from its sling along his right side, he pulled out his combat knife from its sheath on his vest. The same five-inch blade he had used to open window shutters several nights ago.

Hearing the insurgent's subtle snoring, Ty took the last two steps toward him.

Pivoting at the corner of the building to place his shoulders parallel with the wall so the insurgent's right shoulder was just inches from his chest.

He grabbed the top of the insurgent's head with his left hand, and with his right, Ty thrust the five-inch blade into his skull from underneath his chin.

Before the blood could reach his hand, Ty pulled the knife out and inserted it firmly into the left side of his chest, where the heart was located. The guy's eyes never opened from his slumber as he let out a low grunt with his final breath.

Ty pulled the knife out of the guard's chest, wiped it on his pants, and put it back into its sheath before stepping past the lifeless body to the door. It was not locked, so Ty pulled it open slowly to ensure no noise. Once wide enough for him, he stepped in.

Tiller could only see the four one-thousand-pound bombs being stored on the left side of the room. He hadn't seen the other two on the right side, nor the stacks of crates holding RPGs and mounds of AK-47s scattered throughout the back of the building next to smaller crates of what Ty assumed was ammo.

This was a lot of ordnance and weaponry.

The thousand pounders would either be buried along major roads to be set off as a convoy passed or put inside a vehicle and driven by a suicide bomber. Their kill radius could extend over two hundred meters and cause massive damage and scores of casualties.

Quickly moving to the bomb closest to him, Ty dropped to both knees next to the wooden stand the bomb was resting on.

He opened his pack to pull out the blasting charge with its attached timer. Blasting charges were great because they had a sticky backside that would attach to almost any surface. Ty swiftly pulled the film off the adhesive, attached the charge to the side of the warhead where its explosive materials would be, and switched on the timer.

But was sure not to start the countdown.

Ty's open pack was still on the ground beside him, and he needed those few seconds to put it on before turning on the timer. Swinging it on his shoulders, he stood, leaning over the more than seven-foot bomb, and took a deep breath, pushing the button on his radio to activate his mic.

"Initiating countdown in three, two, one…"

TILLER BARKED INTO THE RADIO, "Romeo One, come in. Romeo One. Anyone have eyes on One?"

He had made it over the mountain just when the blast occurred. After momentarily waiting for any secondary explosions, he turned and started back into the valley.

Tiller had waited several minutes into the countdown from his position to cover Ty's run and ensure neither of the HVTs exited the house before the blast. With his haste to clear the blast zone, he had lost track of Ty's ascent up through the dense brush. Coming back down the mountain, he had no idea where his commander was, how much ground he had covered in the countdown's last minutes, or even if he was alive.

The rest of the team had also returned to the camp side of the mountain. Not only to help search for Ty but also to ensure mission success. They still had kill orders, and if, by some miracle, either Black Jack or Babic had survived the explosion, the team were to go weapons hot.

To cover the ground as fast as possible, they spread out in a search formation with ten to fifteen meters between themselves and moved quickly.

As the team descended, Knight took up a new location and pulled out a high-powered spotter scope to assess the totality of the camp's damage.

Looking around, he saw that the storage building that housed the bombs had been vaporized. There were no standing walls, and the foundation was now a deep crater.

Likewise, the house that Black Jack and Babic had been sleeping in was nearly gone. Less than half of the front side wall, where the front door had been, was still standing but engulfed in flames. Only the furthest building from the blast survived. Its roof was gone, and it was also on fire.

Knight noticed two insurgents moving as he scanned the area for life.

One in the middle of the creek near the sole remaining building.

The second, a guard near the front gate, crawled toward the village.

Through the scope, Knight could tell this second insurgent had sustained severe injuries and would likely not survive. However, the one moving out of the creek onto shore was standing upright and only appeared to have sustained minor injuries. Most likely, a late-night urge to take a piss had saved this guy's life after being blown into the water.

From Knight's perspective, this single survivor was not important and was just a lucky guy who would be able to tell the story of the storage building exploding.

"Four, is there any movement?" Newbold asked.

"Two insurgents. One with what appears to be fatal injuries and the other saved by the creek. Do we have eyes on One?"

"Not yet," Tiller said, "What about Babic or Black Jack?"

"No movement from the house. It's been destroyed. Requesting permission to join the search."

"Negative. Keep eyes on the camp, and let me know if you see anything new."

The next few minutes were spent in silence as the team covered as much ground as possible, with half of them now below point alpha.

This was becoming a cause for concern. During planning, they had predicted the kill radius would reach their rally point high up the mountain.

That's what most civilians get wrong about explosions.

If you had asked Ty before he became a Marine what kills a person when a bomb explodes, he would have said the fireball or the shock wave. But that would only be partially true.

The fireball would undoubtedly kill anyone and perhaps even vaporize them. The guard he killed with his knife outside the storage building would have been vaporized.

But, what kills the most people is the lethal debris created by the explosion's shockwave. Fragments of everything from the buildings, vehicles, trees, and even the ordnance become tiny, deadly projectiles moving at ungodly speeds that rip through everything in their paths.

With six one-thousand-pound bombs exploding, the blast radius reached point alpha. And Ty was nowhere to be found.

The forest was on fire as the team reached and moved below point alpha. The few trees still standing had no branches or leaves on them. Several were reduced to ripped, jagged stumps after they had exploded in the blast wave. Putting even more deadly splinters in the air.

"I see him!" Henry yelled loud enough that several team members nearby heard him without their radios.

Henry was about fifty meters below the team when he jumped off a small ledge and, standing back upright, saw boots sticking out from beneath a pile of fallen branches several meters away. Even before he reached Ty's side, he called for the rest of the team.

During his ascent, Ty had covered a lot of ground, but the darkness plagued him. The uneven ground had twice caused him to lose his footing and slide down. In one case, he did several backflips.

Newbold had just announced that there were 'two minutes' before the blast. Ty tried to speed up, knowing he wasn't yet out of the kill zone. Already running like someone trying to escape death, he tried to go faster.

"Thirty seconds," Newbold announced.

He wasn't going to make it. There was no way Ty would clear the blast zone, but he needed to try and hope to find a safe spot before the countdown ended. With his rifle cradled in his right arm like a football, Ty hauled ass up the steep slope.

"Five, four, three..." Newbold said.

That's when Ty felt it.

It wasn't the warmth of a fireball, and he didn't hear it. It felt like Ty was hit in the back by what he was sure was a dump truck going sixty miles per hour without even attempting to apply its brakes. No, the asshole driving it knew he had a full load and was better off running through the Marine than trying to stop the grossly overweight truck.

It wasn't like in the movies. Ty didn't get flung into the air, looking like the cool hero escaping death. Instead, he face-planted into the rocky slope, being crushed into the ground. In one last laugh at his expense, that asshole driving the dump truck decided to stop it with its back tires perfectly centered on Ty's back. Then, with a chuckle, he lifted his bed to drop the contents of the heavy load on him as he slowly pulled away from the hit-and-run scene.

The weight forcing Ty into the ground was the tree branches and other debris from the blast being shoved up the mountainside.

Henry started pulling the fallen forest off his Lieutenant when he reached him. Tiller was the next to arrive, just in time to help lift a massive limb lying diagonally across Ty's back. As they dropped the limb a couple of feet away, Henry knelt and started talking to Ty as he moved smaller trash away from his face and neck so he could check for a pulse.

Henry placed his pointer and middle finger on Ty's neck, trying to find a pulse. "He is alive."

"Holy shit!" Tiller exclaimed.

"His breathing is low."

"I don't see any bleeding or anything broken. Hold his head steady and help me turn him over," Tiller ordered.

Once on his back, Ty reflexively took in a deep breath.

Newbold reached them, "How is he?"

"He's alive, just unconscious. I'm not sure if he has internal bleeding or —," Tiller said.

Cough! Cough!

Ty opened his eyes.

Leaning over him, Tiller asked, "Ty, can you hear me?" No response. "Can you hear me?"

"Yeah," Ty choked out before coughing more.

"Can you move?"

"I think so. But I need a minute. The HVTs?"

Tiller grinned. "Eliminated. The explosion worked. The entire camp's gone."

"Good. Help me up."

The two Marines leaning over him helped Ty sit up. That's when he looked over what was left of the valley. "Damn, that was much bigger than I expected."

Henry tried to diffuse the strenuous situation, "That's what she said."

CHAPTER
ELEVEN

EXHAUSTED, dehydrated, and malnourished would be a gross understatement in describing Romeo Team. The events of the last week had left them in a state of decay, but nothing had yet been as tough as the three-day hike out of Iran.

Stepping out of the Blackhawk at Sykes, Romeo Team was greeted by what looked like the entire 1st Recon Battalion. Aimes and Williams moved out of the crowd of Marines to welcome the team once they had cleared the helicopter's rotors.

"Damn fine job, Hudson!" Aimes yelled into Ty's ear with the noise of the Blackhawk still just feet away. "Seriously, you made this battalion proud."

"Thank you, sir," Ty replied before Aimes turned away to greet Newbold and the rest of the team.

Grabbing Ty under his arm, Williams joked, "Shit, man! You look like hell."

Several other Marines rushed forward from the crowd to grab the team's weapons and gear, lightening their loads and helping them toward the Humvees that would take them to the base hospital.

Before getting in the truck, Ty asked Williams, "Have you spoken with Beth?"

"Several times. We spoke by phone yesterday. I told her you were fine and heading back to base. Let's get you cleaned up and debriefed, and then you can call her."

Ty nodded as he climbed into the front seat of a Humvee.

"Hey!" Williams called out. "What you and the guys did out there was a big deal. Not everyone might know that, but the most important people do. Big things are going to happen for you!"

Ty deflected his Captain's praise. "The team was great and did the Corps proud."

The team's debriefing felt like an eternity for Ty. Despite being safely back at FOB Sykes, it had been a long day. The morning hike to the landing zone to meet the Blackhawk and the hours of debriefings had left Ty near collapse. He got some food in his aching stomach while being questioned by the intelligence officers, but Ty was still hungry and craving hot food.

It had been over a week since he had a hot meal, but he needed to hear Beth's voice to let her know he was safe. As luck would have it, the sun had begun to set in Northern Iraq, with nighttime following fast. That meant she and the kids would be waking to a new day at Camp Pendleton.

The phone rang three times. "Hello?" Beth muttered, getting woken up by the call.

"Hey, love, it's me. Did I wake you?"

"Ty! No, I was in between snoozes. Are you okay?"

"I'm good. Tired after a long hike and need some sleep. But otherwise, I'm good."

"What happened after you-" She asked before Ty cut her off, knowing he couldn't give her a full answer.

"I'm so sorry. We hit the ground at Sykes just minutes after a Blackhawk was shot down in the nearby mountains. My team was first up in the rotation." Ty lied smoothly. "We were wheels up almost immediately after landing and just got back. I asked Marcus to get ahold of you and tell you what was happening."

"Yeah, he called me and then sent me several emails. But he couldn't tell me anything. I would hear from him every couple of days just for him to tell me you were safe and that he couldn't say anything else."

"I know, babe. It's not his fault, just part of the job."

Through tears and a weakened voice, Beth muttered, "I get that. But, for some reason, I've been so worried I wouldn't hear from you again."

"Hey... It's okay, I'm fine. It was just a routine mission, and I'm back safely. You don't have anything to worry about."

Despite wanting to, there was so much about the mission Ty could not tell her. He couldn't say, *'Yeah, I led a team into Iran and eliminated two high-value targets responsible for hundreds of American deaths.'*

And the very last thing he wanted to tell her was that he was the one who placed the charge on a bomb and then ran for his life up a steep mountain only to barely survive. There was no way that adventure was ever getting told.

"So, do you have a handsome boy in bed with you?"

"You caught me. In fact, I have a handsome boy and a cute blond girl lying next to me."

"I miss you all so much. Tell me how things are going at school and around the house?"

The next twenty minutes were perfect.

Ty heard all about Beth's week at work. He listened as Jake woke up and cried out with a wet diaper, and he chatted with Audrey for a few minutes while Beth changed her little brother.

Sure, Marines were big, strong, manly men who were expertly trained to kill and could act as tough as they wanted. But, nothing melted a heart quite like hearing their kid's voice while they were out on a deployment. Maybe it was that Ty had nearly died a couple of days earlier, or perhaps it was just the sound of the sweetest voice in the world, but he started to cry when Audrey spoke.

They were more than seven thousand miles apart, but this was the normalcy Beth and Ty needed. This was how they managed their relationship through his first two deployments. This was how she survived as a single working mom with two young children for months. The heavy burden of being a Marine's wife was something she carried well. At least, Ty thought she did.

When Beth returned to the call with Jake on her hip, just as Audrey was telling her daddy how she wasn't being allowed to watch TV.

Taking the phone, Beth sighed, "I knew she was going to tell you I wasn't letting her watch TV."

Ty laughed out loud. "Yeah, she's pretty upset about that."

"I don't mind her watching a little, but that's all she wants to do."

"I know, love. But she's such a good kid."

With a bit of a snarl, "Easy for you to say. You're not the one she keeps telling 'no' to."

"Audrey, go to bed… No."

"Audrey, eat your dinner… No."

"Audrey, be quiet, your brother is sleeping… No."

"You are a superhero, love," he said, "You're doing the right thing."

"I know. But, enough about what's going on here. When will you call again? Or when could we do a video call?"

"Let's do a video call tomorrow night when you get home from work and have had dinner."

Ty figured that suggesting after dinner would give her plenty of time to settle in at home and feed the kids without feeling pressed for time.

Selfishly, he also knew it would give him more time for sleep.

"That sounds good. I am so happy you called this morning, but I need to get the kids ready for daycare and get to work."

"I know. I'll talk to you tomorrow. I love you with all my heart."

"I love you too, Ty. Get some sleep."

"I will. Bye, my love."

"Bye."

CHAPTER
TWELVE

HOPE IN ONE HAND, *shit in the other. See which one fills up faster,* Ty thought as he sat in front of the monitor and camera for their video call the next day.

There had never been any secrets between Beth and Ty. He found the entire exercise of keeping even the smallest things from her pointless because she could easily see right through him. Ty loved that about his wife.

As the next few days passed, the challenge he ultimately had was that Beth knew him too well. Even in college, when they first met, she could see through his studious, quiet guy mystique that had worked well for him during his first three years at UCF. It might have been the initial attraction for her, but she didn't buy it for long.

During their second date, Beth made it a point to let Ty know she saw through his facade.

After watching Ty bowl his frame, she said, "You know I have you figured out."

"Yeah. You think so?"

"Yep! You're not that smooth. You try giving a cool, smart guy vibe, but you're a romantic and much funnier than you give yourself credit for."

"Romance and humor, are those things you like in a guy?"

"Maybe," she said before turning back as she reached down for her ball, "I'll admit it's working pretty good for you right now."

This small exchange between frames at an old, worn-down bowling alley sealed the deal for Ty. He was falling in love, and it set a precedent of honesty in their young relationship.

While they never talked specifics about his first two deployments, she could always pick up when Ty had a tough day, lost a fellow Marine, or had a close call himself. He didn't know how she knew, so trying to keep things from her wasn't easy.

As news broke of Babic's and Black Jack's deaths, Ty was unsure how the coverage back home would frame it or how much attention it would get. He hoped it was a passing story buried deep in the news cycle. If he were lucky, a celebrity or political scandal would dominate the headlines.

The brutal reality was that Beth was an officer's wife living in a tight-knit group of other wives on a military base. The odds were she was better informed than the president of the United States.

As is their norm, they spent the first twenty minutes as a family. His family crowded in front of the monitor and camera on a small desk in the living room. Beth had dressed both kids in cute pajamas. Audrey had a bow in her hair and was all smiles as she sat on her mom's lap. Jake was in her right arm, and she occasionally lifted him to face the camera so Ty could talk directly to him.

It was early morning for Ty, but it was late evening in Southern California, so Beth eventually stepped away to put Jake in his crib, giving Audrey and Ty a little daddy-daughter time.

After a few minutes of just them on the call, Ty said goodnight to Audrey. She headed off to her bed after giving him the sweetest-blown kiss. This gave Beth and Ty time to themselves, and Ty quickly found out how informed she was.

Once Audrey was out of the room. "So, was your intention to blow yourself up?"

Ty's jaw almost hit the desk he was sitting at. His eyes widened, realizing how much she knew. There was no time wasted with small talk. She didn't try to see if he would offer anything up or confess. She dropped a conversation bomb and put Ty on the spot.

"No, it wasn't the plan, and it wasn't even that close."

With an accusatory tone, Beth replied, "Really! Rumor here is that a team from your company was responsible for it, and the team leader was almost killed."

Ty fidgeted in his seat. "That's just base gossip trying to make the fish bigger than it actually was."

Beth and Ty glared at each other on the screen. She wanted to scold him for taking risks and almost getting killed. He was stuck, knowing he could not move the conversation to another topic until she was satisfied. When she did speak, she took an unexpected path.

Using a softer tone. "Everyone is making this out to be nearly as big as Saddam Hussein being captured. Is it?"

"It's nowhere near that big of a deal, but it was a good win. It's just getting attention because we haven't had a lot of good news about the war lately."

"And it was-" she started before noticing Ty nodding in answering the question he knew was being asked. "Was it close?"

"Not something I want to do again."

They were at an impasse.

Ty decided Beth deserved a little bit of the truth and broke the silence between them. "It was a difficult mission. But I had the best team possible, and everything went according to plan. And at the end of the day, two really bad guys that have killed scores of Americans are dead."

Holy shit! Ty thought, *did I just admit to my wife that I led a team of Marines into Iran, and we killed two high-valued targets?*

This was everything a Marine shouldn't tell his wife about a mission. It was entirely inappropriate and illegal.

With their call ending no better than it had started, Ty decided he needed to blow off some steam. The best way he could do that was with a three-mile run around the perimeter of the fenced airfield, a shower, lunch, and a trip back to sixteenth-century Spain through the pages of *Don Quixote.*

Ty wasn't always a reader. Surely never cared much for the classics. Give him a modern spy novel or crime thriller, and he would flip through the pages out of boredom.

That all changed during his second deployment. 1st Recon Battalion had just fought in the first battle of Fallujah when they rotated out of the city, and Ty found himself with a lot of free time. A copy of Bram Stoker's *Dracula* sat unclaimed on a table in his barracks for about a week before he picked it up out of pure boredom one afternoon. Maybe it was the brilliance of the story or the complete lack of other ways to occupy the hours of the day, but Ty got consumed with it.

His love for the classics was born.

. . .

Sitting in his favorite reading spot, leaning against the barracks wall at Forward Operating Base Sykes a year and a half after finishing *Dracula*, Ty used another classic to escape the war zone where he again found himself.

"Lieutenant Hudson!" Barked the battalion's Sergeant Major in his scruffy, one-tone-fit-all situations voice.

Ty immediately knew who it was and rose to greet him. *This isn't good.*

The Sergeant Major turned to the side and lifted his arm as if to usher Ty from the shade he had been sitting under. "The Colonel wants to see you now."

Walking past him, Ty feared his call hours early with Beth had been monitored, and he was now on his way to get reprimanded by Aimes. For a brief moment, Ty couldn't tell if he was being accompanied or if he was being escorted. As he questioned why Aimes would be sending the Sergeant Major to get him instead of a runner or a lower-ranked Marine, Ty quickly peered down at the man's waist as he stepped by to see if he had a sidearm on him. Much to his relief, he didn't. Ty's nerves were further settled down when he pivoted to walk alongside him.

It had been days since Ty was last in the HQ. At that time, it was a beehive of bustling Marines setting up electronics and communications as the first order of business with 1st Recon's arrival. Today, there was order and an easy feeling of business as usual. The handful of people working at stations along the walls or standing at the end of the room updating a large dry-erase board with troop movements ignored the two men as they walked in.

Inside, Ty was directed to a room at the back. There, he found Aimes and Williams standing around the table. A handful of large maps, folders, and pencils were scattered about. Aimes was leaning on the table with his balled-up fists holding down the largest map. Williams appeared relaxed despite his arms being crossed.

With both of them waiting on him, Ty was sure he knew why he had been summoned.

The initial greetings went as expected. Aimes peppered Ty with a handful of questions about Beth and the kids back home, how his platoon's morale was holding up, and how his recovery was going.

Then the old man got down to business. "Hudson, you've been a Force Recon Marine for two years?"

"Correct, sir."

"What's next for you?"

Confused, Ty asked, "Sir?"

Ty wasn't sure if this was Aimes' roundabout way of telling him he was about to spend his immediate future in a military prison for sharing classified secrets with Beth, but this was not a question he was expecting.

Before Aimes responded, he and Williams glanced at each other. In the odd exchange, Williams gently nodded as if he told the Colonel it was okay to proceed. Ty didn't know what was happening as he observed their glance. Then Williams spoke.

"Lieutenant, the Secretary of the Navy has awarded you the Navy Cross in recognition of your bravery in Iran."

Captain Williams placed an open medal case on the table between him and Ty. In it was the bronze Navy Cross, dangling from a dark blue ribbon with a single white stripe down its center.

Sheepishly looking away, Ty muttered, "Sir, I did nothing the Marines under my command wouldn't have done."

"You are right, Ty. But it was you who risked your life for the sake of the mission and your Marines."

"Thank you, sir. I will do my best to live up to it."

Turning to Aimes, Williams said, "That's not all."

Aimes moved from behind the large table to stand in front of Ty.

His slow trudge and anticipating smile revealed what was happening.

"Lieutenant Hudson, it's my honor to promote you to the rank of captain," Aimes said. Reaching into his left pocket, he pulled out a small black case and opened it to show the pair of silver double bars that indicated the rank.

Shaking his extended right hand, Ty thanked Aimes as he took the black case with his left hand.

Williams and the Sergeant Major, still in the room, congratulated Ty with handshakes and even a long hug from Williams.

As the two returned to their previous places, Ty asked an important clarifying question. "Sir, will I be given a company or remain with 1st Platoon?"

Unless something had changed, each of the five companies that made up the 1st Recon Battalion had commanders. Promoting a platoon leader to captain without giving them the responsibility of leading their own company would be highly unusual.

So, Ty expected Aimes to tell him which company he would be taking over and who would backfill him as commander of 1st Platoon.

He did neither.

CHAPTER
THIRTEEN

WILLIAMS HAD BEEN SITTING with Ty for the last hour. He stood up to leave after Ty suggested he needed time to think. With no objection, Williams reached over with his right hand to take Ty by his left shoulder to get his attention.

With a calculated smile, "Ty, this is a night for celebration. You've been awarded the Navy Cross and been promoted. Let tomorrow take care of itself."

The nighttime sky was clear, with the stars burning bright without the light pollution Ty was accustomed to in Southern California. The half-crescent moon was already high and was bright enough to cast his shadow on the ground. The light breeze blowing in from the western desert had not cooled with the absence of the sun. While not quite like sitting in a sauna, it wasn't a refreshing evening breeze. Instead, it left Ty sticky with sweat, his mouth and eyes dry from the dust being blown around.

Much of the base was already in their barracks. The only noise came from three Marines at a nearby table. Ty was in his usual sitting spot, but he wasn't reading. His head spun as he played out the different scenarios before him.

Williams was right in that tonight was for celebrating. Just a few hours ago, Ty was awarded the second-highest medal for valor that a Marine could get. Then he was promoted to captain a year or maybe even two before he would've expected.

Neither of these accolades had sunk in. Until now, he had not even thought of telling Beth the good news.

No, for the last three hours, Ty had been fixated on what Aimes told him after he gave him the silver pair of bars.

"Captain Hudson, the world is changing. We are fighting an enemy that refuses to wear a uniform and is more likely to attack soft civilian targets than us. It's a changing battlefield, and luckily, we have a Commandant who realizes the Corps needs to change with it."

Standing slightly taller, Ty asked, "Sir, I couldn't agree more. What's the Commandant planning?"

Ty didn't know much about the Marine Commandant. The little bit he did know could be summed up as rumor. And they all suggested he was a better politician than a Marine.

Excited, Aimes replied, "The General has authorized the creation of a Marine Special Operations Regiment. This will be a Tier One unit focused on taking the fight directly to the enemy and eliminating key targets no matter where they are."

"Sir, that sounds like a familiar mission."

"That's right. It's a mission you know how to execute. Which is why we're having this conversation."

Anticipating what was coming. "Sir, I would suspect most of the operators will be pulled from Recon."

"Correct, again. Assessment and selection will start as early as next month. I expect your name to be on the list of volunteers from 1st Battalion."

Wait! What? That wasn't an ask. That wasn't even a suggestion. That was about as close to an order as a Marine officer could give without saying, *'That's an order.'*

Ty didn't know what to think about Aimes' brash approach. The decision to undergo an intense selection process to try to make a Tier One unit wasn't to be made lightly or influenced by commanding officers' expectations.

The feelings that rushed over Ty was a balance of pride in that his Battalion Commander felt he could do it and fear.

Sitting alone against the barracks, the fear was winning.

Can I put Beth and the kids through this?

Being a Recon Marine wasn't easy on anyone. Ty knew how much he had asked of Beth over the last few years. And there was no way this would be fair to her, Audrey, or Jake. *Was this too much to ask?*

He also had to consider if this was something that he wanted to do.

Ty was very close to dropping out of the Basic Recon Course on more than one occasion. His friend Marcus Williams helped steady him and push him through to the end. While Ty had never admitted that he wouldn't have made it without him, he wasn't jumping to put himself back through that level of crazy. The physical and mental effort it would take to make these newly formed teams was insane. Then it's back off to war.

Well, sort of.

As Aimes said, these special operation teams were not being created to fight the war as it was now. They were to fight the small engagements Romeo Team and Ty had just completed in Iran. While he recognized the need for the Marine Corps to alter its approach to winning the War on Terror, Ty was in his third deployment. That he had survived and thus far been unharmed was a miracle.

Was he willing to repeatedly continue to stress test the odds as a tier-one operator? Ty had a lot to consider, but he also needed to try to get some rest. So, he packed it in for the night and headed for his bunk, knowing it would be a long night.

It turned out to be restless. It was the type of sleep that, even when he was asleep, Ty's mind was racing. It felt as if he hadn't lost consciousness. As luck would have it, the barracks came to life just as his mind rested.

After a quick shower to wash the dust and sweat off from the prior night, Ty decided to call home. He needed Beth.

His first few minutes on the phone were spent trying to convince her everything was alright. "There was no reason to be concerned," he pleaded.

After she asked what was wrong the third time, Ty replied, "I got hit with a bad bout of homesickness this morning and needed to hear your voice."

In hindsight, he should have known better than to call home on an off day. They had just spoken the day before by video. For him to call the next day was out of routine, and this put Beth on edge.

"Ty, I always want to talk to you, too. I didn't expect your call tonight. It's just that I have work friends over."

This was unusual for a weeknight. A touch of jealousness swept away Ty's homesickness as his tone shifted from feeble sadness to pointed inquisition.

"On a school night. Who's all over there?"

"Just some fellow teachers. We have testing later this week, and a few of us wanted to get together to complain about it over several bottles of wine."

Ty didn't know what to say. He tried to work through these new emotions. Beth would often have Marine spouses or partners over, and a couple of times a month, she would go out for *'milk and cookies'* with her fellow teachers. They were usually not scheduled. Instead, one teacher would get the inkling to go out for a happy hour and spread the word using this clever code phrase in front of their elementary students.

Ty could tell by her tone and hesitation that he had caught her off guard and that she wanted to return to her guests. Regardless of how he felt, Ty knew he needed to respect that.

With a softer, more encouraging tone, "Go have fun. Everything is good here, and I'll call tomorrow."

"Thanks, babe. I'll talk to you tomorrow. Love you with all my heart."

Beth hung up before Ty had a chance to say goodbye.

This was an awkward feeling.

Ty couldn't think of a single call in their time together when his wife got off the phone so easily. The hint of jealousy that had crept into his feelings was a heavy burden. One that Ty knew could weigh down a Marine and drive them mad.

He had seen plenty of others struggle with it as their spouses or girlfriends were living their lives while they were at war.

Sitting alone in the back of the barracks, Ty struggled to break the grip of these emotions. Staring at the phone, he fought the temptation to call back. It was a tale of two voices battling in his head. One says that something doesn't feel right, and he needs to pick up the phone. The other pleaded that he needed to trust his wife and pull his shit together. In the end, neither voice won out.

"Captain!" A voice yelled from the front of the barracks.

Ty turned to see Henry walking swiftly toward him with a hurried expression on his face. Behind him, members of 1ˢᵗ Platoon started to rush in. Realizing this was urgent, Ty leaped out of his chair and hurried to meet Henry.

"Sir, 1ˢᵗ Platoon, Bravo Company is under fire and taking casualties in Mosul. Force Company is being mobilized to assist!"

"Roger that," Ty said, stepping past Henry to get to his bunk while addressing the barracks. "1ˢᵗ Platoon, gear up for a fight! You have two minutes!"

CHAPTER
FOURTEEN

THE PLATOON EXITED the barracks in a fast jog to FOB Sykes' loading zone. A convoy of trucks was already there for Force Company to load onto. Ty didn't have to worry about giving the order to load. Tiller was already directing Marines towards the first two Cougars in the column.

The Cougar was a favorite among the men. It was a large troop carrier armored to be mine and improvised bomb resistant. Since being introduced a year earlier, no Marine has lost their life when traveling in one.

As 1st Platoon loaded, Ty saw Aimes and Williams huddled near a Humvee at the head of the column. Ty rushed to them to find out what was going on.

"Captain Hudson, we have Marines down. The medevacs can't land until enemy fire is suppressed," Aimes shouted as Ty approached.

"We're getting updates by the minute," Williams said. "We won't know how we will deploy until we get closer. I'm in the lead Humvee with Herrera and Brooks. I'll keep everyone updated as I get information."

"Roger that."

Ty pivoted and ran back to the first Cougar without saying another word. There was nothing to be overly concerned with for the moment. Nothing about the situation was unusual. Force Company was used to responding with little information about what was happening on the ground. This was business as usual.

Landon Brooks was the company's radio operator, and Manny Herrera was its First Sergeant. Both would be in the Humvee with Willimas to help coordinate the deployment, air cover, and the medevacs.

When Ty reached the truck, Tiller asked, "What's the plan?"

"The normal shit! The situation is dynamic, and we'll figure it out as we get closer."

"Has the road to Mosul been cleared lately?"

This question stopped Ty dead in his tracks. He had just reached up to the grab bar on the backside of the Cougar and lifted up on the first of two steps to load. Looking back fast to his platoon sergeant, "I don't know."

From Sykes, there was one main road into Mosul. It was two lanes most of the way but became four for the last five kilometers into the city. Marine and coalition bomb detection vehicles frequently patrolled, but Ty had no idea if it had been done recently.

It seemed like one or two mines or IEDs would be found every week and had to be detonated. Since the fall of Baghdad, the most dangerous part of a Marine's deployment wasn't combat; it was traveling in ground vehicles.

Hanging on the back of the Cougar, Ty pressed the button on his chest to activate his radio, "Captain Williams, come back."

"Go for Williams."

"Has EOD cleared the road into Mosul?"

"I don't know. Let me find out. But we need to move either way."

Ty and Tiller, who had heard the entire exchange in his earpiece, shared a concerned look. Despite not knowing the last time Explosive Ordnance Disposal teams had cleared the road, their orders were to move out. Without saying anything else, they loaded into the Cougar and secured the rear door just as the seventeen-ton vehicle crept forward in first gear and then roughly shifted into second as it cleared FOB Sykes' main gates.

Eight Cougars were in the convoy, with Williams in the lead Humvee and two medical Humvees bringing up the rear. By the time the last one cleared the main gates, Williams informed the company that EOD had not cleared the road today and that the drivers needed to use appropriate spacing.

In the back of the Cougar, a deep hum filled the silence. The personnel compartment, or what the Marines called the 'rear box,' was hot, noisy, and suffocating for long drives. The cost of being protected by an IED was personal comfort. It was a cost every Marine would pay. It was also one they would complain about every time they loaded into the rear box.

On each side of the compartment was a flat bench with seat belts that no one used and three-inch thick ballistic glass windows. Each measured a foot and a half wide by eight inches tall and was large enough for the Marines to safely scan the area during the ride or before they unloaded.

It was still morning, so the day's heat hadn't yet peaked, making the temperature inside the box bearable. But that didn't stop a few of the guys from complaining about the subtle roar of the massive engine as it got up to speed or the humming of the four large tires just below the rear box on this six-wheeled truck.

Ten minutes had passed when the cabin went quiet as Williams started to provide real-time updates of the situation on the ground with Bravo Company. This included the number of known casualties, insurgent positions, and the status of air cover.

By his description, Bravo Company was in a world of hurt. At least six Marines had been killed, twice that number wounded, and ammunition was running low. Their position was on the verge of being overrun. Air cover was ineffective because of surrounding civilian buildings and the proximity of the insurgents to Bravo's position.

As Williams described the situation, it was clear their survival would rest on Force Company's arrival. But they were still ten minutes out.

The mood in the rear box changed. The joking had stopped as each Marine sat on the edge of the bench—most doing final weapon checks. Ty, too, took a moment to make sure he had chambered a round in both his rifle and sidearm. Once confirmed, he did an inventory of the flash bangs, hand grenades, and extra magazines secured to his body.

"Force Company, five mics-" Williams said before going silent.

The other nine Marines in the rear box became the bellows of an accordion, getting squeezed hard as the truck driver slammed the brakes. Everyone was thrown forward against the cab wall. But their grunts and screams did not cover the unmistakable reason Williams' voice got cut off on the radio.

The sound was deafening. Even the direction of the boom was easily identifiable from where Ty was in the Cougar.

The lead Humvee had hit an IED.

Ty was lying on top of two other Marines in the middle of the benches when his situational awareness kicked in. Pushing the guy directly under him on the floor, Ty scrambled to the middle window on the truck's right side to see Williams' Humvee.

He couldn't see anything. There was too much dust and sand kicked up from the explosion. His heart began to race as fear for his friend's life began to take over.

"SitRep! I need a SitRep!" Ty screamed into the radio.

After a short pause, the driver of Ty's Cougar said, "Lead Humvee has been hit. I say again, Lead Humvee has been hit."

"1st Platoon, fall out to set up a perimeter. All other platoons stay put until further orders."

Ty moved from the window to stack up behind Tiller and another Marine just opening the door.

The Marines in Ty's platoon were professionals. They were well-trained and experienced in combat situations. They didn't need further orders about what to do or how to set up a perimeter. It was happening without another word being spoken.

Ty's worst fear was realized as he exited the truck's rear and turned its corner.

Williams' Humvee was severely damaged on the passenger side. There was no sign of life. He and the rest of the platoon started to make their way toward the wreck in a quick step while scanning the area for insurgents or signs of another device.

As he, Tiller, and several other Marines reached the Humvee, Ty yelled, "Medic! Medic!"

The entire vehicle's frame and passenger wall had been bent inwards. The rear passenger door and the vehicle's back end had been ripped off. The front door was caved into the seat where Williams was. Its ballistic glass was blown out.

Reaching its side, Ty looked into the Humvee from the rear door that was missing to see First Sergeant Herrera's mangled and disfigured body. His entire right side, arm, leg, and face were gone. He was dead.

Ty quickly glanced over to Brooks, who was beside Herrera in the rear seat behind the driver—no movement or sign of consciousness. The company's radio man was severely mutilated, with metal fragments protruding from his body. Ty had no idea what his condition was.

He turned to look at his friend through the opening to see Williams' body bent over onto himself. His head on the dashboard above the stick shift. Ty couldn't see any physical damage like what Herrera had suffered. He grabbed the heavy, armored door that was warped in and began to try to pry it open.

Tiller and a corpsman, a Naval medic, who had just arrived, joined in with trying to open it. As the three struggled, the metal-on-metal friction made a high-pitched screeching sound as it finally gave way for at least one person to reach Williams.

Ty instinctively was the first to lean in. "Marcus! Marcus, talk to me, buddy!"

Tiller wrapped his arms around Ty in a bear hug to forcefully pull him back out of the door. "Ty, let the corpsman work. There's nothing you can do. Let him help."

Ty struggled against Tiller's grip. Trying his best to look over the medic's work to see if there was a sign of life. Giving out a heavy grown, Ty relented in his effort to get loose. Tiller released him. Ty stepped to the side to look back through where the rear door had been to see the medic slowly turn Williams's limp body to face him.

Blood was spilling from his right cheek and around his ear as several large pieces of ballistic glass were embedded in his skull. Ty could now see that his right arm was badly broken. The bone ripped through his forearm just inches below his elbow. The right side of his uniform and tactical vest was spotted with dark red stains. No doubt, caused by the blown-out window.

Ty's heart sank seeing his close friend torn apart.

Pulling him back into the situation, the medic screamed, "He has a pulse! But we need to have him airlifted now!"

Ty didn't hesitate. He backed out of the wreckage to press his radio button, "We have Marines down and need an immediate medevac. I say again, Marines down and need a medevac now!"

With his head out of the Humvee, Ty looked at the broader situation unfolding. They had only been there for a minute. In that short time, the two medical trucks following the convoy pulled alongside and pulled the driver from the vehicle while another corpsman looked over Brooks.

Ty looked around for Tiller and found him talking to another radio operator. Noticing, Tiller gave a nod for Ty to join them.

"Captain, Bravo Company is being overrun and needs-" Tiller started to say while holding the receiver to his right ear. Stopping with new information coming in. "They're falling back into a building in a last stand."

A Marine Recon platoon being overrun wasn't something that happened. Maybe not since the Vietnam War. Tiller stared at Ty, anticipating that he would take action, and he didn't disappoint.

Now in command, Ty ordered 2nd Platoon to remain with Williams and the destroyed lead Humvee.

Tiller immediately understood what had been ordered. He began moving 1st Platoon back to their trucks while relaying their ETA to Bravo Company.

But Ty had another decision to make.

The corpsman worked hard over Williams to stabilize him for the flight, which could easily be the difference he needed to survive. Yet, he was 1st Platoon's corpsman, and they were loading back up to go into a firefight. If the platoon took casualties, they would need the medic, too.

Ty kneeled next to him to whisper, "Save my friend."

He glanced up at Ty from his frantic work and nodded. The Corpsman knew the decision Ty had just made and the potential consequences it meant for the Marines in 1st Platoon. Ty had prioritized his friend's life over theirs.

Reaching into the wreck, Ty placed his hand on Marcus' shoulder to give it a loving squeeze. Then, lifting himself off the ground, he returned to the Marines waiting in the Cougar. "Weapons free. Let's take this fucking fight to them!"

CHAPTER
FIFTEEN

NOTHING QUITE SETTLES emotions down like a good old-fashioned gunfight. With every trigger pull, the built-up rage of seeing a fallen Marine flows out of you. Every round put down range at an enemy is a small piece of fury expertly aimed to kill those you feel are responsible.

Seeing his good friend mutilated by ballistic glass and clinging to life gave Ty a stern resolve he had never felt before. The certainty of his purpose was resolute. That purpose now fueled the years of training he had suffered through as a Force Recon Marine.

But none of this could be said out loud.

Not to those in the room with him right now.

For the second time in a month, Ty was being interviewed by Marine intelligence officers for his actions and decisions under fire. The last thing he could say to the two officers sitting across from him was that he felt enraged by what happened to his friend, Captain Marcus Williams, and that he was on a rage-induced warpath.

No. He couldn't say that. But, deep down, Ty knew that was what had happened.

Instead, Ty kept his story vague, not mentioning many of the confirmed kills 1st Platoon had while in Mosul for more than eight hours.

The story was simple.

As the column approached the small village on the outskirts of Mosul where Marines in Bravo Company had been overrun, the convoy came under fire from small arms. The thick armor protected the Marines from the Ak-47 fire by safely deflecting the rounds.

In the rear box, Ty could easily tell when the tires were hit by accident or in an attempt to disable the large truck. The sound of rounds hitting thick, steel-belted rubber was a deep thud, not the high-pitched ping of lead on steel. After a few thuds, he would hear the unmistakable sound of the automatic air compressor under the box kick on to maintain air pressure in the tires. The Cougar was built for this, and as long as it was a small arms fire, Ty and his Marines were safe.

After about a minute of taking fire, the driver radioed to say he was diverting off the main road to avoid burning cars. Once off, he would position the platoon near a wall to provide cover as they disembarked. As he finished speaking, everyone was thrown again as the driver veered off the smooth pavement onto the uneven desert surface.

The sight of nine grown men bouncing around in the Cougar's rear box might have been a comedy stunt if it wasn't such a serious moment. One last heavy bump and then everyone was again shoved against the cab as the driver hit the brakes to make a skidding stop.

"Right side! Right side!" The driver yelled.

The team was to exit the vehicle and go immediately to the safety of the right side of the Cougar to avoid enemy fire.

Tiller and Ty reached for the double doors. Glancing back to see the Maines of 1st Platoon stacked up, Ty ordered, "Go, go, go!"

They both pushed heavy doors open. Ty followed the swinging steel out with his boots hitting the ground first. Pivoting to his left to clear the door, Ty followed the truck's passenger side to the front. By instinct and trust, he knew the other Marines had exited the Cougar and were on his heels as he reached the front wheel to kneel.

He crept forward to peer around the front bumper as he felt Tiller behind him, leaning up to look over the truck's tall hood. The two had neither practiced this nor had done it before, but it made perfect sense. Tiller's height was perfect for peering over the hood while Ty could safely assess the situation from his position behind the tire.

"Three insurgents with AKs on the roof of the center building and another two to four on the right roof," Tiller said into his radio.

Ty followed with his assessment, "Ten to twelve fighters at the base of the buildings behind the short wall. Unknown number in the buildings."

Ty looked towards the truck's rear to see that several other Cougars had followed theirs off the road and positioned themselves similarly. The Marines of 1ˢᵗ Platoon had disembarked and were awaiting orders.

Scanning the area, he couldn't see the Cougars carrying 3rd Platoon. "Lieutenant Jovis, what's 3ʳᵈ Platoon's sitrep?"

"Captain, 3ʳᵈ Platoon is on the North side of the road, about three hundred meters from your position. We are taking fire from multiple positions and recommend moving."

Jovis was in his first deployment as a Recon Marine. He was fresh out of basic recon training and had never been in combat. He had always shown himself a capable commander during training exercises. With only that small sample, Ty had no choice but to believe in his ability to lead his platoon. He just needed to give Jovis the orders he was waiting for.

"Lieutenant, we are five blocks from Bravo's last reported position. Move down the side road just east of the main highway and rally with 1ˢᵗ Platoon at Bravo's position. We will take a similar path up a road further to the east."

This would require the Marines of the 3rd Platoon to cross the four lanes of the main highway to be on the same side as Ty and his Marines. As each platoon moved up parallel roads east of the main highway, they would prevent insurgents from using it to split their positions, potentially overrunning them.

Turning to Tiller, Ty said, "Sergeant, do you see the road to the east with the blue van blocking the intersection? We're moving to the wall and then up that street to Bravo."

"Roger that, sir."

Tiller began giving orders to the Marines behind him and then to the rest of the platoon. Just a moment later, Henry moved to Ty's right and quickly nodded to indicate he was ready. Ty took one more peek past the bumper before yelling, "Move!"

He leaned out from the safety of his crouch behind the tire with his M4 rifle at the ready and aimed at the first insurgent that came into view. Two rapid trigger pulls equaled one less threat. At that moment, Henry and one other Marine ran for the wall as Tiller and another Marine took shots from their position over the hood.

They were in the fight.

Ty's first kill of the day was an insurgent who stood from his protective cover on the opposite wall.

After 1ˢᵗ Platoon cleared the initial set of insurgents, Henry led the Marines past the blue van and down the narrow street toward Bravo's last reported position. Even without radio contact, Ty knew they were still fighting by the distant gunfire because of the unmistakable difference between a NATO 5.56 and the much larger AK-47 round. With Bravo still exchanging fire, there was hope to reach them before they were overrun. But this meant the Marines in 1st Platoon needed to move as fast as they could.

"Henry, pick up the pace!" Ty hollered.

About a block away, he heard a massive outburst of fire ringing out from the northwest where Jovis' platoon would have been coming into the square. The burst indicated that Jovis and his platoon had arrived and that the situation was precarious.

3rd Platoon must have had an easier time getting there.

"Captain Hudson, 3rd Platoon has engaged a large body of insurgents to the northeast and has Bravo in sight."

"Roger that. 1st Platoon is entering the square to the east."

The square was a small park with a fountain at its center. Several tall palm trees were circling its edge, but they provided no cover. From his vantage point, Ty could easily see where Bravo was dug in behind several burned-out cars and concrete barriers that appeared to have been constructed at the building just behind them. The park center and the two three-story buildings on the opposite side were filled with insurgents.

No orders were needed, the Marines immediately went into action by laying down fire on the elevated position as they moved further into the square.

With a steady voice, Ty said, "Command, we have reached Bravo. Estimated battalion strength force. Requesting immediate air support. I say again, requesting air support."

"Negative on air support. Too many civilians in the area," said a calm voice over the radio.

This was complete bullshit, and Ty should have expected the response, but it still pissed him off! He was confident that 1st Platoon Bravo Company had also asked for air support as they were getting attacked and received the same response. It wasn't that Ty knew or didn't know there were Iraqi civilians in the buildings opposite of them. It was that he didn't care.

Call me cold, but I care more about the lives of my Marines and those in the other two platoons than civilians in the buildings we were taking fire from. That part was left out of his story, too.

Ty continued by explaining that was when all hell broke loose. Mortar fire started to pound 3rd Platoon's position. Even from his side of the square, Ty could make out Marines diving into buildings, behind any protection they could find, or in at least one instance, retreating.

Given the fire frequency, Ty suspected two to three mortar teams were being given directional fire support from the buildings across from their position. A well-placed mortar crew could wreak havoc on a platoon. Ty knew this posed a significant threat and that it would not be long before his men were under fire from them.

The two officers interviewing him had already criticized him for ordering the medic to stay with Williams. Ty knew they would disapprove of his next decision to split 1st Platoon, but that's what needed to be done.

Tiller took two fire teams down the street they had come from to move further east to flank the mortar positions. Ty stayed with the remaining two fire teams to make a direct assault on the two three-story buildings across the park.

Aggravated, Ty reminded the two men questioning him of command's decision not to provide air support. "The two buildings we needed air support on were overrun with an unknown number of enemy combatants. Without support, we had to make a direct assault on elevated positions."

The intel officer sitting on his right went to object or comment, but Ty cut him off and continued with his account of what happened next. Or at least the version that was light on details and specifics.

The two fire teams under Ty's command made their way across the park under heavy fire. They first entered the building on the right and worked their way up floor by floor until they reached the roof. Ty was coy in telling them they encountered moderate resistance and that they acted to eliminate all threats.

Once the roof was cleared, Ty ordered two other Marines to set up an overlook position to cover the teams moving to the next building. The rest of them went back down through the building and moved along the street to the next one. Once more, the Marines entered and worked their way to the roof. Ty described the resistance as being a little firmer but manageable for a team of highly trained Marines.

Somewhere in the bottom of the second building, Ty noticed he didn't hear mortar rounds hitting outside anymore. He assumed that Tiller and his teams had eliminated the threat, but this didn't deter his mission of clearing the building.

Upon exiting, Ty's teams regrouped with the rest of 1st Platoon and moved to where Lieutenant Jovis had linked up with Bravo.

Over the next four hours, the combined forces fought off several waves of insurgents while the Cougars made three round trips between the square and FOB Sykes to transport everyone back. Starting with Bravo, then 3rd Platoon, and finally Ty's platoon. As with his boots hitting the ground first, Ty's were the last to step off the ground into the safety of a Cougar.

That was the story of what would become known to 1st Reconnaissance Battalion as the Battle of Bloody Fountain.

CHAPTER
SIXTEEN

WHEN THE COUGAR'S doors squeaked open, Ty saw Aimes roaming between the trucks looking for someone. The Colonel's hurried pace suggested it was urgent, but Ty knew it wouldn't be good news when Aimes found who he was searching for.

"Captain, Williams is being prepped to be flown to Germany. If you hurry, you might be able to see him before they move him out of the field hospital."

Ty didn't respond. Just turned to Tiller to hand him his rifle.

Doctors, even in the Marine Corps, don't much care for rifles to be in their operating rooms, so Tiller took it without saying a word.

Running to the field hospital and bursting through the doors, Ty passed several 1st Platoon Bravo Company members waiting for medical attention. Most of the injuries did not look life-threatening, but there was plenty of commotion in the hallway and adjacent rooms. By his estimate, there were at least fifteen Marines with various wounds. The blood-marked floor was evidence of the severity of the situation.

Weaving through the crowd, Ty recognized several of them and noted that he would want to return to check on them after seeing Williams. But, right now, his friend was his priority.

When Ty came to the desk, the two nurses were using low voices to speak to one another. Neither looked up, but it didn't deter him from rudely interrupting them.

"I am looking for Captain Marcus Williams. Could you point me in his direction?"

Maybe it was his tone, the look on his face, or the fact that these nurses were professionals who were used to dealing with high-strung Marines because they didn't object.

Stepping from behind the desk, the older nurse said, "Follow me."

As she led him down a hall, she gave Ty an update without him having to ask. "The Captain is in critical condition, and we don't have the surgical experience he needs. We are stabilizing him for flight, and he should be moved any minute now to the transport."

"What are his odds?"

"Not great," she replied softly, honestly, as she opened a door and waved him through.

There he was, on a surgical table with two different doctors and the same amount of nurses working on him. One nurse was holding a bag of blood over him and looked to be gently squeezing it to ensure maximum flow. The other nurse supported the two doctors, giving attention to his head.

Ty knew not to say anything. No one in the room needed his distraction, and no one but the nurse holding the blood even noticed his presence.

This lasted for five minutes before the doctor on the left side of the table stepped back, pulled his mask down, and started to remove his bloody gloves. With final instructions to the nurse, he took a few slow, methodical steps toward Ty.

But when he spoke, it wasn't to him.

Looking past Ty, "It's a long shot, but we have done all we can here," the doctor told Aimes.

Colonel Aimes had walked into the room and stood to Ty's right. Due to his fixation on what was happening on the table, he had not even noticed the Colonel.

"He has lost his right eye. I am unsure if he will ever be able to use his leg again, but I am most concerned about the internal bleeding on the brain."

"Will he survive the flight?" Aimes asked.

"His odds are the same on the flight as they would be if he stayed here over the next several hours. At least when he lands in Germany, he will have the facilities and doctors he needs."

Turning to Ty, the doctor said, "We need to move him as soon as the nurse is done, but go ahead and take a minute with him as she finishes."

Ty briefly made eye contact with Aimes before approaching his friend. The young nurse looked up from her work to give what Ty assumed was a sorrow-filled expression. He couldn't be sure because everything was masked except for her eyes. Giving a tight-lipped nod, Ty turned his attention to Williams while taking in the blood-soaked bandage covering most of his head.

Only part of Williams' left cheek and most of his chin was exposed. The uniform along his right leg had been cut up to his hip, and his boot removed. Most of his leg was in bandages. On top of the layers of cotton gauze and wrap was a splint that kept his leg extended and slightly elevated on top of several pillows. His right arm wasn't quite as wrapped but was already in a sling resting on his chest. His frail body, clinging to life, was in drastic contrast to the proud Marine that climbed into the Humvee just hours before.

Struggling to breathe and fighting back tears, Ty knew he only had minutes before losing his composure. *I need to say goodbye.*

Ty took Williams's left hand in his. Feeling the girth and weight of his Naval Academy class ring in his hand, Ty started to cry. First, a single tear. Followed by a second and a third.

Leaning down to whisper in his ear, Ty's face was just inches from the nurse's hands, putting the finishing touches on the bandage wrap. Ty gripped his hand tighter and closed his eyes, pushing more tears down his face.

"Brother, you're a Recon Marine, and your story doesn't end here. Not like this," Ty mumbled into Williams' ear. "You've got this. You have to stay strong and push through this. I'll see you back at Pendleton in a few weeks, and the first round will be on me."

Ty gently leaned another inch in and kissed the side of his friend's head. Opening his eyes, Ty stood up to see that the nurse had finished her work. Both continued to look down at Williams' body. Not making eye contact.

Wiping away the tears, Ty said, "Thank you both for all you did for him."

When he turned to leave the room, Ty expected to see Aimes still there, but he was gone. Aimes had known Williams for nearly as long as he had. The Colonel had been his commanding officer for the last couple of years.

They had a mentor-to-mentee relationship, and it was clear that Aimes was grooming Williams for a successful career as a Marine officer.

Ty thought it was odd that he would leave before he was moved, but then it dawned on him that the Colonel had left for him. To allow Ty a few private moments with his friend, moments that could very well be his last with him.

Ty didn't know Aimes very well, however this kind gesture made him a huge fan.

Walking out of the operating room, Ty passed the two nurses from the desk coming into the room. Together with the two already in the room, they started to work quickly to move Williams to a rolling gurney.

Ty needed to leave. Not that he was in their way; rather, he needed to be alone.

Pushing through the doors, he started back out of the field hospital the same way he came in but stopped just a few steps down the hallway. If he continued this way, he would have to pass a large group of wounded Marines. Including the few who knew him. Standing in the middle of the dimly lit hallway, Ty quickly concluded that he didn't want to walk past them with red eyes, the dirt on his face smeared by wiping tears away, and possibly still crying. They were suffering far worse than he was, and it wouldn't be fair for him to rush by without acknowledging their sacrifice.

There was even a very good chance that this was where Aimes disappeared to after leaving the operating room. The thought of running into Aimes in this condition and possibly having to speak with him about Williams made the decision easy.

He didn't know how to leave the hospital from the back, but Ty would find it. Pivoting on his heels, he went in search of another way out.

Luckily, he found a back door leading out to a loading area for supplies. Coming out of the large open door into an alley between older airport buildings confused him for a minute. Ty knew the general direction of his barracks, so he instinctively went that way.

Turning one last corner, he heard the distinct sound of an Airforce C-17 Globemaster taking off. Looking up to his right to see the giant transport plane lift off the ground and bolt into the air. It wasn't airborne for long before it banked back to the West, towards Germany.

Having been in the Marines for a few years, the sight and sound of jets taking off were nothing more than background noise. They were easily dismissed and rarely looked at because they were common. But, this particular C-17 drew Ty's attention. As it turned over his head, he turned with it and stayed standing there, watching it fade into the distance.

Captain Marcus Williams, his friend, was on this transport. Its due west, heading toward the late afternoon sun, gave Ty hope that he would survive.

CHAPTER
SEVENTEEN

FOR THE SECOND night in a row, Ty struggled to sleep.

He had taken up his normal spot along the side of the barracks. It gave him the privacy he wanted and the space he needed to shed a few more tears. At one point, he nodded off before falling over while leaning against the wall. Jarring him awake, Ty jumped to his feet, not knowing what was happening or where he was.

It took a moment for the fog to clear and for him to realize where he was. Ty looked down at his watch to see that it was after 2 a.m. He had been here in his go-to spot for nearly eight hours. He was not sure when he fell asleep, but he was awake now.

Thoughts of Williams arriving in Germany filled his head. If Ty had been out here for eight hours, he must have landed by now. It was a seven-hour flight to Ramstein Air Base in southwest Germany. While it would be too soon for Ty to know his prognosis, he should be able to find out if Williams survived the flight.

Hustling over to the battalion HQ, Ty drew the attention of a couple of sentries, but none spoke to him. Maybe they didn't say anything because he was in a light jog, or perhaps because he was still in his tactical gear from the incursion into Mosul. Regardless, Ty was appreciative that they didn't slow him down.

Reaching the door, Ty slowed his pace to step into the building in a controlled manner. The last thing he wanted to do was to fly into the door in the dead of night and alarm anyone inside. As he cleared the doorway, Ty looked around to see three Marines. This was typical of late-night HQ duty when there wasn't an ongoing operation or threat in the area. It would have been safe to assume that any of the three sitting relaxed at their stations could have told him if the transport had landed and of his friend's condition. Ty wanted to be respectful and not just ask the Marine closest to him. Instead, he made his way toward the back of the open room to the watch officer, who would have the flight information and the latest condition of the battalion's strength and numbers.

On duty tonight was First Lieutenant Franklin Vassolle, or Franky, as the men in the battalion had nicknamed him. Crossing the room, he made eye contact with Ty. His expression was similar to the sentries on duty outside when they, too, noticed him still in tactical gear. He swept his eyes up and down Ty's ragged appearance but said nothing. Franky leaned out of the chair he was sitting in to place his coffee and the file he was reading on the desk.

Standing, he reached for a clipboard on the left side of the desk and handed it to Ty as he stopped in front of him. "Sir, the C-17 landed about forty-five minutes ago. Captain Williams survived the flight but remains in critical condition."

"Do you know if he has been seen by-."

Franky cut him off, "I am sorry, sir. That's all the information I have at this time."

The clipboard he handed Ty was the flight log showing the exact time the C-17 had touched down. A handwritten note beside the time read, 'alive, but still critical.'

Handing the clipboard back, "Thank you, Franky."

"Ty, if we get any news, would you like me to wake you?"

"Yes, please do. I appreciate it."

Inhaling a deep breath through his nose and letting it out slowly, Ty started back out the front door.

"Captain!" A loud voice from another room yelled.

Turning to his left, Ty saw Aimes getting up from his desk and heading to his cracked office door. Ty had not noticed the Colonel's office light on.

Pulling his door open, Aimes asked, "You got a moment?"

It's not like Ty would say no or as if he had a choice.

Coming to attention at the center of his desk, Ty's heart rate sped up as he did a quick inventory of what he had on his body. A sidearm, three knives, one flash grenade, and at least one hundred rounds of rifle and handgun ammunition. None of which he should have in his possession right now, considering he had been back at Sykes for almost nine hours since the operation into Mosul.

In the most gentle tone he had ever heard from the Colonel, Aimes said, "Relax, Ty. And by all means, take your gear off."

Like Ty's conversation with Franky, Aimes had used his first name instead of his rank and last name. This gave him immediate comfort that this was not going to be an ass-chewing or anything too serious. It was going to be a casual conversation between two Marines. Well, casual for him. There was no way in hell Ty would call him by his first name. He would still be 'sir' or 'Lieutenant Colonel Aimes.'

Ty did take him up on his order to remove some of his gear. He slipped out of his vest and placed it on one of the two chairs. While he was removing the gear, Aimes sat back down. This gave a safe sense that as soon as he was done, Ty could sit, too. So, he did.

Making eye contact with him as they sat across from each other was just about as awkward as it could have been. The two men had spoken hundreds of times since Aimes had taken over the 1st Recon Battalion six months earlier. Yet, Ty couldn't recall a time when it was this informal. Or when they needed to fill the silence with small talk.

Aimes must have felt the same way.

Without saying a word, he reached into his desk and pulled out a half-empty bottle of scotch. Aimes broke the silence by placing it on the desk and pulling the cork top off. "Are you a fan of good scotch?"

With a sly smirk. "Sir, I am a fan of any scotch. But, if you are asking me what preferences are, it's a single malt from the Highlands region, preferably aged eighteen years."

Matching Ty's smile, "Two out of three are covered. This is a twenty-one-year-old single from Speyside."

In their exchange, Ty missed that the Colonel had pulled out a couple of small paper coffee cups from the same drawer. Despite all that had happened in the last twenty-four hours, he couldn't help but find humor in the two of them drinking a fine whisky from paper cups. Aimes poured a couple of fingers into each, placed the bottle on the desk to his left, and passed Ty one of the cups. Ty noted that he didn't re-cork the bottle.

Lifting his cup off the desk and a little towards Ty, Aimes said, "To Marcus surviving."

"To Marcus surviving."

Both took a long pull. As they drank, Aimes' eyes didn't leave Ty's. He was waiting in anticipation for his reaction to the scotch. Ty wasn't sure if this was his personal preference or if a bottle was left behind as a gift from the commander who occupied this office before him.

All he knew was what his palette told him. This was good whiskey.

Wide-eyed, Ty pulled the paper cup from his lips. Looked at it as if he was appreciating its rich color through the clear crystal of an expensive Baccarat tumbler. A glass worthy of such a fine whiskey. "Damn!"

"You like that?"

"Yes, sir! This is really smooth and finishes well."

"Ty, you and Marcus met at recon training. Right?"

"That's correct, sir. He and I bonded being the cool kids in Recon training, having spent time at Pendleton and knowing all the best spots off base."

Aimes gave out a hefty chuckle. Before he could speak again, Ty asked him the same question.

Surprised, the Colonel replied, "Really? Marcus never told you about the first time he and I met?"

"No, sir."

Aimes reached for the open bottle and motioned for Ty to extend his cup. "Well, we'll need another drink for this."

The next few minutes were filled with Aimes using animated hand motions, his best impression of Williams's voice, and lots of laughter by both Marines.

Ty knew they met when Williams reported to 3rd Reconnaissance Battalion at Camp Butler in Okinawa, Japan. But, despite their friendship, he had never heard the hilarious story of the first time he had met Aimes. Listening now, Ty was glad that he could hear Aimes tell it first.

As it went, the Colonel drove onto the base one morning around 7 a.m. and rear-ended Marcus, who was reporting to the battalion for the first time that morning. Now, Aimes admitted the minor fender bender, as it was described, was entirely his fault.

"Oh, I was juggling my coffee mug, a file, and trying to find my badge at the same time. I looked down to see if it had fallen on the floorboard, and WHAM! I hit the back of Marcus' car."

None of this was the funny part, he proclaimed. The funny part was that Marcus exited his car, cursing at the Marine who had just rear-ended him. When Aimes didn't immediately exit his vehicle, Marcus looked at the scratched paint while cursing in the other driver's direction.

"It all was quite embarrassing for me. I was ready to get out and be very apologetic up until Marcus decided to point his finger at me and scream for me to get out of my car so he could beat my ass," Aimes exclaimed, using his fingers to make air quotes for the 'beat my ass' line.

That was when he decided he wouldn't get out to apologize despite being the person at fault. Rather, make an example out of the junior-grade lieutenant talking tough.

To hear Aimes tell it, Marcus went from badass Marine ready to beat someone's ass to being submissive in seconds.

"He was all big and tough until I got out of the car. I don't know if he noticed my rank or my name first. But he set a land speed record with how quickly he shut up and came to attention."

Urging the story, "How did you handle it now that you were out of your car?"

"Oh, that was the best part," Aimes smirked, "I stood there looking at him for a long minute to let it all sink in. Then I stepped closer to him and leaned in so we were nearly nose to nose, and asked, 'Weren't you saying something about beating my ass?'"

Despite being exhausted and emotionally drained, Ty enjoyed listening to Aimes talk about their friend. As Aimes concluded, Ty couldn't help but notice how the Colonel revered Williams as a person and not just as a Marine officer. It never occurred to Ty that the two of them might have formed a similar friendship of a commanding officer and a junior officer the way Marcus and he had become friends. Ty had spent the last six months under their command, yet he had never noticed this from either of them.

As they sat there in silence, sipping their drinks, Ty realized that Aimes needed this emotional outlet just as much as he did. Like Ty, he had at least one friend critically wounded today and fighting for his life.

Ignoring the urge to retire to his bunk for some rest, Ty continued the conversation. After giving a couple more short stories, the conversation took an unexpected turn.

"Did Marcus ever tell you I asked about you?" Aimes inquired while offering a third pour.

Taking him up on his offer for more scotch, Ty replied, "No, sir. When did you ask about me?"

"After our readiness exercises in Nevada a couple of months ago. Your platoon excelled in every aspect, and you crushed the rest of the battalion across multiple scores. So, I asked him what he thought of you."

"And?"

Aimes sipped his scotch before placing it in the desk's center. He leaned forward, resting his crossed arms on the flat surface. "I'll admit, at the time, I didn't agree with his assessment, but he saw in you what I, too, have come to believe."

Ty had no idea where this was going. He had always thought Marcus believed he was a good Marine and a decent platoon leader, but this entire exchange with Aimes felt too dramatic. There had to be something more to the story than Aimes had already shared. Ty sat there in anticipation of the climax of the story.

"He said you have the best instincts of any battlefield commander he had ever seen. And like I told you, I didn't necessarily agree with him then. But I have seen you in action over the last month, and my assessment is now the same."

Ty had no idea how to respond to any of this. Compliments weren't anything that he sought after. Nor did he not like hearing them or getting an occasional pat on the back when he did a good job. Yet, this felt different.

Aimes was a decorated Recon Marine with more than a decade of service, and he just told Ty that he agreed with Williams' assessment. *Did that mean he, too, thought that I wasn't just a good battlefield commander but the best he had ever seen?*

Struggling to find the right words, Ty responded, "Thank you, sir."

The response didn't please Aimes.

"This is the second part of what Willimas told me about you that I agree with. He said it's not an overabundance of humility. It's that you don't understand your abilities."

Ty sat there confused. Noticing, Aimes took their conversation further.

"Hudson," he blurted in a more serious tone. "I was impressed with how you put things together with Newbold back at Pendleton, and that was just the start. You then planned the insertion into Iran in hours on the flight, only to adapt it when we learned the Blackhawk was shot down. Then, you were able to alter the mission again when you found out Babic was on sight. You might think all of this wasn't a big deal, but there isn't a Recon Marine in the Corps that could've done what you flawlessly executed."

"Sir, I do appreciate it. I just really never have thought of myself or the way I lead as anything special. I do what I believe is best in the moment."

Aimes smiled and reached for his paper cup.

Lifting it again, " Here's to doing what you believe is best in the moment."

Both Marines tipped their twenty-one-year-old Speyside single malt back to finish it.

CHAPTER
EIGHTEEN

TY WOKE to a hushed conversation from a few bunks over. A couple of the men were in the barracks changing clothes to go for a run, doing their best to stay quiet. It shocked them when Ty sat up in bed.

All three immediately offered apologies and promised that they were leaving. Ty assured them they were fine and no need to worry. Looking down at his watch, he calculated that he had been asleep for nearly six hours and that the mess hall was open for lunch. Starving, a touch hungover, and needing to get up, he sat at the edge of his bunk. The foul odor of two days of sweat, gunpowder, and dirt made it clear what his first order of business needed to be.

Freshly showered and feeling much better, Ty made his way to the mess hall. Walking in, he joined the slow-moving food line. Chatting with a few Marines from Alpha Company, he noticed a group gathered around a TV on the far side of the hall. Among them was Franky. Stepping out of line, Ty approached him to ask if he had heard more about Williams.

Before reaching Franky, Lieutenant Lauder drew Ty's attention to the TV. "Captain, have you heard this shit on the news yet?"

The headline read, 'Marines Slaughter Hundreds in Mosul.'

It did what it was intended to do. Ty stopped dead in his tracks to stare at the screen, trying to catch up on the conversation between the panel of so-called experts. It was in the middle of the night back in the States, so this coverage had to have been on the evening broadcast and was being shown again.

"What the hell is this?" Ty asked.

"It's been like this all morning on all the major networks," Lauder replied. "What happened yesterday is being covered as us killing civilians."

"What the fuck-" Ty blurted before a Marine sitting closest to the TV told everyone to quiet down so that everyone could hear what a politician had been saying all day.

"What happened yesterday in Mosul was a disgrace and doesn't uphold our values as Americans. Instead, we saw another example of the U.S. Military doctrine of shoot first and ask questions later. Hundreds, including women and children, are now dead, and the Iraqi government is calling, yet again, for the removal of our troops and an international investigation into why Marines are killing innocent civilians. And, I stand with the good people of Iraq in saying that an investigation needs to happen, and those butchered at the hands of American Marines deserve justice."

Ty's mouth popped open with a gasp of disbelief at what he had just heard. The Marines around him must have already heard these remarks because they were not visibly showing the same outrage he was expressing. Instead, he had at least six to seven sets of eyes on him. All of them were eager to see his reaction to how the news of yesterday's insurgent ambush on Bravo Company was being portrayed and what the politicians back in Washington were saying.

It was Senator Andrew Hayes on the screen. The young, ambitious politician from Iowa was known for making headlines by saying absurd things as he gained popularity by bashing the war. It was Hayes on the TV back at Pendleton the morning of the briefing when Williams asked Ty to settle a dispute on whether he was the 'Next president or not?'.

"What do you think?" Lauder asked.

Ty looked at him with an expression of shock still on his face. He didn't know how to respond.

Sure, now that Iraq had fallen and the Taliban were squashed in Afghanistan, politicians were a bit more critical of U.S. military involvement in the Middle East. But, in the aftermath of the Abu Ghraib torture and prisoner abuse scandal, many were starting to use the war as political capital.

But this was something different. Senator Hayes was very misinformed as to what happened in Mosul. Worse, he had just called Ty and the Marines under his command murderers of women and children.

Ty could feel the center of attention drifting from what was being said on the TV to everyone waiting to hear his response to Lauder's question. He couldn't speak his thoughts, but Ty needed to say something to all the men staring at him.

"Well, that's a shame. It's too bad that a senator is so misinformed and then uses fallen Marines as political punching bags."

His words must not have conveyed the expected reaction.

"But, sir! You have to admit this is complete bullshit," proclaimed a Corporal that Ty didn't recognize.

"You're right, Corporal. It is complete bullshit. But, you or I can't do anything to set the record straight."

Other than cursing at the TV or smashing it, Ty could not give any reaction that would satisfy this group. So, instead of giving the small crowd what they wanted, he returned to his previous mission of asking Franky if he had any news on Williams.

"As of an hour ago, he was out of surgery and still listed in critical condition," Franky said.

"Was it for the bleeding on the brain?"

Breaking eye contact, "Yes, sir. They stopped the bleed and drained it."

Franky's demeanor changed. The way he broke off eye contact and was now not even looking at him drew Ty's attention.

"What else, Franky?" Ty asked in a slow, measured tone, trying to encourage him.

"He lost his right eye and two fingers on his hand. But they were able to save his leg. I am sorry that I didn't wake you an hour ago. Colonel Aimes told me not to disturb you."

"It's fine, Franky. Thanks for telling me everything."

Rejoining the lunch line, Ty went through the motions of picking up a tray, putting food on it, and taking a seat. Then nothing.

It might have only been a few minutes, or it might have been a half-hour, but Ty was lost in his sorrow. His only source of time was how cold his rice, black beans, and chicken burrito had become when he finally began to eat his first meal in twenty-four hours.

Leaving the mess hall, Ty ran into the battalion's Sergeant Major and was told to report to the Colonel in HQ as soon as possible.

Assuming Aimes had an update on Williams's condition, Ty hustled to see the Colonel. When he entered, he found most of the Marines in the building huddled around a TV in the right rear corner of the large room.

From what he could tell, it was the top-of-hour reset, during which the two newscasters welcomed a new audience and recycled the breaking stories. By the rundown, they were all about the political fallout of the Battle of Bloody Fountain. The attention given to the screen reminded Ty of a popular sporting event like the Super Bowl, where no one wanted to miss a second of the coverage.

Walking up to Aimes' office door, Ty saw the Colonel standing while on the phone. Noticing him, Aimes waved for him in.

Once in his office, Ty stood silently for several minutes, listening to Aimes' side of the call. Based on what's being said, Ty suspected the Colonel was on the phone with Lieutenant General Hank MacLean, the commanding officer of I Marine Expeditionary Force.

Hank "The Hammer" MacLean was a Marine icon. Twice awarded the Navy Cross for valor and the recipient of three Purple Hearts for wounds suffered in combat helped to elevate his status from a three-star general to a badass Marine. Ty had never personally met the guy and didn't believe he had ever been in the same room, but he knew of his reputation for always putting the mission first.

What Ty couldn't make out from listening in was MacLean's current mission. Was he looking for a scapegoat to appease Washington or getting the facts so he could defend his Marines?

Hanging up the phone, Aimes moaned, "Well, that was fun."

"How bad is it, sir?"

"Don't know yet. A few politicians are using this for political gain and might try to keep it in the news cycle."

"Where does General MacLean stand?"

Aimes gave a deep chuckle at the question. "He is ready to give you another medal and ask Senator Hayes how he feels about the eleven Marines killed. But, he can't do either of those."

Ty's heart sank. All he heard was that the total number of Marines killed in action rose to eleven. Last he had heard, it was eight.

"Eleven, sir?"

"Overnight, we lost two more men from Bravo Company, and this morning Brooks."

Ty had forgotten all about Force Company's radio man. He had been in the rear seat with Herrera and was severely wounded from the IED. Ty had assumed that he did not survive the blast and was already among the KIA.

The somber reminder of the lives lost two days earlier overshadowed the negative news coverage. It was never easy to lose a fellow Marine in combat. Losing eleven in the battalion would have lasting effects on everyone's morale and mental state.

"Captain," Amies said with a direct tone. "Bravo is down; I need your company combat-ready."

"My company, Sir?"

"That's correct. I'm moving you to Force Company Commander. Harrison of 3rd Platoon is in line for Company First Sergeant, but I suspect you'll want to keep Tiller."

"Yes, sir, I want Tiller."

Aimes took a minute to consider this. Tiller was the most junior of the platoon sergeants in Force Company, and seniority among non-commissioned officers was almost always the determining factor. Fighting back the urge to plead his case, Ty waited for Aimes' response. "Alright. But, you'll need to ensure Harrison is onboard."

"Yes, sir. Is there anything I can do regarding the news coverage back home?"

"Not at this time. Honestly, we need to see how the news cycle goes over the next few days."

TILLER WAS DECISIVE, Harrison was expecting, and Ty was left scratching his head.

Despite only being awake for more than an hour, Ty was ready to give up on this day and go back to bed as nothing was going his way.

Tiller was rummaging through his locker for a pen when Ty found him. After retrieving one for him, Ty told him about his discussion with Aimes and that he wanted Tiller to be Force Company's Sergeant.

That's when Tiller was decisive. "Sir, I appreciate it. Your confidence and trust in me mean a lot, but I don't want the job."

This is when Ty's head-scratching started.

Seeing how Ty was taken aback by his answer, "Sir, permission to speak freely?"

"Please, 'cause I don't understand why you're turning this down."

"The events of the last two days have me wanting to do more to win this war. And I don't think I can do that with 1st Recon."

"I get what you're saying, but where will you go that gets you more into the fight than here?"

"I would like your permission to submit my application to the Marine Special Operations Regiment that is being formed."

Ty had forgotten about this.

It had been a couple of days since Aimes told him about the special operations regiment being formed and asked him to volunteer, but a lot had happened since then.

In truth, he hadn't even known that word had gotten out about it among the battalion. When Tiller requested that he sign off on his application, Ty couldn't refuse him.

He wouldn't dare hold Tiller back. "I'm all for it, man. I'd be happy to support you."

That's when Tiller handed the pen Ty had just found back to him with three un-stabled pages that had already been filled out.

Joking as he took the papers, Ty said, "Really? I have to use my own pen to sign your application to leave."

Tiller had already signed everything. All that was needed was Ty's signature, which he scribbled out.

Handing the papers and pen back. "Congratulations, Sergeant."

Tiller looked at the pen and held it up to question why Ty handed it back to him.

Ty joked, "Keep it. If I don't have a pen, I can't sign anyone else's applications."

Ty could see Tiller was anxious to get to HQ to turn in his papers, and now he needed to find Harrison. Yet, his last smart-ass comment now had Ty wondering *who else was thinking or talking about volunteering*.

When he made the mistake of asking, in response, Tiller handed the pen back to Ty, turned, and walked out of the barracks laughing.

Unamused with Tiller's response, Ty went to find Harrison. When the two spoke, Harrison appeared to be expecting to become Force Company's First Sergeant. He was confident in knowing that he was next up in seniority. Yet, he showed humility in admitting that Williams and Herrera's loss was a significant blow to men's morale and combat readiness.

He was correct on both parts.

This was the first time the two had ever talked. Sure, they had been in the same company for nearly two years, and this was their second deployment together, but being in different platoons, they never spent much time together. Ty was pleased to hear his concerns about Williams's health and that he never wanted to get a new job this way. This was something they had in common.

The other big topic was the buzz around the base, particularly among Force Company, about the new regiment. Harrison wasn't surprised when Ty told him he had already been asked by Tiller and had approved his applications. Four different Marines had approached Harrison, too, asking what he knew. Word about it was certainly out, and they both suspected that over the next few days, many of the Marines in the company would inquire about the selection process. Before things got too out of hand, Ty needed to talk with Aimes about the best way to handle what was sure to be an influx of requests.

The Colonel had been adamant that Force Company needed to be combat-ready. Giving out signatures to allow Marines to transfer did not indicate a return to readiness, and they needed a plan.

This was clearly on Aimes' mind, too, because as if on cue, the Sergeant Major found Ty talking to Harrison and told him that Aimes wanted to speak again.

This was the third time in the last twenty-four hours that the Sergeant Major had been sent to summon Ty. The first two extraordinary meetings with Aimes had begun to condition him to expect big things whenever the senior enlisted Marine was sent to find him, and this third meeting was just as big.

When Ty stepped up to the large conference table in the back of HQ, Aimes had twenty to thirty personnel files spread across it. Ty quickly recognized what was going on.

This was his selection process for the Marines in his battalion to be moved forward and downlisted.

On his left side, there were seven or eight files neatly stacked. The tabs on the manila envelope were facing the opposite direction. Ty wasn't sure if this was the move forward or the rejection pile. Until he noticed the four files on the right side of the table. These names he could read with ease: *Cody Tiller, Jackson Henry, Darren Knight, and Tyler Hudson*

Wait! What the hell is my name doing in that pile? And who signed Henry and Knight's applications? Ty was sure that this was the move-forward pile and that he had not submitted his application for consideration. *So, why the hell was his personnel file there?*

"Sir, I see the word is out."

It wasn't what he wanted to say. Ty wanted to ask Aimes why his name was included in the shorter stack. If he were honest, Ty was thrilled to be there because it was another sign of the Colonel's trust in his capabilities.

But most of what he felt was outrage that Aimes had made this decision for him. Ty had yet to discuss it with his wife and had not even considered it due to the events of the last few days.

Not taking his eyes off the open file in front of him. Aimes replied, "Yeah, word is out. But it's taken a different direction than last we spoke."

"Different direction, sir?"

"Earlier today, you only heard half of my conversation with General

MacLean. Before you walked in, he had informed me that I would lead the selection and training of the new regiment."

"Congratulations, sir! That's fantastic."

Aimes held up his hand. "Not quite yet. I am just overseeing the selection and readiness process. The jury is still out on who will command it."

"But sir, it would make no sense for the Corps to ask you to stand up the regiment but not ultimately give you command."

"It would certainly be unusual. But it was not the first time the Corps did something that didn't make sense. Which brings me to you."

And here we go, Ty thought as he prepared for Aimes to tell him why his name was in the smaller pile. Staying silent, Ty watched Aimes reach over and grab the four files that included his name.

"Between the other companies, I have down-selected seven volunteers so far. But I am stuck on these three from Force Company."

Well, this was a curve ball. Ty read the names on the three files and didn't understand why he would be stuck on *Tiller, Henry, and Knight.* He didn't care whose names were among the others Aimes had selected to advance. None of them were as good as these three.

"I don't understand," Ty muttered.

Leaning over, Aimes placed his hands on the table between them. "No, I suspected you wouldn't. Tiller said he wanted to volunteer, but only if you did. If you decide not to, he wants to stay with Force Company. Henry and Knight came into my office about twenty minutes ago to tell me they would only go if you were their commanding officer."

Ty was stunned.

Tiller hadn't said anything like this to him when he signed his forms. This was the first time that Ty had heard Henry and Knight wanted to be considered.

Picking up the file with Ty's name, Aimes tossed it into the center of the table with the other three. "So, Captain, three of the best Marines in the battalion have put their careers in your hands. I'll admit, at first, I wasn't impressed. But, then, the Sergeant Major pointed out to me that this is the exact level of trust and commitment needed in a Tier One team. And that our first team might have just been formed."

Ty glanced over to see the Sergeant Major looking back. He had not even noticed him still in the room. His facial expression was that of a poker player intent on reading the room while not giving anything away. Aimes' words and conclusions about the guy's actions were correct.

As a commanding officer, you never want to be told by a subordinate that they'll only do something *'if.'* Yet, that was the level of commitment you wanted as a team leader.

Ty understood the quagmire Aimes was in.

'Captain," the Sergeant Major began, "the decision is yours, but we thought you should know the respect and devotion your men have for you."

A rush of pride swept over Ty. The devotion was inspiring, and more so, he could relate to it because if Williams had volunteered, Ty believed he would have followed him.

All Ty could think of was to say, "I understand. I'll have a decision tonight after I speak with Beth."

CHAPTER
TWENTY

THE FIRST FEW minutes of their call went as expected.

Beth, once more, knew most of everything.

Without even saying hello, Beth asked, "Ty, how are you? How's Marcus?"

Ty had suspected that by now, at least three to four other wives had called her or even stopped by their house to share the news.

"Hey, love. I am fine. Just heartbroken and torn up."

"Ty, I am so sorry. I know how close you two are. I was told he was in Germany and had lost his right eye.

Ty confirmed Marcus' condition and shared that Force Company lost Herrera and Brooks. But then, he shifted their discussion. He needed to for his own sake.

Ty needed to hear about her, about Audrey and Jake. He needed her to reach through the phone with a comforting hug and a shoulder he could cry on.

Beth could sense her husband's pain and put herself on speakerphone with the kids.

Ty could tell by the echo and background noise that it was breakfast time in Southern California. Audrey would be sitting at the counter in a booster seat on one of the tall stools. Jake would be in his highchair covered with fruit and dry cereal. Beth would still be in her comfy grey pants and an old t-shirt of Ty's that she liked to sleep in.

This was the normalcy that he needed right now.

Holding back tears, Ty talked with Audrey about her friends at daycare and what she was having for breakfast. Every few seconds, she would say something to Jake about making a mess or that he couldn't have that because it fell on the floor. Beth would be in the background, coaxing him to eat whatever food she put on this tray and to stop dropping it. This slice of heaven lasted for five or six minutes before Jake had enough and wanted out of his chair.

While Beth cleaned him up, Audrey and Ty had a few more minutes of daddy-daughter time on the phone. She finished telling him about the new girl at daycare named Sophia and how they were best friends. Ty asked her simple questions about her new friend to keep her talking. *What color was her hair? What games did they play together? Did they sit together at lunch?*

After a few questions about Sophia, he asked, How's Mommy doing?" Ty knew their nearly three-year-old would give him an honest assessment, but he wasn't prepared for what he heard.

"Mommy is good. She has lots of teachers over, and they are all nice. I like Rob. He gave me a doll."

What!?! Ty had no idea what to say.

The honest assessment she was giving scared the shit out of him. He didn't know anyone named Rob from Beth's school. The last thing he wanted to hear from their daughter was that some guy had been over and given her a doll. He quickly changed the subject if she was being nice to Jake. As expected, this sent Audrey into a chatter frenzy.

A minute later, Beth was back on the phone. And Ty couldn't help himself. "So, who's this Rob our daughter likes so much?"

Beth laughed lightly. "She's your little snitch. She tells you everything."

Ty didn't respond. That wasn't an acceptable answer to his question. Beth was smart enough to know that.

"Rob is Julie's husband," She conceded. "Julie, Heather, and I have been getting together a couple of times a week for dinner here at the house, and he joined us last night. They have a son a year older than Audrey."

A huge weight lifted off Ty's chest. His temperature cooled.

It was always a fear of any deployed Marine that their wife would find comfort in the arms of another man while they were gone. It was such a common occurrence and a disturbance to the military that there are laws in place to prevent infidelity on the part of a spouse.

Now Ty had a different problem. He had semi-accused the love of his life of hanging out with another man. This brought on a burden of guilt that he needed to address.

"Beth, I am so sorry. The last time we spoke, you said you had teacher friends over, and then to hear Rob's name without knowing anything, I jumped to a horrible conclusion. Please forgive me."

"There isn't anything to forgive, love. You are under so much pressure, and you're right. You don't know Rob or why he had been around the kids. I should've told you."

After a moment of guilt on both their parts, Beth moved on to the news coverage about Mosul and what was being said around Camp Pendleton about the battle.

For Ty, it was good to hear that the word on base was that Washington, especially 'dumbass Hayes,' as the wives were now calling him, was politicalizing things for their own purposes. The morning news coverage didn't lead with the story and wasn't discussed as much as the previous day. This was music to Ty's ears.

But, now came the tricky part in the conversation when they needed to discuss the new regiment. Ty had no clue how to bring it up, partly because he didn't know how he felt about it.

Listening to Aimes tell him how the guys would only join if he did was inspiring, but this was no light decision. This was life-altering for the Hudson family.

As Beth discussed her and the kids' plans this weekend, Ty kicked around ideas for bringing up the topic. Without any good ones, he decided the best way forward was to drop a grenade in the middle of the conversation. Then, see how it landed.

As Beth paused to breathe in her story, Ty blurted, "Aimes asked me to join a new Special Operations team."

"Okay… What does that mean?"

"It means a lot. The Commandant is forming a tier-one regiment in response to how the war is going, and Aimes has been asked to lead it. The selection process started yesterday, and training will be at Camp Lejeune next month."

In a determined tone, Beth replied, "You should do it."

Ty had not expected this. He thought, for sure, she would ask a handful of questions before objecting to the idea. So when she, after just one question, told him that 'he should do it,' Ty's mind went blank. He struggled to grasp what had just happened.

After a long pause. "Ty, are you there?"

"Yeah, I just don't kn-"

"You should do it. You love being a Marine, and you are good at it. Why wouldn't you do it if your battalion commander asked you to?"

"Because of you and the kids."

"I knew that would be your reasoning. But, like you have said before, if not you, then who?"

Years ago, just after September 11th, Ty wanted to join the Corps, and Beth wasn't sure what to make of it. They had only been dating for a few months, but they both knew how madly in love they were. To help convince her, Ty used the line: if he didn't step up, then who would?

It was a flimsy excuse. Thousands of Americans were rushing to join the different military branches as the embers of the Twin Towers were still burning. But, his statement had its intended effect of wedging his love for Beth between his patriotic call to duty and a possible lifelong feeling of guilt for not stepping up when so many others were.

"The kids and I will be fine. I don't know how, but we'll find a way. This is your opportunity to make a difference. Not only for yourself but for Marcus, Audrey, Jake, and me. I support you."

———

CHAPTER
TWENTY-ONE

HOLY SHIT! Ty thought to himself. *I fucking did it. I'm a Marine Raider.*

Colonel George Aimes made his way down the line of Marines to award each the Raider insignia. The Raider designation for the Corps Special Operations Regiment dates back to World War II and was revived as the unit got closer to operational readiness.

Aimes was standing a bit taller today as he was brandishing, for the first time, the full-bird Colonel rank on the shoulders of his dress blues. Ty had heard last night that Aimes had been promoted, so he wasn't surprised when he saw the distinctive rank polished perfectly for all to see.

Until now, Ty had been composed, but as the Colonel stopped at the Marine to his immediate right, his heart began to race. Like each of the twenty-two Marines standing on the stage today, Ty was facing out to a large crowd here to witness and celebrate this moment with them.

It was late summer in North Carolina, and the ceremony was indoors, saving the Marines and the crowd from the brutal late August heat and humidity. The northernmost aircraft hanger at Camp Lejeune's airfield had been recently built as a maintenance building designed to hold up to ten of the Corps' new F-35B Lightning II jets.

Four of the jets were proudly displayed for the pomp and circumstance of the day. Each was decorated with red, white, and blue streamers and banners. A stage had been installed under a giant American flag, and white folding chairs were arranged in at least thirty seats wide and twenty rows deep. The large retractable doors were shut to keep the cool air in and summer heat out.

Coming onto the stage just a few minutes ago, Ty scanned the wildly diverse audience when he turned to face it. Looking past the Secretaries of Defense and the Navy, past at least three senators, four times that amount of Congress members, and countless other Marine officers of all ranks in the first two rows. He couldn't care less that they were here to witness this momentous moment in the Corps' distinctive history. His family were the only three people he cared to locate in the crowd.

It didn't take him long to spot them. They were seated eight rows deep and slightly to the left where he stood on the stage. Beth wore a perfect curve-fitting white dress with blue trim at the waist and shoulders. She had gotten her long blonde hair cut to shoulder length and highlighted the day before. She looked stunning. Jake was seated on her lap and dressed sharply in a bow tie that had somehow remained on thus far. Audrey was in the chair to her right and in the cutest yellow sundress. Even some thirty feet away, Ty could see Beth wipe tears from her eyes as she gave him the proudest smile when she noticed he was looking in their direction. And then Aimes stepped in front of him.

He reached out with his right hand to shake Ty's while, with his left, placed the Marine Raider insignia on him. "Congratulations, Captain Hudson. You've done your family and the Corps proud."

"Thank you, sir."

Aimes leaned in to whisper, "Come see me when this is over."

"Yes, sir."

As Aimes moved down the line, Ty fought back a tear of his own. The last year had all happened quickly, yet it had been his life's greatest endeavor and struggle. Standing there proudly gave Ty a moment to reflect on his accomplishments.

It seemed like yesterday when he was one of thirty-four Marines from 1st Recon Battalion that was selected during the screening process to attend Assessment and Selection for the new Special Operations Regiments. Of the Marines from 1st Battalion, only five were officers. The thirty-four of them would be joining about the same number from each of 2nd and 3rd Battalions at Camp Lejeune on the North Carolina coast as the first class for the regiment.

At Camp Lejeune, they underwent three weeks of intense physical training and classroom learning to prepare each for what would come next. During these first weeks, nearly forty percent of the Marines in the class dropped upon request. For those that remained, this first phase was just the appetizer for the actual assessment and selection that would occur during phase two.

The next three weeks were spent at an undisclosed location, where they tested the limits of their physical and mental endurance. At the same time, they performed various direct assaults, amphibious reconnaissance, and search-and-destroy exercises.

After being selected to advance past phase two, Ty moved on to ten months of individual training courses hosted at various Marine Camps and other service installations. Each course was designed to develop the critical skills needed as a small team, tier-one operator. Like in the beginning, Marines washed out. The difference was it was now a trickle, not the massive waves of Marines that had dropped during the first six weeks.

Just six days ago, Ty learned he passed his last individual training course and was now rated as a Marine Special Operator. When Ty asked his lead instructor how many other Marines made the final cut, he would say that the 'Targeted attrition rate was met.' If Ty recalled correctly from his first day at Camp Lejeune a year ago, Aimes told the hundred-plus recruits that they expected the dropout rate to be at least seventy-five percent.

When Beth told Ty that 'you should do it,' the enormity of the training and personal sacrifice wasn't fully understood. Like anything new in the Corps, there was a plan, but it was only known to a select number of people. It was such a secret that Aimes, who had been selected to lead the regiment, didn't even know the full assessment and training requirements. In hindsight, Ty should have taken the secrecy or lack of detail as a foreshadowing of things to come. But, the shock of Beth encouraging him to do it and the excitement of a new chapter as a Marine had him in disarray. He signed up without a second thought about what it would take.

As Aimes finished awarding the last insignia, he returned to the podium on the far right side of the stage to congratulate the twenty-two new Marine Raiders again and closed the ceremony.

Everyone erupted in cheers and applause, but none more than those on the stage. Tiller was two Marines down on Ty's left, and the two quickly found each other. In excitement, Tiller pulled Ty into a big bear hug. Their celebration was soon joined by Henry and Knight.

Coming off the steps of the stage, Ty was met by several well-dressed politicians seated in the front rows. He had no idea who they were as he shook hands and said thank you for the many congratulations. Ty smiled ear to ear in politeness while he tried to pass them to get to his family.

But one firm grip held his hand as Ty tried to release it to move to the next. Confused, he turned to see who had started pulling him back in their direction. Ty didn't know the guy looking back at him, but he recognized the face and crooked smile. He couldn't place where he knew the man from.

His puzzlement deepened when the guy spoke as if he knew Ty. "Congratulations, Captain Hudson."

"Thank you, sir. Do we know each other?"

Still holding Ty's hand, he smiled and laughed heavily as he looked around at the handful of other people watching the awkward exchange. Over the guy's left shoulder was an attractive younger woman holding a fancy leather-bound notebook, not looking very impressed that Ty didn't know her boss. While he continued to chuckle and make off-hand jokes to an on-looker, the woman turned the notebook around so Ty could see the guy's name spelled out in large gold font.

Andrew Hayes
United States Senator

Ty's respectful smile shifted to a stern look as it dawned on him that this man had accused him and the Marines of Force Company of killing women and children in Mosul a year ago.

But this wasn't the place for an altercation.

"Senator Hayes, I am pleased to meet you, sir," Ty said with his best attempt to fake pleasure. "Thank you so much for being here today and for your support."

Hayes, laughing and gesturing to the crowd, stopped as he returned his crooked smile to Ty. All while still holding his hand. "Oh, Captain. I wouldn't call me being here as supportive. Instead, let's call interest."

Confused. "Interest in what, sir?"

"You, Tyler."

So, now we are on a first-name basis?

Thankfully, Ty was rescued before he said anything too stupid.

"Ty!" Yelled Beth as she pushed her way to him through the crowd with Jake on her hip and Audrey in tow by her hand. "Oh my God, I am so proud of you."

Hayes was finally kind enough to release Ty's hand. Beth and Ty embraced each other quickly before he took Jake from her, kissing him on the cheek. Audrey let go of her mom's hand to wrap her arms around her daddy's right leg.

Leaning down to hug her, "Hey, little girl. Did you enjoy that?"

"Yeah, but why was it so long?"

Beth and Ty remained eye-locked as he talked to their daughter. She knew who was still standing there, and he could see her trying to gauge the temperature of the exchange. Breaking from her, Ty looked back at the Senator.

"My love, this is Senator Hayes of Iowa."

The two shook hands as Beth greeted him. Ty watched Hayes put his left hand on their clasped hands. A politician's trick to show how warm and trustworthy they were.

"Mrs. Hudson, it's a pleasure to meet you. You must be so proud of your husband."

"I am. What Ty and these Marines have done is something to admire and inspire towards."

"It certainly is."

"Maybe now you'll have a little more appreciation for what they go through."

With an uncomfortable smile, Hayes said, "Ma'am, I've always appreciated our service members; your husband is no exception."

"Oh, Senator. It would help if you remembered actions speak louder than words. And outside of Washington, we voters care more about actions."

The brash politician was at a loss of words. He dropped Beth's hand before giving her a pursed-lipped smile.

And that's why Ty loved his wife. Well, that and how well her white dress fit in all the right places. She knows how to land a proper insult without appearing as a total bitch.

Noticing the turn, the attractive assistant gently touched the Senator's arm. Ty could tell this was a well-practiced move as Hayes looked to his right side, where her hand was on his arm, and gave a simple nod.

Ty got the sense that Hayes had more to say. Perhaps there was a lot more he wanted to get out, but his insistent assistant wouldn't let him, especially in front of the small group of onlookers.

"Captain Hudson, it was a pleasure to finally meet you. I am sure we'll see each other again soon."

His tone and sly smile made this last part feel like a veiled threat. It also confirmed that Hayes had more to say.

"Have a good day, sir."

Both parties pivoted to go in opposite directions.

Stepping away, Ty used his free arm to pull Beth into him while planting a kiss on her lips. Several of the onlookers chuckled.

Looking around, Ty noticed Colonel Aimes twenty feet away, talking to someone, but was more interested in his conversation with Hayes. *Had he watched the entire exchange?*

Ty leaned back into Beth, "Shit. I think Aimes was watching us talk with the Senator, and he looks pissed."

CHAPTER
TWENTY-TWO

THE LOOK that Aimes gave Ty suggested that the two needed to talk. And soon.

But as he held Jake in his arms and Audrey by the hand, Ty decided that his Colonel could wait. He was in his happy place and didn't want to talk shop or politics right now. But he did want to talk with another Marine present for the ceremony.

"Have you seen him?"

"I did when we first arrived, but not since we took our seats," Beth replied.

Ty scanned the room, swiftly passing anyone not wearing a Marine uniform and only briefly observing those who were. He was in search of a Marine with distinctive fashion accessories.

One would think that a Marine with an eye patch would be easy to spot in a room of only a couple hundred people. Yet it took Ty roaming the large open space for a few minutes to find him.

He was next to one of the decorated jets, talking to a small group that included General Louis Marin, the Commandant of the Marine Corps. Several people in the group were smiling, including the General. Ty figured it wouldn't be inappropriate for him to join the light-hearted conversation. He crossed the room with his family in tow through an empty row of chairs.

Marcus Williams was using a black steel cane to steady himself. His once imposing stature was a shell of its former self. While he might measure six feet three inches tall, the damage to his right leg not only required using a cane but has forced him to walk and stand in a slight hunch, making him look several inches shorter. His face was scarred from the ballistic glass shattered by the explosion. Yet, his sunken cheeks and bony facial features were more noticeable to those who knew him prior.

If Ty had to guess, Williams must have lost thirty pounds. He didn't have the extra weight to lose for an already lean, physically fit Marine. If his thin face wasn't evidence enough, the bagginess of his dress blues in how it hung off his shoulders and drooped down his chest clearly showed a man in distress.

Williams gave a huge, teeth-bearing grin when he noticed the Hudson family approaching. The man was talking to the Commandant but hadn't smiled until then. General Marin took notice and turned to see what drew Williams' attention.

"General, sir, may I introduce you to Captain Tyler Hudson," Williams said.

His introduction was a little quicker than Ty had expected and caught him in the middle of handing Jake back to Beth so he could adequately greet the four-star general.

"No, Captain," the General proclaimed, "please hold your son."

Listening to the General, Ty kept Jake on his hip, "Thank you, sir."

"General, this is my wife, Beth Hudson."

"Mrs. Husdon, it is a pleasure to meet you. You have to be so proud of what Tyler has accomplished."

"I am, sir." She replied. "Thank you for starting the Raiders and giving him this opportunity."

"That was the easy part. His making the team was easy, too. It's you, my dear, that deserves all the credit. You and the other spouses here today are the true heroes that must be recognized."

Williams and Ty exchanged a glance.

It wasn't unusual for a high-ranking officer to address a spouse like this, but it felt that the General was laying it on a bit thick. Ty could tell through Beth's polite, yet fake, smile that she was thinking the same thing.

The General immediately turned his attention to the kids and then back to Ty, congratulating him on earning his Raider insignia. After a few minutes of small talk, the General excused himself and walked off with his entourage. With only Williams remaining, the two embraced in a long hug.

It had been nearly a year since they had last seen each other.

With his left arm around Ty, Williams said, "Shit, Ty. You've bulked up."

"That's cause all these damn instructors knew how to do was to give push-ups and make you run. But look at you, man. The eye patch works!"

Taking a small step back, Marcus joked, "Yeah, I tried the glass eye for about a week, and it sucked. This fits better with the scars."

Wanting to shift the conversation. "So, is it true? Are you doing consulting work with the company?"

"It's more complicated than that."

Before Ty could respond, Beth interrupted to say she wanted to talk to another wife she had just seen. Before walking away with the kids, she suggested they get a drink at the newly opened hospitality bar.

It didn't take much more encouragement. Since it was a celebration, several tables were strung across the hangar behind the F35s. Two walk-up bars had been rolled out, and lines formed at both.

Ty wasn't sure if it was the Purple Heart on Williams' chest or his cane. But as he approached, he was ushered to the front of the line. Ty followed.

As Williams asked for a light beer, Ty glanced back at the depth of the line they had just skipped. So when it was time to order, he asked for two beers.

"Shit, yeah," Marcus blurted out. "That's a great idea. Can I have another one, too?"

When the bartender poured the second beer from its glass bottle into a plastic cup, Ty watched Williams' expression turn sour. He realized he couldn't carry the two beers when he needed his right hand for his cane. Before he could speak, Ty grabbed Williams' second to form a tight triangle with the three cups.

Lifting them, "Lead the way, man. What table do you want to go to?"

Ty could tell that this wasn't what he wanted. He knew Williams had too much pride to be cared for this way. But Ty wanted to get him away from the bar and alone so they could chat more freely.

Placing his second beer before him. "So, is it true?"

"Yes and no. Yes, I am temporarily advising, but after last week, I don't know for how much longer."

Confused, Ty asked, "What happened last week?"

Williams looked puzzled. Assessing if Ty didn't know or if he was playing dumb. When he finally spoke, "Seriously?"

"Yeah, is it a secret and something you can't tell me about? Cause if it is, I get that."

"You didn't hear about the air strike that killed several civilians outside Jalalabad?"

"Of course, that was on the news last week. But I don't recall them mentioning civilians being killed." Then it hit him, "Wait, were you advising on air strikes?"

"Sort of," Williams started. "I've been consulting on target acquisition and elimination for the last three months. This was only my second recommended drone strike. And I screwed it up. Bad!"

Since the war on terror began, the military focused most of its drone efforts on close support for troops in contact or hitting hardened targets. The CIA's strategy had been to use them on strikes to take out high-value targets. Ty had heard that Williams had been working with the CIA, but he didn't know he was giving out recommendations or, in this case, kill orders.

"But, you couldn't have been the final decision maker. Why do you think this will blow back on you?"

Williams took a long gulp of his beer. "I recommended using a drone strike, and deputy chiefs don't fall for stuff like this. They find scapegoats."

Ty knew he was right but couldn't say it. "This shit has happened a lot. You'll get clear of it."

In part, Ty was right. There had been several incidences of friendly fire or missed targets that had resulted in civilian causalities.

Taking another sip, Williams replied, "I hope so. I like the work. It makes me feel like I'm still in the fight."

Beth and the kids walked up.

Ty passed her his second beer and played it off like he had waited in the long line a second time to ensure she didn't have to. As expected, she called him out on his bullshit by letting him know that she saw the two of them get moved to the front of the line and that he had ordered a second beer for himself. Not because he was trying to be a good husband.

When he caved, admitting she was right, Ty asked for the beer back. To which she chugged it. Putting the empty clear plastic cup down, she sarcastically asked for another. Being a good husband, Ty went to stand in line for ten minutes.

The next two hours were like old times. Almost all of the dignitaries immediately left following the ceremony, and all that remained were Marines and their families. Beth, Williams, and Ty stood at the same table, laughing and enjoying one another's company. Only stopping to attend to one of the kids playing with others in the hangar or to get another round.

After a last call from one of the bartenders, Ty noticed the time. It had gotten into the afternoon, and they needed to figure out what to do for dinner. There were several popular places just off base, and they were in the process of listing them when Aimes walked up.

"You all seem to be having a good time."

"We are, sir. How about youuu?" Williams slurred.

Beth and Ty laughed, with Aimes joining in at his expense.

Slowly coming out of his laughter, "Cindy and I wanted to invite you all to dinner. Have you made plans yet?"

"No, sir. We were starting to discuss what we were doing."

With a big smile, "Perfect, you're joining us. And please, bring the kids. Cindy would love to spend time with them."

TWENTY-THREE

WHEN AIMES INVITED everyone to dinner, Ty was sure they were going to a restaurant. A family-friendly bar-n-grill or one of the many great BBQ joints around the base. Instead, they met him and Cindy a few hours later at a beach pavilion where Camp Lejeune met the Atlantic Ocean. All Aimes' had asked for was for them to bring the beer. He and Cindy would take care of everything else.

Beth decided it was best to pick Williams up on their way to minimize the number of drivers. After scooping him up, Ty jumped out at a small store to get beer when he ran into Aimes and another guy he didn't recognize buying hotdogs.

Shrugging his shoulders in embarrassment, Aimes admitted, "I forgot the hotdogs for the kids, so Cindy sent me back."

"You should've called, sir. We would've picked them up. I am grabbing the beer and ice now. Do you have a preference?"

"No, I'm not as picky with my beer as my scotch."

In an odd move, considering they were all heading to a BBQ together, Aimes didn't introduce the other guy.

Did Aimes assume that I already knew him? Should I have known who he was?

Opening the rear door of their rented SUV to put the beer and ice in the cooler, Ty asked, "Hey Williams, did you see that guy with Aimes?"

"Yeah, is he going to be at dinner?"

"I think so. Do you know who he is?"

Williams turned in his seat to look at Ty. "You don't recognize him?"

"Should I?"

"I guess not. That's the Deputy Director of Counter Terrorism at the CIA."

Closing the lid to the cooler, Ty looked at him. "Is that the guy who authorized—"

"One and the same. Which means dinner just got a little more interesting."

Jokingly, Ty quipped, "Do I have enough beer?"

Arriving at Onslow Beach a few minutes later, Ty pulled into the closest parking spot to pavilion number five. Williams and Ty unloaded the back of the rental while Beth took Audrey and Jake to Cindy, who was anxiously waiting.

It was the perfect setting for a beach BBQ. The sun barely hung on in the sky, and the temperature had cooled. The breeze off the water carried the smell of salt, and the sound of each crashing wave could be heard in the distance. Aimes and the deputy director were doing what all guys do: standing above the grill and discussing the finer aspects of cooking chicken.

When Williams and Ty made their way up, Ty immediately opened the cooler to offer everyone a beer. Williams didn't even notice him passing him a cold one. Instead, he approached the grill to shake the Deputy Director's hand.

Guess he's getting the awkwardness out of the way.

The greeting was as warm as if the two had known each other for years. There appeared to be no animosity or hard feelings as Williams jumped into small talk with both men. Ty carried four beers over, deciding that he would need to introduce himself since neither Aimes nor Williams had.

The Deputy Director took the cold beer and said, "I've been told you go by Ty."

"That's right, sir."

Aimes turned from the grill, "None of that tonight. I'm George, and he's Sean."

There wasn't anything overly noticeable about Sean. He didn't have any particular feature that stood out. He might have been five foot ten, at the most. He wasn't thin, but he wasn't muscular, and chubby didn't fit either. His coarse sandy blond hair was medium length, and he hid the grey along his sideburns well. Looking at him, Ty couldn't tell if he was thirty or fifty, which might be his best feature. He was more forgettable than he was memorable as a man.

Having heard Marcus and Ty's conversation outside the commissary, Beth helped her husband put the pieces of Sean's story together. She played the curious Marine wife well. So, when she innocently asked Sean if he was also a Marine, she reacted in astonishment when he admitted to working for the CIA. She already knew this but didn't give it away as she navigated through several questions about his education, family, and work at the agency. Ty would bet a year's salary that Sean knew what she was doing but played along to keep the conversation easy. He seemed to relish the opportunity to tell his story.

Assuming everything he said was true, Sean Preston had a law degree from Yale, where he went into the agency right after graduating as a junior attorney in the compliance department. By the mid-1980s, he left a desk to become a case officer tasked with developing human assets in the war between Iraq and Iran. To hear him describe it, Operation Desert Storm in 1991 was perfect timing for his career. The Iraq-Iran conflict had ended years earlier, yet he still had several key assets across both governments that were not being used.

During the first war with Saddam Hussein, he and his assets became highly valuable, helping his stock skyrocket within the ranks of the CIA. By the end of the war, he landed the highly coveted Section Chief job in Riyadh, the capital city of Saudi Arabia.

After al Qaeda claimed credit for the underground bombing of the World Trade Center in 1993, Sean's focus turned entirely to counter-terrorism. He had spent most of the last twenty years in the Middle East. He only recently returned to the United States when he became the controversial pick to be the Deputy Director of Counter-Terrorism eight months ago.

He admitted to all of us at the picnic table that the agency's new director was under immense pressure because of the agency's failures to assess the al Qaeda threat leading up to September 11th. So, when he picked Preston to lead counter terrorism, it was met with a huge uproar from almost everyone in Washington. Most politicians blamed him, since he was the Section Chief in the Middle East, for the agency's failures. Despite the headwinds, Preston secured the position with the backing of the president, the new director, and several key figures within the Pentagon.

Ty mused in astonishment at all that Beth could get from Sean in just ten minutes.

The next two hours were a good ole' American BBQ.

Dinner was split chickens, homemade potato salad, baked beans, and an amazing Serrano ham and arugula salad that Cindy had mastered while living at Naval Air Station Naples in Italy for three years in the mid-1990s.

It was a great time among friends, as the conversation was light-hearted. The food was so good that Audrey had chicken instead of a hotdog. She ate two drumsticks before asking her daddy for the one on his plate, which Ty happily gave up.

As the sun faded into night, Beth held a sleepy Jake and suggested it was time to get him back to the house, bathed, and ready for bed.

Cindy spoke up before Ty could respond and asked if she could return with Beth to help with the kids. Her excuse was to spend more time with them, but everyone knew it was to give the guys time alone. Besides Beth's questions to Sean, everyone had masterfully avoided any reference to work, the day's ceremony, or Ty's encounter with Senator Hayes.

That changed before the women and kids were out of the parking lot.

Looking at Ty with a sly grin, Aimes asked, "So, Ty. What was your impression of the Senator?"

Toying with the bottle cap, he just twisted off his fresh beer. "I have a feeling that I am about to be stepped on by his ambition."

Preston laughed hard before adding, "You and I both."

"Then what's the story?" Ty asked, looking at the CIA Deputy Director, "Because I doubt the four of us are here by coincidence."

Aimes and Sean shared a look. It was reminiscent of the same look Aimes had shared with Newbold over a year ago, just before they told Ty they wanted him to lead the mission into Iran. As he did back then, Williams sat quietly.

"There is a lot to catch you guys up on," Aimes began before asking for another beer.

After last year's Battle of Bloody Fountain, Hayes was a small contingent of Washington insiders who tried to politicalize the war by accusing Marines of slaughtering civilians. This part Williams and Ty already knew. The rumor was that Hayes had unsuccessfully attempted to garner support in the Senate to subpoena Ty, Aimes, and several others to testify before Congress on their actions. To hear Aimes speak about it now, he was posturing as the junior Senator tried to make a name for himself.

Aimes explained that after the stunning revelations of abuse and torture by American service members at Abu Ghraib prison, politicians wanted nothing to do with another scandal leading into the 2006 mid-terms. So, Hayes 'couldn't get enough support at the time to force us to testify.'

Because of the lack of political appetite, Ty was never even informed of what was happening. Instead, life went on with him going through Marine Raider Assessment and Selection.

"So, after my screw-up in Jalalabad, Hayes is back on his high horse," Williams said.

"You didn't fuck up," Sean said in a low voice. "You gave an assessment, and I made the decision. That was on me."

Until now, Ty hadn't known what to think of Sean. He was a smart, accomplished guy with a critically important job that no one should want. In Ty's experience, that meant he was a cheap suit that would do anything or throw anyone under the bus to save his own ass. So, taking responsibility for his decision to release a missile into a crowd in Jalalabad a week earlier was nothing less than jaw-dropping.

Williams, of course, disagreed on whose responsibility it was. Aimes and Ty became bystanders in the conversation as the two rehashed the order's logistics and timing.

Bringing everyone back into a single discussion, Ty said, "So, Marcus is right. What happened in Jalalabad has renewed Hayes' motivation. But, now he has the backing to subpoena us."

With a stern look, Aimes grumbled, "That's right. We'll both be getting subpoenas early next week."

Confused, Ty asked, "Hayes isn't on the Armes Services committee, so who would we be testifying in front of?"

Aimes used his head to point toward Sean, "That's why he is here."

Sean explained that Hayes sat on the Foreign Relations Committee, particularly the sub-committee on counter-terrorism. Since counter-terrorism was predominantly an intelligence-gathering effort in foreign countries, Hayes has the oversight authority.

"He's using this oversight to draw attention to what he calls the failed American doctrine with the War on Terrorism," Sean said.

"And that failed American doctrine is his path to the White House in 2008," Ty retorted, "So, I am about to get stepped on by his ambition."

The four spent the next thirty minutes bantering back and forth about Hayes and the problems with Washington politicians in general. Like everyone else in the country, they had all the answers. But, what astonished Ty was how relaxed Williams had become since he and Sean cleared the air.

His body language was more at ease as he sat on the picnic table bench. He had been as still as a statue, leaning with his arms crossed on the table. Now, he was smiling, using animated hand gestures while describing solutions for Washington, and engaging in much more of the conversation. The guy sitting across from Ty for the last half-hour was his friend, this was Marcus Williams. Not the unsettled, apprehensive guy who had been here for the first three hours.

When it seemed they had solved all the problems, Aimes changed the subject. Looking at Ty, "I am surprised you haven't asked about tomorrow yet."

Ty was also surprised that he had not asked.

Though he wouldn't let Aimes know, he agonized over it all evening. *Better to play it cool.*

"I figured you'd bring it up when you wanted. Or I'd have to wait until tomorrow like everyone else."

The Colonel's mouth turned up in an amused smirk. Knowing Ty was full of shit and wanted to know the team assignments.

It had been all the buzz the last few days at Camp Lejeune. As final selection notices were being made, every one of the twenty-two newly designated Marine Raiders began to speculate about team structures and base assignments.

"There are going to be three teams. Two stationed here at Camp Lejeune and one at Pendleton."

Ty's eyebrows raised in anticipation, "And?"

The Colonel smiled, "And, what?"

"Sir, you are killing me. Do I get my team?"

Aimes was having way too much fun at Ty's expense and appeared ready to make him wait until tomorrow.

"George," Sean said in an insightful tone. "We're all here. I think we can tell them."

Williams and Ty gave each other a confused look, having both caught the pluralism of Sean's remark.

"Them?" Williams questioned openly to both.

"Ty, you got your team," Aimes conceded. "Breaking with norms, you'll be designated as Romeo Team so as not to jinx an already great thing."

Ty was grinning ear to ear with excitement, but this didn't answer Williams' question.

Looking now at Sean, Ty gave him an eyebrow-raised expression to encourage him to expand his word choice.

As not to be outdone by Aimes, Sean laid the proud boss breaking good news or promoting a favorite employee on thick. "Do you remember Newbold?"

"Yeah, of course," Ty responded eagerly.

"He has a few things going on, so Romeo Team will be assigned to him. Williams will start to report to him while running an intelligence team out of Langley in support."

Emotions got the better of both Ty and Williams.

Ty jumped off the bench, and Williams followed at his best speed. They gave one another a blistering high-five before pulling it into a long hug. They acted like two schoolboys who had just won the big game in front of a Deputy Director in the CIA and a Marine Colonel.

They didn't care.

This was as close to a perfect scenario as either of them could have hoped for.

Trying his hardest not to rain on their parade, Aimes reminded, "But, we all have to survive Hayes' Senate hearing."

INDIFFERENT.

That's how Ty felt about lawyers. He had never had a positive or negative experience with one to warrant strong feelings. His perception of the job was impartial.

But a lot has changed over the last two weeks.

The guys were ecstatic to hear Romeo Team was staying together. Their reaction was mildly better than Williams and Ty's schoolboy celebration at the BBQ the night before. There was also an audible sigh of relief when Aimes announced they would be stationed out of Camp Pendleton instead of Camp Lejeune. No one wanted to move across the country. Especially the team members who had families, like Ty.

The mood only soured when the Colonel told them about Hayes and that the team wouldn't go operational until after the Senate hearing. Instead, the team would rotate back to Pendleton 'until further notice.' The energy was sucked out of the room, with lots of vulgar language directed toward Hayes.

For Tiller, Henry, and Knight, the last two weeks had been split between intelligence work with Newbold and conducting readiness exercises to keep their skills sharp.

To Ty's dismay, he spent fourteen hours a day being coached and drilled by several Department of Navy lawyers. More commonly known as JAG Officers. One in particular, Lieutenant Joseph Wooden, was the biggest pain in Ty's ass.

As the team's lead attorney, he would go with Ty to the hearing and be responsible for making sure he didn't screw up. Wooden was a by-the-book lawyer. Ty had initially thought this would be good, but the more time the two spent together, the more disdain he had for Wooden and lawyers in general.

Educated at the University of Virginia Law School, Wooden was as arrogant as he was smart. While he and Ty were about the same height and weight, they wore it differently. The Marine was fit with good muscular tone. Wooden carried his weight as a spare tire around his waist. His pasty white face was round, and he would blush easily when his temper flared, which he tried to cover with overly large square-framed glasses.

Every day, he started with briefings to help Ty learn about the nineteen senators on the Foreign Relations Committee, their sub-committee assignments, historical positions on related topics, and key personality traits. Ty was getting a more in-depth understanding of sitting U.S. Senators than he had ever received on high-value targets. Compared to the three pages Newbold had given him a year ago on Black Jack, the JAG officers had an encyclopedia on Hayes.

Hayes' background included everything from his primary school grades to the name of his senior prom date, how he met his wife, and even quite a bit about her.

The section on his rise up the political ladder included his FBI background checks, voting record, controversial positions, and scores of pages on campaign and Senate floor speeches.

The goal was for Ty to consume so much intel on the Junior Senator from Iowa that he would know what to expect during the hearing and perhaps even be able to predict his behavior.

The detailed dossier on Hayes' Chief of Staff, Luna Copeland, was just as thorough. The attractive woman who had helped Ty at the Marine Raider graduation by turning around the leather folder to show Hayes' name was more than just an aide. Her file was filled with examples of her influence on the Senator's actions and positions. She, too, would be a formidable adversary.

Four days before the hearing, Aimes suggested they go to Washington early. This would give him and Ty time to rub elbows with the Committee members to 'get the room's temperature before they were in the line of fire.'

Wooden loved the idea.

Beth was less enthusiastic as Ty said goodbye to her and the kids.

The good news was that eleven of the nineteen senators on the Foreign Relations Committee had agreed to speak with the two Marines. Another six, not on the committee, had also asked for a few minutes.

Most of these meetings were scheduled to be quick, fifteen-minute office drop-ins that would be enough time for a picture or two, a few good laughs, and for Ty to apply the right amount of flattery and bootlicking. Noticeably, Senator Hayes was not on the list.

Aimes found it odd that the Senator who pushed for the subpoena wasn't willing to speak with them before the hearing. However, Ty saw it as an opportunity.

Hayes had shown up at his Raider graduation in an attempt to intimidate him, knowing that Ty would soon be given the subpoena. *What better way to illustrate that I wasn't intimidated than showing up uninvited at his office?*

While it was likely Hayes wouldn't speak with him, it would send a clear message—*You don't scare me.*

Unsure how Aimes would react to his idea about dropping by Hayes' office, Ty kept the plan to himself. He would have to find a time to sneak away. Then again, there was always the possibility that the two of them would run into each other in the vast halls of the Senate Office Building. He needed to be ready for this scenario because if Ty didn't handle it well, his attempt to disarm the Senator wouldn't work.

While Ty schemed how to rattle Hayes, he failed to remember that he wasn't the only Senator who wanted their pound of flesh—his first meeting started with a brutal reminder.

"No pictures!" Senator Lauren Wrzesinki blurted out with a long, Southern drawl.

Her orders were directed to the young photographer who was tasked with walking around with Aimes and Ty to document their visit.

According to her dossier, Senator Wrzesinki was a hard woman and a talented politician. The good people of West Virginia had just reelected her to a fourth term, making her the longest-serving woman in U.S. Senate history. Before the Senate, she was the Governor of her beloved state. She served as the Ranking Member on the Foreign Relations Committee. Which put her in the same party as Hayes and indicated that she would have been instrumental in getting Ty's subpoena served.

She was a fierce politician. Standing five foot seven inches tall, with a thin athletic frame. Her short grey hairstyle gave off strong Margaret

Thatcher vibes. Her dark red power suit was underlaid by a soft white blouse that tried to add a touch of feminism to her look. Just above her Senate lapel pin was a second, larger yellow gold and black tungsten pin in the shape of West Virginia. Once asked about it by a reporter, she remarked that the 'black tungsten represented her state's most valuable contribution to America, coal.' And that it would always be worn above her Senate pin as a reminder that her 'highest duty was to 'the good people of West Virginia.'

Ignoring her obtuse remark to the young photographer, Ty extended his right hand, "Good morning, Senator. It's a pleasure to meet you."

Without offering her's, "Ah yes, Lieutenant. I forgot I agreed to meet with you."

She knew Ty wasn't a lieutenant; this was a power play. Taking the bait wouldn't do him any good, so he ignored her dig.

Slowly dropping his extended hand. "Is now still a good time for us to speak, ma'am?"

"I am not sure if we have anything to discuss. I just wanted to lay my eyes on you before tomorrow to get the measure of what type of man you are."

"And?"

"Still trying to decide."

Ty was at a loss for words. His head was spinning with what to say or how to respond. She had just given him a small opportunity to persuade her opinion, but he was standing there looking like a fool. Thankfully, Aimes spoke up.

"Senator Wrzesinki, I'm Colonel George Aimes. Perhaps a couple of minutes in your office could help you decide."

Nodding, she said, "Alright, you have five minutes."

She turned and walked into her office. The two Marines followed, as did two of her staff members. Ty suspected one was her Chief of Staff but was unsure who the other was.

Wrzesinki sat behind a large wooden executive desk and gestured for Ty and Aimes to sit. "So, Lieutenant Hudson, why do I keep hearing your name associated with the killing of women and children?"

Again, with the games. It must be a trick that had previously worked well for her with military officers. Call them by the wrong rank a couple of times, and they lose focus by becoming flustered.

"Well, ma'am, that's what I hope to clarify. It's a horrible distortion of what happened. I hope to set the record straight tomorrow."

"I think we all understand what happened. My question for you is, why did you do it?"

"Why did I do what, ma'am?"

A voice from behind. "Lieutenant, the Senator doesn't have time for games."

Ty looked over his left shoulder at the mid-thirties staffer looking resolutely back at him. Like the Senator, he was thin, with thinning hair and oversized round glasses. Oddly, his tie matched the red color of the Senator's suit. Ty suspected this wasn't a coincidence.

With a firm voice, Ty replied, "Captain."

"I am sorry?" The staffer quipped.

Standing up, Ty looked back at the Senator and said, "My rank. I'm a captain in the Marine Corps, not a lieutenant."

Knowing the meeting was going nowhere, he turned to walk out. Aimes, still seated, rushed to stand up before thanking the Senator for her time.

Turning back to the room, looking first at the nerdy staffer and then at the Senator. "You know, what I look forward to the most tomorrow isn't clearing my name. It's hearing what evidence and lies you and Senator Hayes have contrived to smear my name."

"Captain, you wouldn't be in this position if we didn't have the evidence," Senator Wrzesinki snapped.

Taking a big step back toward her desk. "You're forgetting one important fact."

"Which is?" Asked the staffer.

"I was the one there. I know the truth."

No other words were spoken until Aimes and Ty exited her office to the hallway.

"I can't tell if she thinks I did it or if she and Hayes are that committed to their lies," Ty mocked.

"Ty, these people don't believe in truths or lies," Aimes said, "All they care about is what they can sell to the American people and get away with."

Ty knew his commanding officer was right. He wasn't naive to how Washington politicians manipulated truths to gain and maintain power. Yet, conceptually knowing it and experiencing it weren't the same.

"Then, sir, how do we beat them?"

"Ty, you do what has gotten you here. You follow your instincts and fight to win."

BENJAMIN FRANKLIN SAID nothing in this world was certain, 'except death and taxes.' He failed to mention partisan politics.

> *"You're a great American hero."*
> *"I'm disgusted by your presence and will work tirelessly to see you*
> *in prison the rest of your life."*
> *"What you and your Marines did was nothing short of a miracle."*
> *"You're a disgrace to the uniform."*

By the conclusion of his fifth meeting, Ty knew exactly what to expect from the rest. Each senator's position on the matter was already predetermined by which side of the aisle they sat on.

All he had to be thankful for now was his next meetings were after lunch.

"It would be great if they served beer or something stronger in there," Ty mumbled as he and Aimes followed the crowd.

Walking into the cafeteria, they found the place buzzing with activity. Ty looked to the guide escorting them around to ask if it was usually this busy. According to her, it was a slow day for the lunch rush. She then gave them the layout by going station by station to point out the different food options. The place had everything from sushi to ballpark-style hotdogs to tacos.

Separating from Aimes, Ty went to the salad bar to scope it out, still undecided about what he wanted. Looking for another option, he saw a familiar face get in line at a coffee bar just outside the cafeteria. It was Luna Copeland, Senator Hayes' Chief of Staff. She was chatting with another woman as they stood in the long line.

Glancing around to see where Aimes was, Ty noticed he had taken a seat with his back to him. This was his opportunity to approach Luna about meeting with Hayes. At the very least, see what intel he could gather.

Making his way toward the coffee bar, Ty moved to his right to position himself to walk up from behind to Luna. Then, he gradually entered the line directly behind her and the other staffer. As he had hoped, neither noticed him. He stood just a couple of feet behind them, hands to his side, and waited for his turn to order coffee.

Now, part of the line, Ty could make out what the two women were saying. A junior staffer had leaked the Senator's future travel plans to a reporter, and Hayes was pissed. The two discussed salvaging the staffer's job while punishing him for the leak.

Minutes later, Luna received a text message. "Oh, crap! Andy needs the files on the energy bill."

"I'll run them to him if you buy the coffee," the other woman replied.

With a relieved smile, "Done. I will see you back in the office in ten minutes. Well, maybe closer to twenty," Luna said, looking at the twelve or so people still ahead of her in line.

After her colleague left, Luna flipped open a file that she had been holding in her left hand. Something Ty hadn't even noticed her carrying. She flipped past the first couple of pages and stopped on the third to read while moving one step forward.

This isn't appropriate, Ty thought.

It started with infiltrating the line, eavesdropping on a private conversation between peers, and now he was leaning on his left foot, trying to get a glance at the file in her hand. It was more than likely any one of hundreds of topics that a senator's chief of staff would be reviewing and had nothing to do with him.

Finally, getting the peep he was craving, Ty was left dissatisfied. He couldn't distinguish what was in it. So, now he was in the middle of a long line to get a coffee he didn't want instead of eating the lunch he needed. Ty also had about three more orders before Luna placed hers and undoubtedly turned to see him standing behind her.

If he stepped out of line right now, he could easily disappear in the swarm and not be noticed. But then he wouldn't get the opportunity to speak with her and would most likely not be able to see Hayes before tomorrow's hearing. Ty's mind raced through the options as he took another step closer. And another one.

"Hi, I need a medium skinny caramel macchiato with an extra shot and a large iced chai tea latte."

Instinctively, Ty acted. He stepped up to the counter on her right. "Make that two macchiatos, and please allow me."

Luna started to object to him handing his credit card to the cashier but stopped mid-sentence when she realized who he was.

"You really think buying me a coffee is gonna help you?"

Making eye contact and giving her a soft smile, "Oh, no. You ordered my drink, and I thought it would be easier for the barista to make both at the same time."

"I shouldn't let you. It's against the law to buy Senate staff members gifts."

Taking his card back from the cashier. "I won't say anything if you don't."

Together, they moved to the left side of the coffee bar to wait. With how fast the line had been moving, Ty figured they had another five minutes together.

"I never got a chance to thank you for helping me last time we saw each other."

"It's not necessary. It was pretty clear you were confused, and nothing pisses the Senator off more than when someone doesn't recognize him."

Finding that a bit humorous, "So, it was more self-preservation on your part?"

"You haven't figured that out yet?"

Confused, Ty slightly tilted his head to encourage her to explain further. She picked up on his gesture. "Captain, this is Washington. Everything anyone does is all about self-preservation."

"Dragging me before Congress is all about Andy staying in office?"

"Andy? So you were eavesdropping while you were standing in line behind me?"

"Let me guess, only a handful of people call him that?"

"Maybe four in the world. Is that your way of admitting you were eavesdropping?"

"I'll admit that I overheard the exchange, and you calling him Andy caught my attention."

For the next few minutes, they joked about Washington norms and how out of place Ty looked in his dress blues. The conversation was natural as they easily moved from joke to joke. Most of them were at Ty's expense, but it also felt like there was a trace of flirting on her part.

No way she was flirting with me. She's smart by using her stunning good looks to disarm me. Wait, how did this turn into her working me for intel?

The barista called Ty's name as she placed their drinks on the counter. Luna reached for them, passed Ty his medium skinny caramel macchiato, and then picked up her two drinks.

Seeing how he was looking at the hot drink in his hand. "You don't drink those, do you?" Luna asked.

Ty chuckled. "No. I have no clue what this is."

"Then why did you order it and then pay for mine?"

If she was flirting with me, let's see how she reacts when I turn the tables.

"Honestly," Ty began, "I had been eavesdropping behind you for twenty minutes, and I couldn't think of a smooth way to say hi."

She didn't respond. Didn't even crack a smile.

Instead, she returned to the barista to ask for a drink holder and then took Ty's from his hand to place it in the holder.

"Since you won't drink it, I'll give it to someone in the office."

With a smirk, Ty replied, "Maybe Johnny would like it after the day he's having."

Johnny was the name of the junior staffer who had leaked Hayes's travel plans. This confirmed to her that he had been listening to her conversations.

Again, she gave no reaction. Just started to walk away without saying another word. Ty had fumbled the opportunity to gain intelligence or talk his way into meeting with Hayes. It couldn't end that way, so he quickly turned to get her attention without knowing what he would say, but he needed to stop her. That's when she turned back toward him.

"Have drinks with me tonight," Luna said.

Ty tried to disguise his shock. "I would like that. When and where?" "I would like that. When and where?"

"I'll text you."

"Don't you need my number?"

Laughing, "You're really out of your depth in Washington."

CHAPTER
TWENTY-SIX

"HAVE YOU LOST YOUR DAMN MIND?" Aimes scorned.

Of the two people whom Ty told about getting drinks with Luna, he hadn't expected his commanding officer to be the one to call him crazy. The person he suspected would be upset about his agreeing to meet another woman for drinks would have been his wife. That wasn't the case.

"I think you should go," Beth said, "but you need to be careful. She is using you the same way you're using her."

Ty had been dreading telling her for nearly four hours before he worked up the courage to call home. The rest of the afternoon in the Senate offices went about as well as the morning. After his meeting or beating, he and Aimes had a few minutes before their car arrived. Ty used this time to call Beth.

With a knot in his throat, "I saw Luna Copeland today."

"That's great," Beth responded. "Did you see Hayes?"

"No. I ran into her getting coffee, and we chatted for a few minutes."

It was an innocent enough lie. He wasn't sidestepping or avoiding telling his wife about how he snuck into the line so he could eavesdrop. Ty knew he would chicken out if he didn't get to the drinks part quickly.

"How did that go? Did you get any good intel?"

"It went as expected. She knew what I was trying to do, and I knew that she knew. So, neither of us got much from the other."

"Well, nothing gained or lost. And at least she knows you are a worthy adversary now."

Ty paused for a second. Not sure how to bring it up or say it out loud. He had no interest in Luna. Yes, she was an attractive woman who, in another life, might have been right up his alley. But he was head over heels for his wife and wasn't the type of man to cheat just for a meaningless orgasm. Beth, of course, knew this. But it didn't make it easy to tell her that he had agreed to have drinks with another woman.

"Ty, you still there?"

Letting out a low laugh, "Yeah, I am here. Before she walked away, Luna asked me out for drinks tonight."

Now, it was Beth's turn to take a pause. A long pause.

"Babe?" Ty asked, wondering if she had hung up.

"I'm here."

"I don't think it was anything romantic. I think she is still trying to bait me."

"Oh, that's exactly what she is doing. Ty, I'm not worried about you doing anything. She's trying to honeypot you into giving something away."

"Right! That's what I think, too."

That's when Beth said she thought he should go. It felt weird. Unnatural in the sense that it went against what Ty thought a wife should tell her husband in a moment like this.

For the next few minutes on the phone, Ty looked for a reason to avoid going. Yet Beth continued encouraging him to view it as an after-work business meeting or a complex reconnaissance mission—not something to be worried about.

This last analogy helped convince him to stay the course and go out for drinks with Luna. After all, it was a mission to gain intel from someone who was a foe and was trying hard to kill him, albeit professionally. But, if she and the Andrew Hayes' of the world had their way, Ty wouldn't spend another day in a Marine uniform. According to them, he was a cold, calculated murderer who was a disgrace to the uniform and belonged in jail for the rest of his life.

While his wife supported the idea, Aimes ardently objected to him going out with Luna. He brought up something neither Beth nor Ty had thought about. "Luna might be trying to make you an asset," Aimes said.

The Colonel rationalized it by suggesting that she and Hayes knew they didn't have evidence of civilian deaths in Mosul, and after some chest-beating, that would come out. But they had an agenda and could try turning Ty into an asset.

Aimes' theory amused Ty, but knew it wasn't far-fetched. Most Americans don't know about the shadow wars that the CIA and powerful politicians run without oversight. Countless Hollywood hits and popular television shows have been about the concept. Yet, what might be seen as fiction is often very real.

Hayes had been in Washington long enough to accumulate power and a level of influence over American foreign policy that most voters didn't know about. His having access to Tier One operators who could carry out his plans overseas under the disguise of an intelligence mission was a powerful tool. Aimes reminded Ty that he was now a leader of a Tier One unit and could be a target for Hayes.

At first, Ty blew off his suggestion by thinking, like most Americans, that politicians don't have that much influence on black ops or other covert military interventions.

The Colonel laughed at his objection. "Ty, why do you think Marcus is running a small intel team for the CIA's Deputy Director of Counter Terrorism now?"

Giving it more thought, "It's because he has the skill set and knowledge to do the job."

"Really!" Aimes barked. "Sure, he has both the skills and knowledge, but you don't think Preston or Newbold recruited him while he was recovering?"

That's nuts. No way, that's what happened.

"Sir, you can't be serious."

"Alright, next time you see Marcus, ask him if Newbold visited him at Walter Reed."

Not long after that comment, Aimes gave up on trying to convince Ty not to meet Luna for drinks and stormed out of his room. That left Ty about an hour to relax, shower, and make it to the bar where Luna told him to meet at twenty hundred hours.

While he tried to relax after a brutal day, Ty was consumed with what Aimes had said about Marcus. He didn't know if the Colonel knew something that he didn't about how Marcus ended up working with the CIA, but Ty couldn't ignore the possibility. What was even more confounding was his pending evening out with Luna. *Were she and Hayes working me? Was that a thing?*

No way! Ty concluded. Luna was his age, and there was no way a sitting senator would entrust a person in their late twenties with that responsibility. The more likely scenario was that Aimes had lost his mind or was being overly paranoid.

The taxi ride from Marine Barracks Washington to the chic bar Luna wanted to meet at took twenty-five minutes longer than expected because of traffic. Ty had lived in Southern California for several years and knew how to account for local traffic, but he didn't know Washington. Because of that, he arrived late.

Getting out of the taxi, Ty looked to his right to see the Capitol standing tall at the end of the street. This symbol of American government and power reminded him of what Luna had said about him not being in his element in Washington. This was her home turf, and she had the advantage. Ty had no allies in the building before him, whereas she most likely knew all of the D.C. elites drinking their hard day away.

The bar had ground-to-ceiling windows that allowed those driving or walking by to peer in to see all that was happening inside. It was dimly lit by random-sized antique bulbs that gave an orange glow from the low-hanging rustic chandeliers scattered around the crowded room. The small signage hanging off the building over the sidewalk had the same orange glow.

Looking at the handful of people outside waiting to go in and those standing closest to the tall windows, it was apparent that Ty was not dressed appropriately. A woman in a low-cut mini dress must have thought the same thing as she eyed him with disgust before she said something to her friend, who turned to look Ty over before bursting out in laughter. Regardless of his evening with Luna, at least he could entertain these two women.

Walking past the two women still laughing at his appearance, Ty stopped inside the door to look for Luna. Scanning the room, he didn't see her. He did notice all the glances the dress-to-impress crowd of patrons gave him. He noticed that each person was holding a fancy mixed drink, a whiskey, or a long-stemmed glass of wine. There was not a single person holding a beer.

This wasn't Ty's crowd.

And they all knew that he didn't belong either.

Reluctantly, Ty moved several steps further in.

The room was enormous, and a couple hundred people had to be in it. Two bars on each side ran the entire length. Several fancy-dressed bartenders took orders, making and pouring drinks in mere seconds, almost working shoulder to shoulder-on both sides. That was the only way they could keep up with the demands of so many drinkers.

The tables were all in the rear and elevated on three different tiers. So, anyone sitting at the top-tier tables could easily see over the crowd. In the middle of the room, there were no seated tables, just a handful of tall tables to stand at.

He hadn't yet seen Luna, making the situation unnerving. His heart started to beat faster, and the palms of his hands began to sweat as he felt the physiological pull of his fight or flight response building. *Do I try to find her or retreat to fight another day?*

Weighing the decision, Ty remembered the advice that Aimes had given him just this morning. *'Follow your instincts, stand on principle, and fight to win.'*

He took several more steps into the center, looking first to his left and right. That's when Ty saw who he was looking for.

CHAPTER
TWENTY-SEVEN

EXHALING A DEEP BREATH. Ty groaned, "This is a bad idea."

Ty couldn't see Luna when he walked in because she was seated at the bar, surrounded by a huddle of four well-dressed guys. Each was in a smart, expensive-looking suit. They all still had their ties on, but most had loosened them as if that was the more casual look for after-hours drinks. Maybe they were Capitol Hill colleagues or hitting on her using the safety of numbers.

From a distance, it was the typical conversation between a group of guys and a girl in a bar. She was the center of attention, smiling at each guy as he took advantage of his moment to speak. Ty couldn't tell if Luna was genuinely interested or if she was good at faking it.

Of course, there was a third option. Maybe she was too kind to dismiss their advances.

This, however, would seem out of character based on Ty's limited interactions with her. She would have sent these guys running with their tails between their legs if she were bored or uninterested. No, she either knew this bunch or was enjoying the moment.

The most striking part of the scene wasn't a group of guys flirting with her. It was what she was wearing. She wasn't in the same clothes Ty had seen her in earlier. In the office building, Luna donned a dark blue business suit with a long skirt that went below her knees. Her white blouse was buttoned nearly to her neck, her shoes were tidy short heels, and her hair was up off her shoulders in a tight bun. As with her political values, she dressed very conservatively, making sure not to wear anything that would draw unwanted or unnecessary attention.

But this wasn't the office. And the only thing missing from this evening's outfit was a blinking sign that read 'Look at me.'

Sitting cross-legged on the bar stool, Ty could see nearly the entire length of her right leg. The slit in her tight yellow ankle-length dress ran up to her hip. The thin spaghetti straps were barely visible through her mid-back length hair that was down for the night. The last part of her ensemble that suggested she was screaming for attention was how much cleavage was displayed.

And for good reason.

The poor guy standing at the bar beside her shamelessly stole a glance each time she looked away.

Sure, Ty had subconsciously acknowledged that she was attractive when he first saw her a month ago at his Marine Raider graduation.

But she wasn't just attractive.

She was hot!

That internal struggle of fight or flight resumed. Ty was drawn to her as if he were one of the four guys talking with her. If he were honest with himself, a single Ty would be in the middle of that group, fighting for her undivided attention.

However, he wasn't single. No, quite the opposite.

He was a happily married man with two amazing children. Despite what Beth told him earlier about meeting Luna tonight, she would not approve of her husband having drinks with a woman looking like she did. Ty knew the smartest thing he could do would be to take flight and leave.

As fate would have it, he made eye contact with Luna before he could retreat.

They held each other's glance for a moment. It wasn't the 'please come over here and save me' look you might expect from a girl you were supposed to meet for drinks. No, this was an 'if-you-want-it-come-and-get-it' stare.

Ty could say *no* to her tight-fitting dress.

He could even say *no* to her.

But he couldn't walk away from this challenge.

Strolling up to her, Ty squeezed himself between the two guys dominating the conversation. "Yes, I would love a drink."

The guy to his right, the one with wandering eyes, opened his mouth in disbelief. The guy to his left shot him a pointed, side-eyed glance.

"I'm sorry?" Luna asked with a chuckle. "You want to buy me a drink?"

"No, you're buying me a drink. A scotch or whisky would be great."

Luna got the reaction from the other guys she wanted. The guy with wandering eyes stood a bit taller and leaned towards Ty as he looked him up and down. By his expression, he wasn't impressed with the newcomer's worn tennis shoes, blue jeans, and off-white t-shirt from a bar-n-grill.

In a firm voice, the guy said, "Hey man, I don't think she's interested."

Keeping eye contact with Luna while she smiled back. "No, she is. When you sneaked a look at her tits a moment ago, she invited me over here for a drink."

"Yeah? You think that's what happened?"

Slowly turning to look the man in his eyes. "Have you noticed she hasn't asked me to leave yet?"

One of the other guys spoke up from the cheap seats. "Jeff, don't take that shit from this loser."

So the wandering-eyed guy was named Jeff, who was now weighing his options as he looked Ty over again.

Taking advantage of his contemplation, Ty looked back to Luna and nodded in the direction behind her. "I believe the bartender is waiting for you to order my drink."

One of the fancy-dressed bartenders noticed the awkward interaction and quickly approached. Ty doubted it was to take his drink order; instead, he suspected it was to keep the peace or tell them to take it outside.

As Luna turned to see the server, Jeff decided to act.

"Hey! Asshole! You're way out of your league, and you need to move on before I—" he said, grabbing Ty's right arm before coming to a dead stop mid-threat.

Ty didn't bother to look at him. He immediately knew that once Jeff grabbed his ripped bicep, the staffer dressed in an expensive suit was going to retreat. Luna had turned back to see the entire exchange. Ty kept his eyes locked on hers as Jeff reconsidered his next move.

She pulled her eyes off Ty's momentarily to look at Jeff. In doing so, her smile widened as she had also decided.

Swinging back to the bartender. "Ricky, give me a scotch on the rocks and another one of these," she said, holding up her nearly empty martini glass.

Neither Luna nor Ty had to say another word to Jeff and his buddies.

They quickly moved on.

A moment later, Ricky, the bartender, was back with their drinks. She passed Ty a lowball glass of scotch as he took up the bar mantle beside her.

"Did you enjoy that?" He asked, now that it was just the two of them.

"I did, but Jeff might have had a shot tonight if you hadn't walked up."

"I can go get him for you."

"No, it's you that I want."

That caught Ty off guard. He had no clue how to respond. *Was this a blatantly forward sexual advance, or was she trying to disarm me?*

If it were an advance, she would be disappointed, but Ty was afraid he wouldn't get what he wanted if he told her that outright.

Ty sidestepped her comment by changing the subject. Looking around the bar. "Are these all Capitol Hill staff members?"

The question had the desired effect. Luna began a long-winded explanation of who worked for which politician, who had a history with one another, and how this bar was considered neutral ground. She explained that while she had never met Jeff before, he was a senior aide to a Congressman on the opposite side of the aisle. She was sure to mention a few times that his political association wouldn't have stopped her from sleeping with him.

Ty knew she wasn't interested in Jeff. She just wanted him to know how in demand she was and that she was open to getting laid tonight. It would be a long evening if, at every moment, she would pull the conversation back to sex.

But this was also an opportunity for Ty to defuse her by playing along. "So, how many of these guys have you slept with?"

"Guys only?"

Smiling back at her to acknowledge the admission. "Okay, how many people have you slept with in this room?"

"Guess."

"I would say three."

She let out a loud laugh while grabbing his arm.

"Ty, this is Washington D.C. I appreciate you not wanting to suggest that I'm a slut, but seriously, how many do you think?"

"Give me a clue. Remember, I'm married. It's been a few years since I've had to guess something like this."

This wasn't a conversation he wanted to be having. The gentle reminder that he was married was intentional, but he knew it wouldn't move them off the topic until she was satisfied. Ty either needed to be more direct or get this dumb guess right.

After having her hand on his arm for a long minute, she finally dropped it. "How about this for a clue? You're not even close."

Ty looked over the crowd again. It was a beautiful room. Not in the sense that it was a well-designed motif with low-hanging lights, dark wood features, and perfectly placed furniture. No, it was the people in the bar that made it beautiful.

Everyone was under forty and attractive. The only aspect of the room that was more impressive than its appearance was its diversity. There was a near-perfect blend of sexes, races, and ethnicities.

While Ty was used to diversity in the Marine Corps, it wasn't something he had seen in college or his neighborhood outside Camp Pendleton. He couldn't help but appreciate the sight.

As for Luna and her sexual exploits, he needed an answer. She had said he 'wasn't close' when he had suggested three partners.

Does that mean I need to multiply it? As Ty considered by which multiple he would use, *times four or five*, he remembered a line in her dossier mentioning that she had just recently ended a long-term relationship with her college sweetheart.

Ty turned his attention back to Luna with a confident expression, "Zero!"

Her smile confirmed he was correct.

"That's right," she admitted, "I just got out of a long-term relationship, and besides, most of these guys don't do anything for me."

Ty took the offramp to turn the conversation from sex onto her life story. Luckily, she allowed it.

For the next fifteen minutes, she sat on her bar stool, with her legs still crossed, showing off the length of her leg, describing what it was like growing up in the middle of nowhere Iowa. She droned on about how she used to try to run away from her home in her early teen years, trying to make it to the big city, but was never able to make it past the cornfields that surrounded her small town.

Ty listened intently while leaning against the bar's wooden edge, facing out into the room, asking follow-up questions at the right moment to keep her talking.

After graduating Valedictorian of her high school class of forty-eight seniors, she attended Iowa State University on a volleyball scholarship. This was an interesting fact not in her dossier, so Ty asked several questions about being a college athlete and balancing that with her studies. These questions led him to how she met Hayes. Another fact that was not in her file from the JAG Officers.

She explained that Hayes' youngest sister, Jenny, was also at Iowa State on a volleyball scholarship and was a year ahead of Luna. The two became close friends and roomed together during her sophomore and junior years. During a Christmas trip home with Jenny, she met the older brother, who was kicking off his Senate campaign.

Luna described the chance meeting as life-altering, "His passion for the people of Iowa, our values, and how the rest of America should be more like us was so inspiring. It made me start to appreciate my small-town life."

With a new perspective, she immediately volunteered with his campaign. Upon returning to school after winter break, she switched her major from nursing to political science. After graduating from Iowa State, she worked full-time for newly elected Senator Hayes in his D.C. office while studying part-time for her Master's in Public Policy at Georgetown University. Only about a year ago did she become his chief of staff. It was a testament to her brilliance as a political force and her commitment to the Senator.

Admittedly, Ty was impressed. Her life story was inspiring, and her devotion to Hayes was undeniable. Hearing all of this convinced him that she would not let anything slip or give him anything that would be helpful for tomorrow's hearing. But he still had a lot of unanswered questions. Ty took her concluding her story as an opportunity to move in.

"I am curious about one thing."

"Just one?" She replied with a flirty tone.

"Well, no. I have a lot of questions. But the one that's been bothering me all day is why you invited me out for drinks tonight?"

Something or someone in the distance caught her eye. Ignoring his inquiry, she hopped off her stool and waved for Ricky to return. The bartender passed two or three patrons trying to get his attention to reach her.

"Ricky, please send another round to my table for us."

Table? Ty thought, looking to the back of the room towards what might have caught her attention a moment ago. There, he saw an empty U-shaped booth with what appeared to be a hostess standing guard, directing people away.

Luna grabbed Ty by his hand as she guided him to the booth.

CHAPTER
TWENTY-EIGHT

THE BOOTH WAS COVERED with deep burgundy leather and evenly spaced buttons that gave it character. The backrest, lined with the same leather and buttons, was tall. Despite being over six feet, it towered nearly a foot over Ty's head when seated.

The table was weathered and matched the same deep brown wood as the bar. When he and Luna sat down, the only two items on it were a simple black, low lamp that gently illuminated their seats with the same yellow light as the rest of the room and a golden six-inch metal tent sign that read, *Reserved.*

As Luna sat, Ty entered the U-shape from the opposite side. The booth was easily big enough for four people, but as Ty settled on his side of the table, Luna scooted closer. While it might appear to an onlooker that she was seated in the deepest part of the U-shape, she wasn't. She had taken up half of his side of the table and was close enough that her knee rested on his right leg when she crossed her legs.

Ricky appeared with a round tray and their drinks. As he dropped a pair of white bar napkins and placed the drinks down, Ty used his appearance to adjust how he was seated by sliding left and angling his body toward her. This repositioning had its desired effect. Their legs no longer touched, and he looked more directly at her. She matched his move by turning her shoulders to be square with his.

Well, shit! Maybe I should've stayed the way I was. Now that Luna had turned her body to face his, her cleavage was on full display. For a brief moment, Ty felt a ping of empathy for Jeff's wandering eyes.

Ty and Beth had always been secure in their relationship. Neither was the jealous type. Both thought it was petty to get bothered if the other checked someone out. Meeting while in college meant attractive people surrounded the young couple. So early on, they had an unspoken agreement that *you could look but couldn't touch.*

As they grew closer and more secure in their future together, they would even point out a hot person for the other.

Yet, this felt different with Luna.

While leaning against the bar, Ty was facing the room and had to turn his head to look at her. This made it easy to ignore his instincts to sneak a peak and admire her beauty. Now facing her, mere inches away, it had become a conscious effort. One that Ty suspected he would have to struggle with the rest of the evening.

Sipping on her fresh drink, "So, back to your question. Why do you think I invited you here tonight?"

"Honestly?" Ty asked rhetorically, "To get into my head before the hearing tomorrow morning."

"Really? You don't think I could have a different motive?"

"No, I don't."

Her flirty smile dropped as she tilted slightly, "Well, that's disappointing."

Her response was unexpected, and it occurred to Ty that he might have been wrong. *Maybe she was interested.* Thinking momentarily about how to respond, he decided the best path was to get her to say why she had invited him out.

"What other reason could there be for you to ask me out?"

"Ty, isn't it obvious? I'm into you."

Taking a deep breath, "I am flattered, but you know I'm happily married."

This was the moment of truth. Either she would acknowledge that fact by moving on, or the evening was about to end.

Ty was comfortable with either outcome.

With a sly smile. "I know, but a girl can dream."

The two sat there in silence for a moment, each taking a long pull from their drinks, trying to figure out how to advance the conversation.

"Wait, you thought me asking you out for drinks and getting dressed up like this was all about trying to throw you off tomorrow?"

"Yeah."

"So, you thought this was all politically motivated, and you showed up anyway?"

Hmmm… fair point. Is she looking for admittance that there's an attraction, or is she genuinely confused about why I'd show up for drinks with an adversary?

Honesty was the best approach. "That's right. I'm trying to figure out why your boss has it out for me."

With a touch of anger in her tone. "You think Andy is out to get you, and what, you thought I would give something up to help you?"

"No. I know you aren't giving anything up. But, yes, I would love for you to tell me why he is out to get me."

Ty had struck a nerve as her body turned rigid. Her facial expression hardened. "How big of an ego do you have?"

"Ego?"

"What makes you think this has anything to do with you?"

Now, she had struck a nerve.

"Are you kidding me? Your boss is accusing me of committing war crimes. You think this has nothing to do with me?"

"No, he's stating facts. You're being protected by the Navy and promoted for it."

The conversation had taken a dark turn. But Luna didn't realize that she had just given several things up. First, Hayes was fully committed to the lie that Ty had killed civilians. Next, the Senator wasn't after him. His target was the Navy or the entire military institution. As Ty had feared, he was just the stepping stone. And he was going to exploit her anger.

"Luna, you're smarter than this," Ty began, "You know there isn't any evidence of civilian deaths. If there were, the Navy would've acted on it."

She leaned toward him, but not in the flirty way she had been doing just minutes ago. No, this was way more intense, "Wow, you don't have a clue!"

"Clue about what?"

"Ty, this is so much bigger than you. So, let me give you some advice."

"Please do."

"The sooner you realize this is going to happen, the easier it will be for you and the softer the blow."

Matching her emotions, Ty leaned just a few inches away. "I don't live in the same world as you do. So, what do you think is going to happen tomorrow?"

His power move by closing the distance between them had the opposite effect. Ty could almost taste her warm breath as he fought back the urge to lean in just an inch or two further. By how her eyes burned, he suspected she felt the same way.

He was right.

With a heavy breath, Luna whispered, "I want to kiss you right now."

Her words sent Ty crashing backward into the booth, putting space back between them so as not to tempt fate anymore.

Holy shit! That was way too close.

When Ty didn't respond, Luna joked, "Yeah, yeah, I get it. At least you could admit that you wanted to."

They were again at a crossroads. Ty didn't want to go back to talking about Hayes or tomorrow's hearing. Yet, in his heart, he knew he couldn't continue down a lustful path either.

Once more, he changed the topic.

"Tell me how a girl from a small Iowa town has taken over Washington so easily."

This simple question allowed her to talk about herself and avoid Hayes.

Time passed easily as they shared stories of their early lives, the people they spent time with, their regrets, and the dreams they had.

Luna was easy to talk to. Maybe too easy.

Looking down at the table, Ty asked, "Wow, how many rounds have we had?"

Laughing, "I think I'm at five, no six. And you're at four."

"I didn't realize Ricky kept bringing us drinks."

"Yeah, he takes care of me when I'm here. Could I talk you into one more?"

Ty looked at his watch. It was approaching midnight, "You can, but only one more. I think I'm going to have a long day tomorrow."

"Great, let's go!" She said, getting up from the booth.

"Wait, what? Why are you getting up?"

Luna waved in Ricky's direction. "I didn't say we would have the drink here."

"Ummm… Where are we going?"

"Dancing," she replied as the bartender arrived with the check.

This was not expected. He had been sure she would try to lure him back to her place for a nightcap, hoping its privacy would loosen him up. He had not danced in years.

Reaching her hand out, Luna asked, "You coming?"

The nightclub was only three blocks away, so they walked it while continuing their conversation. Coming up to the line of the scantly dressed crowd waiting to get in, Ty wasn't shocked in the slightest when Luna walked past them to the doorman. She kissed him on the cheek as he unfastened the velvet rope to let them through despite the groans and objections coming from the line.

Inside was what Ty expected—bars along the side walls and a wide-open dance floor. The DJ was on an elevated stage at the back of the room as different color lights randomly pierced through the otherwise dark room that smelt like sweat and sex.

Taking Ty by the hand, Luna pulled him out to the center of the floor.

Leaning into his ear, Luna said, "I hope you can dance."

When he started to move with the music, Luna's eyes went wide, and for the first time, Ty saw her speechless.

That's right. I can dance.

TWENTY-NINE

THE ELEVATOR WAS BIG, easily capable of carrying twenty or more. Two sharply dressed women were already there when Aimes, Wooden, and Ty walked up.

Waiting for it to arrive, Ty looked at his reflection in the shiny steel finish of the door. Luckily, looking back, the Marine showed no signs of being hung over. Nor tired. He had operated on less than three hours of sleep before and with more than four drinks.

I'll be okay. I've got this.

When the doors opened, the waiting group stepped in. The two women moved to the back right corner, and the three in Ty's party stood in the middle. Wooden pushed the button for the hearing room floor, and the door began to close slowly.

"Hold the door! Hold the door, please!" A rushed female voice called out.

Ty paid no attention to the elevator being held up. He rubbed his eyes while fighting off the urge to yawn.

When the person calling to hold the elevator reached the door, it was Luna. She rushed in, not even looking around as she thanked everyone for waiting. Looking up, she stopped in front of Ty as they made eye contact.

She had resorted back to the Capitol dress code. Her business suit had a long black skirt that dropped below her knees. Her impressive cleavage, on display just hours ago, was now covered by a chic light blue blouse beneath a blazer. Her heels were short. Her hair was put neatly into a bun. No doubt, the yellow dress was hung up nicely in her closet.

The mood in the elevator had turned on a dime as she and Ty were in a stare-down. Ty felt Wooden's gaze turn to him as he began understanding the tension between Hayes' Chief of Staff and the Marine officer.

Deciding to pick up where they had left off hours before, Ty said, "I'll admit, I was hoping you'd still be in the yellow dress."

Grinning. "It's still on the floor where I slipped out of it."

Her flirty remark made Aimes break his composure as he, too, now glared at Ty.

She moved closer to the center, allowing the doors to shut behind her. The two were now a foot apart. Still facing each other as Luna kept her back to the door.

"I had a great time last night," she smirked.

"No doubt it'll be an evening I might regret."

The door opened on the next floor to allow several others to pile in. Everyone inside took steps backward to make room for six more riders. Ty took a big step, trying to put distance between them. Luna did the same while never acknowledging the new riders.

Yet, when she moved toward the back of the now-crowded box, it wasn't proportional to his move in the way most people would make sure to keep the same distance from each other.

No, Luna had moved closer. Now inches away. Looking down into her eyes, Ty could smell her shampoo. Feel her breath on his face. The scene had to look like two people on the verge of a passionate embrace rather than two opponents getting ready for what was sure to be an intense polit-ical exchange.

She let out a low breath. "I wish we could've met under different circumstances. I think it would have been special."

Her tone was soft, sincere even. Unlike last night, there wasn't a hint of lust.

Despite it happening in an evaluator full of her colleagues, Ty's commanding officer, and one unimpressed JAG officer, this moment felt heartfelt.

Having a little fun, Ty playfully remarked, "Nah, at most, it would have been a one-night stand."

Before Luna could say anything, the elevator came to their floor, and the doors opened behind her. Nobody exited.

Every person was now vested in what was happening. Even the small group waiting outside to get on started to peer in to see why no one had yet rushed off the moment the door pulled open.

Luna placed her right hand on Ty's chest. "I don't think you believe that."

She leaned up on her tippy toes toward his face as she spoke. Fearing she was trying to kiss him, Ty stepped back to create more space between them.

Acknowledging his defensive move, she smiled, turned, and was first off the elevator. Everyone else was staring at Ty, unsure what they had just witnessed.

Leaning over to him, Wooden sneered, "Umm... What the fuck was that?"

And just like that, Ty's day was off and running!

He was sure everyone in the hall outside the small conference room he had been dragged into could hear every word being screamed. Ignoring most of what was being yelled at him, Ty focused on all that had happened in the last twelve hours: the drinks, the flirting, the dancing, and a way too public scene on the elevator.

In his fury, the JAG Officer stepped face to face with Ty, who stood four to five inches taller than him. To make his point, he started to poke the Marine in the chest as he blurted out explicative after explicative. Each of his questions returned to a single theme, *'What the fuck were you thinking?'*

As Ty ignored Wooden, he appreciated that Aimes had not mentioned his evening with Luna earlier. His entire morning would have been like the last five minutes. And his head was already pounding after just a few minutes of the lawyer's disapproval. He might've killed him if Ty had dealt with it all morning.

At first, Wooden ignored the hints to step back. Finally, Aimes gently pulled him back. "Unless you, too, are going to try to kiss him, I think you can back out of his face."

While Wooden was pissed about Ty meeting with Hayes' Chief of Staff, Aimes was more fixated on why she had tried to kiss him.

With a few minutes to go, Ty grabbed a bottle of water from a cart near the door. It wasn't there for him. But he didn't care. He needed something to drink. Something in his hands that wasn't the lawyer's neck.

That's when the Commandant of the Marine Corps, General Marin, walked in.

Standing taller to come to attention, Aimes said, "General, sir. We weren't expecting you."

Extending his right hand, "Colonel, the Secretary, and I thought it best to show a unified front."

Shaking the General's hand. "We appreciate that, sir. This is Lieutenant Commander Wooden from the Judge Advocate General's office, and, of course, you'll remember Captain Hudson."

Marin shook the JAG Officer's hand first, as with the military custom of recognizing the high-ranked officer, before offering his hand to Ty. "Sir, thank you for your continued support."

Ty had learned that the General was influential in helping to squash Hayes' initial pressure campaign after the Battle of Bloody Fountain. It wasn't until Williams and Preston screwed up the Jalalabad strike that Hayes brought Mosul back up.

"Captain, it's good to see you again. How are you feeling about today?"

"Good, sir. I'm well prepared and ready to go."

"That's good to hear. You have a lot on your shoulders, and I'm afraid half of Washington is coming after you."

Interjecting, Aimes asked, "Sir, what are you hearing?"

"Well, that's why I am here. Hayes and a few others will use this hearing to attack the war, the DOD, and the formation of the Raider Regiment. Their goal is to win enough public favor to open an investigation into the Corps by suggesting there's a culture of hiding atrocities with medals and promotions."

Aimes shook his head. "That's bullshit."

"Agreed, but they think Captain Hudson is the perfect example. That's the point they'll push hard to make."

Listening, Ty was finding this unnerving. *Luna was right. This is so much bigger than me.*

Speaking up. "Sir, if all Hayes has is me, why not offer me up? Why let me continue to be his leverage?"

It was a legitimate question. It would have been the easiest course of action for the Corps. If they offered him up as a scapegoat, then Hayes wouldn't have any grounds for this hearing or his ongoing attacks.

Let alone try to disband the Raiders before they even get their boots dirty.

This questioning wasn't something a captain would ask of a four-star general. So, when he did, both Aimes and Wooden looked at him in disbelief. From the corner of his eye, Ty could see Aimes preparing to step in.

Nodding his head in agreement, the General spoke, "Because of that right there, Captain."

Ty tilted his head in confusion. "Sir?"

"It's because you don't hesitate to put your Marines and the Corps first. It's because you just made the leap from thinking this was all about Mosul to understanding the full situation in less than a second. Then, you started to problem-solve. That makes you a special operator, and is why the Corps needs you. That's why Colonel Aimes, myself, and the Secretary are in your corner. Giving you to Hayes was never a thought."

Ty's heart was racing. His hands trembled with excitement as the General finished. He had never been so proud of himself. Never so proud to wear the uniform of a United States Marine as he was right now.

These powerful men were not only on his side but wanted him to succeed as much as they needed him to.

As Ty thought through his words, he began to understand how responsible he was for the fate of the other twenty Raiders who had just graduated alongside him a month ago. To some degree, the future of this special operations unit was riding on his ability to outmaneuver and beat Hayes today.

Excitement and pride instantly turned to apprehension and doubt. *Am I ready for this?*

Ty's head started swirling with different emotions. Knowing this couldn't last, he turned to his training. *Put the mission first*, he reminded himself. *The next few hours were all that mattered.*

"Sir, I appreciate the backing. What does the Corps need from me today?"

Marin gave an approving smile. "Captain, just be yourself today."

Taking a big step toward Ty, the General placed his right hand on his shoulder. "Take the fight to Hayes. Own the room by turning the tables on them and making them pay for their arrogance and stupidity for picking a fight with you. In short, Captain, we need you to be a Raider today."

The General left the room, leaving the three men alone to contemplate his words. The lawyer immediately started to protest the General's advice. Both Aimes and Ty ignored him.

"Wooden, could you give Hudson and me the room?" Aimes asked rather matter-of-factly.

Wooden gave the Colonel a stern look but didn't protest. He reminded them they only had a few minutes before the hearing started and that he would be waiting in the hallway.

Aimes turned back to Ty, "What are you thinking?"

"Honestly? I think the Corps and the Secretary are using me. Just like Hayes is."

"How so?"

Ty considered this for a moment. Was sharing his unfiltered thoughts with his commanding officer something he wanted to do?

He chose honesty. "I can say the things they can't."

"And that's why you think they're supporting you?"

"Yes, sir. And then, depending on the blowback, I'd be offered up as a scapegoat."

Rubbing his chin. "I hadn't thought of it that way. What are you going to do?"

"Well, sir… I was going to ask for advice."

The Colonel didn't respond.

He walked over to the cart to get a bottle of water, twisted off the top, and took a long swig.

He stood there, staring at the opposite wall.

Concerned, Ty stepped over to his right side. "Sir, what are you thinking?"

Turning to make eye contact. "I think you only have one option, Ty. You need to rise above the moment by becoming a celebrity with the American people."

Ty's eyes went wide. *What the hell is he talking about?*

Seeing his confusion, Aimes continued, "Americans hate politicians but love a good hero. If America sees you as a hero, the Corps and the Secretary's hands get tied. Then there's no way this blows back on you."

"So, not only do I need to beat Hayes today at his own game, but I need to look like I'm the hero?"

Laughing. "Sort of. You're a decorated Marine. You're already a hero. But now, the American people need to see you taking on Washington for them. They have to believe you're fighting what's wrong with all of this for them. That's what makes you a celebrity and ties the hands of the Secretary."

There was a hard rap on the door before Wooden stepped in to tell the two Marines that it was time. Everyone needed to get inside.

"Ty, don't overthink this. Be yourself by taking the fight to Hayes. The rest will take care of itself."

CHAPTER
THIRTY

THE LITTLE BIT of confidence Ty had after General Marin's visit began to fade as he walked into the hearing room.

The spectacle before him brought him to a stop at the doors.

The back of the enormous room was littered with TV cameras, all with fancy news organizations' logos on their side. Each was fixated on the intimidating U-shaped desk at the front. On the opposite side of the elevated desk were evenly spaced black executive chairs for each of the nineteen senators that made up the Foreign Relations Committee. Behind them were two or three simple conference room chairs.

These, Ty suspected, were for aids. One would be Luna's.

It wasn't the size of the desk, the number of executive chairs, or the centered name plaques that were intimidating. The desk was a step or two higher than the room's floor. This was intentionally designed so that the senators could project power onto whoever was seated at the table situated in the center—that was the table Ty was heading towards.

In the center of the room were more than twenty rows of conference room chairs. Divided by a center aisle, each side looked to have twenty chairs. Each was already filled up with onlookers.

As he started down the aisle toward his fate, Ty felt like a bride.

Everyone in the room stopped what they were doing to watch. The TV cameras turned to follow him, and for the first time, he noticed the photographers on the floor at the base of the U-shaped desk. They would stay there the entire hearing to capture Ty's every facial expression and emotion as he answered questions.

The rapid double click of their cameras resonated throughout the room. The only difference between this moment and a wedding is that the crowd didn't stand as he descended the aisle.

But someone in the front row did get up as he approached. His best friend, Marcus Williams, dressed in his green service uniform, using a black steel cane to steady himself.

He gave Ty a huge smile. Not the type of grin that was *I'm glad to see you* or *Surprise I'm here.* No, there was more to it than that.

That's when Beth stood up from her chair at the edge of the aisle.

She was breathtaking in a gorgeous ankle-length pale blue and white dress covered with flowers. Her hair was down, with the front curled as it fell off her shoulders. She was a glimmer of beauty in an ordinary room.

Ty's smile rivaled hers as they embraced one another tightly.

"Oh my God! What are you doing here?"

Stepping back after giving him a quick kiss. "We've had this planned for more than a week."

"Who's we?"

"The two of us and the Colonel," Williams said excitedly before Beth could answer.

Taken aback. "Wait, when did you get into town?"

Beth and Williams shared an embarrassed look.

"Well, don't be mad. I got in late yesterday afternoon, and I was in my hotel a few blocks from here last night when you called."

"Why didn't you tell me? I would've much rather spent the evening with you."

"I know. But, you needed to focus on everything going on. And last night, that was her."

Aimes joined their conversation. The four stood in a circle at the end of the aisle. A few feet behind the chair Ty would be seated in.

Taking the room in again, Ty looked back at the cameras and then again at the desk where several senators had begun to arrive. Among them was Hayes, with Luna bending over his shoulder, showing him something.

Nodding his head in Luna's direction. "That's her."

"Wow, she's beautiful."

Williams and Aimes now had to look.

Perhaps sensing what was happening, Luna looked up to see all four of them staring at her. Laughing that they had gotten caught, Williams and Aimes quickly turned around.

Luna, however, did not look away. She stared in Ty's direction but not directly at him.

He knew who she was staring at. Ty turned his head to see Beth in a staring contest with her. Breaking it off, she wrapped her arms around him before giving him a long kiss.

Taking the opportunity to claim her Marine by figuratively peeing on his leg.

When Beth pulled back, Ty looked sheepishly at Aimes. Both trying to decide whether to tell her about the elevator ride just minutes ago. Ty suspected Aimes wouldn't want him to share that particular detail. At least not in this specific moment.

But Ty was dying inside to share it. Against his better judgment, he caved.

"So, Luna was on the elevator with the Colonel and me a few minutes ago," Ty said softly.

"Did she say anything to you this morning?"

Aimes spared Ty, "She said quite a bit and embarrassed herself in an elevator full of people."

"What did she say?"

Aimes started to chuckle.

Ty didn't join in with the laughing. "It wasn't as much what she said as she tried to do. She tried to kiss me."

Beth leaned away from Ty but didn't drop her arm from his around his waist. She needed to create a space between them so she could look up at his face to see if he was serious. "You're kidding, right?"

"No, I'm not."

Beth snapped her eyes toward Luna. Now seated behind Hayes. Thankfully, she was looking down, so she avoided the look Ty's wife gave her.

"As I said, Beth," Aimes cut in, "it was embarrassing for her. Ty handled himself very well in rejecting her advance and put her in her place."

"Bitch, better watch out. A Marine's wife isn't someone to mess with," Williams added.

Laughing at his joke, Beth said, "That's right. I'll cut a bitch for trying to kiss my man."

Wooden stepped into the circle to tell everyone to take their seats because the Chairman had just entered.

Ignoring the lawyer, Ty said, "Thank you for being here. I need you today so much more than you realize."

Beth smiled. "I'm here for you. Now go give them hell." With one more passionate kiss for the whole world to see.

Whack! Whack!

"I call this hearing to order. If everyone would find their seats, we'll get started," proclaimed the Chairman as he slammed his gravel again.

Whack! Whack!

Ty ignored him for a moment to give Beth one more quick kiss. Then turned to sit.

He was seated at the only table in the middle of the room. It was a wide, lightly stained oak with plenty of room for the three of them.

To his right was Aimes, and on his left was the JAG Officer. The senators would not directly address or question these men. They were there solely as advisors and as his legal representation.

The Chairman, Senator John Burgess of South Carolina, was in his late seventies. Fit, energetic, and sharper than most people half his age, he had been in Washington for over forty years. Serving three terms as a congressman representing an affluent part of Charleston before being elected to the U.S. Senate in 1972. He was in his sixth term. In the late 1980s, he unsuccessfully ran in a primary for president.

Burgess had been in D.C. long enough, spending time on both sides of most issues as the political pendulum swung back and forth over the decades. Hayes would've had to convince this aging senator to hold this hearing.

Ty expected the elder man to be hostile toward him.

It didn't take long for that to be validated.

After Ty stood to take his oath, Senator Burgess opened the hearing with a few comments, as was the norm for a hearing with this amount of public interest. What Ty thought would be a handful of hearing rules turned into a partisan monologue for the cameras.

His grandstanding lasted ten minutes. Flawlessly moving between needing to maintain strong foreign relationships in the Middle East to ensuring accountability when atrocities of war were committed.

Burgess never looked in Ty's direction or spoke directly to him. Ty sat tall with his hands folded on the table before him as the Chairman spoke to the audience over his head.

Listening intently, Ty took note of two particular aspects of his speech.

First, Burgess said the words *'truth'* and *'facts'* a dozen times each. Second, it was clear that the Senator was using his opening comments to distort said facts to create his version of the truth.

The blatant lies about what happened that day more than a year ago in Mosul should have pissed Ty off. It should've turned his face red in rage and sent his head spinning in anger. Turning him into the deranged Marine that Burgess was hoping the world would see today.

Instead, the elder Senator and the world would get the Marine who led Force Company into and out of Mosul safely.

The stern resolve that had settled Ty's nerves after seeing Williams blown up on the road returned. Sitting in an uncomfortable chair, being accused by a U.S. Senator of war crimes, Ty decided that any opening comments he had prepared with the help of Wooden wouldn't work for him. Not today.

He had a new purpose.

A new enemy that had to be defeated. He just needed to do it differently than he was accustomed to.

Taking a deep breath, Ty looked over to Wooden, who was staring back at him with his eyebrows raised. Wanting to know why Ty had just ignored the Chairman's second attempt to get his attention to give any prepared remarks.

While maintaining eye contact with his lawyer, Ty finally answered, "Yes, Mr. Chairman. I have a few opening comments."

Then Ty took the smooth sheet of paper with his lawyer-approved remarks resting beneath his folded hands and turned it over.

With a deep breath, Ty turned his gaze to the Chairman. Not scared to make the eye contact the politician had avoided.

Mr. Chairman and esteemed Senators, I have a short statement for you and the record this morning. First, thank you for allowing me to address this committee so I can set the record straight on what happened on April 18th of last year in Mosul, Iraq.

However, before we can get to that, Mr. Chairman, I believe you forgot to mention in your opening comments the eleven Marines who gave their lives for the American people on the day in question. There's no better place to start than for this committee to recognize the ultimate sacrifice they and their families have made for our country. And the additional sixteen Marines of 1st Reconnaissance Battalion who were wounded during that premeditated and coordinated ambush that lasted more than ten hours.

The Marines who lost their lives that day were Second Lieutenant Albert Dire, First Sergeant Manny Herrera, Gunnery Sergeant Luis Perez, Gunnery Sergeant Jackson Volker, Staff Sergeant Micheal Easterland, Staff Sergeant Javon Williams, Sergeant Landon Brooks, Sergeant Marcos Lopez, Sergeant Christopher Micheals, Lance Corporal Billy Codd, and Lance Corporal Andre Salters.

These men proudly served their country by stepping forward against the odds in a war they had not asked for.

I would also like this committee to recognize the sacrifice of Captain Marcus Williams, who sits directly behind me today. Captain Williams was Force Company's Commanding Officer on April 18th. He and Lance Corporal Jason Miller were gravely injured in the IED blast that destroyed their Humvee and killed First Sergeant Herrera and Sergeant Brooks. Captain Williams lost his right eye and two fingers on his right hand. The Captain's right leg was saved by the excellent field triage performed. These men deserve not only your recognition but your respect and for nothing short of the truth to be told today.

On that note, Mr. Chairman, I appreciate that you used the words 'truth' and 'facts' numerous times in your statement. I understand that we are in a town where those words aren't always black and white. But, instead, in shades of grey that are consumed and spoken only when it's politically expedient. Or they're swept away when they must be avoided at all costs.

Senators, I don't live in your world. On April 18th, the truth is really black and white. You'll get nothing from me today other than the truth and the facts about what happened.

But, let me warn you, Mr. Chairman, and to any of you who have taken liberties in altering that truth or are trying to dismiss the facts of that day to fit your political narrative, I will not be bullied. I will not submit to your lies, and I have no interest in being a stepping stone to a higher office.

On the table in front of me are the same sixteen after-action reports completed by Marines in the hours after the firefight on April 18th that you have had access to for over a year. Here with me are also the two field reports for the Commanding Officers of the Iraqi Security Force who relieved our position that evening.

Yet, all eighteen of these reports contrast your opening statement, Mr. Chairman. You said, and I quote, 'The Battle of Bloody Fountain was aptly named because of the scores of civilians, women, and children who were slaughtered by Marines under Captain Hudson's command.'

There were no civilian deaths. There were undoubtedly not scores. I know this because of eighteen after-action reports and because I was there. This committee should remember that while trying to spew lies.

I know there were no civilian deaths at the fountain because, between the third and fourth waves of attackers, five other Marines and I had to scour the area for weapons and ammunition because we had run out.

I know there were no civilian deaths because I was the last Marine to step into the transport after we beat back the fourth and final wave. There were no dead civilians. There were no women or children murdered at the hands of Marines that day. Any attempt by the members of this committee to say otherwise is a complete disgrace to not only the office you hold, to the Americans you represent, but also to the eleven Marines who lost their lives that day.

Marines, Mr. Chairman, that you still have not acknowledged.

So, yes. Let's speak the truth, give the facts, and be done with this charade. Thank you.

CHAPTER
THIRTY-ONE

THE WORLD HAS many great fireworks shows.

Those that come to mind are the cities of Boston or Washington, D.C., on the Fourth of July, or New Year's Eve in Singapore, London, and Sydney. Hundreds, if not thousands, of fireworks rocket into the dark skies over these cities, leaving a faint trail of smoke only visible to the closest spectators, and then burst into colorful and perfect circles.

Yet, despite their splendor, none have ever been quite as impressive as the fireworks that Ty had set off with his opening comments.

The entire opposition erupted in unison. Yelling and hollering at the Chairman and Ty for several minutes. Some screamed for Ty to be held in contempt for not recognizing the committee's legitimacy or its authority.

Others shouted insults.

Once he regained order, Senator Burgess nearly came out of his seat to scold Ty on Senate decorum. He added that if the witness continued to be hostile toward committee members, he would be held in contempt of Congress.

Ty sat back in his chair to get the best view of the fireworks show he had just set off. This included Burgess' grand finale. While enjoying the display, he focused on keeping a straight face. To his surprise, neither Aimes nor Wooden spoke, passed a note, or even looked in his direction.

The hearing was only minutes old. Yet, the tone for the rest of the day had been set.

In keeping with Senate procedures, the Chairman recognized Senator

Bonnie LaSalle of New Jersey and gave her the floor for five minutes. This set up a relatively easy period as the hearing moved ahead with a much less hostile tenor.

Over the next forty minutes, several committee members on both sides of the political aisle questioned Ty about the Battle of Bloody Fountain. As with their party affiliation, some questions were phrased and asked to highlight his heroic actions and those of the Marines of Force Company that day.

Others were more direct and used lead-in questions other senators would leverage during their time.

Ty could feel the intensity in the room building.

"The committee recognizes the gentlelady from West Virginia, Senator Wrzesinki," the Chairman said.

Of the senators who supported Hayes' position, Senator Wrzesinki was his strongest ally. As she now had the floor, Ty knew the relaxed questioning period had ended. She would be his first big test.

She was seated on his left, three over from the Chairman in the center. As she shuffled a few papers and moved her microphone lower, Ty waited patiently.

"Captain, I am concerned that while you stated in your opening comments that this committee would get 'nothing from me today other than the truth and the facts,' you have yet to be honest with us."

"Ma'am, I am sorry you feel that way. Is there a specific part of my testimony you feel is untruthful?"

Looking sternly at him, "Everything you've said today."

Ty didn't speak. He just looked at her, waiting for a question. This was a tip that Wooden had given him.

'Don't get baited to speak when no question is put forth.' He had said while explaining that many witnesses get in trouble by trying to defend themselves with no direct questions being asked.

Senator Wrzesinki hadn't asked a question. She just said that she didn't believe anything Ty had said thus far.

Breaking the silence, she asked, "Do you not have anything to say for yourself, young man?"

"I don't believe there was anything to respond to, Senator. You levied an opinion and didn't ask a question."

"I want to know why you've lied to this committee today?"

"Senator, at no time have I lied. If you have a particular instance where you believe I have, I am happy to discuss that."

"Fine. You had testified earlier that you had not killed a woman during the raid, and that's a blatant lie."

"Correction, Senator, I said I did not kill a civilian woman. Furthermore, as mentioned several times today, this wasn't a raid. This was a quick response action to support a Marine platoon from being overrun."

"So, you admit you killed a woman and lied about it earlier?"

"Madam, I've never denied killing a female insurgent. That encounter was and has always been part of my after-action report."

"Yet, Captain, you have repeatedly claimed that you and your men hadn't killed civilians. Why are you still maintaining this lie if you admit to killing a woman?"

"The difference between what you call a lie and the truth, Senator, is your interpretation of the word civilian."

"Are you calling me a liar?"

"No, ma'am. You are not lying, just misinterpreting the facts to fit your narrative."

Wrzesinki gave Ty a scorching look as her face turned bright red.

After a brief pause, "Then please tell me how I am misinterpreting how you killed a civilian woman?"

"An AK-47, ma'am."

"I'm sorry!" The Senator exclaimed.

"A person, regardless of gender, firing an AK-47 is no longer a civilian. The insurgent woman you're wildly claiming to be a civilian had just fired several blind shots through a wall at one of my men. As the Marine closest to the door of the room the fire was coming from, I broke through it and eliminated the threat."

"So, by your standards, a woman with an AK-47 is no longer a civilian and deserves to be brutally murdered?"

"No, Senator. Those aren't my standards, just the ones I swore an oath to adhere to. The difference between civilians and combatants is clearly defined in the Geneva Convention, the U.S. Military Code of Conduct, and the United States Marine Corps Rules of Engagement. And in all three of these doctrines, a person firing a weapon at you is no longer a civilian, regardless of gender."

Wrzesinki again stared Ty down while she started to tap her pen on the desk in front of her.

It was as if she was unsure where to go with her line of questioning. Ty fought back the urge to speak again to shut her down.

Before he could speak, Wrzesinki asked, "So you're okay with murdering a woman?"

"Again, Senator. You're twisting a scenario to fit your predetermined narrative. A woman—."

"Captain, that is twice you have called me a liar."

Instinctively leaning into the table. "Then perhaps you should stop doing it and not interrupt me."

Matching her glare, Ty was ardent in his position and would not back down. She said nothing, so he spoke again with more fury.

"Senator, you and members of your party have called me a murderer today, called me a war criminal and the only scenario you have been able to point to is unraveling in front of cameras broadcasting this hearing to the world. Under the accepted international rules of warfare, a woman wielding a weapon is not a civilian. She is classified as a soldier if she is in uniform under the flag of a country, like the hundreds of thousands of women who serve in the United States military. If she is not in uniform or under the banner of a country, she is classified as an enemy combatant, as this particular woman was. It is not murder to take lethal action when engaged by an enemy combatant firing an AK-47. My duty as a Marine is to complete the mission and protect the men and women under my command. Ma'am... Which part of this has you confused?"

Senator Wrzesinki lost it. Going on a tirade.

Not directly at Ty but rather pointing her fury at the Chairman for allowing a witness to speak to her in that manner and for his complete lack of respect. She accosted her fellow senator for several minutes for his lack of control. All the while, the elder Senator was hammering away on his gavel, trying to bring order back to the chamber.

Wrzesinki turned to one of her aids and began talking privately with him. Burgess turned his attention to Ty with instructions to respect the committee and its rules. Ty ignored him and continued to watch Wrzesinki.

Aimes pushed a note pad over to Ty. He was certain the Colonel had written a warning for him to back off. But that wasn't the message.

In scribbled handwriting, *Don't let up!*

"Pardon me, Mr. Chairman," Ty said. "My sincerest apologies for interrupting, but before we continue, I feel I could save a lot of time if I address the next bad idea Senator Wrzesinki is concocting over there."

Turning back in her seat to look at Ty, she said, "What are you talking about?"

"Senator Wrzesinki is about to question why I was awarded the Navy Cross. I don't believe that line of questioning should be covered in a public hearing."

The Senator's stern facial expression turned to a look of utter shock and disbelief. "Captain, what makes you think I was going to ask about that?"

"The same reason I know that your egg white, red bell pepper, and feta cheese omelet wasn't a great choice for breakfast. It's been causing you heartburn all morning. That's why your aide had to get you Tums."

Wrzesinki turned to look at her aide, who shrugged his shoulders to answer her unspoken question.

"Forgive me, Senator. But I would remind you and the committee that I'm a Recon Marine. Our government has spent a lot of time and money teaching me how to collect and use information to complete missions successfully. This includes learning to read lips."

"So, you're reading my lips?"

"Yes, ma'am. I have been reading the lips of almost everyone in the room for the entire hearing."

"Sorry, Captain. I don't believe that. You're somehow listening to what I am saying over here."

Ty slid excitedly to the edge of his seat as if it was the bottom of the ninth inning in a close-ball game. The Senator had taken his bait, and this Marine wasn't about to let up.

"I understand you're having doubts. Allow me to show you. Senator Pouter needs a break so he can run to the restroom. He, too, is having stomach issues today. Senator Tillis has been using his time this morning to update the invite list for this Saturday's fundraiser, and Senator Hayes..."

Ty paused momentarily to turn to whom he knew would be his biggest adversary at today's hearing. Hayes looked back at him with raised eyebrows as Ty paused for dramatic effect.

"Oh, Senator Hayes. I hope you have more evidence to use in attacking me today than an article from Al Jazeera News written eight months after the Battle of Bloody Fountain. I hope you will not accuse a decorated Marine officer of war crimes based on terrorist propaganda."

CHAPTER
THIRTY-TWO

IF THE HEARING started with fireworks, it had just gone nuclear.

Senator Pouter, a short round man, started to appeal to the Committee's Chairman but quickly gave up when his voice was drowned out by Wrzesinki, who was screaming at Ty and Senator Burgess. Pouter eventually threw his hands up before storming out of the hearing room.

With his tight, fast-paced walk, everyone knew where he was heading.

As the room came unhinged, Ty looked at Luna for the first time since the Chairman had gaveled the hearing to order. She was staring back at him.

When their eyes met, they exchanged smiles. Although they were different, Ty was cocky and arrogant, while the grin on her face was more appreciative. They didn't linger long. Both of their attentions were pulled to the back of the large room.

A subtle applause had picked up in the rear of the room. The rumble of protests, clapping, and cheers started to carry through the crowd to the front.

Like everyone else, Ty turned to see most of the room standing. These were not members of the Marine Corps or the armed forces in uniform. No, it was civilians and what he assumed to be Washington insiders cheering. At first, Ty wasn't sure why or who they were applauding.

Leaning up from his seat, Williams yelled over the noise, "Ty, they are cheering for you!"

Cheering for me?

It wasn't just a standing ovation. They, too, were yelling at the Chairman and several of the senators. Particularly Wrzesinki.

As Ty looked over the crowd, he saw people waving at him, giving a thumbs up, and even a few *'Oorahs'* from spectators not in uniform. Row by row, more were joining in.

Ty couldn't resist. He stood from his chair and waved his arms up and down as if he were a cheerleader trying to get the crowd to join him in a school chant during the big game.

What was already a loud and chaotic scene turned into pandemonium.

Williams leaped from his seat to give Ty a vigorous high-five. Beth sat watching her husband with a proud expression. After waving his arms for a couple of seconds longer, Ty turned to see what, if any, effect it was having on Hayes, Wrzesinki, and the rest of the senators.

To his disappointment, most had left. At some point in the chaos, the Chairman had called for a recess. Ty had not heard him, but it became apparent as Burgess exited the room.

One senator was still seated at his desk, taking everything in. Hayes had not moved. He had not even engaged in the commotion led by his colleagues. No, something else was going on; Ty suspected he was strategizing about what to do next.

Without sitting back down, Ty asked Wooden if they could speak in private before the hearing resumed. Now that Ty had gone off-script, they needed to have their own strategizing session.

A few minutes later, Wooden shut the door behind him and said, "Well, that was interesting. I assume you realize how much trouble you've caused yourself and the Navy."

"How screwed do you think I am?"

"Bad enough that I suspect the Secretary would advise me to end the hearing and offer you up to Wrzesinki and Hayes."

"I don't see it that way."

"Of course you don't. You're narcissistic and naive as to how much power they have and how little you do."

"No, what happened at the end was power. And that's why Hayes sat there to watch. Those weren't crazy Marines or military guys cheering me on. No, those were his people who had turned on him for the cameras to see."

Before Wooden could speak, Aimes entered the room with a big smile. "Ty, you've kicked the hornet's nest out there."

"The Captain believes that's a good thing, and I was just telling him that he has put himself and the Navy at risk."

"Well, we are about to find out. Luna has asked that Ty speak privately with Hayes before the hearing resumes."

The lawyer and Ty looked at each other with surprise. This was an interesting development.

This meant that one of us was right; Hayes was about to declare total war on me, or he would look for a way out of the mess I had created for him.

Because it was a private meeting, Ty suspected he was looking for a way out. And Aimes agreed.

Wooden wasn't convinced and grew upset when Aimes reminded him that it was a private meeting and that he wouldn't be going with Ty. He even threatened to call the Secretary directly to intervene, but he quickly withdrew his words when Aimes informed him that Luna had not approached him with the request for a private meeting.

No, she had gone to General Marin. The General agreed to the meeting and told Aimes to get Ty there.

Even the JAG Officer couldn't object to the General's orders. He crossed his arms and took on a pouting expression.

Aimes ignored him by sharing with Ty what the General had told him about Luna's request. He rushed through a few minor details, then stopped mid-sentence.

Abruptly, Aimes turned back to the lawyer, who still had his arms crossed, pouting. "Wooden, you're a lawyer, so you should have a dictaphone?"

"NO!"

When Wooden screamed his response, Ty knew it wasn't a simple no, 'I don't have one.' It was a warning that he wouldn't be a party to allowing the two of them to record a secret conversation with a senator.

"So, you do?" Aimes responded, glancing down at Wooden's briefcase on the table.

"Colonel, I can not—"

"Why don't you check on how much time we have before the hearing resumes?" Aimes asked.

The lawyer's jaw dropped open. He was in total disbelief as to what Aimes had asked him.

Reaching to pick up his briefcase to take it, Ty placed his hand on it before saying flatly, "You forgot this in the room."

The three men exchanged looks before Wooden closed his eyes in disbelief and turned to leave.

This was their second time huddled in this smaller conference room off the main hallway. Neither time had Ty noticed there was a side door. This was the door that Aimes took him through right after rummaging through the briefcase. Then, through two more to avoid the cameras and reporters in the hallway.

At the fourth door, Aimes stepped to the side, "Captain, I don't know what he's going to say to you there, but I think you need to protect yourself."

"Understood. I won't say anything that compromises me or the Navy, sir."

Reaching into his pocket, the Colonel pulled out the dictaphone he had retrieved from Wooden's briefcase. "You know this is a crime in Washington, so decide for yourself."

Taking the small device, Ty looked at its buttons. Pushing one with the little red dot to see a faint light start blinking. He then pushed the square button to see the red light stop, and the screen showed that three seconds had been recorded.

This wasn't something Ty had ever considered doing.

Yet, Aimes was right. Whatever Hayes wanted to say was being done behind closed doors for a reason. Ty knew recording the Senator without his permission would be illegal. Nor could it be used in court, but depending on what was said, it could be political leverage.

Leverage. That's what I need.

Aimes opened the door. "Good luck. I'll be waiting here when you're done."

It had not occurred to Ty that the Colonel wasn't joining him. When he pissed off Wooden by telling him he wasn't invited and then asked for his dictaphone, Ty had assumed it was because his commanding officer, not the lawyer, was going into the meeting too.

The look on Ty's face was one of shock, but Aimes just patted him supportively on his shoulder and didn't say another word.

If Ty's face registered shock when Aimes didn't join him, it must have been funny to see when he walked into a staff break room and realized that was where the secret meeting was taking place.

In the middle of the bland room were three circular off-white tables with four plastic blue chairs evenly spaced around them. In the center was a table caddy with various condiments, paper towels, and plastic ware.

Along the wall Ty faced were two refrigerators, a counter with a large steel sink, and two coffee machines.

With no one in the room, he walked to one of the coffee machines. Choosing the fullest glass pot, Ty took a small styrofoam cup and poured himself some. The rich smell of fresh coffee confirmed that he had chosen right.

As he gently blew on the hot black liquid and took his first sip, Hayes walked into the room purposefully, with Luna closely behind. *So, I'm on my own, but he has Luna.*

That didn't seem fair, but it made sense as she and Ty had several interactions.

"Holy shit, Ty!" Hayes uttered as he, too, poured himself a cup of coffee. "I had no idea you had this in you."

The two men stood beside the coffee machine while Luna stayed several feet away in the center of the room. Ty let Hayes's words hang in the air without a response.

Instead, he leaned casually against the countertop, slipped his left hand into his pants pocket, and hit the record button on the dictaphone.

God! I hope this thing works through pants.

Taking his first sip, Hayes filled the empty air. "You've pissed off Senator Wrzesinki. She's already called both the Chairman of the Joint Chiefs and the Secretary of Defense demanding you get discharged from the Marines."

This much Ty had expected. This was the power that Wooden had warned him about. He knew that neither the Joint Chiefs nor the Secretary of Defense had the blanket authority to kick him out without a court martial hearing.

Still, each could easily make life so difficult that Ty would eventually quit. The bottom line was that both men could make Wrzesinki happy by agreeing that he would be dishonorably discharged when the time was right. This was the scapegoat piece he was worried about.

He wanted to know Hayes' thoughts on the matter but, again, chose not to respond.

Acknowledging Ty's thoughts, Hayes said, "I bet you're trying to figure out if I've also called for your court martial or if I will be."

"I suspect that will depend on how this discussion goes."

After another sip, "That's right."

"So, what do you want?"

With a stern expression, Hayes replied, "I want you to admit the truth.

That you and your Marines were so distraught and enraged at the sight of your dead friends that you lost your cool and took it out on the civilians in Mosul that day."

"You know that's not the truth."

"Ty, it doesn't matter what the truth is. All that matters is that my megaphone is bigger than yours. Allowing me to create the truth I want the American people to know."

Hayes was right. As a popular sitting Senator, he had everything he needed to craft his narrative of the truth and get it out there. As a skilled politician, Hayes knew that the more he said something, the more people would believe him.

This was a fight Ty couldn't win. That pissed him off. "I agree with what you just said."

Hayes smiled. "Good, so you'll admit to killing civilians and make this easier on us all?"

"Oh, no. You misunderstood me," Ty corrected, "I believe you don't care what the truth is as long as you get your way."

Luna stepped up to two men and said, "Ty, don't make this hard on yourself and Beth. Admit to it today, and we can ensure that you get dishonorably discharged and don't go to prison for the next twenty years."

"That's right. Think of your wife and your children. Do what's best for them," Hayes added.

Ty's face was burning with anger. His free hand clenched in a tight fist. His breathing was shallow as he thought about his next move.

"I'll consider your offer, Senator."

Ty walked to the door from which he had entered the room and dropped his cup of coffee in the trash bin beside it.

"Ty," Luna called as he opened the door, "Don't be a fool."

CHAPTER
THIRTY-THREE

WHACK! *Whack!*

A red-faced Senator Burgess called the hearing back to order. Moving right into another ten-minute monologue accusing Ty of using his testimony for self-righteous grandstanding. Once more, he threatened the Marine with Contempt of Congress.

When he pointed his long, crooked finger at Ty and asked if he understood, Ty replied firmly, "Yes, sir."

After the stern warning, the hearing continued with a few comments and questions from senators who had yet to have time.

The mood in the room hadn't changed after the break.

If anything, there was a new energy of anticipation for what everyone knew was coming. The fuse had been lit, and it was burning toward a powder keg. It would be up to Ty to let it go off or cut the fuse before it reached its final destination.

Thirty minutes after the Chairman's monologue, he recognized the "Esteemed gentleman from Iowa, Senator Hayes." Who wasted no time.

"Captain," Hayes said, leaning up to his microphone, "it's been quite a hearing thus far. Wouldn't you agree?"

"I would agree, sir."

With a slight grin, he said, "The entire lip-reading trick was pretty cool. The crowd certainly liked it."

Ty said nothing. Just sat with a blank expression. Hands folded on the table.

Holding several papers in the air. "Yet, it changes nothing for you. I still have in my hands a news article that claims that the final body count from your raid was more than one hundred civilians. Most of which were innocent women and children. What do you have to say to that?"

"To confirm, Senator, the article you're holding up is from Al Jazeera, and it was published almost eight months after the day in question. Correct?"

"I'll ask the questions here, Captain!"

"That's fine, sir. I just wanted to repeat you so that the American people know that you're citing a known source used for terrorist propaganda, and it was written eight months after the battle."

"That doesn't make it any less truthful."

With a slight chuckle and shrug of his shoulders. "Okay."

Hayes' eyes burned at Ty's response. It was becoming clear to him that the Marine wasn't taking the advice given to him in the break room.

"This article proves you committed war crimes and led a raid that killed a hundred civilians, and all you have to say for yourself is *'okay.'*"

"Senator, the Al Jazeera article only proves how small-minded you are to believe it. And how little you think of the American people in assuming they, too, will believe it when over eighteen after action reports completely contradict it."

The Chairman hit his gavel twice before Hayes could respond, "Captain, you were warned about your behavior, and you can now consider yourself in Contempt of Congress. Do you understand?"

Ty gritted his teeth as he looked at the table. Collecting his thoughts.

"Do you understand me, son?"

That pushed him over the edge.

Whipping his head toward the Chairman. "Yes, sir. I understand. I understand that you and several members of your political party are using this hearing to lie to the American people, and you, Mr. Chairman, are doing nothing short of abusing your power by holding me in contempt when I am the only one telling the truth. That's what I understand."

Whack! Whack!

"Son, don't you dare tell me—"

"Senator, I wasn't finished!"

"Don't you dare interrupt me when I am talking, or I'll remove you from this hearing."

Ty pointed his finger at the Senator. "And don't you dare call me *'son.'* I am a highly decorated captain in the United States Marine Corps. In my opening statement, I told you and the committee members that I would not be bullied or submit to your lies. Furthermore—"

Whack! Whack! Whack! Whack!

"I'll have order!"

"Furthermore—"

Whack! Whack!

"Senator, I'm falsely accused of war crimes by murdering women and children. I will be heard today. You can either let me speak or keep hitting your gavel. Either way, all this proves is that I am right, and you and Senator Hayes are liars."

The room again erupted into chaos. Several senators were yelling at the Chairman as the crowd started to chant, "Let him speak! Let him speak!"

Half of the committee was calling for Ty to be removed.

The other half joined in with the crowd, calling for him to have the opportunity to speak.

While the Chairman struggled to regain control, Aimes leaned over from his chair to whisper, "Do it now."

Ty pulled the dictaphone from his pocket and put it close to his microphone.

And hit play.

"So, what do you want?"

"I want you to admit the truth. That you and your Marines were so distraught and enraged at the sight of your dead friends. And that you lost your cool and took it out on the civilians in Mosul that day."

"You know that's not the truth."

"Ty, it really doesn't matter what the truth is. All that matters is that my megaphone is bigger than yours, and that allows me to create the truth I want the American people to know."

The two voices were amplified through the speakers in the room.

Everyone went silent as they listened to the short exchange.

When Ty was satisfied that he had gotten everyone's attention. "Mr. Chairman, honorable Senators of the committee, that is a recording of a conversation that Senator Hayes and I had forty minutes ago in a break room a few doors down from here. As we speak, the full length of this audio is being released to each news organization present today. In it, the world will hear that a sitting U.S. Senator asked me to go along with his lies in exchange for him not continuing to use his political megaphone to destroy my career and my life."

Leaping from his chair. Hayes screamed, "How dare you record me! That's illegal and a violation of my rights. I'll have thrown in jail for this."

A hand grabbed Ty's right arm before he could speak.

Wooden cleared his throat as he leaned up to his microphone. "That's fine, Senator. What Captain Hudson did or didn't do might or might not have been illegal, and he's willing to accept any consequences for his actions today. But you and this committee should know that the Secretary of Defense is aware of this and will present the full recording to the Attorney General. At which time, I expect the Secretary will ask her to authorize a full investigation into your conduct and the willingness of several committee members to make false accusations of war crimes against active U.S. military personnel."

Hayes's demeanor changed as he looked over to the Chairman. Then, back at Wooden and Ty before sitting down.

No one knew what to do.

What to say or how to proceed. The Chairman leaned back to consult with an aide while Hayes sat stunned.

With no one speaking, Ty decided he hadn't reached celebrity status yet.

Leaning to his microphone, "Senator Hayes, your mistake wasn't lying to the American people. Your mistake was thinking you were safe while hiding beneath a veil of patriotism."

Hayes' mouth opened to say something, but Ty kept speaking. "You get up every morning and put on your American flag lapel pin before coming to work in this majestic building at the behest of voters. Here, you pound your desk and point your finger at others as you preach about values, the problems with Washington, and how you're the man who can save America. Then you spend your evenings and weekends in front of TV cameras where you blatantly lie to the American people that Marines are war criminals who ruthlessly murdered women and children."

Ty took a deep breath to allow his words to resonate around the room.

"All I did today was lift your veil so the entire country could see who you really are. And an American patriot isn't what we see."

Ty and Hayes stared each other down. While the room full of people waited for whatever they thought would come next.

The Chairman finally decided. "In light of the crimes committed by Captain Hudson today, we will adjourn this hearing to allow law enforcement to do the work they need to do. This hearing is concluded."

Whack! Whack!

Before the Chairman's gavel hit the second time, Hayes, Wrzesinki, and several other senators exited the room.

The only people moving faster than them were the news reporters. They ran out of the room to cut into their respective news feeds to tell their audiences all they had just witnessed.

Jumping up with excitement, Beth wrapped her arms around Ty from behind. Getting to his feet, he gave her a proper hug that lifted her off the ground.

While the couple embraced, Aimes was tugging on Ty's arm.

Turning to him, Ty was instead greeted by General Marin with a strong congratulatory handshake.

"Captain, that was the most impressive and maybe the most courageous thing I've ever seen a Marine do in my thirty years. You did the Corps and your family proud today," Marin said.

"Thank you, sir."

"And as I told you earlier, you have the full support of the Commandant and I. No way Hayes will be pressing charges or getting away with this."

"Excuse me, General," Wooden interrupted. "I believe it would be best to get the Captain in front of the press as soon as possible, sir."

After the General excused him, Ty looked around the room. While it might have seemed that he wanted to take in the scene one more time, he had ulterior motives.

She was there. Standing with both hands on the back of the executive leather chair that Hayes had abandoned. Ty didn't know why she was still there but got what he wanted.

They caught each other's gaze and held it. For him, Ty was taking her in one last time, knowing that he would likely never see her again. He didn't care what she thought of his actions. Of course, she would disapprove. But he was sure that she would have appreciated the boldness of the move.

As in confirmation, Luna gave him a small, pursed-lipped smile and nodded her head.

Beth must have taken notice. She leaned in closer, taking her husband's right hand in hers as she pulled him back in her direction. Lifting on her toes, she gave Ty a quick kiss. When their lips separated, Ty noticed she wasn't looking at him.

Rather in Luna's direction.

Without looking back, Ty grabbed Beth by the hand to make their way back down the center aisle to the wide double doors at the rear of the chamber.

As they escaped down the aisle, all that was missing was the bubbles their wedding guests blew at them as they left the church. Even without the bubbles, the edges of the aisle were pressed with onlookers. Some reached to shake Ty's hand or give him a high-five. Others held cameras to capture the moment.

As Ty approached the open doors, Wooden pulled Ty in close. "Keep things brief and to the point. Don't speak for more than a couple minutes and only take a few questions."

Ty nodded. Then stepped out into the hall.

"Captain!"

"Captain Hudson, over here!"

A swarm of ten to twelve reports crashed down on him.

Each held a microphone and a cameraman just a step behind. As they had done hundreds of times, they formed a semicircle around Wooden, Beth, and Ty.

Wooden spoke, "Captain Hudson will make a brief statement and then take a couple of questions. Please be respectful of that."

Taking a deep breath through his nose. "What a day! This was not how I wanted things to go, but ultimately, I achieved what I came here for. The truth found its way through the lies. Beyond having my name and those of the Marines under my command cleared, I hope the American people recognize that my actions were not out of spite or vengeance. On multiple occasions, I gave Senator Hayes, Wrzesinki, and Chairman Burgess a fair warning that I would not submit to their lies. They chose to continue down that path. It is an unfortunate day for the U.S. Senate and the Americans they represent. But, for me, it feels pretty damn good."

"Captain Hudson."

"Captain!"

"Captain, do you expect to be charged?" A female reporter asked.

"I'll leave it to the authorities to decide. But I'll say this. Regardless of any legal action, I am proud of how I defended those under my command, myself, and the Corps."

Multiple reporters yelled questions. Overtaking each other, but Ty heard something that caught his attention.

Looking at the guy who said it. "Could you repeat your question?"

"Yes! Do you think the Senate Ethics Committee should start proceedings to look into Senator Hayes and Wrzesinki's actions? And would you support the Attorney General opening an investigation?"

"I don't have an opinion on either. My goal is to put this behind me and rejoin my team."

"Captain Hudson, why do you think Senator Hayes did this?" A deep voice called out.

The question shut everyone up as they turned to see who it was coming from. It was a younger black guy standing in the back of the crowd.

He was different than the other reporters in the circle. He wore a simple black and gold polo shirt tucked into khaki pants. No microphone, just a dictaphone, he held up. It was similar to, if not the exact one Ty had used to record Hayes in the break room.

Like Ty, the young man was out of place in D.C.

"That's an interesting question."

"So, do you have an opinion on why he did it?"

"What news agency are you with?"

Hesitantly. "The Daily Iowan, sir. It's the student newspaper for the University of Iowa."

That explained why he was dressed in black and gold and why the professional reporters stared him down when he spoke. He was a student reporter for a small university newspaper.

Ty was impressed with the young man's courage. "That's the best question I've been asked."

Staying on topic. "And your response to it?"

"I believe that question should be addressed to the Senator."

"Come on, sir. I know you have an opinion here, and the students at the University of Iowa should hear from you."

Ty smiled in appreciation for his tenacity.

This was someone he could respect.

"I think the Senator has his eyes on the White House and was using the growing frustration of the war on terror to his advantage by trying to create his lane to the Presidency. That's what I believe."

Blurting out over the other reporters, the student asked, "And how do you like his chances now?"

"I suspect the American voters won't be as kind as I was today now that he has no veil to hide behind."

CHAPTER
THIRTY-FOUR

THREE DAYS HAD PASSED—THE decisions and actions Ty had made had started to catch up with him.

Standing before a group of people getting ready to judge him, he couldn't help but remember what his senior drill instructor had said to another guy during Marine recruit training several years ago at Parris Island, South Carolina.

"You've done fucked up!" The drill instructor yelled in a deep Southern accent. "This was the path you chose. You've gotta be a man now and take the ass whooping."

The recipient was a Marine Recruit who had been a bully during the first three weeks of training.

One night, after a towel-flicking incident, four guys took action. Shortly after lights out, they jumped him. Grabbing the bully by his legs, they dragged him off his bottom bunk and started to pummel him with their pillowcases stuffed with a boot. It only took two or three hits before blood flowed from his nose, and he yelled for help.

That's when the lights came on in the barracks. The drill instructor stood in front, wearing his boxers, a white t-shirt, and a big smile.

After a pathetic plea for help from the bloodied guy on the floor, the drill instructor offered the lesson that Ty was remembering years later. *'You've done fucked up! This was the path you chose. You've gotta be a man now and take the ass whooping.'*

Why did I agree to this? Ty thought as he stood at the front of the room with everyone's eyes on him.

His hands trembled from nerves. When he began to speak, his usual confident, steady voice cracked.

Several onlookers laughed. His face turned a deeper shade of red. Standing by his side, Tiller stepped over to help settle him down.

"Ty, you've got this. Just relax."

Some punishments fit the crime. Others are unjust.

This was the latter. Standing up to Hayes, Wrzesinki, and other Washington elites had put a target on Ty's back, and people were out for him.

When told what he had to do, he protested by arguing that he would never agree to it. *'Hell no! They would have to drag me up there!'* There was never any dragging. But that didn't mean everyone wasn't pressuring him.

Even Beth said, "Babe, it's not that big of a deal. Everyone expects this from you."

Ty didn't care what everyone expected.

He was supposed to have a choice, which was being stripped away by peer pressure.

I can do this. It's not that long.

Reaching up to steady himself with the thin steel pole holding the microphone, Ty began again.

Heart racing through fumbling words, Tiller wrapped his arm around him and leaned close to give his commanding officer courage. Knight, on the other side, wasn't as comforting.

He was bent over in agony, laughing so hard that he couldn't breathe.

Ty had tried to warn them. "Florida's not in the south. Sure, it looks that way on the map. But, the further south you go, the more north it is."

The Kansas-born Tiller and the South Carolinian Knight didn't fully understand what Ty meant until they realized he needed the words on the screen to help him.

"Are you serious?" Knight asked. "How do you not know the words to this song?"

"Why the hell would you think I would've known them? Have you ever heard me listen to country music in the two years we've served together?"

For the two of them, this was an anthem they had grown up listening to and singing along with. The words and tune came easily to them.

For Ty, the only songs he knew by heart were the Marine Corps Hymn and the National Anthem. So, it was obvious that he was out of his depth standing next to Tiller and Knight. He had hoped their experience would mask his shortcomings when he agreed to go on stage.

The crowd cheered excitedly as the melody played. Then, it repeated several times, getting louder with each pass. Ty attempted the first few words.

Tone-deaf and more than a beat off as the first few words moved across the screen. That was when Knight lost it, and Tiller moved in for moral support.

A minute into the song, Tiller waved for the crowd to join. Everyone in the bar joined the three Marines singing the famous country chart-topper.

To Ty's relief, his voice was drowned out. He stepped back from the microphone to wrap his arm around Knight, who had miraculously stopped laughing just in time for the chorus.

The song's gist was a guy who didn't want to cause a big scene because he wasn't big on social graces. This caused him to want to slip down to an oasis among his friends. It was fitting, considering where the team was tonight.

The Sunset Oasis Bar and Grill was less than a mile from Camp Pendleton's southernmost gate. Located on the beach, it has great sunset views over the Pacific Ocean. It had been a staple for Marines wanting to get off base to blow off steam by grabbing a few beers and some decent bar food for over fifty years.

Since tonight was Sunday, it was karaoke night. Luckily, the bar was less crowded than usual.

Ty was thankful for that.

He had officially achieved celebrity status.

So much so that just hours after the Senate hearing, Ty and Beth were invited to a ceremony by the Secretary of Defense down in Mississippi the next day

"I'd be happy to, sir. But, if I might ask, what's in Mississippi?" Ty asked the aide who had called him with the invite.

"The Secretary would like you both to be his honorary guests for commissioning the Navy's newest ship. It's quite a big deal."

Ty understood that if the Secretary of Defense wants you there, you go. But the name of the new ship is what caught his attention.

The USS Makin Island was a Wasp Class amphibious assault ship. While not as big as an aircraft carrier, these ships were similar in size and shape to those of World War II.

It was named after an island in the Pacific Ocean where the Marine

Raiders conducted their first operation. In August 1942, more than two hundred Raiders came ashore from submarines to assault Japanese positions before the battle of Guadalcanal.

Ty appreciated being among the first qualified Raiders of the twenty-first century to pay homage to those of the last World War. He was honored to attend the commissioning of a ship named after their first raid.

After the pomp and circumstance of commissioning the USS Makin Island, Ty and Beth made it back to Southern California. She was ready to relax and forget about Washington, and he was ready to rejoin his team. They were ecstatic when her parents greeted them on the tarmac when they landed with Audrey and Jake.

Audrey ran up to her father, arms wide open, to tell him about seeing her daddy on the television. Jake was waking from a nap and reached for his mommy when he realized who she was.

Just minutes after being back on base, they heard the good news.

Tiller had come to welcome them back and was unusually giddy with excitement.

After giving Beth a quick hug, Tiller said, "So, you guys are back just in time."

"For what?" Beth asked.

"For an engagement party!"

Ty and Beth looked at each other in surprise. Only a couple of the team members were single, and from Tiller's story, they assumed it was him.

"Wait," Ty started, "You got engaged in the five days I was gone?"

Laughing, "No, not me. Knight."

"Are you kidding? Knight's settling down?" Beth blurted out in disbelief.

That's where they were tonight. In typical Marine fashion, Knight's engagement party was at the Sunset Oasis Bar and Grill. All of the friends and Marines who had gathered for the celebration were excited it was karaoke night. Except for Ty.

Once off the stage, Ty vowed never to go through that again. Singing, even if it was karaoke, wasn't his thing. He preferred to watch everyone else.

About an hour later, someone grabbed Ty's shoulder as he was eating a hamburger.

With a mouthful, Ty mumbled, "Hey, Newbold! Holy shit, how the hell are you?"

Ty had not seen the CIA case worker in more than a year. Once they returned from eliminating Black Jack and Babic in Iran, Newbold was immediately transported to Baghdad. The two men never got a chance to speak again.

Pulling up a seat to join the group, he caught up with the Marines of Romeo Team.

After a little bit, he leaned over to Ty and said, "You got a few minutes? I want to chat with you outside."

Ty had expected this. Newbold wasn't there for Knight's engagement party.

Once outside, they reached the edge of the parking lot, far away from the restaurant doors. After Newbold looked around to ensure no one was close, he asked, "What do you know about Basra?"

"It's a large city and port on the Arabian Peninsula in southern Iraq. A British armored unit took it in 2003 after some heavy fighting. But it has never been a hotbed of insurgent activity. As far as I know, it's been a pretty quiet sector. Am I missing something?"

"No. That's all correct."

"So, why are you asking me about Basra?"

Looking around again, Newbold answered, "British intelligence has been picking up chatter in the area, and they are getting ready to pull out. Handing the city over to Iraqi Security Forces and the intel off to us."

"Is the chatter anything of note?"

"No. There isn't anything actionable. But, the British have connected much of it to Karim Muhammad Abdullah Al-Abbasi and Abubakar Esameldin Farhit."

Ty rubbed his chin. "I don't recognize either name."

"No, I suspect you wouldn't. Al-Abbasi was a low-level enforcer for Hani Abd Larif Tilfah and has risen by acquiring his old boss' network."

Ty recognized Hani's name. He had been the Director of the Iraq Special Security Organization at the start of the war and a high-value target until his capture in 2004. The SSO, as it was called, was Iraq's version of the Nazi Gestapo or the Soviet KGB.

They were responsible for spying on Iraqi citizens, kidnapping and torturing those who were outspoken against Saddam's regime—even carrying out blatant political assassinations. For three decades, the cruel members of the SSO worked tirelessly to keep Saddam Hussein in power. Karim would have to be a nasty dude if he had risen to fill Hani's void.

"Ok, he is a big deal. But, who is Abubakar?"

"He is one of Karim's known carriers. And he is most important right now because he has been spotted multiple times in Basra over the last month."

Ty took a sip of the beer he had carried outside. "Has he been seen there before?"

"Not that we know of. But the British believe he's a precursor to a visit from Karim."

"Okay, so is it a wait-and-see scenario? Or is the team rotating back into country?"

"Well, what's your first impression?"

If the U.S. military acted on every bit of intel it received, it would send special operation teams into Iraq every other day.

The British intel was solid but lacked the specifics needed to warrant a deployment for a special operations team. Ty knew Newbold had already made that assessment. It would have been a different conversation if he had thought it was actionable.

Ty arrived at the same conclusion. "Right now, it's a wait-and-see."

THIRTY-FIVE

THE NEXT FEW days were the happiest Ty had been in weeks. No more JAG officers. No more wasting time preparing for a bullshit Senate hearing or having to defend himself against bogus accusations.

He was in his happy place, with his time being split between his favorite people in the world. During the days, he was back with his team training. In the evening, he was spending every moment he could with Beth and the kids.

It was a perfect balance.

Yet, he was struggling this morning.

After almost a week of no news on Hayes or any fallout from the hearing, Ty turned on the TV to see an interview the Senator had given as he was going into the Capitol.

"Despite my legal team and law enforcement encouraging me to, I've decided not to press any charges against Mr. Hudson for his illegal actions last Thursday. Instead, I have asked the Department of Defense to investigate why I and other members of Congress had been given inaccurate intel about the Marine raid in Mosul last year."

It was a bullshit statement, not an apology.

Sitting at the kitchen counter watching the small TV, Ty mused at Hayes' audacity in continuing to insult the intelligence of the American people.

Surely, everyone sees through this guy's bullshit. Ty thought as Beth walked into the room with Jake on her hip.

"Did I just hear what I thought I heard?"

Ty took Jake so she could pour herself coffee. "Yep. That was his first statement since the hearing."

"Does it piss you off that he didn't admit he was wrong?"

"No, I knew there was no way he would apologize. What I find amusing is he's saying that he received inaccurate intel."

Taking a sip, Beth asked, "Why's that funny to you?"

"Because it's complete crap. He was on TV claiming there were civilian deaths before our after-action reports were even finalized. This has always been a political game for him."

There was no reason to dwell on it. The Hudson family had plans to go to the beach, and Ty wouldn't let this ruin his day off.

It was a beautiful Southern California day—blue skies, warm, with a gentle breeze coming off the water.

It had taken a little longer than he had planned, but after digging the trench a few feet further, the incoming wave finally filled the moat.

"Daddy! It worked," Audrey exclaimed.

They had sat together for forty minutes, building her dream castle. The fine, powdery white beach sand was great for sports and relaxation. And easy to brush off when it was time to leave.

But, as Ty was learning, it took the proper water-to-sand ratio to make a castle. Too much water made it a soupy mess, and the towers wouldn't stand up. After several failed attempts, they finally got the mixture right, and once Audrey was happy with the three tall towers, she demanded a wall to protect her toys. As any good dad would, he began building it for his daughter.

Sitting a few feet away, holding Jake under an umbrella, Beth said, "Just saying, it might be easier for you to dig her a moat."

Considering his wife's point, Ty decided he would do both. He would dig out a moat and use the excess sand for a wall. *It's my little girl. She's going to have both.*

Once the water from the gentle waves started to pour in, Ty kissed Audrey on her forehead and joined Beth and Jake in the shade.

Passing him a cold beer from the cooler beside her, Beth said, "You're a great dad,"

"The moat was a great idea."

"And I noticed she got her wall, too."

"Yep! She wanted a wall."

They laughed. Ty knew what Beth was hinting at. She knew she didn't need to mention how their little girl had her daddy wrapped around her little finger, as most do.

He took a long gulp of the beer. "This is heaven."

"Yeah, it's the perfect beach day, and the water looks amazing."

Taking Jake from Beth, Ty sat silent, holding his son for a few minutes while he watched Audrey play in her sand castle. His mind drifted between his family, the intel Newbold had brought to him, and *her*.

It had been a week since Ty had last seen Luna just before he exited the hearing chamber. Yet, that hadn't stopped him from thinking of her. He didn't know why or what it was about her. But, he allowed his mind to wander.

He imagined what it would be like if she sat beside him at the beach.

What would they talk about? How would she look in a bikini? What would she look like in no bikini?

Jake moved in his arms and spit out his pacifier.

Grabbing it before it fell to the sand, Ty felt a wave of guilt. He was holding his son, watching his daughter play in the sand, and his beautiful wife sat beside him while thinking of another woman.

Oh my God, Ty. Pull your shit together!

Ty looked over to Beth as she rummaged around in the beach bag. "Can I ask you a question?"

"Yeah."

"Why did you allow me to join the Raider teams?"

She found the apple she had been searching for, then looked back at Ty, confused. She wasn't sure why he had asked this question, especially after a year.

When she didn't respond, Ty continued, "When I called you from Iraq and spoke to you about doing it, you barely hesitated before telling me to go for it. I've always wondered why."

"I think it was because I knew I had no choice. You were going to do it regardless of what I wanted."

Her words stung. They were not what he had hoped for. Her frank honesty reminded him of the morning before his last deployment.

'It doesn't matter what I want,' she had said, *'You're going to do whatever you want.'*

Sitting on the porch in the rain, Ty tried to protest by claiming they were in this together when she reminded him that he was about to leave her and their kids for a third time to go off to war.

That was when she asked him, ' *What happens from here?*' before the time forced him to head to Camp Pendleton.

They were sitting on a beach in the bright midday sun, about to have the same conversation they had not finished more than a year ago. Ty wrestled with the thought of going down that path. Fearing it would ruin a perfect day.

Throughout their five-year marriage, Beth had always supported him and his desire to serve in the Marines after September 11th. She, too, was a patriot consumed with anger in the wake of the terrorist attacks.

As an officer's spouse, she stepped forward to contribute to the war effort without complaining or asking for recognition of her sacrifices.

Ty knew there were many like her.

After taking a bite of the apple, Beth explained, "It was nothing you had to fear asking me. I've started to slowly come around to the fact you're in this war until it ends. So, when you asked about being a Raider, I knew you had already given it a lot of thought, and it was what you wanted to do."

Ty took in her words.

He hadn't thought about it as much as she might believe.

Sure, Aimes had brought it up when he promoted Ty after the raid into Iran. Maybe the Colonel had mentioned it again after that, but Ty had never considered it until after Marcus' Humvee was destroyed on the road outside Mosul. That's when he felt the pull to do more in the war.

Would she understand? Or would she think I was selfish? That was all Ty could think of as he carefully considered his next words.

Beth added, "I won't lie to you, Ty. I struggle with everything a lot. Five years ago, I had no idea we'd be where we are right now. After your first deployment, I thought you would finish your commission, and we would continue our lives together."

"And then I joined Recon."

Beth nodded. "Yeah, and you went back to Iraq. Twice."

"I never thought of it that way."

"I know."

Those two simple words brought the world down on Ty.

In her way, Beth had just told him he had been selfish. He had put the

Corps above their marriage and their kids. He knew that she wasn't wrong. Worse, he was still doing it as a Raider.

Ty fought back tears. "Five years ago, I thought this war would already be over. Like you, I never could've imagined what it's become. Or what it's done to you."

"I know."

There were those two words again.

Ty recoiled from them. He fought the urge to get upset.

Shooting through his mind was why he had chosen to go to war, join Recon, and become a Marine Raider. Each started with the little girl still playing in the sand in front of them and the boy Ty held in his arms.

He thought Beth understood that he was fighting for them so that they could grow up in a world free of the threat he and Beth had experienced.

They had talked about it many times. He couldn't help but think, *What had changed?*

Looking out at the clear blue water of the Pacific Ocean, Ty caved. "What's changed for you?"

"You have," she replied after a brief pause. "I don't think you love going off to war or that you get off by killing terrorists. You believe you're the only person who can do it."

The woman knows me.

Ty looked at Beth, who had been looking at him the entire time, and gasped for air. He had expected to see her crying like she had that morning on the porch a year ago or, at the very least, have tears in her eyes.

So, when he saw neither, he feared that she had run out of tears for him.

For them.

THIRTY-SIX

ZERO SIX-HUNDRED HOURS came early for Romeo Team, and no one was overly impressed when Ty announced they were doing a rucking march before chow. Hiking while loaded with forty to fifty pounds of gear in your rucksack while carrying your rifle wasn't a favorite for most Marines.

But after his conversation with Beth yesterday, Ty was anxious to forget her comments. He figured the best way to accomplish that was to exercise them out.

He announced the hike just after arriving in a foul mood at the team's headquarters. He was ready to break a sweat, get dirty, and forget how things ended at the beach.

Not everyone agreed.

It was an exhausting exercise that was difficult enough when you weren't hungover. So, when Henry and Knight stayed up late playing poker, Ty wasn't surprised they objected.

After several ignored warnings to stop the complaining, Ty took out his frustration.

The trailhead was more than three miles away. Instead of riding in the back of a truck, they would meet the driver there in twenty minutes. That was a brisk six-minute mile pace. Only to then load down with gear for a seven-mile timed trek through the infamous sand dunes of Camp Pendleton.

This wasn't the first time that Ty had to make a point to the team. But, it was uncommon.

The four Marines were a close-knit group that had served together for nearly two years. They had seen some serious combat in Mosul, and their insertion into Iran was a massive crucible.

As the team started to run, Ty couldn't help but think that *this was just another example of how bored the guys were with no mission and no deployment date to look forward to.* Something had to give soon.

"A hair under seventeen minutes, sir," Tiller announced as they reached the parked truck.

"Well done. Grab some water and load up. We march in five."

Knight quickly stepped away to rush toward the front of the truck, throwing up on the ground. As the team listened to Knight empty his stomach in heaving moans, Ty noticed Henry looked a little green, too. Surprisingly, he held it together.

While looking at Henry, Ty noticed a military-issued white car pull quickly into the parking lot and speed toward them.

Coming to a sliding stop on the gravel, Newbold stepped out of the car. "Damn, Knight! You alright?"

"Did you rush over here to get in on our hike?" Ty asked jokingly, knowing what the answer would be.

The team stood in anticipation, looking at Ty and Newbold greet each other. Even Knight returned to the group to see what was happening as he used his canteen to wash his mouth.

Everyone hoped Newbold's sudden and unexpected arrival brought news of a mission. Or at least something that would get them out of rucking seven miles.

"I got something for you."

"A mission?"

"Yeah. Any chance you can head to HQ with me?"

Ty looked at his team, staring back at him. Henry was still green, and Knight appeared to be holding back another episode of puking. "Is it something you can brief the whole team on?"

"Sure, I am good with that if you are."

Satisfied, Ty pivoted to order his team to load up in the truck to head to HQ but thought better of it. There was no way Knight and Henry should go there looking hungover.

Turning back to Newbold. "Can you, Tiller, and I head there now, and the guys meet us there in thirty minutes?"

"Perfect."

Ty ordered the two hungover members of the team to return to their barracks, shower, change, and grab some quick chow before meeting back up in half an hour.

Surprisingly, there were no cheers, clapping, or high-five this time.

Instead, there was a level of professionalism that hadn't been seen in some time. Knowing that they would be briefed on a possible mission meant something to these guys that didn't warrant a celebration.

It meant a chance to get back in the fight.

For Ty, it was both a relief and a cause for concern. If they were heading to a briefing now, it was not only possible but likely that the team would deploy quickly. Given yesterday's conversation, he wasn't sure how that would resonate with Beth.

Ty knew this was big as they pulled out onto the road for the ten-minute drive. Newbold would've told the guys at the trailhead if he had a simple update. No, this required the security measures for a top-secret briefing at the team's HQ.

Ty gave in to his curiosity. "Can you fill us in on anything during the drive?"

"Umm… I can tell you that you might need to go wheels up in the next twenty-four hours."

"Destination?" Tiller asked.

"The operating area we've been talking about, but more on that when we get to HQ."

Both Ty and Tiller understood what Newbold was and wasn't saying. The details they wanted to know wouldn't be spoken out loud until they were in a secure room.

Ty listened intently as he leaned back in the rolling office chair, picking at the laminate underneath the table.

Newbold had just started briefing the team on the new intel that had prompted him to jump in his military-issued car and rush to find Romeo Team.

The fancy large screens at the front of the room went from black to having the new intel images in seconds.

Ty mused at how fast the technology worked.

The center screen showed pictures of Al-Abbasi and Farhit, while the left had a map of Basra. A photo of two trucks taken from a drone was displayed on the right.

Newbold stood at the middle monitor. "If the intel is accurate, it would be the largest known cache of weapons since the invasion started."

"Is the mission the weapons, the seller, or the buyer?" Henry asked.

"None of them. We want the stash."

Ty leaned forward in his chair to speak for the first time. "So, your theory is that these two trucks were only a small delivery?"

"That's right. We believe that Basra is being used as a staging point to move weapons into and out of the country. This is why there has been little to no insurgency activity in the area last year."

Newbold continued by linking the trucks in the drone footage to pictures from multiple trips into and out of Baghdad and other hot pockets of resistance. He explained that the British had been tracking several trucks to monitor the movement of weapons and allowed them to continue to move freely until they could identify the source.

They had turned over that intel to the CIA when they moved out of the region.

"Why would Al-Abbasi be moving weapons out of Iraq?" Tiller asked.

"Money. We think it's because his weapons stockpile is so large, he can afford to sell off massive amounts while pushing tons north to be used against coalition forces."

Trying to move the briefing forward, Ty asked, "So, what's the play?"

"Romeo Team has been green-lighted back into country. You'll operate out of Ali Air Base in Nasiriyah. From there, you'll be on the main road out of Basra and can cover the entire region."

Ty had never been to Imam Ali Air Base. But had heard it was one of the more favorable places to be stationed in Iraq. Rumor had it that ground forces there saw minimal action while having the amenities of a nicer foreign base.

He was not the only one who had heard rumors about how nice the air base was.

"Wait, isn't Ali the base with the Taco Bell and McDonald's in it?" Knight asked.

This sparked a debate in the room on whether it was a McDonald's or a Burger King.

While the guys argued over which they preferred or hoped was there, Ty flipped through the intel on the small screen at his seat.

"So, when do we spin up?"

The team ended their debate to turn their attention to their commander's question.

"Zero-five hundred hours."

That gave Ty less than twenty-four hours to smooth things over with Beth while also prepping his team for a deployment with an unknown timeline.

After a few more instructions, the team left the briefing room for a quick gear check before heading home. Grabbing his phone from the lockbox, Ty noticed several missed calls from a Washington, D.C. number. Not recognizing it, he dialed it back.

"I was hoping you'd call me back," a provocative voice said after just two rings.

Ty's heart skipped a beat.

He was excited to hear Luna's voice.

Looking around at the guys walking past him to the equipment room, he knew this wasn't a call he could take in their presence. He quickly walked to the team's empty rec room.

Sitting on the arm of the closest couch. "Luna, I didn't realize this was your number."

"It's my office line. I figured you knew my cell and wouldn't pick up or call me back if you saw it."

With an emotionless voice, Ty said, "That's probably true. What do you want?"

"Why are you being so cold?"

"I'm sorry. I didn't expect to hear from you again, and I'm unsure what to make of it."

"Are you alone?"

"Yeah. Why?"

"I don't want to get you in trouble if your wife was there with you."

Ty moved from the couch's arm to the seat cushion. "I appreciate that."

"You left Washington so fast that I didn't get to say goodbye or congratulate you on your performance. You shook things up around here."

"Is this why you called me? To congratulate me for ruining your boss?"

Luna chuckled. "Ty, this is Washington. The news cycle has moved on, and you were never close to ruining him. He's already come out of this stronger than he could have hoped if you had admitted to it."

He knew Luna wasn't intentionally trying to push his buttons. This was her way.

"That doesn't surprise me one bit. So, why are you calling me?"

"Honestly? I wanted to hear your voice. I know you don't like me, but Ty, there is something about you that I can't stop thinking about."

Is she for real?

This was a first. She had never admitted anything like this before. They had a flirty banter that sometimes was a bit hostile due to who her boss was, but this felt like something else. It felt wrong.

The conversation started to remind Ty of the elevator ride the morning of the hearing when she lifted on her tippy toes to try to kiss him in front of Aimes, Wooden, and several onlookers. Once more, he wrestled with an instinctual pull toward Luna and his love for Beth.

Ty, you need to shut this down, ran through his mind as a warning.

Knowing what needed to be done wasn't enough to make it happen. He stayed silent, letting the empty air between them do the talking.

After a quiet moment, she spoke again. "I know. You can't say the same thing back to me."

"It's just not something I am willing to do. I won't go down that road."

"But, you want to? Go down that road, I mean."

Ty sighed. "What I want and what I do don't always agree with one another."

In an upbeat tone. "That's all I wanted to hear."

Weighing his next move, Ty concluded he had said way more than he should have.

"I'm going to go now."

"Wait!" She yelled. "Andy wanted me to convey a message to you."

"And…"

"He wanted me to let you know this isn't over. Sure, he was impressed with what you did during the hearing. He even went as far as to tell me he thought it was inspiring. But you should know he won't stop."

"Yeah, I suspected as much."

"Does that scare you? Knowing that the next president is coming after you?"

Ty thought about her question. She was most likely correct. Hayes was still his party's golden boy and could easily be the next President of the United States despite his trip up in the hearing.

Taking a measured breath. "It does."

"Anything you want me to tell him in return?"

Ty knew what he wanted to say. But he was afraid that if he did, it would point out the chink in his armor. He weighed his fear against the hope that Hayes would respect his wishes.

Sensing his reluctance. "Ty, Adam is honorable. You just found yourself on the wrong side of his ambition."

"Just remind him that this is between the two of us. No one else."

"I will. And he'll understand that. Is there anything else?"

"Yeah… Tell him to bring his fucking 'A' game."

She laughed hard. "I'm sure he'll love that."

Ty knew this was the cockiness that Luna found so intoxicating about him. He liked that about her.

"Who knows, Luna? There might be hope for you and me one day, after all."

"Now you're just being mean."

"Bye, Luna."

"Bye, Ty."

THIRTY-SEVEN

TY'S TWENTY-MINUTE drive home from Camp Pendleton had been spent anxiously bouncing his leg on the truck seat as he thought about his call with Luna. He should have been thinking about how to tell Beth the team was being spun up.

His demons were starting to wreak havoc on his marriage.

Frustrated at himself, he sat in the driveway for several minutes, playing out different ways the conversation could go. With no resolution, he pushed open the door to his truck to head inside.

He found her changing Jake in the nursery.

"You have that look on your face," She said.

"Which look is that?"

"The babe, please don't be mad at me, but I'm leaving again."

Had him leaving for a deployment become so frequent that he had a look she had become familiar with?

With no response from her husband, Beth turned with Jake in her outstretched arms. "Feed your son and put him down. When Audrey gets up from her nap, you need to spend as much time as you can with them before leaving."

She walked out of the room without another word.

With Jake in his arms, he grabbed the bottle off the dresser she had already prepared and sat in the rocking chair next to the crib. There was no reason to chase Beth down the hall in an attempt to talk or apologize to her.

She was right on both accounts. He was being deployed again, and the best thing he could do right now was spend time with their kids.

Jake was asleep halfway through his bottle.

Ty slowly eased his son into his crib and covered him with a small blanket. Stepping quietly out of the nursery, he found Beth standing against the wall outside the door.

In a hushed tone, Ty asked, "Have you been standing here the entire time?"

"No, I came back up a few minutes ago but didn't go in."

"Why not?"

"I didn't know what to say."

Ty took his wife by the hand, pulling her toward their bedroom.

She didn't resist.

Once in the room, Ty slowly shut the door behind them and locked it.

On any other occasion, clicking the push lock wouldn't sound as loud as it had. But it was so boisterous that Ty paused while facing the door, waiting to hear if it had awakened Jake. With no cries reverberating down the hall, Ty turned to Beth, spinning her to press her back against the door in a deep, long-overdue kiss.

She pushed back against her husband's chest. Ty ignored the struggle she put up with her hands because her mouth and heavy panting gave a different signal. Giving in, she reached to undo his belt as he moved his mouth down to her neck.

Each of them had so much they needed to say. But, for right now, Ty needed her in a different way. And she him.

Jake was the first to wake up and cry out. He had peed through his diaper and needed another change. Ty carried him downstairs after cleaning up his son and putting his sheets in the wash. Beth had started to assemble turkey sandwiches for lunch.

Sitting at the table with Jake in his lap, a sleepy-eyed Audrey on his right, and a still-flushed Beth on his left, they enjoyed lunch as a family.

It was almost too easy to forget that by this time tomorrow, he and Romeo Team would be in the air heading back to Iraq. It was barely noon, yet so much had already happened—and more was needed.

"When do you need to be back on base?" Beth asked.

"Fourteen hundred hours for a final gear check and to finalize last-minute details. It should only take a couple of hours."

"Is the team getting together tonight?"

Ty didn't know.

When 1st Recon Battalion deployed, having a large get-together the night before was usually planned by Aimes' wife, Cindy. With the help of Beth and some other officers' wives, of course. But Aimes was already in Iraq, and this was Ty's team that was deploying.

He considered, *Was I responsible for this now? Was Beth?*

He also recognized that he wasn't in the equipment room with the team due to Luna's call. They might have planned something on their own, and he didn't hear about it or was too occupied at the time to listen to what was being discussed. Either way, he needed to figure it out.

This was the team's first mission as Raiders, which deserved a proper send-off. Ty weighed his different options.

Do I ask Beth to put it together on such short notice? Do I call Tiller to ask if the team had discussed anything while he was on his call? Or do they skip it?

Sensing he was thinking through options. "Why don't you let me take care of it?"

"Babe, I can't ask that of you. That's too much."

"It's not. We'll keep things simple and have everyone over here. We have the fire ring in the backyard. All we need is food and beer."

Ty stared at her.

These were the mixed signals he struggled with. He knew she wasn't happy about him deploying, yet she was always willing to volunteer to take on more than she should.

In many ways, he would rather her be upset with him and not offer to host the team or say she didn't want him to go on the mission. It would be much easier if she would tell Ty precisely what she wanted and give him an ultimatum— *the Corps or her*.

Resisting anything more, "Thank you, love."

After the sandwiches, Ty and the kids went to the living room to play on the floor. Jake was crawling everywhere. Audrey was running back and forth from the kitchen with water to have a tea party with her daddy. Beth sat in a recliner, watching amusingly for the entire hour as she made phone calls to arrange the evening's get-together.

When it was time for Ty to head back to base, he put Jake in his playpen, finished his tea, and went upstairs to change back into his uniform.

"Everything is all arranged for tonight," Beth said, coming into the bedroom as Ty tied his boots.

"I have a few minutes. Do you want to talk?"

"I wouldn't know where to begin."

"How about I start?" Ty said as he reached for her to join him on the edge of their still-messed-up bed.

"A lot has changed in five years. Neither of us would have ever guessed we'd be here and how my career would've progressed. But it has, and I'm, for unknown reasons, really good at being a Marine. It comes easily to me, and a lot of powerful people know my name. And as we saw in D.C. and Mississippi, that could be good and bad. But my love for you has only gotten stronger. I don't always show it, but you, Audrey, and Jake are my priority. If you asked me to quit the Raiders and get out of the Corps, I would as soon as I could."

Ty reached to wipe a tear from her left cheek. "Beth, you're the world to me, and I don't want to lose you."

She kissed his hand softly before cupping it around her face. She pushed her warm, wet cheek into the palm of his hand.

"I know you love me, I know you love the kids, and I know you love being a Marine. I'll never ask you to choose, but I don't know if I can do this much longer."

She just asked me to choose.

Sure, she was saying that she wouldn't, but by telling him she wasn't sure if she could continue as his wife, she was telling him to make a choice.

Ty felt part of his heartbreak there on the side of their bed.

Beth's tears were steady now, and his eyes swelled to the point they ran over when he blinked.

This is it. This is what's most important.

He leaned over to kiss her softly. Then, he laid his forehead against hers.

Nose to nose, he kept his promise.

"I can't stop tomorrow's deployment, but as soon as I get back, I'll request to change jobs and get out of the Corps as soon as my commission ends."

Beth broke down into hysteria.

Ty knew that she was torn. He was giving her what she wanted, but she was heartbroken by asking him to leave the job he loved.

CHAPTER
THIRTY-EIGHT

WAR-SCARRED SOUTHERN IRAQ is different than anywhere else in the world.

During the days, the intense sun burns through the layers of desert sand in the air, creating an orange, apocalyptic haze.

The night isn't much better, as the warm air carries eerie sounds from distant oil wells. The city's buildings and roads bear the deep scars of years of war. Tanks, artillery, and burned-out cars are still everywhere. The people are secluded and weary of anyone who doesn't look and sound like them.

A feeling that Ty and Romeo Team could relate to.

Arriving at Ali Air Base, the team quickly found their way to their housing. Aimes arrived shortly after they finished unpacking.

"Team, ten-hut!" Tiller yelled as Aimes walked into the common room.

The team quickly stopped what they were doing to stand at attention.

"As you were," Aimes called out.

Stepping forward to greet his commanding officer, Ty said, "Sir, good to see you again."

The two Marine officers briefly discussed the flight, base logistics, and home life.

Ty wouldn't mention anything to Aimes about getting out of the Raider teams until after the mission was complete. As it had been for the last twenty-four hours, this was a secret he would keep to himself.

Turning his attention to the entire room, the Colonel asked, "You guys want to take the night to get settled in, or are you ready for a sit rep?"

The vote was unanimous. The twenty-two-hour flight with two different stops had meant the team had been in the back of a C-17 Globemaster for nearly thirty hours. Between the jet lag, being on California time, and needing to shake off the pure boredom, everyone was up to preparing for the mission.

Standing above a street-level map of Basra and its port, Aimes briefed the team on the Army's routine patrols, the city's politics, neighborhoods, cultural centers, and past flash points with the population. As Newbold had indicated, the city was relatively quiet. Coalition forces hadn't been attacked in more than three months.

Compared to other large Iraqi cities, this was abnormal. Even nearly five years after falling, Baghdad couldn't go three days without a roadside bomb or an attack of some sort. And American troops were a favorite target.

"Newbold, do we have any intel on the number of trucks the British were tracking or their movements within the city?" Ty asked.

"They started with eleven trucks nine months ago, but a few got destroyed. They turned over intel on eight."

"And known movements in the city?"

"That's where it gets more complicated. Basra is a city of over a million people spread over nearly a hundred square miles. The problem is that we know of at least sixteen spots the trucks visit frequently. But, there isn't a particular place they always return to, leave from, or stay very long at. It's truly random."

"What do you mean random?" Henry asked.

"Take a look here at these pictures and tell me what you see?"

No one replied after looking at six different pictures scattered on the table.

Leaning over to Tiller, Ty whispered, "I don't see anything but trucks."

Newbold's laughter made it clear that the team wasn't following. "All right, guys, let's act like you've done this before. Look at the truck the photo is focused on. It's the same one. Notice how the engine grill has the same indention and the driver's door has the same three bullet holes."

Seeing those details now, the team broke out into jokes about having noticed it but wanted to test him.

Ignoring their quips, Newbold continued, "So, this truck has been traced to four trips in and out of Basra in the last six weeks. It never stopped at the same building, visited the same neighborhood, or went to the same destination after leaving. Each trip was completely random."

"So, how are you connecting that to weapons movements?" Tiller asked.

"Great question! Each time this truck made a delivery to another town or city, an attack took place within forty-eight hours."

"Total coincidence."

Speaking up, Aimes said, "That's what I said, too, at first."

Newbold added. "Sure, there are slim odds of it happening on a couple or even a handful of occasions. But the British tracked it to seven straight attacks before giving it to us. We tracked the four I just mentioned. All with the same truck."

Picking up a photo to examine it more closely, Knight asked, "So, you guys have tracked this truck to eleven different spots in the last nine months where an attack takes place within days, and you haven't blown it up yet? Why the hell not?"

"They want the weapons stockpile, not the delivery," Tiller replied before Newbold could.

"That's right. So, that is one truck. We have similar data on the other seven. Each has different schedules and stops, but after a delivery, there's an attack. And not always on coalition forces. Most have been on Iraqi Security Forces."

"So, why don't we stop one of the trucks, grab the driver, and force him to talk?" Henry asked.

"It's been tried. Remember I said that the British started tracking eleven trucks? They intercepted three loaded with weapons and couldn't get anything out of the driver." Newbold replied as he walked away to grab a laptop out of a bag.

As he fired up the machine, the team started to talk amongst themselves. Ty took the opportunity to get Aimes' read on the situation. "Sir, what's your take on this?"

"There is a lot I don't like about it. I said no when Newbold brought it to me. That's when they showed me this video," Aimes said, pointing at the video on the laptop Newbold had started.

It was a compilation of the interrogations by British Intelligence on all three of the drivers.

They were all the type that wasn't supposed to happen.

The most disturbing part of the twenty-eight-minute video wasn't what was being done to each of the drivers. It was their conviction to their cause.

Each had an unfathomable calmness during an intense interview and didn't give anything away.

Ty understood what Aimes saw in the video. This wasn't arbitrary truck drivers making a quick buck by delivering weapons or a low-level Iraqi insurgent.

This was more sophisticated.

They had interrogation training that rivaled anything Ty had undergone in Recon or Raider qualifications. It was apparent how each driver only gave the same information to the interrogator, how they maintained their breathing, and how none had their composure cracked while they suffered unspeakable pain.

Ty had undergone similar training and had been subjected to small amounts of some of the methods these guys had endured for hours. But, what he had suffered during training was designed to show him what being tortured was like or what to anticipate. It lasted minutes at most.

"Damn," Tiller said. "Where are they now?"

"The first one you saw died during the interview. The other two were later moved to British intel sites out of country." Newbold answered.

Shocked at what he saw. "So, we aren't going to waste our time grabbing a truck," Knight said.

"No, we're not," replied Aimes. "We are going to flip what we're focusing on."

The guys didn't understand what Aimes meant, but Ty knew what he was suggesting. "How do we cover sixteen buildings spread over nearly a hundred square miles?"

"Why the buildings?" Knight asked.

"I would assume none are big enough or protected enough to be the main stockpile," Ty said, looking to Newbold for confirmation.

"That's right."

"Then the sixteen buildings are a staging point for the trucks. Instead of where the trucks go after they visit, we focus on what and who is going in and out of each building before the trucks arrive. Then we trace that back to where the main storage is."

Nodding his head, Aimes replied, "Correct."

"So, back to my original question. How do we cover sixteen buildings spread over nearly a hundred square miles if everything is random?"

"That's why you're here," Newbold began, "If we knew how or

could've done it, we would already have the weapons, or the British would have found them."

Ty didn't reply. He weighed Newbold's words while a few of the guys started to mumble to themselves in dissatisfaction.

"Guys," Aimes called out to get everyone's attention. "I get it. This isn't what you had hoped for, and a lot of intel work still needs to be done. But let me remind you of the last several attacks traced back to these trucks. Eight Americans lost their lives, and another five were injured. That's just in the last two months. It's imperative that you find these weapons. And quickly!"

Newbold had not filled in the team on the American casualties caused by the attacks. But Aimes' knew how to motivate Marines.

Ty looked down at the sixteen spots marked on the map. *This is nearly impossible. It's not finding a needle in a haystack. It's finding a needle in a hundred-square-mile field.*

Clearing his throat, Ty said, "Sir, you brought in the right team. We'll put together a reconnaissance plan with Newbold and have it to you by the morning."

It was after 10 p.m. local time, but for the guys still on California time, it felt like early morning. Ty knew their bodies would take a few days to adjust to the time difference. They could use this to their advantage and troubleshoot the problem tonight.

Aimes didn't object and left the team to do their work.

As Aimes left the room, Tiller looked at Ty. "I assume you already have a plan."

"Nope."

Most everyone was stumped as to where to start.

After a few minutes of kicking around ideas about starting close to the port, working into the city, or dividing the team into sectors, no one had a good idea.

That's when Henry said, "Guys, you're overthinking this."

Growing up in Kentucky's coal country, Henry's dad worked in the mines for the first ten years of his life. After an accident just before his eleventh birthday, he quit mining to start driving cross-country semi-trucks. The way he told the story, most of Henry's summers were spent with his dad hauling loads from coast to coast.

Thankfully for the team, it taught Henry two things.

First, he never wanted to be a trucker. So, when he turned eighteen, he joined the Corps.

Second, it taught him basic logistics and how to move massive amounts of cargo easily from one point to another.

While the team struggled, Henry had already mapped out the best places to start based on points of egress, potential storage and loading capabilities for larger munitions, and ensuring the trucks blended into the neighborhoods.

The most critical clue Henry walked the team through was finding patterns between the type of attack on the delivery end and the origination point in Basra.

This was a game-changer. Henry found that the known attacks that used larger bombs came from only a few buildings. This meant they were the only ones with the storage and loading capabilities for bigger ordnance.

Within three hours, the team had narrowed their focus to three buildings. While they hadn't eliminated the others, these offered the best odds of finding the weapons cache.

Newbold was so impressed with Henry's intel work that he ordered drone surveillance for each target location without Aimes' approval. Following his lead, Ty worked with Tiller to set up ground intel-gathering efforts by rotating the team to recon the different buildings.

Unlike Newbold, Ty couldn't authorize the plan before Aimes signed off on it. With no more work to be done and hours before Aimes would return, he ordered the team to get some rest.

After everyone left, Ty looked at his watch. It was sixteen hundred hours back in California. That meant Beth would have already picked up the kids from daycare and gotten home.

Ty wanted to hear Beth's voice before heading to bed.

Their call was short but satisfying. They spoke for a few minutes with little to report on either end before hanging up.

Walking back to his bunk, Ty felt the urge to make another call.

Stopping as he reached the barracks, he took out his phone and scrolled through the numbers.

When he reached her name under contacts, he froze. *Is this something I should do?*

Struggling against what he wanted, he snapped his phone shut. But didn't go immediately inside. With his hand resting on the doorknob, he again thought about calling her, rationalizing that it wasn't too late in Washington.

Ty knew that any conversation with her would be fun and flirty. All he would have to deal with later was the guilt.

Stepping away from the door, he opened his phone again to scroll to her name.

Pressing the green phone icon button, he lifted it to his ear just as the first ring sounded.

Panic.

Snap!

Ty quickly closed his phone again before shoving it in his pocket as he went inside.

What the hell were you thinking? That was stupid! He thought while pulling his phone back out to ensure the ringer was off. The last thing he needed was for her to see he called and to call him back.

Imagining how difficult it would be to explain to the team why he was receiving a call was one thing. But it would also mean that he would have to take it.

Throwing the phone on his bed, he decided to take a quick shower. Rummaging through his pack for toiletries, he noticed the light on the face of his phone was lit up. Then, it went dark. He had missed a call.

He knew who it was. He also knew she would've left a voicemail. As if on cue, the notification on his small screen changed from 'Missed Call to New Voicemail.'

Ty flipped it open and held down the voicemail button.

"Hey Ty, I noticed I missed your call. I'm not sure why you called me after the last time we spoke, but I'm glad you did. I would love to talk, so if you can, call me back. If not, I understand."

He wasn't going to return her call. At least, not tonight.

CHAPTER
THIRTY-NINE

"ROMEO TEAM, hold what you have. Two trucks are pulling out and heading west toward the main highway," Tiller said from his overwatch position some two hundred meters away.

"Roger that," Ty responded. "Romeo Four, confirm eyes on."

Knight whispered, "I have eyes on two trucks heading west."

Three days ago, a nervous Henry laid out the plan for Romeo Team to narrow their focus to just three of the sixteen possible buildings in Basra. Ty stood quietly by the Sergeant's side at the large map while he applied logic to a problem that Newbold could not solve.

After Henry circled the third location, he looked up and saw Ty and the Colonel smiling. He had done a brilliant job, and after only a few tactical questions, Aimes authorized the team to go into the city.

The plan was simple.

They would conduct small team reconnaissance during the day, and Newbold would arrange drone coverage at night. This would give them twenty-four-hour coverage of all three locations. Since this was a recon-only mission, each would be in civilian clothes and only carry a sidearm—no tactical gear, no rifles.

When the team went into the city for the first day, Ty was surprised by what he found. Sure, there was plenty of evidence of war, but unlike Mosul or Baghdad, this city was on the rebound.

Most of the roads, telephone, and electrical lines, as well as the central government buildings, had been repaired. They passed schools in session with kids playing soccer on dirt fields. Local markets were a beehive of activity. There were signs that even tourism had returned.

Seeing the city's progress compared to other parts of the country was encouraging. Yet, it was equally alarming that major arms movements were taking place in the middle of such a peaceful city.

Like the first day, nothing happened on the second, either.

It was the morning of the third day when the team got their first break.

Knight was reconning the city's dry docks along the Shatt Al-Arab river when two cars carrying four men crossed the only bridge onto the island and pulled up to the target building.

The building was one of a handful on the island that made up the dry docks. It was on the island's south side, nestled among rotting boats on land, shipping containers, and machinery.

An off-white color peppered with bullet holes, its handful of windows were boarded up, and the main door faced the island's interior. It was the last in a row of three single-story buildings that appeared to be small offices with similar damage.

Its only distinguishing feature was the three truck loading docks on its rear along the riverside. Due to damage and a partial collapse to the roof, Henry had determined that only one of the loading docks was still functional.

All of this was a typical scene for a building in a war zone.

The entire area was shaped like a square, less than two acres in size. Its main riverbank was parallel with the surrounding city shoreline. The man-made U-shaped waterway that created the island provided more dock space for tugs and other boats.

At its center was a long, wide ramp into the water, through which large boats could be pulled onto land.

The city's most extraordinary attraction was at the mouth of the ramp. One hundred meters off-shore.

Resting on its side in the river's mud was the capsized al-Mansur.

Coalition forces had bombed the once magnificent personal yacht of Saddam Hussein in the early months of the war. The hundred-and-twenty-meter al-Mansur was later looted before rolling over on its side in the middle of the river. Becoming a popular tourist attraction as she rusted away.

The sight of the luxury yacht lying on its side in a state of decay was ominous.

From his position on the city street, Knight knew that a car stopping to let out passengers wasn't a big deal. But it was the first action at any of the three target buildings in days. Having no visibility of where the men got out of the cars, he went on foot to walk down the main street across from the island to discreetly look down its center road as he passed.

What he saw prompted the team to collapse into the area.

"Verona, this is Romeo Four. Come back," Knight said into his radio.

"Go for Verona."

"Verona, six military-aged males got dropped off by two civilian cars at target location two. While walking by, I saw the nose of a large truck sticking out of a previously unknown rolling door. Recommend support be moved to my location."

"Hold, Romeo Four."

A moment later, Newbold got on the radio with Knight to confirm what he saw and if the truck was still visible.

"Unknown. No longer in a position to see down the road. But it hasn't crossed the bridge. Requesting additional eyes."

"Romeo One, this is Verona. Are you copying this?"

"Good copy, Verona. Agree with Four. Two move to join Four," Ty ordered.

Before Tiller could arrive, the truck crossed the bridge to head west toward the main highway.

With the truck gone, Ty stayed at his position and waited for any news from Tiller and Knight.

They gave regular updates, but nothing else happened for the rest of the day.

Frustrated with the lack of news and with the sun setting, Ty ordered the team back to Ali Airbase.

As Ty got into the beat-up, rusted truck he was using to travel between the city and the airbase, Tiller's voice cut through the engine's noise. "Romeo Team, hold what you have. Two trucks are pulling out and heading west toward the main highway."

Shifting his truck into gear, Ty did a U-turn to head toward the river district. He wasn't sure what he would do when he got there or why he was heading that way. It felt like the right action since he was already in the truck.

"Two, any other movement?"

"Nega—" Tiller began before stopping. "Hold Romeo One."

Ty increased his speed to thirty miles per hour. Unless he or another team member was in distress or under attack, this was the fastest he could drive without drawing too much attention to himself in the narrow side streets.

Running out of patience. "Romeo Two, sitrep."

"Romeo One, this is Four. Two isn't talking because three men are standing near his position. Hold for them to move."

Ty passed several blocks before Knight said on the radio, "Movement on the water! I say again, movement on the water. There's a large boat pulling to the dock. I see at least five, no six military-aged men on it."

"Roger that Four. Are they carrying anything on the boat?" Ty asked.

"Negative, no sign of cargo."

Hearing there was movement on the water, Ty turned north toward the river on the next street. Moving now at forty miles per hour, he could see the river bank four blocks ahead when he came to a screeching halt due to traffic.

Wedged in, Ty pulled the truck to the side of the road, turned it off, and got out. With the traffic backed up, he would be quicker navigating the next several blocks on foot.

"Three, what's your sitrep?"

"One, I'm in the same traffic you are. You passed me a few blocks ago, so I followed you. I just saw you exit your vehicle, request permission to do the same to follow you on foot to the river." Henry replied.

"Granted. Stay behind me not to draw attention to us."

"Roger that."

Reaching the river, Ty turned west up the road along its bank. Henry stayed a hundred meters behind.

The few street lights along the sidewalk started to buzz as their lights turned on. The river was barely visible in the fading sun, with Ty still a klick from location two.

He stopped as he approached a large intersection with a bridge. If the boat was heading in this direction, this might be his best location to see it.

"Romeo Four, do you still have eyes on the boat?"

"Roger that," Knight replied. "The boat is docked. No one is on it."

Ty crossed the street to walk to the edge of the bridge span. He stopped just before crossing the river and looked toward the dry docks to see the boat in the distance.

"I have movement on the loading dock," Tiller said.

"Nice of you to rejoin us," Ty joked.

"Yeah, the guys on the street wouldn't shut up. But they've moved on. I have five guys moving three large crates toward the dock. Four, are you seeing this?"

"Confirmed. I have eyes on them."

Frustrated he wasn't closer, Ty did the next best thing. "Verona, any chance we have a drone in the vicinity? We need to track the boat down the river."

"Roger that Romeo One. We can repurpose one. Hold for ETA."

"Team, how long do we have before the crates are loaded on the boat?"

"One, they just got to the edge of the dock. I say we have ten minutes, maybe less," Tiller said.

"Roger that. Verona, you have less than ten minutes to get a drone above us."

CHAPTER
FORTY

AS TILLER HAD PREDICTED, loading the three crates onto the boat took ten minutes. Impatiently, Ty asked Newbold for the status of the drone and was disappointed by the response he got.

"It's still several minutes out. We should be able to pick them up on the river, pass along the direction and boat's description," Newbold said.

The Shatt Al-Arab River wasn't a hotbed of boat activity at this hour. Still, there was enough water traffic this evening with fishermen returning from the Gulf to complicate things for a drone operator trying to identify a single boat.

In a stroke of luck, the men did not push off immediately.

Once they had covered their cargo with tarps, they returned to the dock to chat for several more minutes. This allowed the drone to reach the location in time.

Once the men boarded and pushed off, they turned back in the direction they had arrived from. In Ty's direction.

As the boat started down the river, Ty looked around to notice he was one of only a few pedestrians on the bridge. In his current position, he would stand out like a sore thumb.

With just a couple minutes before they reached the bridge, he quickly looked around for a better spot.

Hmmm… That's perfect.

Ty reached into the garbage can on the street corner to pull out a newspaper and started to unfold it as he sat at the edge of the bridge's wall. He put the unfolded newspaper over his head and leaned back. In the fading evening light, the men on the boat would make him out as just another homeless person taking refuge for the night.

As Ty hoped, the position gave him a clear view of the boat as it passed.

Holy shit! That's Farhit. Ty whispered when a man stepped out of the wheelhouse as it reached the bridge.

As the boat moved out of sight, Ty pressed his mic, "Verona, Farhit is on the boat. Is the drone in position?"

"Roger that, Romeo One. The drone has eyes on, and we have confirmation on Farhit," Newbold replied.

"Can we get authorization for an airstrike?" Tiller asked.

"Negative, Romeo Two. The mission isn't Farhit. It's the weapons and finding the cache."

"Yeah, but if those are bombs, they're going to be used to kill Americans. An airstrike will take out Farhit and the boat." Knight interjected.

Getting to his feet, Ty settled the debate. "Romeo Team, return to base. Our work is done here for the day."

Ty watched the boat float down the river for a few more minutes before returning to his truck.

He was the last to get back to base. The other three team vehicles were already there. He walked into the mission room as all hell was breaking out.

Tiller and Henry were restraining Knight as he shouted at Newbold.

"Not the mission! I'll show what the fuck the mission is!" Knight yelled as he came out of his seat to rush Newbold, standing by a monitor showing the drone feed over the boat.

Tiller was seated next to Knight and quickly grabbed him.

Henry had to join Tiller to hold him back.

To his credit, Newbold didn't flinch. He just stood there looking at the Marine.

Henry was the first to notice Ty walk into the room. "Sir, maybe you could talk some sense into Newbold for us."

Walking up to the table the team had been sitting at. "Nah… It looks like you guys have a good handle on it."

As Ty hoped for, his sarcasm cooled the temperature in the room, and Knight was released by his teammates.

As everyone settled down, Ty asked, "Sitrep?"

"The boat is in the gulf and has turned east along the Iranian coastline. No indication yet as to its destination."

"Is the drone armed?"

"It is. But—"

Ty held up his hand to cut off Newbold's response.

Taking a deep breath. "Is it in Iranian waters yet?"

This was an olive branch.

Ty knew neither he nor Newbold had the authority to order an airstrike, but they could ask for one as long as the boat was still in Iraqi waters. If it wasn't, the strike was off the table.

Newbold turned to an operator at a computer screen behind him. "Where's the boat?"

"It entered Iranian waters about ten minutes ago, sir."

In a measured tone, Ty said, "Then there isn't anything we can do."

No one objected. The team knew the rules of engagement, and no one in command would authorize a strike in the waters of a sovereign country for a messenger and what may be a few bombs heading away from the war zone.

"Guys, it's been a long day, and there isn't anything more we can do tonight. Get some chow and sleep. We'll regroup at zero-six hundred hours."

With what came off as an order, everyone started to file out of the room.

Ty followed the team outside. "Knight."

The wide-shouldered, muscled Sergeant reluctantly returned to stand face-to-face with his commanding officer.

Speaking first, Ty said, "I get it. I really do. Those bombs will be used to kill Americans, but that's not how this works. And you know that."

Knight didn't respond as he looked away, irritated.

Ty recognized that his soft words weren't resonating with the stubborn, low man on the team. So, he decided to make his point using language the Marine could understand.

He took a step closer. "If I ever see you lunge at another team member again, you're fucking done. Do you understand what I am saying, Sergeant?"

Making eye contact, "Yes, sir."

Ty understood Knight's frustrations because he felt the same way.

There was a very high probability that if there were bombs or weapons in those crates, they would be used to kill Americans. Maybe not in Iraq, but they were being moved for a purpose.

The difference was that Ty believed Newbold in that these three crates were only a tiny piece of a much larger weapons stockpile. And while Farhit would be a good kill, he was a small potato compared to his boss, Al-Abbasi.

Ty had his eye on the long game of eliminating the weapons cache and getting Al-Abbasi. That would be a mission worthy of retiring after.

But, you couldn't tell a gunslinger like Knight that. You had to keep him focused on the mission and then unleash him at the right time.

Preferably toward the enemy and not your team's CIA handler.

With nothing more he could do about Knight, Ty walked back into the mission room to chat with Newbold about the drone coverage and when he could expect a sitrep during the night. Satisfied, he left the intelligence team to do their work while he went to eat and get some sleep.

It was a restless night.

His head hit the pillow a little after 11 p.m. local time, but he couldn't fall asleep. Tossing and turning in his bunk wasn't working as he checked his watch regularly to see the late-night hours tick by. Frustrated by the anxiety from not being able to sleep, Ty gave up and got out of bed just after 4 a.m.

Sitting up, he considered his options for the next few hours. There was a book he had brought from home on the small table in the corner of his room, which doubled as a desk.

Laying on its face with the hardcover binding frail from use was *Master and Commander* by Patrick O'Brain.

While not considered a literary classic by most, it was one of Ty's favorites. He opened its pages during his sophomore year at UCF and has reread it twice since. While he thought the Hollywood adaptation that came out a few years ago was good, he still preferred the complexity of Jack Aubrey's character as the author told it.

It was fitting that part of Aubrey's challenge as the master and commander of his two-masted brig was keeping his men's morale high as they chased a much larger Spanish frigate along the South American coastline thousands of miles from home.

Looking at the title on the spine, he mused at the irony that this was the one he had brought with him out of the hundreds of books in his home library.

After a half-hour in the first few chapters, he again became restless. It was time for something else to occupy his mind.

Putting on a pair of shorts, a simple grey t-shirt, and his tennis shoes, Ty slipped out of the team's bunkhouse for a run around the airbase's outer parameters. He still had an hour and a half before he was due back in the mission room. This was plenty of time.

He took a brisk pace, targeting a sub-six-minute mile to get in at least seven miles before he needed to return for a shower, get some chow, and still be on time to meet the team.

On this return, he noticed a growing crowd gathering along one of the runways.

This was unusual, but even more so that it wasn't even 6 a.m. In the distance, he could make out a C-17 Globemaster, similar to the one Romeo Team had arrived on a few days earlier, coming into land. Curious, Ty picked up his pace toward the crowd.

As the giant transport plane landed, it taxied toward everyone gathered near one of the remaining intact hangers. Now jogging along the runway, Ty could see Aimes and Newbold among the fifty to sixty people.

Walking up, short of breath and covered in sweat, Ty asked, "What's going on here?"

Aimes and Newbold shared a glance. But neither answered.

Noticing the awkward exchange, Ty turned to see several people coming out of the plane's now open rear door.

Among them was Senator Andrew Hayes.

"Shit, Ty. You two have something else going on we should know about?" Newbold asked sarcastically.

"What the hell?"

"I just found out about fifteen minutes ago. I went to your barracks, but Tiller said you weren't there," Aimes said.

"So, what's this?"

Aimes sighed. "He is part of a Congressional delegation that's touring several facilities. They are starting here and then going to Baghdad to meet with the interim government."

As others came off the plane, the crowd started to clap and cheer. The base commander, in uniform, walked forward to greet the new arrivals.

Naturally, the crowd pushed closer.

Moving with it, Ty stopped only about ten meters from Hayes. This was close enough.

He was fuming at the sight of Hayes in person so soon after the Senate hearing. His eyes narrowed, and his fist clenched as he watched the Senator greet the base commander.

To Ty's dismay, Senator Wrzesinki was also with the delegation being warmly welcomed to the airbase.

Stepping back to allow someone else to shake hands, the elder Senator looked over the crowd. That's when she made eye contact with the only person not clapping.

Stunned, she nudged Hayes' left elbow and pointed with her head in Ty's direction. He slowly turned to lock eyes with Ty.

The two of them held each other's gaze for a long moment.

Neither was willing to back down.

Noticing, the base commander looked in Ty's direction. By his facial expression, he quickly put together the cause of the stare-down. He mouthed something to the two senators and then started to usher them in the opposite direction.

Hayes broke eye contact with Ty before walking away.

Taking a deep breath, Ty exhaled it slowly to calm his nerves.

Glancing around to see if anyone else had noticed his tense exchange with the Senator, he spotted her.

Luna had been standing at the rear of the plane the entire time.

Walking over to Ty. "Of all the gin joints, in all the towns, in all the world," she said provocatively.

FORTY-ONE

WHILE GLARING DOWN AT HAYES, his rage for seeing the Senator had not allowed him even to consider that Luna would be traveling with him.

Now that she was standing right in front of him, his rage turned to something altogether different. His heart beating fast for a different reason.

He had listened to the voicemail she had left him at least a half-dozen times in the last few days. In the handful of private moments he had found, he flipped open his phone to hear the desire hidden in her words: 'I would love to talk, so if you can, call me back.'

Each time, he was hit with a splash of curiosity about what she was doing at that particular moment or what their conversation would be like if he caved to temptation. But he knew better than to let his thoughts roam too far. Not only was there desire hidden in her voicemail, but there was also a subtle warning.

'If not, I understand.'

Those four simple words gave Ty the escape route he needed to try to forget her. They signaled that Luna knew there were, or at least there should be, boundaries to whatever they had going on. She said she would understand that he had chosen Beth and their two kids over her.

She would understand why I didn't call back. Ty had rationalized with himself after each time he listened to her short message.

But this wasn't a voicemail.

"I'm sorry I called you the other day," Ty said. "I don't know what I was thinking."

Luna lifted her hand to place it on Ty's sweaty chest. "I didn't mind. I was only sorry I missed your call."

This was a softer version of her. One that he had not seen before.

She was sincere.

Her expression wasn't sinister or lustful as it had been the night they danced or in the elevator before the Senate hearing.

Looking into her deep brown eyes, he could see a different burning for him.

"You're hearts beating like crazy."

"I was just running."

She clenched his chest with her fingers while ignoring his sweat-drenched shirt. "No, it's more than that. I feel it, too."

And with those words, his heart went from racing to stopping.

Luna has just pushed out the edges of their boundaries from welcomed flirting to improper overtures.

Ty knew he had to control the direction of this conversation. "What brings you and Hayes to Iraq?"

Luna gave him an understanding smirk and dropped her hand from his chest. "We're touring several bases and meeting with members of Iraq's new parliament."

Ty already knew this, but it gave them something else to talk about.

"How long will you be here?"

"At least a day. Will you make time to see me?"

"I should be able to. I don't know when, but I'll make it work."

Ty noticed her glance over his right shoulder, the way a person does when they acknowledge someone else is waiting to talk to the person they're talking to.

Shit! The last thing he needed was Aimes standing behind him, watching this.

Before he could say anything, Luna leaned in to kiss him on his left cheek.

She had just spent the last eighteen to twenty hours in the back on a C-17, yet her hair smelled as enticing as the night they met for drinks. With her leaning in, touching his cheek with her lips, Ty's heart returned to racing.

"Come find me later," she said before heading in the direction that Hayes and the rest of the delegation had gone minutes ago.

Ty forgot about whoever was standing behind him.

Instead, he admired Luna as she walked away.

She was twenty feet away when she whipped around to catch his eyes locked on her ass.

It took Ty a second to respond. Realizing he had been caught, he jolted his eyes up to see a big smile on her face.

Luna knew what she was doing.

Like any red-blooded man, she knew Ty would be staring at her in those jeans as she left.

Ty stood in place as she turned and walked away without looking back again. She was fading out of view, but he was afraid to turn around to see Aimes standing there.

On more than one occasion, his commanding officer warned him about Luna and the possible consequences of continuing their charades.

"Captain, nothing about this ends well for you. Not your career and not your marriage. So, you need to think long and hard about keeping anything going with her," Aimes said minutes after they exited the elevator before the Senate hearing.

Aimes was right. Ty knew it then, and he knew it now.

As he built the courage to turn around, the man who drew Luna's attention stepped up beside him.

"That was a bit intense," Tiller said.

Looking first at the ground, Ty turned to see his First Sergeant looking at him with his eyebrows raised inquisitively.

Ty knew what Tiller was thinking and what he was fishing for. *Have you slept with her?*

Taking a deep breath, Ty replied, "Yeah, it's complicated."

"Is that who I think it is?"

"Yeah, she's Hayes' Chief of Staff. We met—"

Interrupting Ty, "Oh, I remember her at our Raider graduation."

Ty hadn't ever talked to anyone other than Marcus about meeting Luna.

It wasn't something he would share with the team.

Tiller had just acknowledged he knew who she was and when they met. That would mean that whatever was going on between them wasn't as big of a secret as Ty had thought.

Narrowing his eyes, "How do you know when we met?"

"Seriously? A woman looking like that, and you think we didn't notice you talking to her and Hayes."

"Wait! Who's we?"

"All of us. The entire team noticed. We also saw her on the TV during the hearing. She couldn't take her eyes off of you."

Ty had no idea. He felt the blood rush to his face with embarrassment.

He looked away. Not towards anything in particular, just in another direction as not to face Tiller when he asked his next question. "Do the guys think I've cheated on Beth with her?"

"No one has said anything to me."

"Okay."

A moment passed as Ty stared out into the distance.

Tiller stood there all the time, watching his commander's facial expressions. Giving in to curiosity, "How bad is it?"

"Pretty fucking bad. And no, we haven't slept together. But I can't stop thinking about her."

"Does Beth know?"

"No."

"Want to talk about it?"

Ty resisted at first. He wasn't good at sharing his personal feelings. He preferred to keep them bottled up, releasing them in small amounts to Beth and maybe his best friend, Marcus.

However, this was different.

The intensity of their moment wasn't lost on Tiller. Unlike Aimes, he knew there would be no judgment. Nor any underlying concern for political fallout. Tiller would listen and advise a friend.

The same way Marcus would do if he were standing here.

Nodding his head in silent agreement with himself, Ty glanced over at Tiller, "Alright. Let's talk."

He unloaded everything.

The coffee line, the drinks, the dancing, the elevator, her call to him just before Romeo Team deployed, and even his call several nights ago. Ty even admitted that he had listened to her voicemail multiple times to hear her voice.

Breaking the silence between them after he had finished his story, Ty said, "I'm an asshole for what I'm doing behind Beth's back."

Nodding his head in agreement, "Yes, yes you are."

Ouch! The sting of his words hurt.

"Can I speak freely?" Tiller asked.

"Seriously? I think we're well past that."

They both chuckled.

"Fair point." Tiller continued, still chuckling, "Ty, you have a crush. And I get it. She's as hot as she's an adversary. There is fun in the chase. Especially when it's after something so forbidden."

"Okay..." Ty replied, unsure of where his First Sergeant was going.

"But, here's where I'm at on this. You haven't done anything yet that you can't come back from. And sure, you know you need to cut this off. I just—"

Tiller stopped mid-sentence. Ty looked around to see if someone was walking up, which forced the conversation to be cut off.

There was no one.

Raising his eyebrows in anticipation, "Well?"

"So, she's here. You're here. I'm willing to bet that if you spent a little more time with her, you'll realize that she's not that great, and what you have with Beth is way better."

Rubbing sweet off his forehead, Ty replied, "Wait, your advice is if I spend more time with her, I'll realize the grass isn't greener?"

"Yeah! The best way to get over her is to test the waters a little. I know Beth, and I know this woman won't measure up. But you need to come to that conclusion yourself. The only way to do that is to spend more time with her."

"Wow!"

"Pretty good idea, right?"

"No! It's the dumbest fucking thing I've ever heard!"

"Alright," Tiller said, "Let me put it another way. If you don't do this, you'll always wonder if you missed out on something. That's what will drive you away from Beth."

Damn, he might be right.

Seeing Ty was considering his idea, Tiller added, "Besides, it's not like you are going to sleep with her at an airbase."

Ty had not made that leap. Did Luna think they would in the time she was here?

CHAPTER
FORTY-TWO

WHEN TY WALKED into the team's mission room, it was as he had found it the night before.

Emotions were high, and voices were raised.

After his admission to Tiller on the runway, Ty ran to take a quick shower, grab a bite to eat, and made it to the scheduled meeting with minutes to spare.

Walking in, he was shocked to find it was Aimes doing the yelling. "How the fuck did we lose the only lead we've had in days?"

Under distress, Newbold replied, "Sir, the drone pilot followed international law. We couldn't track the boat once it was out of sight in Iranian waters. It stayed on mission for four more hours but could not relocate it. Low on fuel, it returned to base."

"Are you saying we don't fly drones into Iranian airspace?"

"No, sir. I'm saying we didn't have clearance for this particular mission."

The heated exchange told Ty all that he needed to know.

The boat entered Iranian waters to make a delivery or because it knew a high-altitude drone was tracking it. Either way, it didn't matter.

The team saw firsthand how weapons were being moved into and out of the city, which was most important.

"Colonel," Ty interrupted, "Sir, I understand the frustration. But we still have a lot of strong intel about the dry dock and how the river is being used. If we continue to focus on the three locations, it won't be long before we dig up more."

Newbold gave Ty an appreciated nod for defusing the intense situation.

Aimes considered his points. "Alright then, let's get back to it."

Ty took the Colonel's words as permission to proceed with the morning briefing.

The team would be deployed again to the target locations. But Ty wanted both Knight and Tiller back at the dry docks. He and Henry would split the other two locations.

That's when his plan took a detour. "Captain, I want you here with me today," Aimes said.

Ty's eyebrows pinched in confusion, but he had no choice. "Yes, sir."

He had no idea why he was being ordered to stay back. Regardless, the team could only cover two of the three locations.

The briefing took another five minutes to finish. Once complete, everyone loaded up to depart to Barsa for the day.

Seeing them off, Ty took the opportunity to speak with Aimes. "Sir, I didn't want to ask in front of the team. But…"

Ty didn't pose a question, yet Aimes understood what he was asked. "Sorry, Captain. I know you want to be with your team. But I need you to do something for me."

As he had suspected, it had to do with Hayes being on the base.

The two senators would speak to a crowd of soldiers this morning. While no one knew the topic or what would be said, Ty was expected to be present to show his support.

"Call it a goodwill gesture," the Colonel said, "Don't oversell it. But, clap at the right moments. Laugh when you're supposed to and appear genuinely over the hostility from the past month."

Begrudgingly. "Roger that, sir."

Ty was pissed. Aimes was only partially right. He did want to be in the field with the guys. But, what he wanted more than that was to avoid Hayes. And Luna.

The base turned out in droves to hear them speak in an empty hangar.

Looking around, Ty guessed there had to be nearly a thousand soldiers crammed, shoulder to shoulder, to hear a couple of politicians spurt out nothing but bullshit.

In place of a stage, a flatbed truck was pulled into the center of the vast space. The base commander was standing in the back, using a microphone and a handful of small speakers sitting on top of the truck's cab to project his voice.

The first up to speak was Wrzesinki.

The four-term Senator wasted no time in working up the crowd. "From what we hear back in West Virginia, ya'll are over here kicking some ass!"

The crowd ate it up.

It didn't matter that at this particular airbase, no one had flown a combat sortie where they released a weapon in more than three months. Or that there had not been a recorded insurgency attack in Southern Iraq in twice as many months. None of that mattered.

No. Senator Wrzesinki knew her audience and how little it took to get them hollering and clamoring for more.

She didn't disappoint.

For nearly ten minutes, Ty stood in amazement as she spoke about the great march of democracy and how this room of heroes was the tip of the spear.

As Aimes had asked, he clapped at all the right moments and smiled so all those around him could see the past month's events were water under the bridge.

To help sell it, he occasionally joined in with a *whoop* and even a few loud *oorahs*.

That much would be expected from a Marine officer.

While he projected excitement, Ty's stomach wrenched. His fists were clasped once more at the sight of the two politicians.

If Wrzesinki is talking this much crap, I can't wait for the bullshit Hayes spews; Ty thought as the Senator from Iowa stepped onto the truck's bed to thunderous applause.

The clapping and cheering lasted several minutes as Hayes started to speak before being cut off twice. Ty played along with a steady, half-assed clap as he looked over the crowd in disbelief.

Does no one remember what Hayes did a month ago?

As Ty scanned the crowd, he found Aimes just a few rows from the truck. Like him, the Colonel clapped slowly to maintain pretenses.

Once everyone calmed down enough for Hayes to be heard, like Wrzesinki, he fired them up again.

Yet, the next few minutes of Hayes' speech differed from his colleague's pro-American, pro-democracy lines.

No, Hayes' speech was a politically charged assessment of the current president's job and how *'he was failing soldiers, like all of you, by not doing more to bring you home faster!'*

That line got the biggest applause.

After a few more critiques of the administration's role in what Hayes called a *'mortally flawed Iraqi policy,'* he did something unexpected.

"Now, you all might have seen me recently in the news. Something about a hearing and some bad intelligence: I'm here today to set that record straight. And I need help."

The crowd didn't know how to respond. There was no clapping nor any hollering—just confused looks.

Hayes continued in a softer tone. "So, when I got off the plane, I saw someone in the crowd I needed to speak with."

SHIT! No way!

"I wonder if he's standing amongst you all right now. If so, I would love to invite him up here."

Several Marines and soldiers in Ty's vicinity looked at him, knowing exactly who Hayes was talking about. Yet not one of them outed him.

After a long silence in the hangar, Hayes asked, "Is he here? Is Captain Tyler Hudson in the room? If so, please, Captain, join me up here."

Now Ty had no choice. He couldn't escape through a backdoor to avoid the spectacle Hayes had thrust on him.

Instead, Ty straightened up, pushed his shoulders back, and stepped toward the truck.

Since he was the only person moving among the crowd, it didn't take long for Hayes to spot him. "Yeah, there he is. Ladies and gentlemen, a true American hero, Captain Tyler Hudson!"

The crowd cheered but with apprehension this time.

No one understood what was happening. Or what to expect once Ty climbed into the truck with a politician who had accused him of so much.

As he made his way through the parting mass, Ty looked over to see a wide-eyed Aimes. There were no words mouthed or gestures. Yet Ty understood what his commanding officer's look said: *keep it cordial, brief, and go with it.*

As Ty reached the truck's rear, a hand extended to usher him.

"Up you go," Luna said with a flirtatious tone.

As he placed his right foot on the steel step to lurch up, Luna put her hand on Ty's back. Unnecessarily pushing him upward. He couldn't help but notice her hand gradually run across his butt as she dropped it.

Glancing down at her, she gave him a quick wink.

Ty rewarded her with a flirty grin for her audacity.

Once the Marine was on the truck, Hayes extended his right hand to him in his own gesture of goodwill.

Shaking hands, Hayes pulled him in closer to wrap his left arm around his back.

"Captain," Hayes started but paused. "Actually, can I call you Ty?"

As if he had a choice. "Sure."

"Thanks. Ty, I owe you an apology. And I'm not too big a man to admit when I'm wrong, and I was wrong. I was given some bad intel and took it at face value. I accused you of horrible things. For that, I'm sorry."

The crowd went wild. Their applause was twice as loud as it had been before.

Wow, he's really good. Full of shit, but he knows what he's doing.

It took a moment for the applause to turn into a deafening chant.

Hayes for president! Hayes for president! Hayes for president!

Ty knew he had lost this round. Hayes had accomplished what he wanted by bringing him forward. And he couldn't do anything about it.

Ty said into the microphone, "Thank you, Senator. I accept your apology."

In a final gesture, Hayes pulled his arm from around Ty and opened both wide, gesturing for a hug.

With no choice, Ty embraced him.

In a public show of forgiveness, Hayes showed his true colors again in a hushed voice, "I'm still going to ruin you."

"Make sure you bury me 'cause you never want me to be this close to you again."

With a laugh, the Senator pulled back to raise his and Ty's arms as if he were a referee recognizing a champion boxer after a title fight.

CHAPTER
FORTY-THREE

TY HAD BEEN HUMILIATED.

Hayes had used him to, once more, advance his political aspirations.

Worse, Luna was privy to her boss' plans. Ty didn't expect loyalty from her, but that didn't lessen the sting of her betrayal.

How can she flip back and forth between us so easily? One moment, she's coming on to me. The next, she sets me up. It's all a game to her.

Off the truck, Ty made his way through the crowd. Shaking hands, giving high-fives, and faking a smile all the way to the back of the hanger. Once there, he turned to hear Hayes' closing words.

As the Senator was wrapping up, Ty slipped out a side door to escape before the clapping and chanting started again.

Briskly walking to the team's mission room, Ty took a deep breath and slowly exhaled. He knew he needed to calm down before Aimes caught up with him. The Colonel would have a strong opinion on what had happened, but Ty needed to show that he was unfazed by Hayes' actions. He needed to show that he was mission-focused with his team in the field without him.

Entering the mission room, Ty blurted out, "Sitrep?"

"Nothing to report. Everyone is in position. No movement yet at any location."

Just as Newbold finished speaking, the wooden door flew open.

Exasperated, Aimes barked, "That son of a bitch! I can't believe the balls on that guy."

In confusion, Newbold glanced back and forth between Aimes and Ty. "Wait, what happened?"

Recognizing the CIA's analyst wasn't there, Ty told him what Hayes had done.

Waiting for Ty to finish, Aimes asked, "It looked like he said something to you at the end."

Ty knew his commanding officer would have paid close attention to all the small details that most in the crowd would not have noticed. He also understood nothing was to be gained if he told the truth.

Making it up on the spot. "He thanked me for playing along."

Aimes didn't respond. He took in what Ty had said as he weighed Hayes' comment or took a moment to consider whether Ty had told him the truth. "Sorry you had to deal with that."

"Not a big deal. We all know what type of man he is."

Aimes laughed, "Oh yeah, he's a piece—"

Knock. Knock.

The loud double wallop on the door cut off Aimes. Drawing everyone's attention.

No one had ever knocked on the door before.

It was a mission room. The people on the base who had permission to enter didn't knock, and those without permission knew they shouldn't bother attempting to enter.

Since no one said anything, Ty spoke, "Umm… Who is it?"

"It's Luna. Can we talk?"

Are you kidding me? Ty thought, with the other men in the room looking in disbelief.

Answering before Ty, Aimes announced, "Come in."

With an aura of confidence, Luna stepped in. "Oh, I didn't mean to interrupt anything."

"Not at all," Aimes scowled, "We were just talking about the shit your boss just pulled. Maybe this is perfect timing, and you could tell us what he was thinking."

Luna stopped in the doorway to look at Ty for help.

The look that Ty returned as he crossed his arms and tilted his head in anticipation let Luna know she was on her own.

His response to her silent plea wasn't missed.

Luna didn't disappoint when she spoke. "I think the Senator made a public apology. It's time for you boys to move on."

Ty was unable to conceal his shock as his mouth dropped open. *Holy shit! I can't believe she just said that!*

Aimes let out a bellowing laugh. "Captain, I think we have this all wrong. She's the one with the big balls."

Newbold joined in on the laughter.

Ty didn't as he worked through ways to excuse himself so he could talk with Luna alone.

This wasn't the sort of time with her that Tiller had suggested he find. No, this would be a much easier conversation about what happened and the role she had played in it.

Turning to face his commanding officer, "Sir, permission to be dismissed?"

Aimes nodded.

Walking out, Ty noticed the sun was still low in the mid-morning sky. So much had already happened, and it wasn't even time for lunch.

Stopping between buildings, Ty asked, "Did you know he was going to do that?"

"Who's idea do you think it was?"

Ty fumed in anger. "It's all a big game to you. Isn't it?"

"No--"

He cut her off, "I wasn't finished. You flirt with me, act like you have feelings for me, and then help your boss by trying to destroy my life. Why?"

"Ty, I'm a bitch. I'm the type of girl who wants my cake and eats it. I thought you understood that."

Her honesty was shocking.

Pinching the bridge of his nose and rubbing his eyes. "I understood that you would never choose me over Hayes, but I never thought you would be the one coming up with the plans to ruin me."

Luna reached to take his hand, but Ty pulled away.

His cold gesture didn't phase her. "I'm sorry. I truly am. But, I have the opportunity to be the chief of staff for the next president. And right now, he's after you. I have to do my job."

"I have a job, too. And right now, my team is in the field."

When Ty stomped back into the mission room, neither Aimes nor Newbold said a word.

The heavy footsteps and scowl on his face were enough for them to know not to ask anything.

Stepping up to the table Aimes was standing at, Ty asked, "Sir, permission to join the team?"

There was no objection.

Arriving at location three, Ty ordered a coffee and sat at the corner cafe. Of the three locations, this was the preferred post for the guys.

Adjacent to the single-story, abandoned retail strip Henry had circled on the map was a string of stores, restaurants, and the small cafe that Ty was sitting at now as a high-probability target.

Much to his delight, the place served a respectable cup of coffee.

It was easy for the team reconning this building to blend in with people on the street while enjoying the local food and street market atmosphere the other two locations didn't have.

Sitting alone, in civilian clothes, Ty looked like any other foreigner who had come to Basra. He was there to make a lot of money by helping rebuild the city or exploiting its proximity to Southern Iraq's oil fields.

To help pull off the look, Ty purchased a British newspaper being sold in the cafe and had it opened on his small round table. But he wasn't reading it.

Nor was he paying much attention to the building across the street.

His thoughts were still on Luna, Hayes, and that morning's events.

How could I have been so stupid? Was the question he kept going back to as time passed.

As he had said to her, he *'never thought she would be the one coming up with the plan to ruin him,'* so how did he miss that she was his biggest adversary, not Hayes?

Ty had not only fallen for the honey-pot but genuinely thought Luna had feelings for him.

This was as bad as getting a private dance at a gentleman's club and convincing yourself that the dancer was into you.

How could I have been so stupid?

"Romeo One, this is Two. Come back," Tiller said.

"Go for One."

"Drones are inbound for the night. The team is returning to base."

Ty looked down at his watch to double-check the time. He had been in the city, alone in his thoughts, for more than eight hours. "Roger that. I'm going to sit on location for a bit longer. I'll be back later."

Tiller objected, asking to join his team leader, but Ty insisted he return to base with the rest of the Romeo Team.

Ty had found solace in his time alone.

Free to think.

Free to do just as Tiller had suggested earlier that morning. He had concluded that the grass wasn't greener.

After two more hours, Ty rose from his seat to start the long ten-minute trek back to where he had left his truck. The only bad thing about this location was that you couldn't park near the target building.

Looking at his watch, he noticed it was just after 8 p.m.

That's perfect.

It was mid-morning in Southern California, meaning his family would already be out and about for their Saturday.

Whether it was the guilt of deciding that Luna wasn't right for him or the burning need to declare his love, Ty jumped into his small truck, flipped open his phone, and found Beth's name in his contacts.

"Hey, love, I figured you and the kids were already at the zoo, but I had a few minutes. I wanted to call to tell you that I love you all. Everything is going good here, so there isn't anything to worry about. I'm just missing everyone and wanted to leave you this voicemail. Have a great day in San Diego, and take lots of pictures for me. I love you!"

The disappointment of Beth not picking up didn't outweigh the relief of being able to bring closure to all that had happened with Luna. With his phone still open, sitting in a truck in Basra, Iraq, Ty decided to free himself from her as best he could.

He scrolled down to Luna's name in his contacts.

And deleted it.

FORTY-FOUR

THE RIDE back to Ali Airbase was quick.

Alone, feeling free of Luna's gravity and recommitted to the love of his life, Ty did something he had never done before.

He sang as he drove.

He could only remember a few lines from the famous song he had karaoked to at Knight's engagement party, but it didn't matter. He repeated those lines at least thirty times on the road between Basra and the base.

With each pass, he grew louder. More confident he had figured out the rhythm.

Luckily, no one would ever know.

Pulling up next to the team's other trucks, Ty noticed two guys coming out of the building in his direction.

Oh shit! Ty swung open his door to jump out.

"Williams, when the hell did you get in?"

"Bout an hour ago. The walls in Langley were closing in on me, so I asked to come out here to work with you guys."

Williams hadn't been in Iraq since his Humvee was destroyed by a roadside IED. He was a welcomed sight.

Ty looked over to Tiller, who had also walked outside, "Yeah, Newbold said it had been a few days in the making, and he wanted it to be a surprise."

"Shit, this is awesome! Welcome back to Iraq, man," Ty exclaimed.

"Thanks. But Newbold filled us in on what Hayes did. You okay?"

"Yeah! It was a bullshit move, but all good on my end."

"Are you?" Tiller asked. "Cause it's not like you to stay out on mission without the team."

Tiller was right. Staying out without the team's support was dumb, and Ty wasn't one to make dumb choices.

"You're right. I needed to clear my head, so I stayed on location longer to work things out. But I'm good."

They started to walk toward the mission room when, in the distance, a voice called out. "Ty!"

The three men turned to see Luna walking quickly toward them.

"She's been here three times in the last two hours looking for you," Tiller said.

"I'm over this shit."

With raised eyebrows, Tiller asked, "Really?"

"Yeah, I took your advice, and you're right. It's not greener. I thought I had made myself pretty clear to her earlier."

Trying to play catch up, Williams asked, "What the hell have I missed?"

Before Ty could respond, Tiller blurted out, "It's complicated!"

As with their inside joke, Ty joined his bellowing First Sergeant in an uncontrollable laugh. Williams stood clueless, waiting for someone to explain.

But, before they could, Luna reached them.

"We'll see you inside," Tiller said before walking away.

Still feeling left out of the joke, Williams added, "Yeah, make it a quickie. We're expecting Aimes in a few minutes."

Playing along. "I'll be quick."

Having waited for the guys to walk away. "Hey," Luna started, "I was worried I wouldn't see you."

Ty didn't speak. Just stared at her with a blank expression on his face.

Nodding to acknowledge the cold shoulder she was getting. "I get it. You're still mad at me, and I don't blame you. But, before I left, I wanted to tell you again that I'm sorry. It was wrong of me, and I shouldn't have done that to you."

Softening his expression a little, "I appreciate that, but... Luna, it doesn't matter. We are on opposite sides of this, and whatever little thing I thought we had, it's over."

Luna took Ty's hand. "It's not over for me."

Not giving Ty a chance to speak, she leaned forward to kiss him.

Her lips meeting his, she let out a passionate breath as they parted, and her tongue pressed forward.

Ty's initial shock faded. Feeling the heat of her breath and the moisture of her tongue on his lips, he parted his to allow her in.

Pulling his hand out of hers, Ty embraced her right cheek before curling his hand to the back of her head, where he buried it in her hair.

His left hand found the small of her back, and he used it to pull her in tighter to his body.

They had forgotten the world around them. They were new lovers in a kiss of passion, teetering on the verge of something more.

It was Luna who pulled back first. "I'm not over you."

Breathing heavily. "I can tell."

"I want you so bad," she said before rushing in for a second kiss.

This time, Ty pushed back. But not before they had shared another long, wet embrace.

"Luna, this isn't right."

"It feels right. And I think you feel it, too."

In a few short minutes, Ty had reversed everything he had thought about and decided on during his long day alone. He was the spinner at the end of a yo-yo, and Luna had pulled on the string.

Damn, I want her. Bad.

Stepping back, Luna said, "I have to go. I was able to delay our flight to Bagdad, but I have to go now."

Ty struggled with how to respond.

He wanted to ask when he would see her again. But that went against his decision less than an hour ago when he called his wife and deleted Luna's contact from his phone.

Forgetting everything, he asked, "What is it about you that has me so twisted?"

"We fit together, Ty. It's that simple."

There was no argument.

There were no words to protest that they did or didn't fit better than he did with Beth. *Is she right?*

Giving him a flirty smile, "Besides, if you think you're twisted now, wait til we sleep together."

Ty let out a defensive chuckle. Refusing to admit that's what he wanted.

Luna, having to go, moved in for one more kiss.

This one was softer, less in the heat of the moment.

Instead, it felt loving. The type of kisses Ty shared only with Beth. His wife.

With her gone, Ty stood at the door and wiped his mouth again, ensuring it didn't look like the two had just had a teenage make-out session.

Entering, the team, now including Williams, turned to him.

Williams spoke first. "Wow, you were right. You did make it quick."

For five minutes, the team piled on Ty for Luna's puppy-like attachment to him and said that since he was married, he should *'pass her off to Williams, who would at least give her more than a couple minutes of love.'*

After taking everyone's crap, Ty said, "Alright. Alright. I deserve all of this, but she's gone. And Hayes along with her."

"Yeah," Williams said, "you're a better man than I am for not punching him in his smug ass face in front of everyone."

"Oh, I wanted to kill him. WAIT! Shit, I can't say that."

Everyone broke back out in laughter. Ty had just told a group of Marines and a CIA officer that he wanted to kill a sitting U.S. Senator. He could be brought up on charges if spoken to a different audience. So, when he realized the meaning behind his words and tried to backtrack, the team lost it.

"What's so funny?" A deep voice called from the doorway.

In their moment of amusement at Ty's expense, no one had noticed Colonel Aimes come in.

Straightening up, Ty answered, "Sorry, sir. Just celebrating Hayes leaving with a few jokes."

"Are you done? Or should I come back?"

"Done, sir."

"Alright, then. Why doesn't someone tell me about moving day at our prime location?"

His question brought the room back to reality.

But none came crashing back as hard as Ty. He hadn't been told about any activity at the dry dock, and his commanding officer, knowing more than he did, put Ty in a precarious position.

Tiller recognized that Ty didn't know anything, so he started from the beginning. "Sir, around thirteen hundred hours, two small trucks crossed the bridge to pull up to the front of the building. Four men unloaded several boxes and a few furniture items."

Ty tried to listen, but his thoughts were elsewhere.

They were still on Luna.

It had only been a few minutes ago, but he was already reminiscing about how good of a kisser she was. Fantasizing about what might have happened if they had kissed the night they had danced in Washington.

As they said goodnight outside the nightclub, she had hinted, *'My apartment is only a few minutes away.'*

Ty had resisted that night but now wondered if he would be so strong.

Clueless to what was going on around him, Ty concluded two things. First, he wasn't over Luna.

And two, he might have missed his opportunity by not taking her up on her offer that night.

"Captain Hudson, I would love to hear what you think," Aimes said.

Ripping Ty from his thoughts, he said the only thing he could think of. "Unless I'm missing something. Today was a bust."

With a pointed tone, Tiller asked, "How so?"

"Four guys unloaded some boxes, a couple of chairs, and what, you believe to have been curtains. Is that it?"

"Yes, sir,"

Ty had brilliantly recovered from not paying attention. Now, he had put Tiller and the rest of the team in an uncomfortable position by downplaying their intel.

Ty cleared his throat. "Yes, it's worth noting since it was activity at the only building we've had any luck. But I don't believe this is actionable, and it doesn't give us anything new on the weapons cache. Do you guys feel differently?"

"Well, not when you put it like that," Knight remarked sarcastically.

The room chatted about the significance of the intel for a few minutes. Ultimately, Newbold and Aimes deemed it non-valuable despite, as Ty had pointed out, occurring at the one location where the team had verifiable movement.

After the briefing, the team made their way to the mess hall.

Williams pulled Ty's arm to get him to slow down so the two could walk behind the team.

"So, what's this thing with Luna?"

Ty stopped. Allowing the team to move out of hearing distance.

"Shit, Marcus. I've fucked up!"

Ty told him about everything that had happened. Starting with Luna coming to see him after Hayes pulled him up in front of the crowd.

In typical fashion, Williams narrowed in on two details.

"So, this bastard told you he was going to ruin you as he hugged you, and then you kissed his chief of staff?"

"Yeah, I told you. I've fucked up."

Shaking his head, Williams said, "No, Ty. You're ruining yourself. Hayes doesn't have to do anything but let you continue down this stupid path."

CHAPTER
FORTY-FIVE

TY VAULTED OUT of his bed.

Flipped on his light and rushed to get dressed. All the while screaming for Romeo Team to "move your asses!"

Together, the team stacked up at the door in their barrack's common room. Henry, as he usually did, took point with Ty right behind him.

With a firm hand, Ty grabbed the Gunnery Sergeant's right shoulder.

Henry pushed the door open without a word and stepped out into the night. He moved to the right. Ty swung left out of the building with his M4 pressed tight to his cheek as he stared through its sight at the ready.

"Clear!" Knight yelled as the last person to exit the barracks.

It was just before midnight, but the entire airbase was lit with bright flood lights and a buzz of major activity. The loud sirens had just moments ago come to life with the blaring alarm of an imminent attack. As was the protocol, the team quickly loaded out for a potential firefight and exited their barracks.

"Move to HQ," Ty called out.

With no looming threat, the team lowered their weapons to jog the two hundred meters to their mission building.

In the background, the sirens' screams gave way to the deafening roar of fighter jets taking to the sky, the rumble of armored vehicle engines accelerating toward the base's perimeter walls, and the shouts of commanding officers ordering their Marines and other soldiers into positions.

Ty had experienced insurgent attacks on bases before.

In his first tour, during the battle of Fallujah, mortar attacks were a nightly occurrence. The enemy would lob a few mortar rounds inside the base's walls from predetermined sites and then break down and flee before they could respond.

While the attacks rarely resulted in casualties, they were always enough to bring the entire base to combat readiness for the rest of the night. This tactic was a much more effective form of psychological warfare than causing any meaningful damage or loss of life.

Tonight was different.

This wasn't some tiny base at the edge of a known hostile insurgency zone or a far outpost in the mountains. This was Ali Airbase, the second-largest coalition military installation in Iraq.

Any attack here would be quickly squashed.

Rushing into HQ, Newbold and Williams were already there. Neither looked up from their computers as the team came piling in.

Looking for answers, Ty walked over to Newbold. "What's going on?"

Not taking his eyes off his screen, Newbold replied, "Major explosions within the Green Zone. There are reports that insurgents have breached the walls and have engaged in a massive firefight."

"Holy shit," Tiller said.

The Green Zone was a vast area located in the heart of Baghdad and the center of the newly established Iraqi government. While the U.S. or any other coalition military didn't consider it an active base, it was heavily fortified and housed tens of thousands of troops.

It had been touted as the most secure area in Iraq and the only place in Baghdad free from insurgency attacks.

"Any direct threat to us?" Ty asked.

"None. Well, that we know of. But, we're on high alert until things are figured out in Baghdad."

"Hey! Check this out," Williams hollered.

He moved his laptop over to a tall table next to a large screen and plugged a cord in. After a moment of light flickering, the screen came to life.

"Oh my God," Newbold said.

The live drone footage was of Gate Seven on the western side of the Green Zone. What was supposed to be a large checkpoint, with three different pill boxes supported by armored vehicles and numerous concrete barriers to slow incoming traffic, was now a massive crater in the ground.

The night vision imagery from the drone showed the body heat of scores of insurgents charging through what remained. They were not being met with any resistance.

"That had to be two one-thousand-pound bombs to wipe out the gate and leave a crater that big," Henry mumbled.

"Yeah," Williams said, "Shit, I can't count how many there are."

Aimes stormed into the room. "What's the sitrep from Baghdad?"

As Newbold started filling in the Colonel, Ty looked at Tiller and nodded toward the back of the room.

By themselves, near the door, Ty asked, "Does this make any sense to you?"

"Which part? The full frontal attack on the Green Zone or sending what appears to be hundreds to their death?"

Ty nodded in agreement. "Exactly! This doesn't add up. There is no way they can take the Green Zone or reach any of the HVTs inside. So, why do it? Why waste so many lives?"

"Classic diversionary tactic, but what are they planning that would require that big of a red herring?"

Noticing the two of them chatting near the door, Williams walked over. "Whatcha guys thinking?"

"We're thinking it is a precursor to something bigger," Ty said.

Pointing back at the screen. "You don't think that's big?"

Tiller replied first, "That's it, sir. That's too big of an attack on the most fortified area in the country. There's no way they win that battle. It's a diversion."

He gave it no thought before loudly saying, "I'm lost. You think they're attacking the Green Zone as a diversion?"

The entire room turned to the three Marines standing in the back. Ty didn't think Williams intended to bring that much attention to their conversation, but his tone and elevated voice did just that.

Ty approached Aimes. "Sir, these are pawns being moved on a chessboard as a distraction while the queen gets into position. It's a rope-a-dope in boxing waiting for our forces to collapse into the Green Zone. Something else is about to happen."

"What?" Newbold asked.

"I don't know, but whatever it is, it'll be bigger than this."

"Ty, they are storming the area with hundreds, if not thousands of men. Are you suggesting they are all running to their deaths as a coordinated effort to distract us?" Williams sarcastically asked.

Ty twisted to look at his friend. "Yes! That's exactly what I'm saying."

Aimes had stayed quiet through the entire exchange.

Ty had no idea if his commanding officer was considering their points or waiting for Williams and Newbold to talk some sense into him.

The Colonel turned his attention back to the screen. "Are there similar attacks at other gates?"

"Yes, sir," Newbold answered. "Reports are that Gate Five has also been bombed and is being overrun. And at least one of the north gates has been attacked, but thus far, have repelled the enemy."

The room was quiet as everyone waited for Aimes' assessment and orders.

"Alright, Captain. I get your point. So, what do you propose?"

Ty had been considering this while deflecting jabs from Williams and waiting for the Colonel to conclude his assessment. "Sir, we need to put together a short list of potential other targets in the area and ensure they're prepared."

Aimes looked around at Romeo Team. "There's nothing else we can help with from here, so get it done."

The team jumped into action.

After stowing their weapons along the wall, they gathered around the large table in the center of the room.

"Ty, where do we begin?" Tiller asked.

He considered this for a moment.

"Let's break into small teams. That way, we can work the problem from multiple angles. Williams, take Henry and Knight to identify possible infrastructure targets. Newbold, take Tiller to look for anything new in the region. I'll take—"

Newbold cut Ty off. "Sorry, what do you mean by anything new?"

"Any event, recent movements, or new arrival of dignitaries. You know…"

Ty stopped mid-sentence.

The metaphorical light bulb turned on for everyone at the table.

"No way," Henry said. "That's impossible."

"Breaching two Green Zone gates was supposed to have been impossible, too," Tiller quipped.

Newbold flipped open his laptop to start banging its keys to log in. "I don't think the company would have their travel itinerary, but I'll make some calls."

Seeing the team's flurry of new activity, Aimes walked over. "You guys have something?"

Williams and Ty shared a look across the table. Each asked the other if they should share their thoughts or keep their mouths shut until they had more intel.

"Sir, just a theory as of right now. So, we are running it to ground," Williams said.

Aimes wasn't going to let that flimsy excuse get by. "A theory on what could be bigger than this Green Zone attack."

"Sir," Ty started, "the most significant event happening right now is the arrival of the Senate delegation in Baghdad."

Aimes' eyes went wide. "And they were heading to the Green Zone. Have they arrived?"

"Not that I can tell," Newbold said.

Just as the CIA case worker completed his sentence, his phone vibrated in his pocket. Pulling it out to look at who was calling, "Shit, I need to take this."

Aimes turned his attention to Ty and Williams, "We need to find out if they've landed in Baghdad."

Before anyone could speak, Newbold repeated the words spoken to him by the other person on the phone, "Their convoy has been hit!"

"What?" Ty asked.

He held up his finger to tell Ty to hold as he got more information.

"Sir, hold on, I'm putting you on speakerphone with the team here. Repeat what you just said."

"Okay, can you hear me?" A familiar voice said.

"Yes," Newbold said.

"Less than ten minutes ago, a convoy carrying the Senate delegation was ambushed. They had landed at Baghdad International and were en route to the Green Zone when this attack started. They were rerouted back to the airport for security," Preston said.

Sean Preston, the Deputy Director of Counter Terrorism, whom Ty had met at the BBQ with Aimes, was in Langley getting real-time intel.

"What happened?" Aimes asked.

"Initial reports are that it was a well-coordinated attack. They disabled the two lead and the rear armored vehicles. Then, they collapsed on the others in large numbers. Right now, we can confirm that both senators have been taken hostage."

Ty's thought drifted to Luna. "Any other casualties or known KIAs?"

"The entire detachment," Preston replied. "ETA for boots on the ground is three minutes, but from the drone footage, everyone is down."

Ty was afraid asking specifically about a young, dark-haired woman would be too obvious, so he refrained.

"Sir, this is Newbold. Is there any effort to relocate the senators before they're lost in the wind?"

"Yes! Forces have been redirected from the Green Zone attack to support finding them."

Looking at Aimes, Ty said, "If it was that coordinated, and ten minutes have passed, then they're in the wind."

FORTY-SIX

"I CAN'T BELIEVE that I was kicked out, too," Williams scoffed.

Ty took a sip of coffee from a styrofoam cup. "I can't believe how pissed Aimes was. Did you see his face when Newbold told him he couldn't stay either?"

"Yeah. I've known the man for four years; I've never seen him turn so red. I bet he's still mad."

After the call with Preston, the team watched drone footage from over the Green Zone. As expected with a diversionary assault, the insurgents withdrew as soon as the primary mission was completed. They had breached two well-guarded gates while making their way several blocks before retreating.

For over an hour, there had been no word on the kidnapping of Senators Hayes and Wrzesinki.

Ty had been doing a great job keeping a stern, emotionless facial expression, but he was starting to get aggravated. With no news from the response team that had arrived at the ambush site, he was getting frustrated with Tiller and Williams' constant attention to him.

After the second time, Williams asked *'how are you doing,'* Ty replied, "Marcus, you ask me that again, I'm going to stab you in the neck."

Just after that exchange, Newbold got a second call from Preston.

Ty watched his face intently as he listened to whatever was said on the other side of the phone. Either noticing he was being watched or in response to something that was said, Newbold's eyes darted up to Ty's before they scanned the rest of the room in a look of bewilderment.

What's that look for? Ty thought as he glanced around.

"Hey guys," Newbold said, snapping his phone shut. "There's no news on Senators Hayes and Wrzesinki. But, we do know that Luna was also taken hostage, along with two Army soldiers."

Ty suddenly felt relieved that Luna was alive and not among those killed during the ambush.

But the feeling didn't last.

His fear abruptly turned to knowing that if they took her hostage, they would torture her before either killing her or using her as leverage.

"What do you mean by *'I can say'*?" Aimes snapped. "Is there intel you can't share?"

Ty had not picked up on the words Newbold had chosen to use.

After taking a moment to think about how to respond, "I'm sorry, sir. But I have been told to clear the room of everyone, so I need the team to clear out."

"Understood," Aimes said. "Captain, move your team out."

"Not just them, Colonel. You and Williams need to go, too. I need the room cleared of all non-essential CIA personnel."

That was when Ty saw Aimes lose his cool for the first time.

The Marine Colonel came unglued, berating Newbold for keeping secrets and not being a team player.

To his credit, Newbold took it.

He didn't argue, fire back at Aimes accusations, or try to reason with the man verbally assaulting him.

He kept a straight face while he listened to the five-minute temper tantrum.

Ty didn't wait until it ended before securing his rifle and heading for the door. Romeo Team followed.

That's when Aimes took a breath, and Newbold swooped in to speak. "Sir, this was a well-organized plan. We haven't had this level of organization since 9/11. They knew the Senate delegation was in the country and their route from the airport to Green Zone. We need to find out how they knew that."

"So, you're assuming that information came from someone with that knowledge? Possibly, someone on the base or, perhaps, in this room. Is that what you're saying?" Williams asked.

"No, I'm not. But that's protocol, and I don't have a choice," Newbold replied.

As the sun rose, the threat level at Ali Airbase was lowered.

Ty instructed the team to return to their barracks and get a few hours of sleep before regrouping to head into Basra for the day.

It had been five hours since Newbold had kicked the team out, and Ty was still on edge.

As everyone strolled toward the barracks, Ty asked Williams if he wanted to grab breakfast. The mess hall was empty. Most base personnel opted to go back to sleep rather than get chow. With no line, it took two Marines seconds to get food and grab a seat.

"Do you think it was an inside job?" Williams asked before shoving a fork full of scrambled eggs into his mouth.

"I don't know. It would make sense given how it unfolded."

With a mouth full. "You know—"

"Yeah, I know."

Williams alluded to something Ty understood when Newbold asked them to clear the room.

He would be their primary suspect.

Having been accused of war crimes by Hayes and their public battle during the hearing put Ty in the agency's crosshairs. The coincidence of his being at Ali Airbase when the delegation arrived would be difficult to ignore.

His concern for Luna had grown throughout the early morning hours. But Ty was also fretting about what Newbold was digging into. Every aspect of his life would be examined, reexamined, and then looked through a third time, trying to find the smallest detail that could link him to the ambush.

Exhausted and with nothing more to say, they ate in silence.

Still hungry, Ty got up for seconds. "Hey Johnny," Ty said, reading the name tag of the soldier serving breakfast, "can I get a few more sausages?"

The young man dropped four sausage links on Ty's plate before asking with a New England accent, "Anything else for you, sir? It's slow this morning, so we have time to make you a latte or a macchiato if you'd like."

Ty stared at him for a moment. There was something about him that felt familiar.

It wasn't deja vu, but a recent memory was stubbornly not returning to him. Ty thought it through, trying to place the soldier. He might have seen him while getting served food before, but that wasn't it.

Ty looked again at his name tag and then over to the two fancy coffee machines. It all came together. Ty's eyes widened as he remembered why Johnny's name and the fancy coffee felt familiar.

Grabbing the sausages by hand. "Thanks, Johnny!" Running past Williams, "I think I have something!"

The two Marines barged into the team's mission room—startling Newbold, whose head was buried in his computer.

"What the hell, guys!" Newbold yelled.

Choking on his last piece of sausage, Ty spit out, "Johnny! The staffer's name who leaked Hayes' travel itinerary to the media."

"Slow down. Who did what?"

Ty told Newbold and Williams about his eavesdropping on Luna in the coffee line the day before the Senate hearing. She and another woman were complaining about a lower-level staffer named Johnny accidentally leaking Hayes' travel schedule to the media.

"Yeah, apparently Hayes was super pissed, and Luna and the other woman were trying to figure out how to save the guy's job."

Newbold looked back at his laptop while Williams asked a few follow-up questions. Neither appeared to be taking the information seriously.

Completing what he was doing, Newbold said, "Sorry, Ty. There isn't a staffer named Johnny on Hayes' website."

"Then maybe he was fired."

"I could look into it, but it's not a priority right now."

Seeing Ty's conviction, Williams asked, "Is there any chance I could look into it? You can continue your work, and I can chase this down."

Waving his hand, dismissing the two, Newbold said, "Sure, go for it. But not in here."

Williams grabbed his laptop, and the two exited the building.

Walking toward the barracks, Ty asked, "Do you think this is a good lead?"

"Sure. It has to be better than anything they have right now."

"What makes you think that?"

"Cause Newbold didn't dismiss it right away. He looked up the name on Hayes' website."

"But he didn't do anything more after it wasn't there."

"Yeah, but that doesn't eliminate it as a lead. Let's do some digging and see what we find."

Ty was impressed with how methodically his friend approached the work. He asked Ty to repeat the story. Digging in with questions about every little detail.

Williams logged into his computer after asking questions for twenty minutes and started working silently.

"Here you go. There was a media specialist named John Meadows, added to Hayes staff a year ago, but as Newbold said, he's not on the website anymore."

"Okay, maybe Hayes doesn't put his entire staff on his website, or, like I said, he got fired."

"Let me cross-check his name in the system."

A few more minutes passed, and Ty's anxiety got the better of him. He got off the bench and started to pace.

On his sixth or seventh pass, he heard Williams gasp for air. "What! He's dead. A news article in a local Iowa paper reads, '*John Meadows, 31, died Friday evening in a car accident.*' It also mentions that he had worked for Hayes before recently taking a job at a local news station."

"Friday evening, as in two nights ago?" Ty asked.

"Yeah."

"That has to be more than a coincidence, right?"

"Umm… it has to be. Let's take this to Newbold."

This time, the guys didn't barge into the building. Instead, Williams stepped in alone as Ty waited outside. "Hey, I think I have something."

"What?"

Williams read Newbold the same lines from the news article that he had to Ty.

When Newbold didn't respond, he asked, "That's something, right?"

"Yeah, that's something. Is Ty outside?"

"He is."

"You two go find Aimes and get back here. Something has happened."

COLONEL AIMES WASN'T AS contentious when he returned to the mission room. As they rushed back, he shared a few pointed quips about getting kicked out of his own HQ. Ty acknowledged the comments but didn't add to them. Instead, he filled Aimes in on what Williams had found on Hayes' staffer, John Meadows.

"What did Newbold say?" Aimes asked.

"Just that he agreed it was significant."

"Has he cleared you yet?"

Ty hadn't thought about that.

He knew he would be under investigation, but not that he would have to be cleared for duty by someone. "Not that I'm aware of, sir."

Walking in, this was the first question Aimes asked, "Has Hudson been cleared?"

Nodding, Newbold replied, "He has. I have informed Deputy Director Preston of the intel he and Williams found on John Meadows, and he's making inquiries."

With a pointed tone, Aimes said, "Good. So, what do you need from me?"

"A video was posted online twenty minutes ago."

Again, with a hostile tone. "Are you going to allow us to see it?"

"That's why you are in the room, sir."

Ty was relieved he had been cleared. But now he was concerned about what he would see in this video. Insurgents were known for posting videos torturing hostages or worse, executing them.

Walking to the large screen, Ty asked Williams, "Have you seen it?"

Whispering, "No. I didn't know it existed until he just told you guys."

The video started to play.

"Just a warning, guys, it's pretty intense," Newbold said.

Ty controlled his breathing as Luna appeared on the screen with the other four hostages. She was seated in a chair next to Wrzesinki.

Behind the two women were the three male hostages.

Hayes stood in the center, flanked on both sides by Army soldiers.

All five were blindfolded, with their hands tied in front of them. Each showed different signs of being in a firefight.

Ty immediately noticed the dried blood along the right side of Luna's head. It appeared to be coming from her ear. Most likely, it was a ruptured ear drum from head trauma.

Hayes also had blood on him. But, the blood that covered his light blue dress shirt didn't appear to be from wounds he had sustained. Rather splatter from someone else.

Behind the staged hostages, a rug or tapestry was being used as a background. In the center was a black flag with a large white sword and Arabic words. Nothing or no one else was visible.

After a moment of just the hostages on the screen, an Arab man wearing a blue turban, a tan shirt, and a mustache stepped into the frame from Luna's side.

He didn't have a mask on, but Ty didn't recognize him.

"Shit, that's Al-Abbasi," Williams muttered.

This was the low-level enforcer for the Iraq Special Security Organization that had risen to power and whose weapons Romeo Team was tracking. Putting the name to a face, Ty knew of his brutal reputation. His heart started to beat faster as he feared the worst.

Al-Abbasi started to speak in Arabic. Having been in Iraq several times, Ty had learned some of the language but did not know enough to follow along.

Reading the room, Newbold started to translate. "This should be a lesson to the West that you are not as safe as you believe. While you think you're winning this war, Allah has reminded you that your sins will not be forgotten. We will fight on and outlast you. We will..."

Newbold stopped speaking to look toward Ty as Al-Abbasi continued in the background.

Looking over to make quick eye contact, Ty's heart filled with fear as he could think of only one reason Newbold would be looking at him now.

Something terrible was about to happen to Luna.

Slowing, turning his attention back to the screen, Ty saw Al-Abbasi reach down and grab her by the hair. Lifting her off the chair, he reached to clutch her chin with his other hand as he pushed her head forward toward the camera.

Luna cried out in fear.

Tears streaming down her face as she was powerless against her captor.

Newbold picked up with the translation again.

"You insult Allah by sending your whore women to do your bidding and are fools not to expect retribution. As his hand, I will do his work!"

Al-Abbasi threw Luna on the ground in front of the chairs.

Luna let out another cry, "No, please don't. No, please don't kill me!"

In the background, the other four hostages started to cry and shake in fear as they heard Luna's cries for mercy.

Someone outside the frame reached in to hand Al-Abbasi a long, curved knife.

Ty started to tremble. His head spinning.

Less than a day ago, he had spent a heated moment of passion with Luna. Slipping his fingers through her long dark hair in a completely different scenario than how Al-Abbasi had in the video.

While he didn't know how he felt or what the future had in store for them, he knew he had feelings for her. Yet, he was as powerless as he was about to witness her death.

Al-Abbasi pulled her up to her knees. Standing behind her, he held the knife above his head and screamed, "Praise be to Allah!"

From off the camera, several other voices join in on the chant.

"Praise be to Allah! Praise be to Allah! Praise be to Allah!"

In an unexpected move, a masked man stepped into the camera frame to grab ahold of the Army soldier standing behind Luna at the beginning of the video. He pulled the trembling, young black man to the front next to Al-Abbasi, who shoved Luna back to the ground.

"No! Please God, No!" She screamed.

Al-Abbasi and the masked man moved swiftly to position the soldier in the center of the frame. Ripping off his blindfold and shoving his head down so that he was bent at the waist over Luna. The young soldier's eyes blinked rapidly to orient to the light before becoming fixated on the camera.

Al-Abbasi screamed, "Praise be to Allah!"

In a quick movement, he pulled the long, curved knife across the soldier's throat as if he were cattle being sacrificed to an ancient God.

A deep red wave of blood spit out over Luna as she cried out.

The masked man struggled to hold the soldier up as his body went limp and his blood gushed.

Watching, Ty could see the moment his life expired as the young soldier's body went motionless.

Once satisfied enough blood had been spilled, Al-Abbasi waved his free hand to the masked man, who dropped the soldier's lifeless body onto Luna.

The video went black.

Ty was speechless. He stared at the dark TV screen, completely lost.

Aimes broke the silence. "When was this taken?"

"Our best guess is within the last hour. It was posted online twenty minutes ago. I was watching it for the first time when Marcus came in with the intel on John Meadows," Newbold replied.

Taking his eyes off the large screen, Ty said, "What now?"

Newbold ran his fingers through his short hair. "I don't know. Of course, we're analyzing it, but I suspect we won't find anything to help pinpoint a location."

"What makes you think that?" Aimes asked

"Just my opinion, sir. Preston is running lead, and, as you can imagine, all resources are being pulled in, but there's not much to go on."

The room moved into side conversations. Each person needed to process what they had seen in their own way.

Ty walked over to Williams. "Can you play it again?"

He nodded and hit play.

Williams must have noticed how difficult it was for Ty because, after a moment, he walked away—leaving him alone to watch the video.

And, then, a third time.

Seeing Luna's fear, her cries for mercy, and then seeing her get covered with the blood of the slain soldier didn't get easier for Ty the more he watched it. After the third viewing, he rejoined everyone gathered around a table.

Aimes and Newbold discussed the possibilities of the hostages still being in Baghdad or if they would have been moved. Williams had his head buried in his laptop. At the same time, the rest of Romeo Team chatted about the level of planning and execution that had to have gone into the diversion at the Green Zone and the ambush on a protected convoy.

Although everyone appeared to be consumed in their work or conversation, Ty could sense the subtle looks he was getting.

Each tried to hide it, but everyone was glancing in his direction to see how he was holding up.

Listening to the discussions, Ty knew the best thing he could do was act normal and join in on one.

Inserting himself into the conversation between Aimes and Newbold, Ty said, "It wouldn't have been that difficult to get five hostages out of Baghdad immediately after the ambush."

"It would be nearly impossible with the response on the streets and the amount of assets we had in the air," Newbold replied.

"None of which would've been looking for vehicles or trucks leaving the city. They would've been too focused on the fight."

Before Newbold could reply, Aimes said, "So, you don't think they're in the city."

"Sir, it would be easier to keep them in the city. But, if they were going to be moved, the best time would be while the fighting was still happening. Which also means we have work to do here."

Ty hadn't noticed the entire team stepping closer to listen to the exchange. So, when Tiller spoke next, it caught him off guard. "What work?"

Aware that he unintentionally gave a darted look to his First Sergeant, Ty tried to use a measured tone, "Think about what we know right now. We know that Al-Abbasi led this operation and that he has been using trucks to move weapons. Is there an easier way to move five hostages?"

"So, you think he would have used a truck if he moved them out of Baghdad?" Tiller asked.

"I do. So where are all the trucks we've been tracking right now?"

With an upbeat tone, Aimes agreed, "He's got a great point."

Newbold sighed as he reached for his laptop. "Yes, he does. I need to run this by Preston. In the meantime, Williams, I want you to work with a team back in Langley to get the locations of the eight trucks we've been tracking."

Aimes looked at Ty, "What are you going to do?"

"Sir, I'm putting my team back in Basra to sit on the three target locations. It's a long shot, but we can't rule it out."

CHAPTER
FORTY-EIGHT

"WELL, SHIT," Ty said. "I guess some things only sound good in theory or are too good to be true."

Tiller let out a low chuckle. "Yeah, but it was a damn good theory. Besides, it's given the team something to do that has made them feel like they've been helping."

The two Marine Raiders were returning to their truck after another long day in Basra.

The sun had set two hours ago. The city streets had settled in for the night. Exhausted and hungry, they were the last to leave their positions.

It had been almost three days since Luna and four others were taken hostage. In the nearly fifty hours since the first and only video was released online, Ty had only slept for a few hours.

The horrors of seeing Luna so vulnerable, pleading for her life, had plagued him in every quiet moment.

Even Beth could tell her husband was deeply bothered by what had happened. After news of Hayes and Wrzesinki's kidnapping broke in the States, she called Ty and left him a voicemail.

The two had spoken every day since.

Ty was cautious about what they said, knowing that the CIA monitored all calls into and out of the country.

During their morning call, Beth said, "Ty, I can tell you're upset about Luna. I don't know what you want me to say or how I can help you."

Ty didn't have an answer for her. All he could do was convince her that he wasn't upset for just Luna but for the entire situation.

He knew Beth too well to think she had bought his bullshit. Anytime Beth changed the topic of their conversation from Luna or Hayes to him, she was doing it because she didn't want to get upset. She, too, knew that they had people listening in.

Beth would tell Ty a story about the kids whenever she needed to change the conversation. That's how he discovered that Audrey had been given the lead role in her dance recital at the end of the month.

It was the first good news he had received in days.

"She'll never be a professional ballerina, but she looks adorable on stage," Beth joked.

"Will you be able to record it?"

"Yeah, the studio does it professionally, so I'll get a DVD afterward. You won't be able to see it until you get home."

It was an innocent enough comment, but Ty felt the sting in his wife's words. Once more, he was not there for a special moment.

Some fourteen hours later, Tiller and Ty returned to Ali Airbase with no word on the search for the hostages.

Frustrated, exhausted, and emotionally drained, Ty retired to his bunk.

I need a shower. But it's going to have to wait. He thought as he sat on the edge of his bed and took off his boots before something caught his attention.

On the small table in front of him was a picture of Beth and the kids. It was taken at the beach before Ty deployed. Beth ran to the local drugstore to have it printed, and she put it in a cheap black frame for him to take with him.

Seeing his family, his two girls with huge smiles, and his infant son with sand around his mouth, Ty broke down in tears.

He had been so obsessed with Luna that he had forgotten what he had. Not just trying to find Luna over the last few days. His infatuation with her began a month ago when he stepped into the coffee line behind her. What might have been an arbitrary decision had caused him to spend more time in the last month thinking of her than his wife and children.

Wiping snot from his nose, he began to bawl.

Stupid dumbass! What the fuck were you thinking?!?!

With tears flowing down his face, Ty lost his composure and started to hit himself in the face with his fist.

Whack! Whack! Whack!

The force of his third punch to his jaw cut his lip. His mouth filled with the taste of blood. He was a mess. Snot, blood, and tears flowed freely as he collapsed onto his flat pillow. And cried himself asleep.

"Ty! Ty! Wake up!" Tiller yelled from outside his door.

Opening his eyes. "What?"

Tiller pushed open his door to step into the room before coming to a dead stop. "Shit. You okay? What the hell happened?"

"Nothing. What's going on?"

Tiller paused for a moment to look over his Captain. "Ummm... A new video just hit the internet. Newbold is downloading it now."

"Okay, let's go," Ty said, getting out of bed.

"Hey," Tiller said, taking Ty by the arm, "Why don't you take a minute to get cleaned up?"

"Nah, I'm good to go."

Holding tight onto his arm. "No, seriously, Ty. You look like hell. You don't need Aimes to see you like this."

His tone suggested it was more than a suggestion. Ty agreed and walked into the team's bathroom. Seeing in the mirror what had alarmed Tiller.

A mixed stream of snot and blood had dried along his chin, creating a crusted patch of white and red-tinted residue. Worse, his right jawline had started to show shallow blue bruising.

Shit! This isn't good! Ty washed his face. Cleaning off the flaky remnants around his mouth and chin.

There was nothing he could do about the light bruising. The team's mission room wasn't well-lit, so all he could do was hope that no one would notice. Without a better option to hide his bruised face, he needed to get there.

Walking in, Ty found everyone in the room with anxious energy. It was just after midnight local time, yet intense discussions were happening.

Aimes, Newbold, and Williams were gathered around a laptop on the center table. Tiller and the rest of Romeo were broken into small cliques around the table.

"Why would they release a video this late at night?" Williams asked.

"It's only late for us," Aimes said, "Back in Washington, the prime-time evening news is about to start."

Absorbing this fact, Ty spoke for the first time, "Then there's a good chance this is going to be bad."

Newbold agreed, "Yeah, they'll somehow try to escalate or outdo the first. We should expect to see another execution."

"What's taking this so damn long?" Aimes snarled.

Newbold looked down at his laptop. "Sorry, Colonel, the internet sucks here, and this must be a larger file than the first."

Ty joined in on the nervous actions around the room by starting to fiddle with the simple gold wedding band on his left hand. When out on the field, he didn't wear it. It was the first time he had put it on in days.

As the minutes passed, Tiller stepped over to Ty, "Did you get any sleep?"

"A few hours. Thanks for the heads up back there."

"Of course. I got you."

Understanding Tiller's concern, Ty was about to respond further when Newbold yelled, "About damn time!"

As the video started, the team pushed forward to crowd around the large screen.

Just as with the first, it opened to hostages at the center.

"Holy shit," Knight called out, "They're torturing them."

Luna and Wrzesinki were seated side by side in two chairs. Hands bound in front of them but with no blindfold this time.

The two women were the only ones in the frame.

Wrzesinki's left eye was bashed in. So badly that it wasn't black and blue. It was swollen shut with a sizable blood-filled lump.

Ty had seen wounds like this before.

Wrzesinki's orbital bones in her skull had been fractured. Her eye was preeminently damaged. Her neck had a thick, deep red mark around it, as if she had just been hung in the last few minutes. Her clothes were torn and soaked in blood. She had no shoes.

Luna was in equally bad shape.

Her face, too, showed signs of being beaten. Unlike the elder Senator, Luna had no shirt on, just her black bra. At first glance, there appeared to be minor bruises on her body. Newbold suggested that they *were not bruising, rather burn marks.*

Looking at Luna's condition, Ty fumed angrily at what had been done to her. Equally upset that he wasn't in a position to help her. To save her.

As the seconds passed by, neither woman said anything.

They sat there, trembling.

Al-Abbasi stepped into the frame and started to speak.

Newbold translated, "As you can see, your women are frail. They bleed like fat pigs and scream for mercy. But, none will be given. Like the women and children you have murdered in your false war, each will meet their deaths."

Two masked men came into the frame to grab ahold of Wrzesinki. Forcing her to stand, they cut the rope that bound her hands together and pulled her forward.

"God, please no!" She screamed as she was forced to her knees. "Oh God!"

Al-Abbasi was handed a long sword.

Luna started to scream in the background. "No! You can't do this. You'll get what you want. You can't do this!"

The two masked men shoved Wrzesinki's head down toward the ground as they bent her arms backward. One of them placed his boot in the middle of her back as he took ahold of her arms.

Luna continued to scream.

The Senator's face could no longer be seen as it was facing the ground. Through Luna's cries, Ty believed he heard Wrzesinki saying the Lord's prayer just as Al-Abbasi swung the sword down.

And then a second time. A third. A fourth.

The Marines in the room gasped for air when Wrzesinki's head separated from her body after the fourth hit.

With her body on the floor, Al-Abbasi reached down to pick up her severed head by the hair. Holding it to face the camera.

Speaking, Newbold again translated, "I am the hand of Allah! Praise be to Allah!"

From off-camera, chants began. *"Praise be to Allah! Praise be to Allah!*

The insurgent leader walked off camera, carrying Wrzesinki's head.

Luna, alone, looked directly into the camera. "Save us."

CHAPTER
FORTY-NINE

TY WAS in an emotional spot he had never been to before. After this second video, he felt lost, helpless, and on the verge of losing control.

Fuck! I need air.

He turned without saying a word to walk out in the warm night air.

No one protested as he left. As the door shut behind him, he heard someone ask for the video to be replayed.

With his knees feeling like they would give out, he took a deep breath, trying to steady himself. Knowing he only had a moment to be alone before Williams or Tiller came out, he walked to the back of a truck and pulled the tailgate down.

Hopping on it, he stared at the distant dull lights of the airbase's runway.

Get it together. Get your shit together, Ty.

Lost and confused, he had only one choice- one person he would rely on for support. With trembling hands, he reached into his pocket for his cell phone.

"Oh my God, Ty," Beth said, picking up his call. "They just showed it on the news. Have you seen it?"

"Yeah, just a minute ago. Did they show everything?"

"I don't know. It was cut off when they shoved Senator Wrzesinki to the ground. Did they kill her?"

"Yeah."

"And Luna?"

Ty rubbed tears from his eyes, "No. Not yet."

"I am so sorry, love. I can't imagine what you're feeling. You know her and are having to see this."

He struggled with what to say. Guilt weighed heavy on his decision. Do I *tell her about the kiss? About how I've been fighting back feelings for Luna for the last month?*

Opting not to, "It's awful here for everyone. The kidnappers haven't asked for anything, so we think they'll continue to torture them and ultimately kill each in a video like this."

"Is there no intel on where they are or a rescue plan in place?"

"Not that I know of."

They stayed quiet for a moment on the phone. Each contemplated what to say next.

The first to speak again, Beth asked, "How can I help you?"

Her simple question tore at Ty's heart. While he struggled with his feelings for Luna, all his wife wanted was to help him. He had been selfish. So intoxicated by Luna that he had put his marriage at risk. Ty knew he would need to tell Beth the truth one day, but that couldn't be today. "I don't think you can. Just pray for Luna and everyone else and tell the kids I love them."

"And me?"

Whispering. "I love you most of all. I'm done with this war. I want to come home."

Beth started to cry. "I can't tell you how long I've waited for you to say that."

"I'm sorry it's taken—," Ty said before noticing Tiller and Knight walking up.

"Ty, you there?" Beth asked when he stopped mid-sentence.

"Yeah, sorry. The guys are walking over to me."

"Do you need to go?"

"I don't think so, but hold on one moment," Ty said, lowering the phone from his ear.

Tiller gave Ty an apologetic look. "Is that Beth?"

"Yeah, is everything okay?"

The two Marines hesitated before Knight spoke, "Sir, I think we have a lead."

This was not what Ty had expected. He was sure they had come out to check on him. Or give him a pep talk.

Turning his attention back to Beth, "Hey, love."

"I heard them. Go, Ty. Go stop this from happening."

Hanging up from his wife, Ty jumped off the tailgate. "So, what do you have?"

"Okay, so stay with us for a second," Knight began, "Remember a few days ago when we saw a couple of trucks moving stuff into the building at the dry docks?"

"Vaguely, I remember no one thinking it was anything."

"Right. It wasn't anything at the time," Knight said.

"Okay, so why is it important now?"

"The chairs," Tiller said

"And the backdrop," Knight added, hitting his First Sergeant on the shoulder for forgetting about it.

"Right, both the chairs and the backdrop. We saw a couple of guys unload two chairs that looked just like the ones in the video. And in the other truck, a guy pulled out what I thought were window curtains. But they were identical to the backdrop in the video," Tiller said.

"How sure are you?"

Knight and Tiller gave each a quick look.

"Very sure," Knight said.

Tiller, wide-eyed, added, "Ty, we wanted to bring this to you before the Colonel and Newbold. We know it's thin, but it feels significant."

Ty played the debriefing back in his head.

"Walk me through everything again. Start with the trucks pulling up to when you noticed the items in the video."

The two Marines took Ty through everything a second time, apologizing several times for not noticing the chairs or backdrop during the first video. But when Wrzesinki got pulled out of her chair in this video, Knight thought it looked familiar.

It dawned on Ty that it was Knight who had asked for the video to be replayed as he walked outside.

During the replay, Tiller also recognized the chair. The two started to examine the other items in the video. Thinking they had something, they came out to speak to Ty.

"Tiller, could you go inside and get Williams out here without making it too obvious?"

Tiller turned on his heels to march back inside.

Clearing his throat, Knight asked, "Sir, what are you thinking?"

"I think we need to review the drone footage from the night of the ambush. See if there was any activity at the docks."

Filled in on the story, Williams agreed that it was solid intel and that he could look over the drone footage.

"Best case," Ty said, "a truck or a boat pulls up, and we have evidence of them being unloaded."

"And worse case, there's nothing in the footage," Williams said before heading inside.

Playing catch up to the conversation, Knight asked, "Sir, why are we only focused on that one night?"

"The first video was released late that night. So, it would've been then if they were moved from Baghdad to Basra."

The three Marines stayed outside for a few more minutes, chatting about the possibility of it being the location and what would happen.

Coming out in a rush, Williams blurted, "Well, shit! There isn't any footage from that night."

"Wait… Why?" Tiller asked.

"With all the bases, including this one, going on high alert because of the attack on the Green Zone, all air assets were pulled back to protect the bases."

Knight asked, "What now?"

Determined to look into this, Ty ordered, "Nothing changes. We take this to Aimes and Newbold."

Neither were easy to convince.

Newbold questioned the ability to move the hostages from Baghdad to Basra between the time they were ambushed and the release of the first video.

Aimes thought some chairs and drapes were too thin to push up the command chain. Citing that Romeo Team had been *sitting on the location for the last couple of days without anything out of the norm happening.*

Ty went to object, but Williams cut him off, "Sir, I agree with your assessment. We haven't reviewed the drone footage for each of the last two nights. I want to view that before we dismiss this."

Aimes didn't object.

Williams and Newbold pulled up the nightly footage on two different computers, and the team began the ardent process of watching a building at night from ten thousand feet above.

This is going to take a while. Ty mumbled to himself as he put on a pot of coffee.

Returning to pour himself a hot cup, he was cornered by Colonel Aimes. "Hudson, are you squared away?"

Ty turned to see a concerned look on his commanding officer's face. "Sir, I'll admit it's been a rough couple of days, but I'm good to go."

He couldn't tell if Aimes was convinced but knew he didn't need to say anything more. The Colonel should speak next.

He poured himself a cup. "Let Williams and Newbold watch the videos. I want you and the team to work up an assault plan on the location if it turns out."

Tilting his head to the side, "Assault plan, sir?"

"Yeah, did you forget what one of those looks like?"

"Not at all, sir. We'll pull options together."

It was a long shot that the hostages were being held in a building already under surveillance. Yet, Aimes was right in that if it turned out to be the location, then an assault plan to rescue the hostages would be needed.

The prospect of taking the fight to the enemy energized Ty. When he shared the Colonel's request, the rest of the team jumped on the task.

They pulled aerial pictures of the dry docks, the target building, and a street map. Thrown across the large table at the center of the room, the team started to determine how they would execute the mission.

Williams screamed out two hours into their planning, "We have it! We have confirmation!"

Everyone dropped what they were doing to rush over to him, sitting at his computer.

"Here, look, guess who that is?"

"Holy shit, that's Al-Abbasi," Henry shouted.

The drone's angle to the building was just enough to make him out. The footage showed the insurgent leader standing under part of the loading dock roof that had not caved in.

"When was the footage taken?" Aimes asked.

"Twenty-four hours ago," Williams replied.

"What about him leaving the site since?" Newbold asked.

"I haven't gotten that far."

The idea that Luna had been in the building Ty and the team had been watching was a punch in the gut. They could have prevented everything that had already happened if they had known.

Newbold turned frantically to Aimes, "I need to report this to Preston right now."

Turning to his team, Ty said, "Romeo, we aren't done planning. Let's get back to it."

FOR ALL THE crap Washington gets, there are times when the wheels are well-greased. It had taken Newbold less than ten minutes to run the intel up the ladder, and the team was now awaiting a call from Sean Preston, the CIA's Deputy Director of Counter Terrorism.

Ty had met Preston less than two months ago when Aimes invited him and Beth to a BBQ on the beach at Camp Lejune. While the Yale-educated lawyer was initially intimidating, it didn't take Ty long to appreciate how down-to-earth and non-political he was.

Ty recalled thinking Preston was a guy who understood the war and how to win it.

So, when Newbold made the call, Ty was pretty confident.

Ring! Ring!

"This is Preston."

"Sir, this is Newbold. I have you on speaker with Colonel Aimes, Captains Hudson, and Williams. We have a possible location for the hostages, and the Raider team has a plan they can execute tonight. "

The Deputy Director didn't ask questions as Newbold explained how the team confirmed Al-Abbasi's presence on site.

When he cleared his throat, Ty knew what Preston would ask. "Do we have anything more recent?"

"No, sir. But, we also don't have any intel that shows him leaving."

"That's not the same as him being there."

"Understood, sir, but the belief is that the hostages are there. Worst case, we hit a known weapons depot."

Newbold's assertion created an awkward moment of silence.

Aimes spoke up, "Sean, it's George. What Newbold is suggesting is there's a minimal downside to hitting this location."

Aimes and Preston had a relationship where the Marine Colonel could address the Deputy Director by his first name. No matter how awkward it felt for everyone else in the room.

"I get that, George. But, this will still need presidential approval, and I'm not sure we have the intel for that."

Frustrated with the direction of the discussion, Williams leaned over the table so his voice would come through clearly on the call.

"Director Preston, Captain Williams here. Sir, we've executed missions on far less intel. Given the magnitude of the last video, we feel any action is better than no action."

"I agree, Captain. But, the President will need more."

"Other than a more recent photo of the man who just beheaded a senator, what other intel could we help you get? Sir." Ty said sarcastically.

This prompted Williams, standing next to him, to place his hand on Ty's shoulder as a gentle nudge to remember who he was talking to.

Quiet again. "Assuming the hostages are there, and right now I feel that's a big assumption, walk me through the plan. I'm looking at an aerial photo of the area.."

Aimes nodded for Ty to do it.

The Marine Captain took a deep breath before starting, "Sir, the location and terrain are ideal for an assault from the water. Romeo Team will requisition a local fishing boat upriver and use it for our infill. As we pass behind the wreck of the al-Mansur, we'll use the ship to shield our entry into the water. From there, we'll move on to shore. Any questions so far, sir?"

"I agree with an amphibious assault, but why not fast boat in?" Preston asked.

The team had worked through this scenario. "We considered that. But the river is at its widest point at the dry dock. There is too much risk the boats are spotted for us to come ashore unnoticed. The local fishing boat blends in with other nightly river traffic, and the shipwreck is perfect coverage."

"Okay, go on."

"Once onshore, we are thirty meters to the target building. Two teams will simultaneously breach, one from the north-facing main door and the other from the riverside cargo dock. Flashbangs go in, and we'll eliminate any threats before securing the hostages and remains."

"Exfil?"

"Well, sir, that's where we use the fast boats. Three boats from the USS Bataan in the Persian Gulf will make their way upriver to be our primary. Secondary will be by helicopter three clicks north, by northwest in a large empty lot."

"Probability of success?"

Before Ty could respond, Williams said, "Sir, we don't know the number of insurgents inside or the layout of the building. There's a risk they kill the hostages once we breach."

You asshole! Ty thought as he glared at Williams, but his friend wouldn't look in his direction.

In just those few words, Ty's plan might be rejected, and Romeo Team might not be green-lighted.

Also, giving Williams a what the hell look, Aimes said, "Yes, but that's a risk with every building we breach."

"Besides that, there's also the possibility of this turning into a significant firefight. Especially if you have to move to your secondary exfil," Preston added.

"Correct, sir," Ty said, "we'll need multiple air assets on site."

"Such as?"

"A high-altitude drone the entire time, along with Apaches and a gunship for close-fire support, should do the trick."

The request wasn't as big as it sounded. Ali Airbase was home to two Army UH-60 Apache squadrons and a wing of Air Force AC-130 gunships.

"How do we get better intel over the next twenty-four hours?"

Ty looked confusingly at the phone on the table.

"Twenty-four hours?" Williams asked.

"You're not expecting to do this tonight," Preston replied.

Holding his hand up to stop Williams or Ty from speaking, Newbold said, "The timeline is compressed, but it's the belief here that this plan can be executed tonight. Preventing a possible third video from being released."

Preston objected, arguing the timeline was too short and the intel not strong enough to confirm this was where Hayes and the hostages were being held.

While the Deputy Director made his case for holding for another twenty-four hours, Ty's frustration was building. He knew in his heart that this was the right location and that his team was in a position to do something.

It needed to be tonight!

It needed to be now!

Ending the back and forth between him and Newbold, Preston asked, "Colonel Aimes, your thoughts?"

"It's a solid plan. Minimal risk during the infill and the assault on the building depends entirely on the number of insurgents inside. The timing of the exfil will need to be coordinated, but nothing that can't be achieved. I recommend we go tonight."

"I agree it's a good plan."

"Sean, I feel a *'but'* coming," Aimes said.

"I'm still struggling with how to convince the President."

Ty got very pointed looks from everyone in the room when he chuckled.

In an aggravated tone, Preston asked, "Am I missing out on something funny?"

A wide-eyed Newbold shook his head toward Ty as if he were screaming, *don't speak!*

Ty glanced toward Aimes, who gave the opposite, approving nod.

"Sir," Ty said, "that's the easy part."

"How so?"

"Make the decision about the President, not the mission or its risk."

Silence.

After a moment, "I'm not following," Preston said.

"If he sits on this intel for a day and, heaven forbid, we get another video of an execution, the President won't even get his party's nomination during the next election. If he acts, and we save the hostages, he wins reelection tonight."

"And if the hostages aren't there?"

"We raided a known weapons depot as part of an already planned operation."

"Captain Hudson has a great point. This is low risk, very high reward for the President," Aimes added.

With a softer tone. "And how do I address that elephant in the room?"

"Sorry, sir," Newbold said. "We're not following."

"How do I tell the President that a Marine Raider team led by Captain Hudson will rescue Senator Hayes? Let's be honest. Everyone in Washington knows the history and what happened a few days ago with you and Hayes' speech."

Ty was approaching this mission as rescuing Luna.

Hayes was there, but he was a secondary objective. Someone else on the team would grab the Senator. But he couldn't say that out loud.

For the President, making the decision and taking the political risk, Hayes was the mission.

"Ty," Aimes said solemnly, "What do you say to the Director's question?"

Ty pressed his lips together, feeling the sting of the fresh cut from punching himself just hours ago.

"Sir, I'm an American patriot. And you're right. Hayes and I are in the middle of a family scrap right now. But, I'll be damned if I let Al-Abbasi, or anyone else who's not an American, get away with laying their hands on my family."

Out of the corner of his eye, Ty saw the Colonel give him a look he had never seen before. It wasn't a smile of approval. No, this type of expression would come from a father having a proud moment with his son.

The four stared at the phone, waiting for Preston to respond.

"Newbold, I'll get you permission within an hour. Right now, you need to get the resources the team needs. Colonel, you have operational control."

Newbold answered, "Roger that, I'm on it."

"Sean, I recommend Captain Hudson and his team move now to requisition a boat and hold there until we receive the green light," Aimes said.

"I agree, make it happen."

CHAPTER
FIFTY-ONE

"THIS ONE SHOULD DO," Williams whispered to Ty.

"Yeah, it's perfect. Can you hot wire it?"

"Shouldn't be a problem. Give me a couple of minutes."

She was an old trolly that looked and smelled like it was being held together by blood and fish guts from decades of use. At least thirty feet in length, it had a single cabin in its center with outriggers secured in place. The sides were tall enough to conceal the team but not so tall that they could easily slip over the side when they passed behind the wreck of the al-Mansur.

She was perfect.

Ty didn't turn around. He didn't need to when he waved his right hand to signal the rest of the team to move to the dock.

When Ty and Williams walked into the team's barracks thirty minutes ago, they were met by an eager team ready to go.

The team had wasted no time waiting for Ty to return with news of the assault being approved. They had already geared up and were going over the plan again when the two captains walked in.

"Plan is being taken to the President. We are to move to the docks to find a boat. From there, we'll hold for a *'go, no-go'* decision," Ty said.

"I need a sidearm," Williams said.

Tiller looked at Ty first but quickly pulled his M9 Barretta from his holster and handed it to him.

Reading the room, Ty explained, "Slight change of plans. We need every one of our guns, so Henry, you'll go in with the rest of us. Williams will drive the boat and meet up with the fast boats further down the river as planned. "

Excited about the news, Henry stripped from his civilian clothes to hand them to Williams before gearing up.

"I need two minutes. Load the team up," Ty told Tiller before darting to his room.

He changed into combat fatigues, strapped on his body armor, and switched boots. He was securing flash bangs, grenades, and extra ammo when he noticed the picture of his family on the bed.

Just hours ago, he held it tight to his chest as he cried himself to sleep. Picking it up now, Ty said, "Last mission. I promise, my love."

It was as if Beth was in the room with him. Ty wanted her to hear the commitment in his voice that she would have him for the rest of her life after tonight. Kissing it, he returned the picture to the bed and grabbed his rifle and helmet before leaving.

The drive from Ali Airbase to the fishing dock on the north side of Basra was twenty minutes.

As suspected, no one was out and about this time of night. Anyone heading out to fish had done so hours ago and had not yet returned.

Now that Williams and Ty had found a boat, Romeo Team moved down the long dock to board it.

"Last man," Tiller whispered as he climbed aboard.

With the team in position, the waiting started.

It was the hold until authorization that was always the toughest part.

The adrenaline never wore off during the long moments waiting for someone thousands of miles away to tell you that you can now do your job.

As a Marine Raider, you had to learn to stay mission-focused and combat-ready. Every Marine found a way to handle the anxiety.

Knight pulled out a picture of his new fiancee and started to write a letter home—the type of letter that would be delivered in the worst possible scenario.

Henry, as only he could, would drift into a light sleep.

Ty always coped with it the same way—daydreaming of his family time back home.

Not days spent at the beach or celebrating birthdays or other holidays. No, his go-to moments were bedtime when the entire family gathered in Ty and Beth's room for uninterrupted, undistracted time.

Audrey started it shortly after Jake was born. Beth would feed him before putting him down, and she would come into the nursery to sit next to her mom.

It didn't take Ty long to realize that his entire family was gathered in the nursery, and he began joining them. Everything moved to their bedroom after a couple of nights in the nursery.

Each night, Audrey told her mommy and daddy about her day before Ty read her and Jake a short story as Beth rocked him to sleep.

When both were sound asleep, they would be carried into their rooms and tucked in for the night. These were the favorite moments Ty turned to occupy his mind as he waited for word from command to execute a mission.

Kneeling, Williams asked, "It's after zero-three-hundred hours. At what time do we call this because of sunrise?"

"I don't know. We hold in radio silence for another thirty minutes before asking Verona for a sitrep."

Satisfied, Williams crawled back to his position inside the cabin.

Time ticked away.

Ty's patience was wearing thin as concern about not getting the green light to go started to weigh heavily on his mind.

Laying flat on the deck, smelling the foul odor, he was powerless to convince the President of the quality of the intel or the need to act now. He had to rely on Sean Preston, a man he had only spoken to twice, to convince a Washington politician to take quick, decisive action.

Not an easy feat.

With a crackling in his ear, Ty's radio came to life for the first time in an hour. "Romeo One, come back."

Ty's heart started to race.

This was it.

This was the *go, no-go* decision.

"Go for Romeo One."

"Romeo One, this is Verona. We have POTUS with us. Hold for orders."

The old fishing trolly gently rocked beneath Ty as some of the guys moved in anticipation, hearing the same thing in their earpieces.

A new voice spoke next.

Well, new in the sense that Ty had never heard him on the team's radio, but with a Texas draw, everyone knew who was speaking. "Romeo Team, this is the President. You have the go-ahead to begin your assault. Please bring everyone home. May God be with you all."

Closing his eyes while taking a deep breath, Ty replied, "Roger that, sir. Romeo Team is starting our approach."

No signal or words were needed for Williams. Ty felt the boat engines roar to life as their vibration radiated through his body.

Pushing off the dock, Tiller dropped the stern line and Henry the aft. Williams steered the old boat toward the river's channel as Ty looked back at the shore to ensure that no one had witnessed them abscond with it.

The team had ten minutes upriver until they would have eyes on the dry docks. Minutes later, they would pass the capsized mega yacht, al-Mansur, as it concealed them for a few seconds. In these crucial seconds, the team would slip down the sides of the trolly into the water before slowly treading to the wreck. Then to shore.

As planned, Williams would continue downriver toward the mouth of the Persian Gulf. Along the way, he would meet up with three boat crews from the USS Bataan, an amphibious assault ship in the region. They would be the team's exfil once the hostages and remains of the two slain Americans were secured.

The irony wasn't lost on Ty that they were using the capsized luxury yacht of former Iraqi Dictator Saddam Hussein to cover the team as they began their assault on the dry docks. Once one of the world's richest and most feared men, the rusting yacht was once the symbol of this power and wealth.

Not only had it been looted and stripped bare of all the features and furniture that made it luxurious, but now it was being used as little more than a prop in a raid by U.S. Marines.

Oh, how the mighty have fallen. Ty thought as the wreck came into sight.

From behind the boat's cabin, Ty looked over his right shoulder to see Tiller and Henry move along the starboard side. Then, he saw Knight on the port side.

The team was ready. But Ty wasn't.

Reaching to his chest to activate his radio. "Never in our country's history have elected leaders been kidnapped and murdered by a terrorist. No matter what happens, they come home tonight. No team has ever done what you're about to. No team in America's great arsenal can do what you're about to. You're already heroes. Now, all you need to do is follow your instincts and watch out for each other. Romeo Team, this is for Senator Wrzesinki and those killed by these men."

FIFTY-TWO

THE FOUR MARINES OF ROMEO TEAM slipped into the Shatt al-Arab river behind the wreck of the al-Mansur as the fishing trolly cruised by at a slow four knots.

The water was colder than Ty had expected as it soaked through his uniform.

As they had done hundreds of times in training, the team started to tread water away from their drop point, using the wake of the trolly to mask their movement toward the capsized yacht.

Most of the thirty-meter swim was done underwater to disguise their approach. If anyone noticed movement from the shore, they would only suspect marine life.

The cloud-covered moon and lack of street lights in the area made for perfect conditions for the late-night assault from the water.

As the team reached the wreck, they formed a circle along its hull for one last check and clipped their night vision goggles into position. Without speaking, they each gave a 'ready to go' hand signal. Once his eyes adjusted to the faint green optics, Ty waved his left hand to signal his team to move out.

Tiller and Knight moved to the rudder. From there, they would float ashore. Meanwhile, Ty and Henry would make their way around the stern.

The two-prong approach minimized the team's exposure to enemy fire. It also helped to create a kill zone onshore if a firefight broke out while they were still in the water.

Because of the al-Mansur's angle to the shore, Ty's team had just over a fifty-meter swim, while Tiller's team had double that. To ensure they arrived at the same time, Ty and Henry held in place for two minutes while the other team slowly floated in.

The docks were dark.

Their intended target building had one exterior light near the loading doors. There were two more dim street lights further inland. None provided good illumination of the water's edge.

From the water, the team would have to make their way up a long, wide ramp to flat ground. During this, they would be exposed as the river's cover quickly became shallow.

"Romeo two is in position. One tango out for a smoke with his weapon slung," Tiller said.

"Roger that, Romeo One ready. Make final approach."

Ty started walking his way up the dry dock. "Hold," Tiller ordered, "Second tango walking out toward your position."

With the water now only to his knees, Ty crouched down, using the wooden seawall behind him to blend in.

He couldn't see the first guy, but the second one was coming into view.

Pressing his body tighter to the wall, Ty watched the insurgent walk along it, stopping a mere ten feet away.

All Ty could make out in the dark was the AK-47 slung on his shoulder.

A trickle of pee hit the water, with the steady stream turning to sporadic drops and then stopping. Ty soon saw the guy walking away.

With the insurgent heading away, Ty looked over his shoulder to Henry, who smiled back. Suggesting to his Captain, *You almost got pissed on.*

"All clear," Tiller said.

Ty moved further ashore. "Romeo One in position."

"Romeo Two in position."

Ty took a quick, shallow breath as he scanned the area.

Between him and their entry point into the building was the smoker. No other insurgents were visible. "Romeo Two, execute."

The guy pacing outside, getting in a quick smoke, had no idea he was taking his last breaths. When the bullet from Tiller's rifle hit him, he collapsed to the ground, dead.

There was no verbal order to move.

Once the smoker fell lifelessly, both teams moved out from their cover to make their way to their entry points.

As Ty ran by the fallen body, he slowed to grab it and drag it out of the center of the open space.

Disposing of it behind a truck, he rejoined Henry along the back wall of the building.

Giving him the signal, Henry placed the entry charges on the metal door.

This was the moment.

The moment Ty had wanted for days.

His pulse was steady. His breathing was measured.

He had once more reached absolute certainty of purpose and resolve.

With honed senses, he announced, "Romeo One ready."

"Twenty seconds," Tiller said, indicating that his team was still working to place their charges. "Romeo Two ready."

"Executing in three, two, one."

Bang! Bang!

Ty was the first to step into the room, sweeping from left to right, as Henry came in just behind him to sweep in the opposite direction.

Through the smoke-filled room, Ty whipped his eyes around the open space. The backdrop and chairs in each video were on his side of the room.

To the right of the production set was someone hanging by their wrists just off the ground. Bloodied by torture, Ty could barely make out that it was a male. And not Luna.

With his rifle target continuing to move rapidly, scanning the room, an insurgent was getting up off the ground. Ty squeezed the trigger of his suppressed M4 twice.

Thump! Thump!

The man slumped back to the ground before he could reach his feet.

In the background, Ty heard the distinct *thump* sound several times as the team cleared the room.

Just as Ty lowered his rifle from his shoulder, a man rushed out from behind the backdrop with a knife in his hand.

Pulling his rifle back up to place his target on the fast-approaching man, Ty recognized who it was. *That's Al-Abbasi!*

Reacting, Ty dropped his slung rifle to his side to hang freely and rushed forward to meet him.

Stepping to the left to dodge Al-Abbasi's attempt to stab him, Ty kicked his assailant's right knee on its side. The ligaments tore as the knee collapsed with the intensity of the kick. Al-Abbasi fell to the ground on the damaged leg while letting out a scream of pain.

Ty drove his knee into the man's back, forcing his chest and face to collide hard with the floor. Al-Abbasi let out a second cry as his head bounced off it.

Within seconds, Ty had pulled out a thick plastic zip tie handcuff from the back of his belt and bound his hands.

Coming to support, Henry shoved Al-Abbasi's head into a black bag. Then he took Ty's position by kneeing the now-bound insurgency leader's back.

"Verona, ring leader. I say again, ring leader!" Ty barked into his mic.

Ring leader was the code phrase assigned to taking Al-Abbasi alive.

Getting to his feet, Ty scanned the room again.

Tiller was searching for hidden tangos.

Knight had made his way over to the body hanging by ropes and pulled him down. Glancing urgently at Ty, "It's the Army soldier. He's in bad shape and needs to be moved now."

"Roger that, prep him to move. Romeo Two, you're on me."

Tiller moved to cover Ty as they began to search rooms along the south side of the building.

Approaching the first door, Tiller breached it by kicking it, while Ty was the first one in.

Stepping in, he came under fire.

Firing his AK-47 from his hip, the insurgent missed Ty with several rounds hitting the wall behind him.

Thump! Thump!

The insurgent fell backward.

Shit, that was close! Ty's subconscious reminded him he almost got killed.

Thump!

One more in the head for good measure.

As the two Marine Raiders stepped out of the cleared first room, Knight radioed, "I have both bodies. I say again, I have both bodies."

Ty felt relief that there were only two. With only two bodies located, that hopefully meant that Luna was still alive.

It was also good news because one of the critical mission objectives was recovering Senator Wrzesinki and the slain Army soldier's bodies.

Remembering that Al-Abbasi had walked off camera with the Senator's head, "Romeo Four is—"

Cutting him off because he knew what was being asked, Knight replied, "Negative, it isn't here."

Outside the second room, Ty could hear cries coming from inside. Tiller kicked in the door. Ty stepped in, prepared to be shot at again.

Instead, on the ground to Ty's left was Senator Hayes.

Along the back wall was Luna.

Alive! Thank God!

CHAPTER
FIFTY-THREE

TY POINTED to Hayes as he rushed to Luna.

Tiller understood what he was saying and reported to Verona as he moved to attend to the Senator. "Iowa. I say again, we have Iowa."

The code phrase for finding Senator Andrew Hayes alive.

Kneeling beside her, Luna threw her hands at Ty, hitting and pushing him away.

"Luna, it's Ty. It's Ty. I'm here now," he said, trying to calm her down.

Her screams turned to hysterical crying as he wrapped his arms around her. She pushed back on him, but Ty wouldn't let go.

Pulling her tight against him, Ty whispered, "It will be okay. I have you. I'm not going to let anything else happen to you. It's okay."

Her struggle to escape from him faded as her body became limp in his arms.

"One!" Tiller called out, "the Senator's foot is in bad shape. He won't be able to walk."

"Okay." Pressing his mic, "Romeo Four, collapse to my location."

Coming into the room, Knight said, "Remains have been secured in body bags and are ready to be moved. No sign of… Never mind."

Knight noticed what neither Ty nor Tiller had seen. Senator Wrzesinki's severed head was on the ground next to Hayes. Picking it up, he secured it in a bag.

Ty lifted Luna up from the ground and leaned her against the wall. "Luna, can you walk? I need you to be able to walk."

She nodded her head, but Ty kept one hand on her as she struggled to find the strength to stand.

Ty put Luna's arm around his left shoulder as they moved into the main room. Reaching Henry with the two body bags, the injured Army soldier and Al-Abbasi still tied up, Ty placed Luna along the wall next to the loading dock door he had entered through just three minutes ago.

"Verona, this is Romeo One. All objectives are green. ETA on exfil?"

"Romeo one, exfil is four mikes out," Newbold said, using military slang for a minute.

"Roger that, Verona. We have two severely wounded—"

Ty cut his message off when Knight hollered for help.

Knight and Tiller were moving Hayes into the room when the Senator collapsed.

Running to them, Ty asked, "What happened?"

"He passed out," Knight said calmly, "He's in bad shape and needs to be carried."

Ty looked at Knight, "Move to the front and get everyone prepared to exfil. I'll help Knight."

Without a word, Knight moved to join Henry while Tiller and Ty worked to stop the bleeding from Hayes' right foot.

The radio cracked. "Romeo team," Newbold barked, "You have incoming. Three trucks just crossed the bridge with another thirty to forty insurgents on foot."

Like the President and his Security Council, Newbold and Colonel Aimes were watching a live feed from two drones high above; this was the warning that Ty feared the most. A large number of incoming insurgents would turn this already difficult mission into a firefight.

"Verona, move in air support to engage incoming targets. I say again, move air support in, now!"

"Copy that, Romeo One. Assets are inbound. Thirty seconds."

Not using his mic, Ty screamed, "Prepare to repel borders!"

Needing to move the Senator, Ty leaned under Hayes' arm, lifting him onto his back.

Just as Ty lifted Hayes, Tiller hollered, "Contact!"

Two insurgents had come through a door at the end of the hall.

Tiller opened fire.

"Contact right! Contact!" Henry yelled from the main room.

Ty moved with Hayes on his back toward the main room when he took fire from several men entering the door Tiller's team had breached.

With his M4 in one hand, he returned fire before jumping back behind the safety of the hall he had just stepped out of.

Seeing Ty taking fire from the main room, Tiller yelled, "One, move to the side hall!"

With fighting in the main room and the inevitable possibility that more insurgents would be coming through the door at the end of the hall, Ty had no choice.

With Hayes over his left shoulder, Ty moved quickly to the hallway just past the room where they had found the hostages.

Tiller covered his move from behind.

As he reached it, an insurgent, followed by two more, entered.

Ty exchanged fire with them as he ducked down the side hall.

Dropping Hayes on the floor, he leaned out from the cover of the corner to kill one insurgent before the other two took cover in a doorway.

"Two! Two!"

"I'm alright," Tiller yelled back.

"Verona, we're pinned down, I say again, we're pinned down!"

"Romeo air cover is on-site, but tangos are too close. You're in the kill zone. Boats are one mike out. You'll have to fight your way out."

Fuck!

"Romeo Three, sit rep!"

"One, we're taking heavy fire. We have moved out of the building to the cover of the loading dock, with only the living in tow," Henry said.

Before Ty could reply, he heard someone scream from outside, "RPG!"

Then, an explosion.

And a second.

"Two, move to support the team?"

"Roger that. I'll need cover."

"Copy. Move in three, two, one!"

Ty leaned out on his right knee, aiming down the hallway toward the door, and opened fire. Emptying his magazine, he hit at least three insurgents before leaning back into the safety of the cover to reload.

Several bullets hit the wall right next to his head when he leaned back out to fire.

Crap, that's twice. This isn't good, Ty!

Peeking back out, Ty saw four more men entering the building.

He had seconds before being overrun.

Looking at Hayes, still unconscious on the ground, Ty smacked the Senator. "Wake up! Wake the hell up."

With no response, he lifted Hayes off the ground and pulled him toward the door at the end of the short hall that led outside.

It had been a miracle that no insurgents had already entered it.

Ty wasn't worried about what fight awaited them outside. It would have to be better than the one he was about to lose in the hall.

While holding Hayes up, Ty rushed to the door.

Reaching it, he felt a hard hit on his back.

Knowing he had just been hit in his body armor, he shoved Hayes through the door before swinging around to return fire on who had just shot him.

Hayes flopped to the ground. Letting out a whimper as he hit it.

At least he's alive, Ty thought, hearing the Senator's moan.

Ty grabbed a fragment grenade off his vest. Pulling the pin, he tossed it toward the main hall. "Frag out!"

Rushing outside, Ty slammed the door behind him just as the grenade exploded.

Swiveling his head and rifle to the left, then right, he saw no danger in the pitch black of the late morning hour.

For now.

He rushed over, grabbed Hayes by the armpits, and began dragging him to the cover of a nearby junk pile.

Hayes struggled in his hands for a moment. Almost as if he was trying to fight loose from Ty's grip.

Ignoring it, Ty stared at the door, waiting for it to burst open.

Reaching the pile of old pallets, machine parts, and trash, Ty leaned Hayes against it. The Senator had regained consciousness as he looked around, confused, trying to piece things together.

On his knee facing the door, waiting for someone to come through it, Ty said, "It would be a lot easier on you if you made an effort to move instead of me dragging you."

"I don't have it in me."

Looking at Hayes, Ty noticed blood running down the left side of his head.

This was a fresh wound.

With no one immediately attacking them, Ty took a moment to look over the Senator's head. He moved it from side to side to see if he had been shot or got a ricochet from a stray round.

Ty found a cut just above his ear. *Whew. Only a cut.*

Glancing back at the door, he noticed a trail of blood in their direction. Hayes' foot was still bleeding.

Ty put his rifle down and hurried down to look at his foot. "Your foot is in terrible shape. I'm going to have to carry you."

Hayes replied with as much energy as he could muster, "No…"

Ty let out a gasp of frustration, and he looked at Hayes.

To his surprise, the Senator was not looking at him.

He was staring at Ty's rifle on the ground next to him.

Amused. "Are you thinking about grabbing my rifle to shoot me?"

Hayes looked at him now, "Why did it have to be you?"

"It was always going to be me, Senator. Our fates have been tied together."

As the two men looked at one another, a single tear, and then a second, fell from Hayes' eyes.

He turned his attention back to the rifle.

"Are you going to kill me now?"

Realizing what Hayes was thinking, Ty said, "No, Senator. You're going to live many more years."

"ROMEO TEAM, EXFIL IN THIRTY SECONDS!" Newbold blasted in Ty's earpiece.

It snapped him back to the reality of their situation. "Copy. Romeo Two, sitrep?"

Not waiting for Tiller to respond, Ty pulled Hayes over his left shoulder, picked up his rifle, and turned toward the boat ramp.

They had a little over a hundred meters to get to the three boats that Ty could now see arriving as their guns started to engage the enemy.

"Romeo Two, sitrep!" Ty screamed.

"Moving to the water with ring leader, one hostage, and the two body bags. We got separated. I don't have eyes on her."

Ty knew who Tiller was talking about without him saying her name.

There was only one person that his First Sergeant would tell him he didn't have eyes on. Luna had been lost somewhere in the middle of the fight.

"Roger that. I have Iowa. I'm a hundred meters out along the south side."

"Copy. Moving to exfil."

With Hayes in tow, Ty approached the corner of the building. There was a large open field between it and the water's edge. The same area that the man smoking was pacing in before being killed ten minutes ago. Fearing they would be defenseless with Hayes on his shoulder, Ty ducked them behind a shipping container with its doors open. Placing Hayes on the ground against the container, he peered out from the corner.

Not ready for what he would see.

Luna was sitting behind a small forklift, facing the water with her knees in her chest, screaming in fear.

To her left was Henry, engaging targets further inland. They were less than twenty meters away.

Leaning further out, Ty could see at least a dozen insurgents firing at Luna and Henry's position. He aimed and opened fire.

"Romeo Three, I'm engaging from the south."

"Roger. We have thirty to forty more coming down the road. We need air cover."

Ty emptied his magazine before leaning back to reload.

As he did, he could see Tiller and Knight arrive at the first boat.

"Verona, we're clear of the building, and the first hostages have reached boats. We need immediate fire support on the road north of the target building."

He didn't hear the response.

Movement in his peripheral drew his attention away from what was being said on the radio.

Two insurgents had come around the corner of the shipping container. They must not have known they were there because neither had their weapons ready.

Swinging his rifle around, Ty didn't aim. He shot from his hip. Dropping both men before they could fire.

Hayes and Ty made eye contact. Wide-eyed, they both knew how lucky they were that the two men were not ready. If they had been, the two of them would be lying dead on the ground right now.

Shaking his head, Ty turned back just in time to see Henry jump on Luna to cover her with his body as the ground began to shake.

The AC-130 gunship above them started to pound the road with its 40mm Bofors cannon.

With each round having a kill radius of three meters, Henry and Luna were at the edge of danger. If a round went astray, they could become casualties of friendly fire.

For the next minute, the aircraft rained fragmenting rounds on the insurgents every second. Taking advantage of the air cover, Ty picked up Hayes and stepped out from the protection of the shipping container.

Two steps out, he took fire from alongside the building. With no choice, he dove back to the safety of cover. Landing on Hayes, who let out a gasp of air.

Ty pulled himself out from underneath Hayes's arm and took a defensive stance. Ready to fight off the approaching insurgents.

Looking to his right, he made eye contact with her.

He could read Luna's lips as she reached out her hand toward him. *'Ty!'*

With Henry's back to her, Luna got up off the ground and started to run towards him.

Oh God, no!

"Luna, No! Stay there! No!"

She must not have heard him. She continued to run in his direction with her arms out.

Ty didn't think as his emotions took over.

He leaped from his position to start running to her.

Leaving Hayes alone.

With bullets hitting the ground at his feet and whizzing by his head, he ran as fast as he could.

He couldn't reach her in time.

A round hit Luna in her right leg.

She let out a scream and started to fall forward to the ground. Before reaching it, she was hit twice more on her body.

Reaching out for her as she collapsed, Ty could see her eyes as clearly as in the moment after they shared their passionate kiss outside the team's HQ just days ago.

This time, it wasn't lust that burned in her dark irises.

It was fear.

Then they closed.

Without warning, Ty was slammed backward to the ground. With all the wind he had left in his lungs, Ty cried, "Luna! Luna! No, let me go! Let me go!"

In his fixation on reaching her, Ty had not seen Henry chasing her. Once Luna went down, Henry's mission became saving his Captain.

"Sir, she's gone! She's gone!" Henry pleaded with Ty as he struggled to go back out to her.

"No, no, she's not! I can reach her."

Frustrated, Henry grabbed Ty by the jawline with both hands to force his attention on him. "She's dead, sir. I need you here. The Senator needs you here."

Seeing the seriousness on Henry's face, Ty took in a deep breath. He glanced over to see Hayes staring at Luna.

Slowly releasing his breath, Ty turned to look in the same direction. Luna's lifeless body was halfway between the building and the protection of their cover. She lay flat on the ground with her head turned toward the waterline.

There was no movement.

No signs of life.

She was so close. I could've reached her.

"Sir, I need you!" Henry said, pulling Ty's gaze back to him.

Nodding his head, "Let's get to the boats."

"I got the—"

"No," Ty said, grabbing Henry's arm. "I'm alright. I can carry him. We need you to provide cover."

Henry didn't object.

Ty picked up Hayes. He held the Senator by the back of his legs as his body was bent at the waist over the Marine's shoulder.

With his rifle in his right hand, holding Hayes in his left, Ty said, "Ready."

Henry leaned out and opened fire.

Ty moved, glancing down at Luna, before he began to run toward the second boat.

In front of him, Tiller and Knight formed a firing line to give him cover.

Ty knew the team could still be overrun, and he needed to get Hayes to the waiting boat.

A couple steps further, Ty felt a sharp pain in his left thigh just before the wind was knocked out of him.

Breathlessly groaning, he fell forward to the ground. Hayes landed on top of him.

Shit, I'm hit.

Pushing Hayes off his back, Ty felt a sharp pain radiate deep in his back. He could hear Tiller and Henry calling for him.

But what caught his attention was what Hayes said. "Like you said. Our fates are tied together."

Laying chest down, trying to catch his breath, Ty turned his head to see Hayes on his side, looking back at him. To his surprise, the Senator was calm. Accepting his fate.

Reaching his left hand out, Ty took Hayes' hand. "No. You and I aren't done yet."

Getting to his knees, Ty saw blood starting to soak through Hayes' shirt just to the lower right of where his heart was.

The Senator had been hit, too.

Before Ty could lift Hayes back up, a hard punch hit his chest armor just before a discomforting prick to his left bicep.

He had been hit twice more.

Ignoring it, Ty lifted Hayes back to his shoulder and pressed upward from his knees.

"Ahhhh!" He screamed as the pain in his left thigh became unbearable.

Steadily taking a step forward, then a second, a third, Ty slowly descended the boat ramp.

Tiller met the two of them just feet away from the team's firing line. Trying to help by pulling Hayes off his back. Ty grunted, "No, I have him. Get us to the boat."

Shuffling down the boat ramp into the water, Ty's left leg gave out. Dropping to his knee in agony, he yelled, "Shit!"

With tears filling his eyes from the pain, he lifted back up. "We're almost there."

Reaching the boat, Williams was the first person to grab Hayes off his back. "Ty, I have him. Let him go."

With all that had happened in the last couple of minutes, Ty reflectively wasn't loosening his grip around the Senator's legs.

"Ty, it's Marcus. You did it. Let him go."

Tiller rushed over to help Williams pry Hayes from Ty's grip.

When he finally let go, Tiller wrapped his arm around Ty's waist and attempted to lift him into the boat.

"Wait, no," Ty said, turning to face back toward the fight on shore.

"Ty, you're wounded. You need to get in the boat."

"No, not without her."

From behind him, Williams called out, "No, Ty. Get in the boat. The guys will get her."

Ty didn't acknowledge his best friend's voice. Instead, he pulled up his rifle, looked down to see a round chambered, and started back up the ramp.

Tiller grabbed him again, "Ty, you're hit! Let me do this."

Ty spun around to glare at Tiller.

The two Marine Raiders held each other's gaze for a moment. It could've been the determination to fulfill the mission that Tiller saw in Ty's eyes. But, most likely, it was the vengeful rage he saw in his Captain's eyes that prompted Tiller to release him.

"Williams, get the Senator out of here. I have Ty. We'll get out on the third boat."

"LEAVE HIM ALONE," Tiller warned in a low voice.

Knight didn't know how to respond. He looked over to Ty, sitting along the boat's starboard side. With blood trickling out of the corner of his mouth, a hole in his left bicep, and a bullet lodged in his side, someone needed to attend to him.

Despite all that, the reason Tiller instructed the team not to bother Ty was lying across his lap.

Luna's lifeless body, her corpse, had been carried by Ty into the boat and pulled onto his lap as he dropped in exhaustion.

He wasn't ready to release her.

Tiller understood this.

The rest of the guys did not know of Ty's struggles over the last month as he wrestled with his love for Beth against Luna's intrigue.

Henry and Knight exchanged confused looks as the boat was pushed back from the dry docks and headed downriver toward the USS Bataan in the Persian Gulf. They didn't understand why Ty was visibly distraught with Luna's death.

This woman was the chief of staff to a politician who had caused him great personal distress. She was supportive of her boss in accusing him of war crimes.

So, why was he taking her death so hard?

Knight didn't know the answers to the questions everyone was asking through shared glances, but he understood the tone Tiller had used when he moved to treat Ty.

Without protesting, he slumped back down on the floor of the boat.

I'm so sorry. I shouldn't have left. Ty apologized as he brushed dirt from Luna's face. *This was all my fault. You didn't deserve this. I'm so sorry.*

Ty's started to cry as he placed his arm around her.

Not the sobbing, snot-running episode he had less than ten hours ago when he saw a picture of his family beside his bed.

This steady stream of large, heavy tears would mark his face by removing the dirt and gunpowder residue caked on from the fight.

Wiping off his face, he took a deep breath before turning away from Luna to stare off the side of the boat as it rushed down the river. Basra's buildings and industrial dockyards soon faded to open marshes as they approached the mouth of the river.

Ty's mind drifted.

He reminisced about seeing Luna for the first time at his Raider graduation when she turned an embroidered folder around to show him Hayes' names. Reliving the moment in his head, a particular detail of their brief interaction stood out. One that he had never picked up on because he had been too consumed the moment he met his nemesis.

It was the smile she gave him.

It was the same one she had when she spotted him through the crowd at the fancy Washington bar. She flashed it again as she turned the corner to see him standing at the center of the elevator the morning of the Senate hearing. And, just a few days ago, she gave it to him for the last time when she exited the C-17 at Ali Airbase.

It wasn't a game or playful lust for her. This smile was a heartfelt expression of interest. Of intrigue.

Ty had attributed it to a powerful Washington aide playing games to disarm her ambitious boss's target.

Salt water splashed his face as the boat exited into the gulf and bounced through the rough sea chop, pushing into the narrow river channel.

Instinctively, Ty tightened his grip around Luna as the boat hopped from swell to swell.

He cringed in pain when the muscle in his wounded arm burned from use. He looked back into the boat to see a concerned Knight wanting to come to his aid. And a team itching to understand what was happening between their commander and this woman.

Tiller scooted over, "Sir, Hayes is safe aboard the Bataan and receiving medical care. We need to patch you up."

"Not yet. The team needs to know."

Tiller tilted his head in confusion before looking down at Luna. "Yeah, you should tell them."

Ty nodded. Not just in agreement but permitting Tiller to call the team over.

With all eyes on their team leader, everyone moved at once when Tiller reached up and gave the rally hand gesture.

As Luna's body lay lifeless in his lap, Ty looked at each of his Raiders before speaking over the hum of the boat's engine. "I met Luna at our graduation, and I've formed a close relationship with her over the last month. It was never inappropriate, but I won't lie by telling you I didn't have feelings for her."

Pausing to allow his words to sink in, he tried to build the strength to say what would come next.

Exhaling. "For me, this mission wasn't about Hayes. It was always about her. And I failed. Luna should be alive right now, not me. I don't know how I go on as a Raider or how I go home to Beth."

Ty started to cry again. This time, he did not try to hide it from his team.

Henry was the first to speak, "Sir, I was with her. I failed to stop her from running to you. This is on me."

"No. You were keeping her alive. I left her in the building. Her death is my burden to bear."

"Ty, you know better than most that shit happens in combat. Neither you nor Henry are to blame. But the team has your back. You'll figure out how to go home and be back in the field before you know it," Tiller said.

Ty appreciated Tiller's words, but the team needed to hear the truth. "Thank you. But guys, I'd already decided this was my last mission and told Beth. I need to start taking care of my family."

Looking out over the bow, the dim lights of the USS Bataan could be seen in the distance.

With nothing more to say, Tiller reached for his pack and pulled out a body bag.

Seeing the rolled-up black plastic bag, the finality in its meaning caused Ty's heart to sink deeper into agony. "I'll do it."

Unsure how to respond, Tiller handed Ty the bag as the rest of the team returned to where they had been sitting.

Placing the body bag on his side, Ty looked down at Luna. *I doubt we would've ended up together, but I don't know what would've happened. All I know is that you became special to me in a very short time. I hope you can forgive me for not being able to save you. We'll meet again.*

Ty leaned down to kiss Luna on her forehead. Lingering there, he could still smell the intoxicating scent of her hair despite all that had happened to her over the last few days.

With no more tears to shed, he leaned her up to get to his knees. Unfolding the body bag, he unzipped it and placed Luna in it. It was something he had done a handful of times in training. But never after combat. And never to someone, he felt so deeply for.

Zipping it closed, he stopped at her neckline to give her one last kiss on her lips as a final goodbye.

As they reached the USS Bataan, the team was greeted by cheers and applause from scores of the ship's crew and its Marine detachment perched along the rails of the landing well.

It was a magnificent triumph that should have been a moment of celebration for Romeo Team. The rescue of a United States Senator and an Army soldier and the recovery of the three others who had been slain at the hands of terrorists could have been a defining occasion for any special operations team.

Still, as they arrived, the fanfare was ignored.

With the boat tied up, Ty lifted Luna off the deck. Handing her to the outstretched arms of the sailors there to help the team aboard.

As they took the body bag from him, Ty's body gave out. Fainting, he collapsed back into the boat.

CHAPTER
FIFTY-SIX

TY WASN'T on the USS Bataan when he woke up.

As his eyes adjusted to the bright lights above him, Beth came into focus.

"Ty, can you hear me?"

Reaching to rub his eyes, he muttered, "Where..?"

"Love, you're at Walter Reed Hospital in Washington."

"What? How did I—" Ty said before trailing off.

Tearing up. "It's been two days. You collapsed when you got onboard the ship because of blood loss and are just now waking up. You had me so scared."

"The guys?"

"They're all here. So is the Colonel. The guys went crazy when the Navy tried to deny them from flying home with you. They got their way, and you'll see them soon."

"Where's Audrey and Jake?"

"At a hotel with my parents. Audrey has been lying in bed with you almost all day, but my mom took her about an hour ago. I'll call her so they can come back in a little while."

"Okay, I want to see them. How are you?"

Beth choked out a laugh. "You're waking up after two days in a hospital, and you're asking about me?"

"What's so funny?"

Beth leaned in to kiss her husband.

Tears running down her nose onto Ty's face. Seeing this, she wiped them off.

When Beth spoke again, Ty didn't answer. He had drifted back to sleep.

Hours later, a different voice greeted him. "Shit, man, you going to stay awake this time?" Tiller asked.

Barely recognizing his First Sergeant, "Hey…"

Tiller got up from the chair he had been sitting in and made his way to the side of the bed. "Do you remember what happened?"

"I remember handing Luna to a couple of sailors, but that's it."

"Well, yeah, that's when you passed out. I didn't let Knight work on you, so no one knew you were bleeding out."

"From my arm?" Ty said, looking down at the bandage on his left bicep.

"No, you took a round in your left side while carrying Hayes that lodged in your lung. The doctor on the ship thought it was the same round that went through the Senator, and that's what saved your life."

"What?"

"When you had Hayes over your shoulder, he was hit in the back by a round that went through him into you under your arm. The doctor thinks it would have killed you if it hadn't hit him first."

"Damn."

Confused, Tiller asked, "What do you mean?"

"That means Hayes saved my life."

Letting out a deafening laugh, "Yeah, I guess he did. Which would make you guys even, but I doubt a politician will see it that way."

Tiller's heavy laugh signaled the rest of the team that Ty was awake.

After coming in, they shared how they were stopped from getting on the helicopter that was air-lifting Ty and Hayes.

"Ty, you should have seen Tiller's face when the ship's XO put his hand on him and told us no one was going with you. I swear he was about to tell us to take the ship," Knight said while trying to impersonate Tiller's facial expression.

As the team made fun of Tiller, Beth walked in with Audrey and Jake.

"Hey guys, let's give them some time," Tiller said, ushering Henry and Knight out of the room.

Before they could leave, Ty spoke up, "Henry."

Ty raised his right hand for Henry to grab as he approached the side of the bed. "Thank you for saving me."

"Brother, that's what we do."

"Daddy, you awake!" Audrey called out as Henry dropped Ty's hand to help her climb onto the bed.

Ty was in his happy place. Audrey was nestled next to him on one side, telling him all the latest gossip from her daycare. At the same time, Jake was pulling at his oxygen tube while lying on his other side.

Beth stood at the bedside with shallow tears forming as she watched.

"Captain Hudson," a doctor said, coming into the room, "Glad to see you're awake. How are you feeling?"

Before Ty could answer, Beth said, "This is Doctor Kagan. He was the one who did your surgery."

"Sore and tired. But what surgery?"

Looking at the chart in his hands, he said, "That's understandable. You've been through a lot these last couple of days."

Exchanging a look with Beth, Ty asked again, "What surgery?"

Peering from the chart, "Ty, you were touch and go there for about thirty-six hours. After the bullet was removed, you had a pulmonary hemorrhage. Your lungs were filling with blood, and we had to go in to find and then stop the bleeding. But the good news is that you're stable."

Holding Audrey and Jake, Ty asked, "How bad was it?"

The tears swelling in Beth's eyes broke loose as she rubbed the side of Ty's head, "Ty, when you first arrived, they were asking me about end-of-life plans."

"I'm so sorry. I didn't—"

Beth started to laugh through her tears, "Why are you apologizing? You didn't do it on purpose."

"Ty, again, the good news is that you appear in stable condition," the doctor said. "As long as you progress in the right direction, I imagine a full recovery and be back in the field before you know it."

Ty recognized the meaning in the doctor's words. "Thanks, doc, but my fighting days are over."

Nodding his head. "That's understandable. You and your team are heroes. You've certainly earned it. I need to see the Senator, but I'll return in the morning to check in. In the meantime, make sure to get some rest."

Alone as a family, Beth told Ty about her experience when she arrived at the hospital two hours before he landed. Upset that the staff didn't stop asking about his end-of-life plans and if he had a do-not-resuscitate order. "It was the worst two hours of my life."

She never stopped crying as she told the story.

Wiping the final tears away. "Ty, you look like you're fighting to fall asleep. I'll take the kids back to the hotel for the night. I'll return in a few hours to stay with you overnight."

"You don't have to come back. I'm just going to be sleeping. Stay at the hotel with the kids and get a good night's sleep. I'll be alright. I can only imagine how difficult this has been for you."

Beth smiled in agreement, and after kissing goodbye, she and the kids left.

Ty stared at the analog clock on the wall. The black hands showed it was just after 2 a.m.

The night nurses would all be occupied with whatever they did during the long overnight hours, so the hallways would be empty.

This was perfect. Now, the only question was whether he could get out of bed. And walk.

Shit! This was a bad idea.

It took Ty five minutes to sneak down the hall to the corner room where the name *Hayes, A.* was written on the small dry-erase board. He stepped in, slowly pushing the heavy wooden door open and closing it quietly behind him.

There was Hayes, sleeping with all the same tubes and gadgets hooked to him that Ty had to remove before he could get out of bed.

He slowly crossed to the other side of the room to sit in a wood-framed armchair just under the window. In the distance, the outline of Washington, D.C.'s skyline was easily seen. *Of course, he has a better view than I do,* Ty mused.

Seeing the city in the distance reminded Ty of his first trip to the nation's capital.

In fifth grade, his parents scraped up enough money to send him on his school's safety patrol field trip. Traveling overnight by train, ten-year-old Ty was awakened by classmates shouting when the city came into view.

It was magnificent! The glowing lights illuminated all he believed to be great about the country. The scene burned an almost biblical image into Ty's mind as the true shining city on the hill.

A decade and a half later, that image had faded. This was no longer a shining city for Ty. Instead, it represented the depths of hell. He would never again be able to travel here without thinking of Luna. Without reliving the moment, the bright light of her life faded from her eyes as she fell, arms reaching out toward him.

"It's not quite as beautiful as you remember, right?" A voice asked.

Ty turned to see Hayes looking at him. *How did he know what I was thinking?*

"What makes you think that?"

Pushing the button to raise the back of his bed into a seated position, Hayes replied, "I've been in Washington long enough where I've had that same look. It's more common than you'd expect."

"Did she ever?"

"No, she believed in its majesty. Luna was a true idealist and never let D.C. corrupt her like it has so many others."

Ty found this amusing coming from Hayes. "Like you?"

In a solemn tone. "Yeah, like me."

Ty turned his attention back out the window.

They sat silently. Neither looked for an angle or for the other to be the first to break the quiet. The two adversaries remembered a woman who meant a lot to them both, but neither knew how to say it out loud.

Breaking the emptiness in the room, Ty asked, "How did you first meet her?"

It was a simple question. One that helped to find common ground that had not previously existed.

The next hour was spent sharing stories. Poking fun at each other for how they had allowed her to control parts of their lives. And how she would be missed.

After Hayes shared a story of Luna setting him up on a disastrous blind date, the conversation turned more serious. "Ty, in the years I knew Luna, she never spoke about a guy like she did you. I know you're married, but you should know she was in love with you."

Ty didn't know if he loved Luna. He knew something was there, but the word love was only reserved for Beth. All he did know was that she was special. That he felt he could share.

"I've often wondered what life would be like if she and I had met under different circumstances. Despite it all, she found her way into my heart."

"Is that why you risked your life and the lives of your men to go back for her?"

There was no reason to lie. And it wasn't that he could trust Hayes. No, Ty didn't care anymore about their ongoing fight.

Looking at the Senator, Ty admitted, "My mission was her. I wasn't going to leave her behind."

Hayes sighed, "I wish I would've died and she lived."

Ty fought back, saying, *Me too!*

Slowly getting up from his chair, "No, Senator. This was the way it's supposed to be."

"How's that?"

"Because it was our fates that are intertwined. Not hers. She's now our common purpose. I'll continue to do my part if you do yours."

"What's my part?"

"Live up to what she wanted. Pull back the veil. Show the American people a renewed commitment to a brighter future by running for president. If you do that, I'll vote for you."

EPILOGUE

TY'S LIFE had drastically changed in the three weeks since he woke up at Walter Reed Medical Center. Not for the better.

After the night talking to Hayes, it took eight more days before he was released from the hospital—four longer than the Senator's.

Doctor Kagan was concerned that if Ty suffered another internal bleed in his lungs, no one could detect it until it was too late.

When Ty pressed to be released, the doctor said, "It's best to be cautious in this situation."

He didn't have a leg to stand on to argue with either the doctor or Beth. But it didn't take him long to suspect there were ulterior motives.

Ty's room became a turnstile for Washington elites who came in to get their photo opportunity with the wounded hero who had saved one of their own.

Members of Congress from both sides of the aisle brought flowers, fruit, and fancy gift baskets for Ty and Beth. Not to miss the photo op, they all showered Audrey and Jake with stuffed animals, clothes, and books.

The most elaborate gifts came from the senators, who, along with Hayes and Wrzesinki, had accused Ty of war crimes. Shockingly, they sang different tunes during interviews and on the Senate floor.

Not to be outdone, members of the President's Cabinet and the Vice President visited. Even the man himself stopped by to shake Ty's hand, kiss Beth on the cheek, and hug the kids.

For three days, Ty was the biggest attraction in Washington.

With all the publicity Ty was getting, Hayes was doing good for himself, too.

As Beth and Ty packed to leave the hospital, Aimes walked in carrying a magazine. Dropping it on the bed, the Colonel said, "I'll give it to Time Magazine; they know how to catch a moment."

Vividly laid out within the borders of the famous red-framed cover was a picture of Hayes taken while being carried off the boat onto the USS Bataan.

Along his side was Willams, holding a blood-soaked bandage where the bullet had cut through him and lodged into Ty.

The photo showed all the pain and suffering Hayes had endured. The mutilation of his left foot by a hammer, the holes drilled into each of his hands, and the facial cuts and bruises from the beatings.

As Ty and Beth read the story and flipped through the pictures, it became apparent that quite a few photos had been taken as Romeo Team came aboard the Bataan. The anxiety Ty felt about seeing himself in one of the pictures was justified.

On the story's last page were several pictures in chronological order.

The first showed Ty handing the body bag carrying Luna over to the sailors.

The second was a close-up of his face, showing the tears and the emotional toll as they took her from him.

The third captured the moment his body broke, and he began to collapse to the boat deck.

Sitting next to her husband on the bed, Beth didn't comment on this montage as she had with every other photo. Instead, she got up and left the room.

Nothing more was ever said about the photos.

Even after returning home to Southern California, Ty wasn't done with Washington.

News organizations, the Department of Defense, and even the Smithsonian Museum called on him while he started his recovery from home.

Of all his visitors, those from the Smithsonian helped Ty realize how big of a sensation he had become.

"Yes, the bullet," the stuffed-up curator said after Beth asked her to repeat what they wanted.

Looking confusingly at his wife and then back at the woman sitting on their couch, Ty asked again, "The Smithsonian wants the bullet that went through Senator Hayes and got lodged in my lung?"

"That's right. It's a true treasure of American history. It should be cataloged and displayed for all the world to see as a symbol of your heroism and our society's struggle against extremists."

"Well, I'm sorry. I don't know what happened to it. I guess the hospital threw it out," Beth said.

The curator argued with Beth by saying that the hospital had told them that they had given it to the Marine's wife.

And they had. Beth knew exactly where it was. It would stay there. Not in a museum for *'all the world to see.'*

Unsatisfied with the answer she was getting, the smug woman continued to argue. That's when the phone call came in, ordering Ty to return to Washington.

Ty had been dreading this particular call. Not in the sense that he expected it or felt that he deserved it. He had served long enough as a Marine to know that any act of heroism that a politician could grab the coattails of always ended in a high-profile medal ceremony.

He wasn't wrong.

But he didn't expect this much pomp and circumstance when he and his family arrived back in the nation's capital.

"Excuse me," the White House Event Coordinator said. "Captain Hudson, I'm sorry, but the President is being delayed. We will start at the top of the hour."

Ty didn't know if he was delayed or if someone thought waiting another thirty minutes would get a bigger television audience.

He didn't care. He also couldn't spend the next thirty minutes in this room.

He and Beth had already been sitting in the front row, holding hands for over an hour. Frustrated, he lifted her hand in his and kissed it. "Love, I need a few minutes. I'm going to step outside."

Ty stood before she could respond. He needed to escape all the politicians, dignitaries, and military guests.

Seeing him walking out, Tiller, sitting next to the rest of the guys and Williams two rows back, got up to follow but sat back down when Ty waved him off.

At an exterior door, a Marine Sentry opened it to allow Ty to step out into the fresh air.

The rain had not let up for hours. It wasn't the drizzle of an afternoon shower that accomplished little more than getting the ground wet enough to track dirt into the White House on your dress shoes. Nor was it the torrential downpour Washington D.C. needed to help keep the grass at the National Mall green.

No, these heavy drops of water were the worst kind of rain.

It moved in from the east with a prophetic feeling, deciding that the White House was the best place to take up residence. Thus, it contributed to the somber mood that was always part of a medal ceremony.

Ty stood alone along the sidewalk's edge, looking over the rose garden. The beautiful red and white buds were in full bloom. With each heavy raindrop, they bounced from the force of the impact.

As he watched, Ty became captivated by their resilience. Despite the constant assault of the rain, they always returned to their upright position. There was a symbolic meaning in what he was seeing.

Slipping her fingers between his, Beth asked, "Why's it got to be raining?"

"Do you know what this rain reminds me of?"

Beth laid her head on Ty's shoulder. "Yeah, that morning we sat on the front porch together before you deployed to Iraq eighteen months ago."

"That's right," Ty said, kissing his wife on her head.

"That's when it started for me."

Ty didn't want to ask what *'had started'* that morning for her. *If I ignore it, maybe it'll go away.*

"Ty, look at me," Beth said tremblingly.

He turned to see his wife's eyes swollen with tears. Immediately starting to fight back his own.

"You know what has to happen now," she said as her voice cracked.

Shaking his head defiantly. "No, it doesn't. I'm going to get out of the Corps."

Beth placed her hand on her husband's cheek.

Ty leaned his head into it, allowing his tears to flow freely as they began puddling along her fingers.

"No. You're where you belong. I didn't realize it until recently."

"There's nothing to realize. I belong with you. With Audrey and Jake."

"And we'll always be here. But you have a calling that is more important than me. With all that has happened, it's become clear that the world needs you more than I do. It's time for our chapter to end and for you to start a new one."

Ty knew she was only partially right. He had been holding her back and putting the three people he loved the most through so much pain and suffering.

"You're the love of my life," Ty said as he leaned down to kiss her.

"And you're mine and always will be."

From behind Beth, the Events Coordinator cleared her throat. "Excuse me, Captain. The President is ready to start your Medal of Honor ceremony."

www.ingramcontent.com/pod-product-compliance
Lightning Source LLC
Chambersburg PA
CBHW071240300726
48975CB00002B/503